The Random Killing

Kevin Boyle

Copyright Page

The story, all names, characters, and incidents portrayed in this production are fictitious. No identification with actual persons is intended or should be inferred.

Book Cover by author, Kevin Boyle.

1 Awkward

1987, Friday, May 8

Albany, New York

No. 1 Pop Song - Bangles, Walk Like an Egyptian

She would have stood five foot nine in her high heels, but the cage was too small. Her only crime was witnessing the naked woman lying on a table with her chest cut open.

She had no idea what time it was when she awoke. A single bulb lit the stairs up to the mansion above. The darkness smelled of urine, mold, and the rot of decaying flesh. After sleeping and waking many times a door opened far above. Light footsteps descended awkwardly with a sloshing sound. She finally saw a small boy carrying a heavy bucket.

"Please, please, help me get out. I must get out of here!" she called with her heavy Italian accent, thrusting her hand through the bars.

The boy walked to the side of her cage and put the bucket down. Celestina Cassanzo's hopes were crushed. In the dim light, she saw a dirty, hopeless face looking back at her. The boy looked just as trapped.

As she looked into his eyes, a dirty finger went to his lips, "Shhh, please don't cry. If they hear you upstairs ..." He looked around and whispered, "They have smaller cages when they don't like you."

The boy reached down into the bucket and handed a cup of water through the bars. She drank eagerly. Handing the cup back, their eyes met again.

"What is your name?" Celestina asked.

His head fell touching his chin to his dirty shirt, "They call me Trash or Mistake."

She moved closer and reached her hand through the heavy iron squares of the cage. The boy jumped back reflexively.

"No dear," she soothed, "you are not trash, nor are you a mistake. You are a beautiful work of God. Like me, you are lost in an ugly place, but you are precious in God's sight. Never forget this."

A shy smile almost broke out but then faded as the boy replied, "My name is Andrew."

"Andrew," Celestina smiled and asked, "Can you help me get out of this place, to get away?"

Andrew's head sunk again, "No."

Celestina continued patiently, "Can you make a phone call for me? I can give you the number."

"I'm not allowed. They always watch. They watch down here too," Andrew whispered.

Celestina lifted his chin again and smiled, "You are such a handsome boy. I think I like you, and I don't care if they hear. You are a sweet boy."

Celestina saw the edge of a smile sneak across Andrew's face.

He leaned sideways to the cage, "I like you too. I have to go. The others need water, and I have to get back upstairs."

Celestina was then aware of other cages farther into the darkness, and she heard movement from somewhere out of sight. Before she had hated the feeling of being alone in the dark. Now she wished she was alone. Other lost souls had been down here longer than she wanted to imagine.

After some time Andrew came back toward the light.

"Andrew," Celestina asked calmly with a smile, "would you mind getting me some soap and a little more water?"

Just then the door above opened, and a deep, harsh male voice demanded, "Trash, what's taking you so long?"

"I'm coming," Andrew replied and quickened his step.

He stopped and whispered back toward Celestina, “Maybe. I’ll try. I’ll be back.” Andrew started climbing the many echoing steps.

“Remember Andrew, even if you can’t get them, we are still friends, all right?”

At the top of the stairs, Andrew turned his head back toward the dark with his hand on the closed doorknob.

He whispered loud enough for Celestina to make out the word, “Friends.”

Upstairs Carlo, her date, argued for her life. He had seen the naked woman also, but he had seen many before.

2 Seattle Police Department

2001, February 20

West Precinct, Interrogation Room B

No. 1 Song - Lifehouse, Hanging by a Moment

The weather was as dreary as the economy. Boeing followed through on its commitment to lay off another ten thousand workers. The entire nation and all the major markets were still reeling from the dot-com bust. Stress brings out the worst in people.

FBI agent Donald Hayworth and his tall partner, Thomas Edwards, spread photos out across the table in the interrogation room where Todd Morgan Fisher sat with his hands chained to a ring bolted to the table and feet chained to a similar ring bolted to the floor.

"Yeah, she was sweet," Fisher said as he rocked in his chair. "Her screams were like music. That one was like, amazing."

Agent Hayworth put another photo in front of Fisher, "Tell us about this one."

"Heh, heh, heh. She was funny. Look at her ears."

"You mean the ones you cut off and stuffed in her mouth?" Agent Hayworth asked.

"Yeah; heh, heh. They were really big."

"Ok, Todd, tell us about this one."

Fisher looked at the photo, shook his head, and looked again, "That's not mine. You're trying to get me in trouble for something I didn't do!"

"Relax, Mr. Fisher. We'll take this one away," Agent Edwards said, "We saw the ink on the wrist and thought it was you."

"NOT MINE! THAT'S NOT MINE!"

Agent Edwards put the photo away in the folder, and Fisher calmed immediately. Fisher looked quickly across the photos and started laughing.

"What's so funny Mr. Fisher?" Agent Hayworth asked with a weary tone.

"You're missing the best ones! The best ones aren't here! You have to find them! YOU HAVE TO FIND THEM!"

After the interview, Don Hayworth spoke to the precinct captain, "Bill, you've got your work cut out for you, but at least you have some clues to work with."

The captain shook his hand, "I appreciate the help. Are you sure you don't want to take over?"

Agent Edwards stepped forward and shook the captain's hand, "Glad to help. With the budget cuts, we are focusing on being more of a resource for you."

The captain shook hands with Agent Edwards and got a puzzled look on his face, "Aren't you Tommy Edwards?"

Agent Hayworth rolled his eyes.

Agent Edwards paused and then nodded, "Yeah, that was a few years ago."

"I'm a big Penn State fan," the police captain added. "The one tackle you had in the Syracuse game, man! I can still feel it. You and Hendricks practically won the game by yourselves. Hendricks ran in the fumble, and you intercepted and scored ... and you and Donelly got the safety. It's no wonder they called you guys the 'Hit Squad.' We couldn't believe you didn't turn pro."

"Thanks for remembering Captain. We need to be going," Edwards concluded.

As Hayworth got into the car he asked, "The 'Hit Squad?' Ok, so now I gotta ask, why didn't you go pro?"

Agent Edwards puzzled at the ink on the victim's wrist replied automatically , "I had more important things to do."

3 Kissena Corridor Park, East Flushing

2002 August 2

New York, New York

No.1 Song - Nickleback, How You Remind Me

"*Mi tio Jorge*! It is so good to see you!" The petite beauty with dark hair and big eyes gave the elderly Hispanic gentleman a big hug.

"Vivian! Congratulations! New York City Police! When do you start?"

"I started two weeks ago. Didn't you know? I'm already studying to be a detective."

"No one tells me *nada*, and I mean nothing! But sit, sit, tell me everything. I'll bet this beats running your father's cement crews."

Vivian nodded, "It does. I think Papa's relieved. Now Julio won't have to split the company when Papa retires."

"And what about the tall man you were with last Christmas?" Jorge said smiling.

Vivian swept the air with her hand, "He is long gone and good riddance. But Uncle Jorge, what I really want to know is do you know if Andrew will be here?"

Jorge looked at her with a grave expression, "I am glad you asked me and not Uncle Julio. Whooo! He still gets very angry *y muy peligroso*."

"He has no reason to be angry," Vivian said. "Andrew was his son, and he still needs family."

Jorge shook his head, "After all the hell he put Julio's family through, little Elena is thirteen now. She still has scars on her face from the dog. It kills her father to see them every day."

"Andrew did not put them there, and he killed that dog! He saved her life!"

"Vivian, my brother does not see it this way. How could a little boy kill a dog that way? How could he bring all the ghosts into their house?"

"Uncle Jorge," Vivian chided, "do you really believe a little boy could do all that?"

"With my own eyes, Vivian, I saw many strange things in their house. These all started after this foster son came to live with them. No one would visit. Not me and not your father. Even the priest living with them had to retire after Andrew left."

"He needs us, Uncle Jorge. Andrew is all alone."

Jorge Vasquez shook his head again, "You are a sweet girl, Vivian. I liked Andrew, too, but no, it won't be me. Todavia me asusta."

4 Chicago

2003, October 3

Grand Boulevard Police District

Prisoner Holding Area

No. 1 Song - 50 Cent, In Da Club

The big German was the worst kind of killer, large, muscled, quiet, methodical. He beat his victims to death with massive, bare hands, picking victims at random.

"Kurt, we have you connected with eleven deaths in Chicago. The police have all the evidence they need. I believe you have also killed people in other cities, Seattle, for example."

Kurt had not answered any questions to this point. The FBI was brought in to see if they could connect him to other cases. At the mention of Seattle, Kurt looked confused.

"I have never been to Seattle," he said quietly.

Agent Edwards showed Kurt a photograph, "Kurt, this man you killed had a drawing on his arm. It was fresh. There was a similar drawing on a victim in Seattle. Look at this picture."

Kurt slowly looked down and nodded, "Yes, they are similar, but I did not kill either of them."

"We have eyewitnesses placing you in the area at the time of the Chicago killing."

Kurt looked at Thomas for several seconds before speaking, "He was already dead when I found him. I kept walking."

After the interview, one of the sergeants came into the hallway, "Hey, Tommy Edwards!"

Thomas sighed and turned toward him, "Yes, can I help you?"

"Yeah, you can tell me why you didn't go pro. The Bears had you lined up for their first round pick. You could have saved their defense."

Tommy shook his head, "No one could have saved their defense. Too many holes."

"So why didn't you go pro?"

Tommy forced a smile, "I had more important things to do."

A couple more uniforms walked up. One of them asked, "Can you do the King Kong for us?"

Tommy stared blankly and replied, "No. Excuse me." He walked away troubled by what he just learned.

5 Fishing Creek Road

2007, July 24

Clinton County, Pennsylvania

No. 1 Song - Beyoncé, Irreplaceable

Tommy Edwards sat in a rocker on the front porch of the log home looking up at the ridge towering above the valley. The limestone ridge created a perfect flow of water for fishing with deep pools and fast streams. This was fly fishing paradise.

"I hear you're going by Tommy instead of Thomas."

"Yes, Sir. I couldn't get away from it. People kept remembering the football days."

"Hey, you can drop the 'Sir' crap. Name's Hank out here. I'm not the director any more. How's that *father* thing of yours coming?"

"I guess it's better. Every time I put someone away, I think dad's looking down on me. I'm hoping he's proud."

The older man wearing a fly-fishing hat and vest smiled, "Never knew your father, but I'm proud of you. I'm sure he would be too. But what really brings you out here?"

Tommy Said, "Hank, I moved around to different cities in the bureau like you suggested. In the process I ran into homicide cases where a victim with the same MO as the rest couldn't be tied to the case. Each one had a small blue ink design on one wrist. The first one was in Seattle in 2001, the second one in Chicago two years later was a little bigger, like a tattoo, but just ink from a pen."

"So far it's a coincidence," Hank said.

"Then I ran across one in Philadelphia with similar markings. Each time the markings were larger and more ornate. I researched older cases and found several where a killer confessed, and then denied that one or more of the killings were his."

Hank leaned forward, fully engaged, "So you took your evidence to Bill Cooper's office in the Criminal Investigation Division?"

"Right," Tommy continued, "but no one there was convinced. None of the MOs were the same, and they ran the gamut from poison, gunshot, beating, rape, some with torture. With all the budget cuts going on, they were too busy to care. It occurred to me that we needed a task force focused on this kind of serial event. So I filed a recommendation to the Critical Incident Response Group."

Hank leaned back again, "Whew, you're talking about carving out a part of CIRG's budget. That won't be popular."

"I know, Hank. That is why I came to you. I could use some advice on how to pursue this."

"You probably want me to recommend this to Washington too."

Tommy smiled, "Really, you have friends in Washington?"

"Real funny, smart ass," Hank sneered.

6 Serial Crimes Task Force Office

2009, May 15

FBI Offices

23rd Floor, 26 Federal Plaza, New York City

No 1 Song - Black Eyed Peas, Boom Boom Pow

"Sorry Tommy, this was too good to pass up."

"Not what I want to hear, Franklin," Tommy said, "If the situation were reversed, I'd do the same."

Franklin left and Tommy sat in his small office wondering how much longer the team could last. Everything was falling apart from staff to budget to office space.

"Hey! Knock, knock."

"Hank!" Tommy said rising from his chair with a rare smile on his face. "Man, you couldn't have come at a better time. What're you doing here?"

They shook hands and Hank took a seat in front of Tommy's desk. "We'll talk about me in a minute. First, I want to find out what's going on with you. How's the task force coming?"

Tommy leaned back in his chair and looked at the ceiling. "May has been the month from hell, and we're only two weeks into it."

"Tell me all about it," Hank asked.

"Hank, I really appreciate you helping get this started, but McNamara gave me his six worst agents. One quit to work for a security firm. I can't get rid of a former Army Special Ops who doesn't get along with anyone. I had to fire one agent for cause, and I'm not allowed to replace him. And now the one agent who really made things happen just told me he's taking the top white-collar spot in L.A. Now I'm down to three agents, and I know they won't let me replace Franklin. They're tying my hands!"

Hank said. "Nope, you're wrong, and you can't count. First off, no one is tying your hands. Everyone's budget got whacked. You just have to do the best you can with what you've got. Second, there are four agents on your team. You need to get your butt back on the street and quit whining. I'm not sure where you learned this, but knock it off. It's not like you."

Tommy threw up his hands, "Even four agents is not enough manpower and Tammy, the lady that left, was our team profiler. How can I replace her?"

"There are psychologists and psychiatrists available as resources. You can borrow them short term without cost."

"But how would ..."

"Hey! Shut up! Listen to yourself. This does not sound like the 'Can Do' guy I brought into the bureau. Tommy, have you ever heard of the law of attraction?"

Tommy was feeling whipped and ashamed. He knew he sounded like a big crybaby. The task force was his idea. He hated being wrong. "No, what does that mean?"

"You have heard of it," Hank said, "The law of attraction means that problems attract answers, needs attract resources, evil attracts heroes. It doesn't always work out because we quit before things come together, or we get greedy about it."

"I've never heard of it before," Tommy said suspiciously.

Hank said, "Sure you have, but it usually sounds something like believing is seeing, or when the student is ready, the teacher will come, or sowing and reaping. Things like that."

Tommy put his head in his hands, "Well, I don't think it's going to be enough. I don't know how much longer we can last."

Hank grinned and tossed a budget extension form on Tommy's desk. "I think you are good for another year."

Tommy looked in disbelief, "Hank, I don't know what to say! How many strings did you have to pull to get this?"

"All the strings I had kid," Hank said sternly, "but it wasn't enough. It's the law of attraction like I told you. People saw your commitment to the team, and they want you to win this fight. The big 'but' here is, some of the strings I pulled are now attached to you."

Tommy stood up in his excitement, but sat back down, "Uh oh. Whose butt will I be kissing for this one?"

Hank's face didn't change, "It's not too bad, but I have a message for you from on high. Don't treat this as your own personal kingdom. Be flexible and work with others, especially local law enforcement. And most of all, get out from behind the desk and back onto the streets."

Tommy threw his hands up again, "But how do they expect me to get all this paperwork done! I've got incident reports, expense reports, manpower utilization reports for people not even working for me, and ..."

Hank interrupted, "Tommy, be smart use the resources at hand. Give the white-collar group in this office credit for some of your work. Get them to take over some of the paperwork. They are good at it. Use a shrink from the resource pool. Some of those psychs are pretty good. Share your office space. You don't need as much as you have. Negotiate. Adapt. You can do this!"

Tommy said with a heavy sigh, "Okay, I know you're right. I can do this."

Hank stood to leave, "Tommy, one year. Don't give up and quit. Promise?"

Tommy stood and grabbed Hank's outstretched hand, "I promise."

They shook on it.

7 The Rossetti Crime Scene

2011, July 7, 9:25 AM

Cobble Hill, New York City

2 Years Later

No. 1 Song - Adele, Rolling in the Deep

The door of the brownstone stood open as police and forensics team went in and out. Detective Vivian Vasquez brought two coffees up the sidewalk to the bottom of the steps and handed one to her boss, Lt. Dick Hanson.

"So why exactly did you leave the paperwork to come out here?" Viv asked over the top of her cup. "Is the body count making people nervous?"

Viv's partner, Hugh Thomas, came down the steps, "What body count? Our numbers are down from last year. Where's my coffee?"

"Lieutenant's drinking it," Viv smirked into her cup. "You can arm wrestle him for it. And it's not the numbers. It's the style."

Hugh reached for Lieutenant Hanson's coffee. Hanson gave him the 'are you serious?' look.

Hugh shrugged and said, "What? Four slice and dice cases in a month is just bad timing. Spread 'em out over a year, and no one notices. And Viv, I paid for the coffee. Next time give him yours."

Hanson scanned the scene. "Nobody wants to hear the 'S' word, so we aren't jumping to conclusions."

Hugh screwed up his face, "The 'S' word?"

Viv said without looking up, "The 'S' is for serial."

Dick Hanson continued, "Just do your job down here and leave city hall and the press to me. So give me the run down."

Viv flipped her notebook open and started reading,

"The victim is Frank Rossetti, Caucasian male, 43

Bound and tortured, wrists and forearms sliced all over

No forced entry into this VERY nice brownstone

Cause of death, single shot to the head

Checking into financial problems and family issues

Prints still need to be processed

No gun or casings found

Neighbors heard nothing until the gunshot at about 8:27 this morning

No one was seen leaving

May be a mob hit

No immediate connection with the families

Might be the Russians or somebody else."

Dick Hanson scanned the street scene again and noticed two men dressed like Feds approaching. Vivian kept reading, "Nothing seems to be missing, and there's no sign of a search. Looks like he had some information somebody wanted bad."

The two suits walked up holding FBI badges, "Who's the officer in charge?"

Dick Hanson spoke up, "Lt. Dick Hanson, senior officer. Det. Vivian Vasquez here is the officer in charge."

The crew-cut Fed gave Dick Hanson's outstretched hand a quick shake, "Agents Haskins and Barrera."

Viv squared up to Agent Haskins, "And on what grounds are you claiming jurisdiction?"

Haskins, at six feet plus, looked down at five-foot four-inch Vivian. Vivian didn't budge, flinch, or feel the least bit intimidated. She didn't play well with bullies.

Haskins looked up and over Viv's head to Lieutenant Hanson, "We are not here to take over or interfere with your investigation. We have reason to believe this murder is related to another case we are investigating. We would ..."

Here Haskins paused, "appreciate your cooperation and sharing your reports, especially any prints you've taken."

"Make the request through channels," Dick Hanson said, "I'll have them ready tomorrow. Where do you want them sent?"

Agent Barrera handed a business card to Lieutenant Hanson. Hanson gave the card to Viv.

The crew-cut added, "It may take twenty-four hours to get jurisdiction. Try not to compromise the evidence," as his gaze lowered to Viv standing toe-to-toe with him.

Viv glared at the agents as they turned and left.

Hanson turned to Viv, "Don't let 'em get to you kid."

Viv Vasquez replied, "Oh, GI Joe didn't bother me, but that Barrera guy is goooood looking, and no wedding ring. By the way, Lieutenant, my cousin from Colorado is in town. He flew in last night. You said you wanted to meet him."

Hugh Thomas gave Vivian a look, "Your cousin Andrew, the guy who found the lost dog and then shot the owner?"

Viv rolled her eyes and ignored him, "Dick, you want him to look this over?"

Dick Hanson looked up the steps, "No, this isn't a freak show, at least not yet."

Hugh continued his version of the story: "He pulls up to this guy's trailer to give him his dog back. The guy's all grateful, and your cousin blows the guy away standing in his own doorway. They didn't even prosecute."

"Yeah, we got the news, Hugh. Thanks," Viv's sarcasm dripped, but she continued.

"Dick, if those Feds come back, you'll never get a chance to see what he can do. They'll probably try to link this with the 'hack and sack' on the west side last week.

Dick said, "Viv, you can bring him out tomorrow morning, but do it early before the Feds have time to drive over here and take our little playground away."

"Sure Dick, thanks."

"And then I want to talk to him," Hanson trailed as he started walking away.

Hugh followed Vivian back up the stairs, "Is he as weird as they say?"

Viv punched Hugh's shoulder, "When you meet him, you can tell me."

8 FBI's CIRG

2011, Friday, July 8, 9:30 AM

Critical Incident Response Group Headquarters

Washington, DC

The Next Day

"Agent Edwards?"

"Yes," Tommy said as he stood and quickly stepped toward the desk.

The receptionist gave him a professional smile, "The director will see you now. Go right in."

"Thank you," Tommy replied and reached for the door handle.

Regardless of the efficiency or competency of the people in the office, everything Tommy saw screamed "bureaucracy" from every gray, drab, straight-lined desk, cabinet, and book.

Tommy strode up to the desk, but before he could offer a hand to shake or any pleasantries, the man behind the desk stated without looking up, "Agent Edwards, you're busy; I'm busy. What do you want?"

"Director McNamara, thank you for seeing me."

The look from McNamara over the top of his glasses said it all: *Don't waste my time any more than you already have.*

"I'm here to bring you the evidence you asked for. Our Serial Crimes Task Force made some major arrests, and here are the reports for them. We have been training police forces in several major cities on tactics and forensics."

McNamara was still looking over the top of his glasses when he said, "You spent the bureau's time and money to bring them to me personally. Why didn't you just scan them to me as I requested?"

"Sir, because there is more to our unit then helping the local police deal with these issues. Some of these cases would have remained unsolved or gone undetected without our direction and assistance. We believe a serial killer has been operating for more than a decade by hiding in the shadow of other murders, for example."

Tommy straightened up and gave the straight pitch, "Sir, we believe our task force is well worth the small budget we were given and have proven our value to the bureau and the cities we have served. I believe you should keep us on the budget at the same level of funding."

McNamara looked over his glasses, "Agent Edwards, budgets are being cut everywhere. Your task force is an unnecessary diversion of funds from the CIRG budget. Your work will be rolled up into the Northeast CIRG Division."

"But Sir, our function will be lost. We have made some major arrests, gotten good publicity for the bureau, and ...," Tommy struggled for a third point to throw into his argument.

"... and the New York Police are expecting us to step in on several major murders."

Director McNamara understood publicity. He also understood complaints from New York City went high up the bureau's chain of command quickly, but budgets are budgets.

McNamara sighed, "Agent Edwards, I will give you one month to complete your work with New York. After that, you will disband and report to Assistant Director McCarthy."

"One month won't work, Sir," Tommy had his foot in the door, and now it was time for hardball. "The latest case is very random. The murders are in multiple states over at least an eleven-year span, using multiple MOs. There is no discernible pattern yet and New York is the latest crime scene."

It was a stretch. The Rossetti murder could be one of them. Tommy's Serial Task Force had no evidence that allowed them to take over the case, but he needed time.

"What makes you think this random killer exists?" McNamara asked.

"I uncovered the evidence in several cases we cracked. The perpetrator confessed to all but one of the murders and then confessed to other murders we didn't know about. They insisted one of the killings we had on our list was not their's. Our team researched several other serial murders and discovered that ten other serial episodes had a single murder that could not be tied to the killer. The first victim had a small pen drawing on one arm. The second victim had a slightly larger drawing. Each drawing got bigger and more ornate."

McNamara nodded, "Okay, I'll give you three months, and you have my permission to request senior sponsorship to keep you operating. That is all you will get from me."

Tommy stepped forward and towered over the desk and the little man sitting there. He stuck his hand out almost under McNamara's chin and held it there. Director McNamara reluctantly shook his hand.

"Thank you, Director McNamara. I appreciate your time."

The inspector went back to his paperwork while Tommy strode out cautiously optimistic. He was hoping and praying Haskins and Barrera found something interesting to keep their team alive. His last thought before the elevator doors closed was, *I should call them*.

9 Andy

2011, Friday, July 8, 11:00 AM

76th Precinct Squad

Brooklyn, New York

Viv walked briskly between the desks and officers spread around the room. No one looked up or noticed the stranger following. Viv interrupted Hugh Thomas and a uniform reviewing Rossetti paperwork with the lieutenant.

"He's here, and did he piss off the Feds!" Viv said.

The first thing Hugh noticed about Viv's cousin he wasn't Hispanic, not even a little, white as Truman Capote. The second thing he noticed was how average he looked, blue button down shirt, khaki pants, tennis shoes, but his eyes darted around the room, fixing uncomfortably on each person and some objects. Hugh saw the lieutenant clench his teeth, quickly putting both hands on the desk. The lieutenant stood and reached his hand out, "Dick Hanson, I'm the Lieutenant around here."

The visitor paused momentarily and then shook the hand while looking around, "Andrew Glover. Call me Andy."

Hanson sat and motioned to the others and said, "Hugh Thomas is your cousin's partner, and this is Sergeant Varga."

Andy looked at each of them in turn then nodded but said nothing.

"So what's this about you pissing off the Feds? And why were they hanging around? They can't have received reports and prints yet," Hanson said to Vivian while re-taking his seat.

Viv said, "The Feds were waiting in their car when we got there. I guess they think this case is theirs already. Anyway, me and Andy here walk up to the front door, and they yell at us to keep clear. I told 'em to shove it unless they owned the building. By the time I got the door open and walked in, the Feds were running up the steps like they think they was gonna push us out."

Hanson put a finger up to interrupt Viv's story, "Varga, did the finger print report get sent to the bureau yet?"

Varga nodded, "Sure Lieutenant, I sent it myself an hour ago."

Viv said, "Probably right after we left."

Hanson pointed at Viv, "So what pissed 'em off?"

Viv continued, "Well, Andy here is looking around the room when they follow us in claiming jurisdiction and all. I told 'em they didn't own the case yet so until then just go wait in their car. They started huffing and puffing and then Andy asks if we checked the toilet. He don't wait for no answer. He just starts walking down the hall."

Viv hooked her thumb at her cousin, "Andy here stopped 'em cold. He walked into the bathroom, and sure enough, the water in the toilet was way down. Ya know, like it's plugged. Andy here tells the Feds it's probably the killer's shit stuck in there."

Viv stands back with her hands spread out, "Whoa, now they want to know how he knew it was the killer's."

In the Lieutenant's office Andy stood calmly listening to Vivian's version of the story while his eyes searched the faces of the office staff looking at him through the office windows.

Hugh Thomas bumped Andy with the back of his hand, "So give, how'd you know?"

Viv gave Hugh the nod and said, "Andy tells 'em torture like that takes time. The killer enjoyed it so much, just like sex, that he forgot to shit. He had a big meal before the torture, so by the time he finished up, he had to go real bad and dropped a big one."

Hanson was interested, "What did the Feds say?"

Viv raised her eyebrows, "They wanted to know how he knew it was one guy. They wanted to know how he knew the killer had a big meal, and they wanted to know how he knew the sequence."

Hanson turned to Andy, "How did you know?"

Viv took the question for Andy, "He told 'em the guy probably does this for fun, and you could still smell the rosemary and garlic."

"How do you know so much about eating and torture?"

There was an uncomfortable silence broken by Viv, "I told 'em Andy here was a deputy sheriff in Colorado. They still wanted to know where he was two nights ago. Andy showed 'em the boarding pass for his flight to New York."

Vivian continued, "I told those guys they were a pain in the ass, then Andy here says 'No, they need to be here.' Andy says we will need the FBI to find the other murders."

Viv rolled her big brown eyes, "Now they are really pissed and asking Andy if he is the perv doing this and if he was challenging them."

Varga couldn't wait, "So what did he say? What did you tell 'em, Andy?"

Viv put her hand up in a stop motion, "Andy told 'em, 'No.' That's it! That's all he said."

Hanson frowned, "So now what?"

A uniform leaned into Hanson's office and said, "Lieutenant, FBI is here. They're taking charge of the Rossetti murder and want to talk with someone named Andrew Glover."

10 Interrogation Room 2B

2011, Friday, July 8, 2:00 PM

76th Precinct Squad

Brooklyn, New York

"Mr. Glover," FBI Agent Haskins started, hard-nosed, all business. The high and tight haircut said military, and the simple efficiency of movement told everyone he was in top shape and no one to screw with.

"Mr. Glover, you are not a suspect ... at this time, but it's more convenient talking in here. It gets you away from prying eyes and ..."

"And you can video tape the conversation," Andy finished for him.

Agent Haskins looked the part of an FBI agent right from central casting. His manner was casual but threatening. Andy didn't look, but knew the shoes were shined to a high gloss.

Haskins leaned on the table towering over the seated Andy, "You have knowledge about this murder that might help us. What can you tell me about the murder scene you were at this morning?"

With just the two of them in the bare, dirty white room, Andy could hear the echo of the words, "... not a suspect at this time ..."

Andy gestured toward one of the open chairs across the table, "Please have a seat Agent Haskins."

Agent Haskins leaned slightly closer and spoke through a tight smile, "I prefer to stand."

"Yes, I know," Andy returned without emotion, "but I prefer you sit while we have a conversation, because I am not being interrogated."

Haskins charged toward the table, "Think you're funny? You think because you were a deputy in some little town that fired you, you can run your game here?"

Haskins' tone got louder, and his face was close enough for Andy to count nose hairs.

"Well creeper, not here! I'm running this conversation, not you! So answer my fucking question!"

Andy's eyes watered involuntarily, and he shook his head, "For a spit and polish guy, you really need a rinse or mint or something."

Then Andy returned to staring into Haskins frothing face.

"Answer my damn question!" Haskins slammed his fist on the table.

Andy's face did not move. He showed no emotion. His voice did not even sound controlled when he responded with, "I intend to ... as soon as you are seated ... over there." Andy pointed to one of the chairs.

Behind the one-way glass, Lieutenant Hanson turned to FBI agent, Tommy Edwards, and warned, "If he lays one finger on Andy, who is not an official suspect, I will arrest and detain him for assault."

Tommy Edwards, Haskins' boss, paused, nodded, and then took the phone Lieutenant Hanson was handing him.

Andy heard over the speaker in the corner of the ceiling, "Sit down, Steve."

Haskins couldn't believe his ears. He glared toward the glass, ripping his hands away from the desk with a short guttural sound, "Fine!" he shouted, and he reached for a chair.

Andy jumped and half stood "No, not that chair!"

Haskins jumped back at Andy's shout.

Andy pointed, "I need you to sit over there."

"Are you kidding me? What kind of shit are you pulling?"

Behind the glass, Hanson spoke low to Edwards, "He doesn't have to talk to you, but I think you will want to hear what he has to say."

The speaker on the ceiling spoke again, "Steve, sit in the other chair."

"Fine!"

Steve picked the metal chair up and turned it around as he sat on it backwards. He slammed it down and yelled at Andy, "I'm gonna sit in the dammed chair like this!"

Andy shrugged, "I don't care. It's just a chair."

Haskins put his hands on the metal table lightly, "Now, we are all settled. Can you answer my damned question!?"

Through the glass, Andy looked as serene as Viv had ever seen him, as if nothing in the world was wrong.

Andy responded, "I believe your specific question was 'What can you tell me about the murder scene you were at this morning?' I'm not sure how you want this, so I'll just put this in the order I remember it."

Andy leaned back in his chair, "Well, first of all the flowers outside the door were freshly watered. With the heat over the last week, I would say Mr. Rossetti had watered them at least the day before his murder. There was no newspaper from that day, but there was a newspaper from the day before. I saw the paper guy down the block about 8:35 AM. So the psychopath probably took Mr. Rossetti captive after watering the flowers and before getting the paper the day before. The psychopath probably got the paper from the morning of the murder to read, or maybe he used the newspaper to hide or wrap something. I didn't see it in the home."

Andy took a breath and continued, "The hallway had all the doors open which is unusual because those brownstones are drafty. You keep the doors closed to keep the air conditioning cost down. The house was orderly, well organized, but some of the order appeared to have been changed. For example, the bookshelves in the living room were organized alphabetically by author first and then re-sorted by varying heights. It gives a balanced look to the room while allowing you to find books relatively quickly. It would be asymptomatic for Mr. Rossetti to order his books this way. I would guess the the psychopath was re-arranging items in the house to suit his preferences, the way he thinks ..."

Haskins held up his hands, "Whoa there, Dr. Freud. So you're an expert on interior design as well as a psychiatrist. And why do you call the perpetrator a psychopath? How about a hit man or sociopath?"

"Well," Andy explained, "a sociopath and a psychopath have similarities in their disregard for the feelings of others, unconcern for consequences, etc. A sociopath tends to be less violent, more disorganized, disregards personal hygiene. They tend to be more emotion based. The cut marks I saw on the body show a high degree of order one would expect in a highly intelligent psychopath. A hit man would have made a quick kill and not taken the time for torturing unless there was some information he was after. If this were the case, you would find broken bones or bones out of joint. The time required is short and the pain maximized without killing the victim. As for the decor in Mr. Rossetti's home, you can see he lives well, but you can also tell he is also frugal."

"Can you prove any of this shit you're shoveling?" Haskins said with hands flat on the table.

Andy remarked, "Proof, let's start with his clothes. The suits and shirts are tailor-made but his belt was from a cheap rack. The boxed food in the kitchen was all generic. The tissue and toilet paper were the cheapest you can buy. His book collection in the living room was all hardback, but in the bedroom, it was paperback."

At this point Haskins started checking out little by little knowing the recordings would be analyzed later. He, however, was stuck listening to Andy drone on about Mr. Rossetti's financial papers on the desk, the smells lingering in the rooms, indentations in the carpet where furniture had been recently moved, pill cases in the bathroom, no dust on the computer desk, on and on and on.

Haskins did not know exactly how long Andy droned on, but he snapped to attention when Andy again mentioned the cut marks on Mr. Rossetti.

"Wait!" Haskins ordered, "You said it showed that the perpetrator was very organized and that the cut marks showed it. I saw the body. The cuts were everywhere, totally random. There was no order to it. And when did you see the body?"

"Yes, there was order, a high degree of order," Andy stated pointedly. "There were photos of Mr. Rossetti's arms on Lieutenant Hanson's desk. I didn't get a close look, but it looked like the cuts were all the same length and the same spacing, using multiple cuts to create the illusion of longer lines. The lines formed a complex pattern without ever crossing. Also, the spacing of the lines never varies. This is pattern has taken a lot of study and practice to perfect and a lot of ability to execute."

Haskins glared at Andy, "It sounds like you admire the work ... or are you bragging?"

"No, I don't admire the work. I just can tell a lot of effort went into it."

Then Andy sat up, looked sideways, and said, "Oh, right. Thanks."

Haskins instinctively looked around the bare room.

"The trash was emptied throughout the home. You need to check when the garbage men come. If they haven't come yet this week, you might find the psychopath's trash in the cans outside. I wouldn't think so, but you never know."

After two hours of Andy's recollections of Mr. Rossetti's home, the FBI called it quits. They asked Andy for a DNA sample, which he provided.

11 FBI Offices

23rd Floor, 26 Federal Plaza

New York City

Monday, July 11, 2011, 10:15 AM

She guessed him to be a few years younger than his age of thirty-two. He looked startled. She moved a loose ringlet of her dark brown hair behind her ear. A move to calm the person to be profiled. Andy looked quickly around. Even after he found whoever he was looking for, the psychologist could see he was still uncomfortable. Carmen Andriano, PhD, with an emphasis on Criminal Psychology, did not want to approach yet, giving him space to get comfortable.

Not bad looking, though, she thought, *good build, but you don't get involved with people you work with, especially the nut cases.*

Agent Steve Haskins introduced Andy to Dr. Andriano.

There were only the three of them in the foyer of the FBI office, twenty-third floor, Federal Plaza, plus the agent behind the security desk thirty feet away.

"Andy," she said.

Andy must have heard kept looking from Dr. Andriano to somewhere else. The doctor could not tell. It looked like Andy was looking past the empty sofa or maybe the sofa itself.

"Andy?"

Andy mumbled something.

"Hey Glover!" Haskins growled, "Are you flipping out?"

Turning to the doctor, Haskins said, "His cousin Vivian said to phone her if Andy had any 'problems.'"

The doctor watched Andy closely.

Haskins continued, "I asked her what she meant by problems. She said Andy gets confused sometimes. Confused my ass, the guy's a basket case. Look at him!"

The doctor looked up at Haskins and smiled, "Steve, could you leave us alone for a few minutes."

"With this guy? Not a chance. He's losing it Doc."

"Steve, the guard is right there," she said pointing to an armed agent behind a desk. "You can sit across the lobby if you like."

She knew Steve was a bit AD/HD and would not like sitting for long. Haskins had one session with Andy on Friday. The FBI wanted to give Andy a low-level security clearance but could not verify his place of birth, parents, or anything else before Andy was ten.

Steve was ordered to bring Andy over to the shrink for psych analysis and let the brass push the security clearance through. This wasn't going any better than the interrogation.

"Fine," Haskins said throwing up his hands and spinning on his heal, "I'm sure you have this under control. I need coffee!"

Haskins marched toward the security checkpoint and was gone.

Andy looked up and shook his head slightly, "He says 'Fine' a lot.'"

"Andy," Dr. Andriano said softly, "Are you trying to make Agent Haskins angry?"

Andy jerked his head toward her at the first word out of her mouth with questioning eyes and open mouth.

"Are you afraid of me, Andy?"

Andy looked around and then back to her. He was tense, and she needed to address the situation quickly.

"Andy, you keep looking at the couch. Is someone sitting on the couch?"

A sudden troubled look, followed by a brief half smile told Dr. Andriano that she guessed correctly. "Andy, can we sit over here," the doctor pointed to two overstuffed chairs at a right angle to the couch.

Andy shrugged, "Sure."

They walked over to the chairs and sat. The doctor smiled, and Andy weakly returned the smile. He looked like he was starting to relax.

"Andy, I watched the video of you and Agent Haskins talking about the murder scene. During your conversation, you kept looking at the empty chair and other places in the room. I could not tell what you were looking at. Were you looking at someone? Is someone sitting on the couch right now?"

Andy stole a quick look to the couch and then Carmen had her answer.

"Mr. Glover, you are a very bright man. I see in your record you have been to several very fine psychiatrists in New York City. You must know the term schizophrenia."

Andy looked down and rubbed his forehead with both hands, "Yes, *schizo* means split; *phrenia* means mind. It means a split from reality. Contradictory evidence to schizophrenia, Doctor, would be the amount of details I noticed at Mr. Rossetti's home, also my ability to carry on this conversation without becoming angry."

Carmen calmly said, "Don't worry, Andy. I'm not your doctor. I'm only here to find out if we can work with you. You gave us more evidence in one hour than we were able to gather in months. So tell me, who is on the couch."

"No, I can't tell you. As you said, you are not my doctor," Andy raised his head and looked directly at Dr. Andriano, "There is no doctor-patient privilege."

Carmen's eyes narrowed as she stood up, "The doctor-patient privilege does not cover everything."

Andy stood up following her lead and replied directly to her, "It covers enough."

12 In Tommy's Office

Agent-in-Charge, Tommy Edwards' Office
23rd Floor, 26 Federal Plaza, New York City

Monday, July 11, 2011, 10:35 AM

"He won't discuss it with me unless I take him as a patient."

Steve Haskins cut the air with his hand, "Out of the question. He's just playing us."

Carmen looked over her shoulder at Steve sitting in a chair facing the desk, "He's not playing us, just you."

She was standing in front of the desk of the Agent-in-Charge, Tommy Edwards, and turned to face him, "As you said Sir, Andy has given us more evidence in one hour than we have collected in several months."

Steve stood and stepped up next to Dr. Andriano and said sideways, "You're not even on this team. You're just a resource. Look Tommy, I'm not saying he's not useful. And even if I did believe in some mystery copycat out there, we don't need this civilian of questionable character," here he looked sideways at Carmen again, "not to mention questionable sanity, distracting us from our real objective and current successes."

Agent-in-Charge, Tommy Edwards, sat behind the desk, his large frame leaning back in his chair weighing the arguments.

Haskins continued drilling his view, "Also, think of the crap we'll get from on high when it gets out we hired a psycho."

Carmen followed suit, "Tommy, we train agents to observe everything from street scenes to crime scenes. Where can we find someone, anyone who can sort through a scene and analyze details fast enough to start reaching second and third stage conclusions before he even crosses the room. He counts like a savant. The body didn't make him sick or even slow him down."

Haskins turned and faced Dr. Andriano, "And another thing about Mr. Glover. Why don't bodies bother him? He couldn't have seen many bodies in Lake County, Colorado."

Dr. Andriano continued facing Tommy, "His record is clean from what we have except for the dog owner in Colorado. Even he turned out to be a serial killer. Tommy, this is the one we, or at least you, want working with this team."

"Ok," Tommy Edwards said leaning forward, "Good points all around. You've made this an easy call. We want his abilities."

Dr. Andriano relaxed.

"But we can't ignore the bizarre nature of this guy and the heat we'd catch from our association with him."

Haskins folded his arms and smiled.

"So here's what we are going to do. Carmen, you take him on as a private patient. This way you can keep his secrets and let us know when we need to sever ties. Steve, as soon as Carmen meets with and clears Mr. Glover, you take him to the other site and see what he can find there."

Haskins' smile slipped away, "Sir, I have to ask, are you serious?"

"Yes Steve, I am serious. Work with him. He may be able to take our investigations to another level."

Haskins looked morose.

Tommy continued, "Carmen, I want you to find out how he processes information," Tommy held his hand up to stop Carmen's objection, "without violating his right to privacy. He is seen as and may very well be a nut, but he's the best nut I've ever seen at reading a crime scene."

Haskins and Carmen turned to leave, but Tommy stopped them. "Oh, one more thing. I think you should both know. Our requests to investigate Mr. Glover's background were canceled."

Haskins turned back around at the doorframe, "You mean it was denied?"

Tommy shook his head, "I mean it was erased from the system, all four requests. I looked for them just before you walked in. I have asked around to find out what happened."

Carmen spoke from behind Haskins, "A computer glitch? Can you create a new request?"

"I can try a fifth request," Tommy Edwards said. "I've asked Carlos to look into it. Maybe he can find out what's going on. The lack of information makes me want to know why, why the silence? Carmen, pay attention, and start a dossier for me on facts I am allowed to have. Let nothing slip on Mr. Glover. If there's a problem, I want to see it coming, not after it's run us over."

"Yes, Sir."

Haskins and Carmen looked at each other with raised eyebrows before they went separate ways. Tommy sat in his office wondering if this was the law of attraction or distraction.

13 Dr. Andriano's Office

96 Baxter Street, New York City

Tuesday, July 12, 2011, 9:00 AM

"Andy, let's get started," Doctor Carmen Andriano said as she walked away from her desk and high-backed leather chair. She was wearing her FBI uniform—black pants, blazer, and white shirt buttoned at the neck.

Her office in a steel gray stone building on Baxter, was two blocks from the federal courthouse. A very official setting except for the framed crayon drawing from her nephew next to Dr. Andriano's doctoral diploma and board certifications. The sun shone in the large window on a cool July day. The warmth and the light were welcome.

Andy saw her warm smile and relaxed. They sat in the area away from Carmen's desk with two low-backed leather chairs and a matching couch.

"Andy, I would like to get to know you, but first can you tell me about the person sitting on the couch?" Carmen was pointing to the couch nearest to Andy.

Andy shook his head, "Not there. She's over there on the far side."

Carmen leaned forward in the chair, "Tell me about her."

Andy said, "I've been through this discussion a few times with other doctors so let me tell you what I think you want to know."

Carmen nodded, "If you like."

"I have two invisible companions. The 'Lady' on the couch is always with me. Her name is Celeste."

At this, Andy saw Celeste bow of her head to Andy acknowledging his introduction. Her smooth, rich brown, silky hair was pulled back in a kind of knot at the base of her neck as it always was, her skin a flawless Mediterranean olive color. The contrast of her beautiful dark features and dark hair with the white evening gown and dark red lipstick was, Andy thought, always stunning.

"The guy in the crappy mood, he's behind you at the moment, but he's always pacing when he's around; that is Warren."

Warren gave Andy the finger. Andy answered with, "Thanks Warren, real class."

To Carmen Andy said, "He's what you call 'vindictive.' If you cause him any trouble, he will make sure you pay for it."

Carmen asked in her professional calm, "And they are always with you? No, you said Warren was not always around, but Celeste is always with you?"

Andy nodded, "She is always with me."

Andy could see Celeste dabbing at a tear in his peripheral vision. He looked sideways at her and smiled.

Carmen leaned back and folded her hands on her lap, "What do you and Celeste talk about?"

"Oh, she doesn't talk, not anymore. You see, she's dead."

Carmen leaned forward, eyes looking around.

Andy explained, "Oh, don't worry. It was a long time ago."

The explanation did nothing to dispel the weird looks the doctor gave while continuing to look around. growing in the room.

Carmen said, "How old were you when she died?"

"I was eight," Andy could not help but look at Celeste. She wore a look of profound sadness on her perfect face.

"How did she die?"

Andy's thoughts snapped back to Dr. Andriano, "Oh, very peacefully."

Celeste smiled sweetly at him, but Andy also remembered the knife and all the blood.

"Would you mind, Andy," the doctor asked, "what is she doing now?"

Andy looked at Celeste and said, "She's smiling at you. You spoke of her as if she were real. She liked that."

Carmen puzzled, "As if she were real?"

Andy turned back to Carmen, "Sure, like I said, she's dead."

Andy felt the temperature drop and the light in the room seemed to change slightly.

Carmens looked around frantically. She said to Andy while scanning the room, "I am a realist. I don't believe in spirits, the un-dead, or anything of that sort." Her eyes went wide as she gripped the arms of her chair tighter. Andy sat calmly while she tried to jump out of the chair but could not move.

"Something is here! It;s getting closer!"

Andy gave a heavy sigh as he watched Warren moving his hands closer to Carmen's ears, blowing on the back of her neck, tilting her chair, and a few other gimmicks. Cheap tricks, but from the look on Dr. Andriano's face, it worked well.

14 FBI Headquarters

Washington, DC

Tuesday, July 12, 2011, 9:15 AM

"Agent Edwards, thank you for coming," the quiet voice called from behind the massive desk.

Tommy Edwards thought to himself, *as if I would turn down the executive director of the FBI for anything!*

"Please have a seat," the director said, waving to a padded leather chair known to many agents as "interrogation central."

Tommy crossed the spacious office with the long strides of his six-foot seven-inch frame. His suit was still sharp from the pressing it got at the laundry minutes after Tommy got the call or "invitation" to be at the director's office in three hours. There was a private jet waiting for him at Teterboro to take him to DC.

Tommy saw they were not alone. A man was looking out the window with his back to Tommy, to avoid being recognized. Tommy instantly knew the White House Chief of Staff, James Robins. Up to this point, Tommy was determined he was not going to worry until he knew what was at stake. When he recognized the man at the window, all calm failed. Now he was scared.

The director had his hands spread out on the desk in front of him and waited for Tommy to settle in the chair.

"Agent Edwards, you are very busy so I won't keep you. As you know, the funding for your special task force was not supported by many in the agency, but I have seen good reports. Keep up the good work, and I will personally authorize your funding for the next year."

Ok, Tommy thought, *these are the introductory remarks. Good, but introductory.*

The director continued, "We, uh, I have heard you have a subject matter expert working with you, a Mr. Andrew Glover."

"Yes Sir," was all a confused Tommy could get out.

The director pressed his lips together while his eyes never left Tommy, "Is he helping?"

Tommy glanced at the window then back to the director, "Yes Sir. Andy, Mr. Glover is quite amazing. He was able to ..."

The director held up his hand cutting off the conversation, "Agent Edwards, you may use Mr. Glover or not, as you see fit. You have been looking into his background. Those are sealed records not to be opened by your requests. Also, you may not contact the Office of Homeland Security about him. I don't want you talking to his foster family either. Am I clear on this point?"

Tommy nodded, "Yes Sir, crystal clear."

The director continued, "You will find the driver waiting for you to take you back to the jet. You will not discuss your trip here with anyone or the content of this conversation. Am I clear?"

Tommy nodded again, "Yes Sir. I understand."

"I doubt it," the director said waving his hand dismissing Tommy.

In the car back to the airport, Tommy's first question to himself was, *What the hell was that about?* The director did not rule out questioning Andy. Tommy and his team would start there.

15 Still at Dr. Andriano's office

New York City

Tuesday, July 12, 2011, 9:30 AM

Carmen was still seated, but her eyes silently screamed with terror. She reached into her pocket and pulled out a small vial. She removed the stopper and was trying to shake out what looked to Andy like water.

"Dr. Andriano, it was just Warren being a butt-head. I'm sorry. I can't control him, and he has no manners."

Carmen stared at Andy who was his usual calm making her feel even more frightened. She continued to wave the vial in his direction also.

"Dr. Andriano, what is in your hand?"

"It's, it's holy water," she responded shakily.

"Well, it may be water, but there is nothing holy about it."

"How would you know!" Carmen shot back with fire in her eyes.

"I just know, and it's not having any effect on Warren either."

"You mean to tell me what I just experienced was Warren?" Carmen asked with a rasping voice.

Andy said, "Yep, that was Warren."

Carmen's mind was working hard to catch up with her senses, "You mean he's real. How could he ... how did he do that?" she stammered.

"It's a cheap trick, works pretty well though," Andy chuckled. "He blows on the back of your neck and holds his hands a few inches from your ears and moves them closer. It makes you feel like something's getting closer. He gave you a little extra nudge by twisting your chair the tiniest bit while rocking it back. It unbalances you, gives you goose bumps, and makes you feel 'creeped out.'" Andy wiggled his hands and fingers to give a spooky effect. "Seriously, Dr. Andriano, you are in no danger. Like I said, he's just a butt-head."

Carmen leveled a hard stare at Andy, "So Warren does this all the time?"

"Naw, not anymore. He used to do it all the time when I was a kid to my foster family. He didn't like them too much. And dating was impossible."

Carmen finally stood trying to get away from the chair.

She hurriedly said, "Well Andy, this has been a most interesting session. I think we've covered enough ground for one morning. Let's pick up more of your story tomorrow. Same time? 9:00 AM?"

It sounded like a question, but it wasn't. Carmen almost pushed Andy toward the door.

"Sure Doc. I'll see you tomorrow," Andy sighed.

Andy held the door for Celeste, then he walked out. Warren found his own way out.

16 Maxwell Crime Scene

New York City

Tuesday, July 12, 2011, 10:35 AM

Agent Haskins had strict orders not to leave Andy alone at any time in the house or let him handle anything. He also had to have Andy wear a wire. It was the best way to record him.

It was a large house in West Village, a block from Hudson River Drive.

"And don't touch anything! Are we clear?" Haskins demanded while blocking access to the front door of the house.

Andy sighed, "Yes, it's clear."

Haskins poked Andy hard in the shoulder, "And don't think for one minute I buy any of this bull shit about any special ability! I see you take one sideways step, and I will drop you. You're just some weird, creepy-ass fairy trying to pull some scam but," and he poked Andy harder causing some pain, "It won't work, got it! I'm not buying it!"

Andy shook his head and then turned and walked away toward Seventh Avenue.

"Hey! Where are you going?" shouted Haskins.

Andy turned to face him again, "I'm going to get a pastry and coffee. Then I am going to do some research. I'll meet you here again tomorrow at 11:00 AM."

Haskins gripped his fists and clenched his teeth. Tommy Edwards and Carmen had been fooled, but not him, oh no, not him, but he knew he would have to come back tomorrow. He was probably going to catch hell for hurting the little prissy's feelings.

17 Back at Tommy Edwards' Office

23rd Floor, 26 Federal Plaza, New York City

Tuesday, July 12, 2011, 11:45 AM

"Not good, Agent Haskins. Not good at all."

Tommy didn't look upset, but you could never tell with Tommy. He gave Haskins the punishment of meeting with Andy again and threw in a "Don't screw it up this time."

Carmen's verbal report sounded like she was conflicted. "He has some signs of schizophrenia, but there was also strong evidence against it," Dr. Andriano told the assembled team in Tommy's office.

Carlos Barrera and Angela Ricchetti sat in office chairs against the wall. Along with Steve Haskins, this was the entirety of the Serial Crimes Task Force.

The Psychologist continued, "Andy could be brought in on a temporary basis but should not be trusted with anything stressful. I would need more time to assess the possibility of any long-term relationship."

"A 'working' relationship,'" she added, "with the FBI," she added again. All three of the Serial Crime team members were surprised by the stumble. Even Carmen was unsure where it came from.

Tommy stood up behind the desk and leaned forward glaring, "Carmen, pull it together! We need this guy. Also, our requests for background information are denied. It is *critical* that we learn as much as we can from Andy himself, and I don't give a *damn* about client-doctor privileges. I won't subject my team to potential internal threats. We have more than enough external threats already."

18 Night Patrol

Wednesday, July 13, 2011, 2:00 AM

Steve Haskins heard the running footsteps again. The echo on the linoleum floor was getting closer. The night was dark, and the inside of the condemned building was darker. Steve saw the runner dash by the doorway where he was waiting. Steve reached out to grab him but missed. He ran flat out just behind him. The runner dashed into an open door on the left, and Steve was right on his heels. He reached out but could only touch the runner's jacket. The runner turned right through another door with Steve right behind, but this door crashed closed against Steve's body before he could get through it, pinning him to the doorjamb.

Steve reached awkwardly for his gun but could only touch it with his fingertips. Then a hand from inside the doorway reached inside his coat and jerked the weapon free. The weight on the door was crushing him against the doorjamb. Steve used both hands to keep the door from breaking his ribs, suffocating him.

A shadowy man stood close enough for Steve to smell his breath. It smelled like rotting bodies Steve had seen too many times in places like Kosovo, Iraq, jungles in Africa and Central America. The face could not be made out in the dim light, but the low, sneering laughter could. Steve grunted as he forced the door off just enough to get a breath.

A pistol, Steve figured it was his own, was forced against his cheekbone. The hammer was drawn back with a loud click. There was a pause. Steve waited for the explosion ending his life. He had faced death before. He would not let his fear control him.

"You're nothing," the deep growling voice said. "You're an insect. I can crush you any time I want."

"Then do it!" Steve screamed, "Pull the trigger!"

"You're a cockroach, an ugly, fucking cockroach."

Steve felt something crawling up his leg. A huge cockroach came out of his sleeve. Steve hated bugs especially cockroaches. This one was walking quickly toward Steve's face. He let go of the door with one hand to knock it down, but there was another one and then another. Steve could feel things crawling on his legs, arms, and neck. The shadow man held one out to Steve's face.

"Don't screw with my friend Andy," the voice growled, and the hand shoved the cockroach into Steve's mouth and forced his mouth shut.

Steve felt the insect clawing at the inside of his mouth and moving back in his throat. Steve let go of the door with both hands and was frantically brushing cockroaches off his face with one hand and trying to grab the one in his throat with the other hand while he gagged. He couldn't breathe, and he couldn't get them off. He was flailing with his hands, but his hands were snagged in a cloth and wouldn't move. Steve became crazed with fear. He struggled frantically to get his hands free as he sat up in bed and rolled onto the floor. He was covered in sweat and retching. He ran to the bathroom and flipped on the light. The feeling of the bug in his mouth was still there even though the mirror showed nothing.

Steve had many nightmares over the years, haunted by bodies and faces of enemies and friends in burned out villages or roadside vehicles, but never like this.

He brushed his teeth, rinsed, gargled with mouthwash, flossed, and brushed his teeth again.

19 The Same Night

Andy's New York Townhouse

329 West 89th Street, New York City

Wednesday, July 13, 2011, 3:27 AM

Andy woke up crying. The clock on the nightstand said 3:27 AM. A profound sense of loss always came with his dream.

In his dream, the night was cold. His face was against something soft he was trying to push, but it wouldn't move, and he was crying. Dry leaves on the ground caused his feet to slip. He felt overwhelming loss and frustration and started crying. Then he woke up.

Andy opened the nightstand drawer and took out the journal. He wrote down the same description he always wrote along with the date and time. He wasn't sure why he kept documenting this dream. His childhood psychiatrist asked him to keep track of the recurring dream. The doctor was long dead, but Andy kept writing it down. He filled up many journals over the years.

20 Dr. Andriano's Office, Take Two

New York City

Wednesday, July 13, 2011, 9:00 AM

Carmen thought she was ready, but as soon as Andy paused in the doorway to let his imaginary lady friend into the office, her confidence wobbled.

Before Andy sat down, he turned to Carmen, "Dr. Andriano, I am sorry about what happened yesterday."

Carmen's face darkened, "You could have warned me. You could have done something!"

Andy held out his hands, "If I had done anything, said anything, stood up, sat down, closed my eyes, you would have thought I was manipulating you. I just had to let it happen and then try to explain."

Carmen pointed at Andy with gritted teeth, "Next time I want a warning!"

"Okay Doc, sure."

They sat and Carmen said, "Andy, I don't believe in spirits or ghosts. If what I experienced was real, can you ask Warren to ..."

Andy was already shaking his head, "No, Warren won't do anything I ask, and I've tried the reverse psychology thing a thousand times. He never falls for it. Also, the only thing affected was your perception. It would be a stretch to call it real. You and I want physical evidence, but in this case, there wasn't any."

Carmen leaned forward, "Well, then tell me about him. Tell me about Warren."

"Okay. I didn't notice him at first. He was just one more face in the crowd. The first time I noticed him was at the Vasquez home."

"Do they have a big family, extended family?"

"There are three children, the parents, Uncle Jorge, at least I think he's an uncle. That's what they called him. They also had Mrs. Vasquez' mother living with them."

Carmen counted out loud, "Three kids, parents make five, uncle and grandma make seven, and you were eight, a pretty full house. Vasquez, I assume they are Hispanic."

"Oh yes, very! Oh, they also had a priest living with them."

"So you were the only white face there," Dr. Andriano pointed out.

Andy looked puzzled but answered, "I guess so."

"Then how did you not notice Warren? Is he Hispanic?"

A light came on in Andy's head, "Right, you're a shrink and an FBI agent. I mentioned all the people, but there were others."

Andy said apologetically, "If you don't believe in spirits, this is going to be tough to explain. I brought a crowd of 'em with me."

"Go ahead and tell me about them."

"There were about twenty? Maybe more. I called them 'The Invisibles.' None of them had names. I gave names to some, others I just ignored. The worst one I just called Big Ugly. He had big hairy arms with lines and faces. He could have several heads and he would, well he did bad things. There was the bleeder, Harriet, Fatso and Mama, the Goblin, Jack, and Headless. Those were the main ones. Some came and went. After a while, I stopped keeping track of them."

"And now you only have two?" she asked.

"Yeah, the others left."

"Where did they go?"

Andy smiled, "This is going to sound weird, but there was a man standing on a street corner in Jamaica. He was crazy. He told people they were all going to burn in hell. He wasn't very nice, but there was someone with him, an invisible, that was nice."

"Andy, what were you doing in Jamaica? I assume you mean Jamaica, New York."

"I was scared all the time, but I found out the drug dealers and gangs were afraid of me. It was kind of cool, gave me a sense of power in a way. So I used to take the bus to some pretty bad neighborhoods and just walk around. I got to meet some interesting people. It's funny the bad people were afraid of me, but the kids in my own school weren't."

Andy continued, "Anyway, this other person, the nice one with the preacher, didn't say anything or do anything, but all the voices stopped talking when I was around him. Most of The Invisibles left too. It was great. I never heard the voices stop before. Whenever the preacher was around, I would go sit by him because the nice one with him made the voices stop. One day the preacher looked at me and told me that if I said a prayer, all things would be made new, the old things would pass away. It sounded great. I wanted that."

"Did you pray the prayer?"

"Yeah, I prayed the prayer he told me to pray."

"Did the 'old things' pass away?"

"Kind of. Most of The Invisibles went away. The voices and the night screams stopped. I finally got to sleep through the night. That was awesome! I knew other people did, but I had never experienced it before. I still have one reoccurring dream but nothing like before."

Carmen made a few more notes and asked, "The Invisibles, do you think they are spirits, demons, angels?"

"Some are bad, like I can't explain how bad. You just want to hide from them."

21 Dropping the Background Check

Tommy Edwards' Office

New York City

Wednesday, July 13, 2011, 10:30 AM

Agent Carlos Barrera leaned into Tommy Edwards' office, "Hey chief, I dropped the miscellaneous agency checks on Andrew Glover. Most of them failed anyway."

"Thanks Carlos," Tommy Edwards said without looking up from his laptop. Then his head popped up. He glanced at the walls and ceiling then stood and walked into the hallway.

"Carlos, wait a minute."

Carlos turned back in the hallway, "Yeah chief?"

When Tommy got close enough for a whispered conversation he asked, "You said most of them failed. So some of them worked."

"Yes, but not much."

"Show me what you got."

They walked to the open workroom the Task Force shared with a white-collar crime unit. All the information Carlos collected was reduced to three sheets of paper. Carlos recognized the conspiratorial tone from his boss and said nothing but spread the three pages on his desk.

Tommy looked at a copy of an ATM slip from First Republic Bank for one hundred dollars and two pages showing copies of property tax statements from Andy's New York and Colorado addresses. Both of the properties were owned by the same trust.

Tommy Edwards pointed toward the ATM receipt and spoke low, "Do you know about this bank, Carlos?"

"No Sir."

"You need a quarter of a million to even open an account. I want you to take a cab to city offices. Pay cash. Go to the City Register's

Office. Find out all you can on this property: 329 West 89th Street. Use only their old records; the micro fiche machine is still there."

"Sir, I can find it online in five minutes."

"No," Tommy whispered, "I don't want this on anyone's radar or even discussed. Write everything by hand or make copies. Bring it back here, and hand it to me only. Are we clear?"

"Yes Sir," Carlos said.

Carlos pulled his coat off the back of his desk chair and headed out.

Tommy walked over to the accountants in the White Collar Crime Unit, "Hey guys, which office is your boss using these days?"

22 Exiting the White House

Washington, DC

Wednesday, July 13, 2011, 11:10 AM

"Jim, what was the deal with the rush diplomatic pouch yesterday?"

"Mr. President, the pouch was for compliance with a codicil of the Euro-Atlantic Partnership Agreement, the NATO expansion," the Chief of Staff explained.

The president and his chief of staff walked briskly down the corridor of the East Wing.

"But what was it? Is this something I need to know about?"

Jim Robins could not explain it in thirty hours let alone thirty seconds walking to the waiting helicopter, Marine One. This was one of the many duties left to Jim by his predecessor. The phone call days earlier on the CIA secured line to the White House came from an apologetic Assistant to the EU Commission President telling him several key things: the assistant had no more clue than he did, powers above him were pushing this hard, and compliance to the simple request was the best course.

"Ah, Mr. President, it was just an administrative task required to assist our European partners. It goes both ways. They also help us."

He's lying again, the President marked mentally. *Every time he starts an explanation with "Ah," I know he's lying. There are more secrets they keep from me than secrets they share with me. How can anyone manage this office?* he thought again for more times than he could count.

23 General Butt-head

Carmen's Office

96 Baxter Street, New York

Wednesday, July 13, 2011, 11:20 AM

"So this 'someone' you saw with the preacher, was he an angel? And he made 'The Invisibles' go away?"

Andy made a thoughtful frown, "Well most of them. I still have Warren."

"So Warren is a demon?"

"I'm not sure."

Carmen's head raised from her notes, "What do you mean 'not sure'?"

"Well, he's annoying. He's rude and a general butt-head, but I've seen him do some pretty cool stuff too."

"Tell me about the cool stuff."

Andy put his hand to his forehead to think, "Yeah, he saved the Vasquez' daughter from the dog that attacked her. He's stopped people from hurting me a couple of times. And a few times when I was at my lowest point, he shut up and left me alone."

"What does Warren say about why he helped you?"

"He reminded me just now about the dog. It was a big deal for him for some reason. He also told me he's really gonna drill me next time I'm in the dumps. Pretty typical stuff for him."

24 Maxwell Crime Scene, Take Two

New York City

Thursday, July 14, 2011, 9:00 AM

The Maxwell murder scene was three weeks old but had been kept pristine due to the ongoing FBI investigation and a separate investigation by the life insurance company. The day was overcast, and a cold mist was falling. Celeste never got cold. Andy felt colder just seeing her bare arms without a coat. He always did. Warren was mumbling complaints as always and fit right in with Steve and Angela Ricchetti complaining about the weather.

The group stood in front of the large house where Andy had met Haskins the day before, "Why am I here, exactly? Andy asked. You've had your team look at everything already."

Carmen stepped onto the curb with Steve and Angela. Angela was the forensics expert on the team.

Carmen said, "This task force believes there is a serial killer hiding his murders inside other serial events. The circumstances are so random across all the serial killings no pattern has shown up except blue ink on the wrist."

Andy looked up at the upper windows, "Nothing is random. You either need a larger or smaller perspective, or you need a different point of view."

Angela set her case on the sidewalk and added, "There's some kinda freako out there trying to look random but he makes these marks on his victims. Why would someone go to all the trouble to look random but leave identifying marks on the vics?"

"There is a reason. There is always a reason," Andy said. "Finding the reason might not help us identify the killer, but it might. Besides, if the killings were spread around the country, what are the chances anyone would connect them?"

Angela said, "If Tommy hadn't put the pieces together, no one would know about this random killer."

"So smart guy," Steve verbally jabbed Andy, "how do you know so much about murder and torture?"

Andy looked at Steve and then looked back at the house, "I've seen some. I know no two people kill in the same way."

"Bullshit! All the guys in my unit always did it the same way."

"If it's at close range, then killing another person is always personal. Even if you don't know them, they become part of you. At the moment of death everything is stripped away, all pretense and façade. You can look right into another person's soul and connect with them. It can be a very heady experience. Some people get addicted to it."

Steve Haskins' mind slipped into a night scene in a jungle long ago. The guard he had just cut was bleeding out. Steve's hand was on his mouth, but their eyes locked.

"Steve!" Angela's yell brought him back. "Are you gonna answer your cell? Man, I been talking to you. Where did you go?"

Steve's private cell was chirping on his belt clip. Steve listened then said, "Okay, Tommy. We'll get started."

Steve Haskins turned around and addressed the group, "Tommy and Carlos will be late. Tommy said to start the walk through without him."

"The sooner we get started, the sooner we'll catch up with Mr. Random," Angela said, picking up her case.

All started moving to the steps leading up to the front door.

Andy walked into the entryway and stood there trying to orient the main room and doors with the photos of the crime scene he was holding. Celeste stood at his right elbow as usual. Agent Angela Ricchetti stood in the middle of the spacious room, about 20 feet away waiting to see if the genius savant could see anything she and the CIRG forensics team had missed. She was good at her job and knew this clown wouldn't find anything. Nevertheless, she also had been through the house twice since she read the transcript of the *conversation* between Steve Haskins and Andy at the police precinct. She had to cover a lot of areas she had not considered before.

"Why is an insurance company investigating?" Andy asked, looking up from the photos.

"Not your business. Just look at the room," Steve barked.

Steve Haskins looked around the room but mostly kept an eye on Andy. Carmen had come along at Tommy Edwards' request in case anything needed smoothed over. Warren wandered around looking into rooms in the back of the first floor.

Andy started moving slowly through the large living room comparing photos with what he saw. Before he reached the hallway leading to the dining room, he looked up at Steve.

"This isn't the same person. There's no way the person who did this killed Mr. Rossetti."

Steve said, "How do you know, smart guy?"

Andy shook his head, "It's simple. The Rossetti killing was elegant. This is a hack job. The room is neat but not compulsively neat."

Andy held up a photo of the body in a heap. "Look at how the body looks like it was just dumped here. There was no concern for form. There's no statement being made unless ... hmmm."

"Okay, out with it asshole. What do you think forensics missed?"

Angela knew it as soon as she heard Andy say it. She blurted it out before Andy could, "He wasn't killed here! He was dumped here."

Steve turned his glare on Angela, "What the hell are you saying? There is blood spread all over!"

Andy pointed to Steve while thinking it through, "He bled out here, and he may have had some life left, but he was dropped in a heap and never moved. Meanwhile ..."

Angela cut him off, "They spread blood around to make it look like they cut him up here, and they might have cut him here, but look at the splatters here, here, and here."

Steve looked where Angela was pointing. He shook his head. He didn't see it. Carmen didn't catch what they were so excited about either.

"When you stand here," Angela said pointing to a clean spot on the carpet, "Some blood spatters radiate out from here, and some from there." She pointed to another spot.

Andy joined Angela pointing to another spot with some blood on it already, "Here's another one, but this was a secondary spot because some blood was here but then they stood here and threw more. Look at the radiating pattern there and there."

Now even Carmen could see the overlapping patterns.

Angela pointed at where the body lay, "The bruising showed blood pressure, but I thought the bruising looked insufficient for the damage to the underlying tissue."

"Steve, how many adult children did this guy have?" Andy asked.

Steve Haskins answered, "He has three children, ages twenty-five to thirty-one."

Andy spoke without looking up from blood patterns, "When you find the location of the original attack, you will find who killed Mr. Maxwell."

The front door opened, and Tommy walked in followed by Carlos. His face was tense.

"Hey Chief, I think we have a break," Angela called out.

Tommy walked over to the group, "Before we get into that, Andy I have a few questions for you."

Andy replied, "Uh, sure, okay."

Tommy Edwards took a breath to calm himself before going into action.

"Andy, have you ever hurt anyone, other than the man with the dog in Colorado?"

Andy couldn't tell where this was going so he just answered, "No?"

"Andy, do you have a history of violence?"

Andy was getting scared but answered, "No."

Tommy kept the pace of his questions tight, "Dr. Andriano, is Andy Glover schizophrenic?"

Surprised, Carmen answered, "I'm not sure, I actually . . ."

Tommy cut her off, "Dr. Andriano, was schizophrenia your primary diagnosis during your first assessment of Andy Glover?"

Carmen recovered herself, and her professional demeanor kicked in, "At the beginning, the diagnosis was schizophrenia, but I have strong evidence to the contrary."

"Andy, tell me truthfully, how many faces do you see in this room?"

Andy was trapped. He hung his head and said, "I see seven." Everyone else counted six. Warren had wandered off.

"Andy, did you ever kill a dog by tearing it in half and stuff cockroaches in its mouth?"

Steve got a weird feeling in his gut at the mention of cockroaches. He looked hard at Andy.

"No, I never did!" Andy protested.

"Andy Glover, did you ever beat any classmates unconscious and stuff cockroaches in their mouths?"

"No, I ..."

The words were choked off by Steve jumping forward and grabbing Andy by the throat.

"You, you did it to me, you piece of shit! You put a gun to my head and bugs in my mouth!"

Andy grabbed Steve's wrists and was only able to make a small gurgling sound. He saw Carmen next to Steve. Celeste stood behind

Steve with a look of fear, and she held her hand out to Andy like she was trying to reach him.

Andy's eyes rolled back in his head just when Tommy yelled, "Agent Haskins, let go of him!"

Steve knew his business. He knew Andy was not permanently injured. He let go, and Andy slumped to the ground.

A sudden noise startled everyone. It started in the back of the house like a roaring wind. Everyone saw was a blackness moving rapidly toward them slamming doors as it moved past. The doors slammed so hard that wood splinters could be seen flying out until the moving darkness covered them. The storm was almost on them. Papers and dust swirled in the vortex of whatever was rushing toward them. Carmen pulled her service revolver and hammered the back of Steve's head. Steve crumpled to the floor.

The force coming at them immediately dissipated, but the wind and dust in its wake shook them all as it blew past.

Angela and Carmen turned to look at a wide-eyed Tommy Edwards.

"What the hell was that?" Tommy asked wide-eyed, looking around but afraid to move.

Carmen said, "I'm not sure, but I think it was Warren."

25 Cards on the Table

Two Floors above Dr. Andriano's Office

New York City

Thursday, July 14, 2011, 2:30 PM

Andy's throat still burned, but he could talk. They were gathered in an empty office space two floors above Carmen's private office. The building manager liked having the FBI in the building, so he quickly volunteered the space for the afternoon. It didn't stop him from asking for a rental fee. They all had started to leave, so he said, "Never mind," and left.

Tommy opened the conversation with, "Andy, Carlos and I talked to one of your old neighbors. This neighbor told us about the dog you killed and the boys you hurt at school. After what we witnessed at the Maxwell house, it's probable there are other explanations. This is your opportunity to explain why you should not be a suspect."

Standing around the freshly carpeted and painted room, all eyes were on Andy.

He rubbed his throat, "I'm not sure how long I can talk. My throat still hurts, and I can't tell you everything, but I can answer some of your questions."

"Trust me, Andy," Steve said holding an ice bag to the back of his head, "You got the better end of the exchange."

Carmen protested, "It was all I could think of to save your life."

Carmen turned to Andy, "Andy, start with your first memories."

There was respectful silence in the room as Andy started, "I remember a bright room. I'm pretty sure it was my bedroom. There was a stuffed bear. There are a few more memories of nice things, toys, and blankets. I have no idea how old I was. Then I remember crying a lot. It was dark all the time. I remember bad smells and being afraid. My parents owned a mansion. It was very large. They had no time for me. There were parties all the time. If there was no party, then important people came to talk to my parents."

Andy took a drink from a water bottle. He winced and continued, "I had jobs to do during the day and at night. I slept in different places so the bad people wouldn't find me."

"Who were the bad people, Andy?" Tommy Edwards asked.

Andy swallowed. Things he tried hard to forget were coming forward. "I don't know who they were exactly, but they scared me or hurt me or touched me. I hid from them all the time when I wasn't working. There was someone there who was nice to me. He protected me. I don't have a mental picture but I'm pretty sure it was a man. When I was with him I was safe."

Steve said, "Andy, you said you were working. What kind of work were you doing?"

Andy took a breath and blew it out and looked down at his hands, "I carried water down to the people in cages in the basement. I cleaned up in the party room. They, the adults, would tell me they spilled red Jell-O, and I would have to clean it up. I knew it wasn't Jell-O from the smell. Sometimes there was a lot of it. Everyone would stare at me. I had to take the garbage out to the burn pile and throw wood on it. They called the body parts garbage. Then one of the servants would come and start the fire."

"You were only a kid," Steve pointed out, "How could you lift a body?"

"I only carried pieces—a hand or a leg or buckets with organs in them."

"Andy, why were people in the cages?" Carmen asked.

"I was told they were being punished. I do know they were from all over the world by their clothes and language. Many of the people upstairs were foreigners too."

Steve looked in his water bottle then up at Andy, "How many cages were there?"

"There were about a dozen. The big ones were about five feet high and across. There were smaller ones too. I would have to help clean up the mess after they took the people out of the cages."

"What happened to the people they took out of the cages?" Angela asked.

They would take them upstairs to one of the parties and tie them down to a table. They would do things to them, rape and mutilation mostly. Eventually they would cut their throats and dismember them. Sometimes I had to hold a bucket or bowl for the blood."

A silence hung in the room. After a time Carlos asked, "How many people were in the party room?"

Andy replied, "It was a big room, and it was crowded most of the time—people and invisibles."

Tommy looked up, "What's an invisible?"

"Invisibles," Andy repeated while rubbing his forehead, "Those were things I could see most other people couldn't see. Some would call them ghosts, but they weren't like people."

Tommy followed with, "Andy, did you recognize any of the people?"

"I don't remember many faces. I was not supposed to look at their faces, but I remember some of the invisibles."

"Andy, tell them about the invisibles," Carmen prompted.

Steve's eyes narrowed. After the incident at the Maxwell site, he was beginning to think Andy wasn't the complete worthless priss he thought, but he still did not believe in ghosts.

Andy looked up at Steve as he spoke, "They are like people in some ways, but they usually don't look human, though some can look human for a while. Some are big, some small. Some are smart, and some are just as stupid as they can be. They fight with each other, and then other times they work together. They are usually angry and mean or they were to me, but they didn't hurt me too much like they hurt other people."

Steve looked out the window and spoke with his back to the room, "All right, let's get on with this. What did they look like, how did they move, did they walk through walls?"

"Mostly they are ugly. They feel dark, maybe vile is a better word. Some of them make you want to throw up when you see them. Some you can feel before you see them. They have different abilities. All of them move in and out of rooms in any direction, no doors or windows needed. Some can move physical objects, but mostly they use people to move things. Some can make a person crazy strong. I've seen them go into a person and talk through them, but they have limits too."

"What kind of limits?" Tommy asked.

"I believe they have laws that they can't break just like we have physical laws. Sometimes they can't hurt people even when they want to. They don't like some people, they are afraid of them and will run or fly away. Sometimes their movements are blocked."

Steve spoke up, "You say 'sometimes'. When are they blocked or can't move?"

Andy shrugged, "I couldn't always tell, but sometimes I could. There was a crazy street preacher who had an angel with him. The Invisibles that were always around me wouldn't go anywhere near him so I used to sit next to the angel whenever I could find him. I've noticed that the invisibles keep away from me now, with a few exceptions, the day I prayed with the preacher."

Tommy stood forward, "Andy, I appreciate your candor, but I need to ask you a few questions about what happened today."

26 Cambourne Hall

A Private Estate Near Oxford, England

Thursday, July 14, 2011, 9:30 PM GMT (5:00 PM EDT)

"My Lord, your guests have been seated and brandied in your private study as you requested," the butler announced and then withdrew.

Lord St. Claire answered, "Thank you, Martin."

William Sutton, who had inherited the title, Lord St. Claire, got up slowly due to constant back pain. He didn't like taking pain pills. He felt it dulled the senses. He told the last doctor to "Quit treating the symptoms and fix the damn thing!"

William, now in his late sixties, ambled through the main section of the manor, with its drafty stone walls and carved oak timbers, wearing an ornate robe instead of a suit coat. He made his way toward the study. He liked this room for private conversations, brandy, and a smoke if anyone liked.

As he entered the study, the two men stood. The dark skinned man with the Hispanic accent held out a hand.

"Lord St. Claire, good evening. Thank you for seeing us at this late hour."

Lord St. Claire did not take his hand completely but only shook the tips of his fingers.

The other larger man merely bowed his head, and Lord St. Claire returned the bow. Both of the visitors wore impeccably tailored suits.

"Please sit and tell me what brings you 'across the pond' as we say," Lord St. Claire said gesturing to the wing back chairs Martin had arranged around the fire burning on the hearth.

"If you would like more brandy, please help yourself. I've asked that we not be disturbed."

The two men seated themselves. Lord St. Claire knew Señor Castillo personally, but the German, as Lord St. Claire referred to Gustav Eberhard, he knew only by his reputation for having risen to prominence in the Uruguay/Paraguay families in a short time. The larger man started in a German/Spanish accent.

"Lord St. Claire, we are being sent here by the families we represent and the other families requesting our assistance."

Lord St. Claire winced at the broken English and replied, "*Ach, mein herr, können wir sprechen Deutsch?*"

Mr. Eberhard shook his head, "*Nein,* Señor Castillo does not speak German, and I am believing you do not speak Spanish."

"Then if you do not mind, and I mean no disrespect, could you do me a great favor and let Señor Castillo do the majority of the talking?"

Mr. Eberhard turned and nodded to Eduardo.

Lord St. Claire added, "That's a good fellow. No hard feelings."

Eduardo Castillo faced Lord St. Claire: "Sir, we are all aware that the Hollingsworth child is now grown and will soon reach the age where he will gain control of his inheritance. We have been hearing rumors that there may be people interfering with this transfer of control. We do not mean to imply that you have anything to do with this or even have any influence on those that do. Our purpose here is simple. We would like you to request that this transfer take place without interruption. Can you do this for us and those we represent?"

Lord St. Claire pondered for a moment then spoke, "You come to the point quite succinctly Señor Castillo. Thank you for that as it is quite late for guests. I have been hearing rumors about the Hollingsworth boy, some quite disturbing rumors. I am not entirely certain that it is in anyone's best interest that the inheritance falls into his hands."

"Sir, it is the business of the American powers. They must decide these things for themselves."

Lord St. Claire stood from his seat, "Yes, I believe you are quite right. I will do as you ask."

Both men stood as well. Lord St. Claire shook the fingers of both men.

Eduardo replied, "Thank you Lord St. Claire; we can ask no more of you than this."

The door to the den opened revealing Martin holding each man's overcoat.

"Martin will show you out. Thank you for coming. Good evening."

Later in the private jet, Gustav said to Eduardo, "*Si él toma el control de Hollingsworth los bienes los Europeos tendrán una ventaja sobre todas las otras familias. ¿Qué piensan los Italianos?*"

(Gustav: If he gets control over the Hollingsworth estate, the Europeans will gain an advantage over all the other families. What do the Italians think?)

Eduardo sat back in his chair and spoke with his eyes closed, "*Espero que alguien en Italia se ha hecho cargo. Si esto no, se ponen muy mal.*" (Translated, "I hope someone in Italy has taken charge. If not this will get very bad.")

27 Cards on the Table (Continued)

Two Floors above Dr. Andriano's Office

New York City

Thursday, July 14, 2011, 5:00 PM EDT

Tommy Edwards stood and asked, "Andy, tell us about the dog, not the one in Colorado, the one in Queens. Also explain about the two boys at your school."

Tommy had taken off his jacket and rolled the white sleeves of his dress shirt. Everyone except Steve had found something to sit on. Carmen had even pulled up an extra box for Celeste. Andy had to cover it with his coat before she would sit. Carlos, Angela, and Steve watched the box intensely, but when the box didn't move or show any signs of weight on it, they relaxed.

Andy had dreaded anyone ever finding out about his past, but now he found he was relieved to share it and more relieved Tommy and his team accepted him.

"Yeah," Andy started, "The little girl was the Vasquez' youngest daughter, Elena. They were my foster family. The dog, the one in Queens, was trouble. He had bitten people before in the neighborhood and, oh yeah, it was a bull mastiff, a huge dog. I was in a tree in the side yard and I saw the dog jump over the fence and head straight toward the girl. I was thinking of jumping down to help her, but I was twelve when this happened. The dog was bigger than I was. I chickened out."

"Anyway, I see Warren rush over to the dog. The dog had already bitten the girl twice before he got there. Warren picked up the dog's back legs and just pulled them apart. You could hear the ripping sound. The one leg landed in the neighbor's yard. The other leg was still attached to the body kind of. That part landed about ten feet away. People came running from everywhere. The little girl was screaming and had blood all over her face and hands and clothes."

"Mr. Vasquez thought I had hurt his daughter at first. He had a hammer and was going to kill me right there, but I pointed to the dog, and he ran toward his daughter. No one else had seen what happened so Mr. Vasquez assumed I did it. The dog's body had all kinds of bugs crawling all over it. They had a priest living there, so he came out and sprinkled holy water on me and the dog. People already thought I was strange. This didn't help."

Andy paused to drink some water and then continued, "There were people trying to help me deal with anger and other issues. I had four different shrinks. There was one priest who was pretty cool, not the one living with the family."

Angela asked, "What about the two kids at school?"

"That was similar to the dog. I wasn't completely innocent. Like I said, I had serious anger issues. The two kids were friends even though the incidents took place a year apart. They both picked on me every day, stole my lunch, you know how it goes. Then the first kid wrecked my bike and told me to eat dirt. He broke my arm trying to make me. I told him about Warren trying to scare him. The kid called Warren a fairy. That's when Warren attacked. The kid went up in the air and came down on his back spitting up insects. My arm was broken. No one could figure out what happened. He was really messed up. You are the first people I've ever told this part of the story."

Tommy pointed at Andy, "So Warren protects you, from everything? Is that what happened yesterday?"

"No, not everything, I got my arm broken. I never got another bike until I left the Vasquez house and moved to Colorado. I never know when he will do something. What happened today surprised me too. I don't know what sets him off. I do know this. If you piss him off, you're gonna pay for it. He's not the forgiving type."

"Is this Warren an evil spirit like your personal mojo?" Carlos asked.

"I don't think he's an evil spirit. He's more like a cranky, pissed off, rude spirit."

28 New Hope Homeless Shelter

Sutter Avenue, East New York City

Thursday, July 14, 2011, 5:20 PM EDT

Steve Haskins and Carlos Barrera walked into the New Hope Homeless Shelter for Men on Sutter Avenue in East New York. Dark clouds moved in from the northeast giving a somber mood to the city.

"He's over there," a toothless man with a two week beard said as he handed out towels to men standing in line for showers.

In their way stood an older, mountain of a man in a sleeveless t-shirt, biker gang tattoos, a faded red bandanna, and a few serious scars showing. The man looked them over before snarling, "What do you want here, lawman?"

"We're looking for Father Rand," Carlos said looking up at the man.

"He ain't here!" the big man sneered.

Agent Haskins stepped forward, "We were told that he is here."

"He ain't here for you, and I don't care WHAT kind of badge you got."

Steve noticed that men around the room were looking and starting to move. Retreat was their only option.

"Okay, you win. Tell the Father that Andy needs to talk to him."

Big man looked puzzled, "Andy? Andy Glover?"

Steve turned back to face him, "Yeah, Andy Glover."

"Well, why didn't you say so!" the big man said with a smile and put a huge paw on Steve's shoulder. The big man stuck his hand out, "Father Rand, how can I help Andy?"

Carlos was shocked, "You, you're a priest?"

Father Rand pulled out some old wooden chairs and smiled at them, "Yep, I think so. I took orders about ..." here he waved his head while thinking, "about twenty-one years ago. Went to seminary fresh out of Sing Sing."

Then Steve remembered what Andy had told them, "Father Rand, Andy told us to give you the secret code, Merry Christmas."

Father Rand laughed out loud, "That ain't a secret code. It's a private joke between Andy and me." Then Father Rand got serious, "So, you guys must be CIA too, right?"

Steve and Carlos looked at each other briefly while pulling out their badges.

Steve said, "No, FBI. Why do you say CIA? Do you think Andy is CIA?"

Father Rand's booming laugh echoed out of the room as he rocked back on the little desk chair. "Oh, that's a good one. No, Andy can barely hold any job. Good kid, but you know, weird follows him everywhere."

Carlos followed with, "Then why did you think we were CIA?"

"'Cause they been around twice asking about Andy. Same guys both times, but since you dressed the same, I figured ..." he shrugged.

"What did the CIA want with Andy?"

"Don't know. All they asked about was if I knew anything about his real family, his foster family, or his adopted family. Oh, and they asked if I had heard the name Hollingsworth?"

"Do you remember what you told them?" Steve asked.

"Not word for word, but it hasn't changed any, so here's what I know. Andy's foster family, the Vasquez family, were, I mean are, real decent people. Andy weirded 'em out pretty good, but I don't hold it against anyone. As far as real or adopted families go, I never heard anything. It would be unusual to be adopted and then end up in a foster family. I suppose it happens, but at least in New York that's tough because of the adoption laws."

Carlos was writing in his notebook while Steve continued, "That's not why we came. We need you to verify part of Andy's story for us. He told us you helped him deal with some anger issues."

The Father chuckled, "Yeah, I suppose you could say that, but if you want my opinion, all I did was ask Andy questions like 'Do you want to be scary and mean all your life, or do you want to have friends and a family?' He did all the dealing with issues."

Father Rand waved a big arm and hand around, "Man, when I met him the first time in the Bowery, he scared the hell out a me ... me! And I seen it all. He had demons climbing all over him. His eyes were like, on fire. No flames or nothin', but you couldn't stand to look at him, in the eyes. The second time I ran into him, no. wait. he tracked me down through the parish office. At the time, we had a coffee house on Fulton in the Bed-Stuy neighborhood. He still scared people, but I could tell he was better, calmer, sort of. Still freaked people out though. That's why he won't come down here. Some people remember him, and then there's some never met him and still get weird."

"So you just see him at Christmas?" Carlos asked.

"No man. We meet at this bar-b-que place on Delancy every Fourth of July. Best ribs in New York. It's when he gives me my Christmas present."

Steve looked hopeful, "Mind if we ask what the present is?"

"Naw, I don't mind. You'll find out from the bank anyway," Father Rand waved the air. "It's a check to keep this place running. I wouldn't be surprised to find out he owns this building too."

After the interview, Steve and Carlos ran to get inside the car before the big storm hit. They could see it coming from the northeast. As soon as they were in the car, Carlos started dialing his cell phone. Lightning flashed as large drops started falling. The thunder rolled overhead, and the rain increased.

Carlos said, "We need to go straight over to the White Collar Director's office. He and Tommy got some deal worked out for sharing office space and resources."

Steve looked straight ahead as he drove through the driving rain, "I think you mean for hiding resources."

"That'd be my guess," Carlos said.

Carlos spoke into his cell phone, "Tommy, I don't care what plane he was on. I can place Andy Glover in New York City the day before the Rossetti murder."

29 Joe, The Art of Coffee

Joe, The Art of Coffee

405 West 23rd Street, New York City

Thursday, July 14, 2011, 5:30 PM EDT

Carmen said into her coffee mug, "So, what you are saying is if I want something, I just have to think about it?" Faint morning light filtered through the window behind her. Discussions from the coffee crowd made a wall of sound holding the world out. Celeste sat between them on the curved bench.

"Yes," Andy said, "but I'm not talking about a casual thought. The idea has to consume you. You have to want it bad." Coffee of all flavors scented the air, and the young man with the Persian coloring yelled out the latest order in his Farsi accent.

Carmen sat forward, elbows on the table holding her coffee with both hands, dark brown hair in ringlets hung down, framing her face unlike the bun she usually wore. A cream silk blouse buttoned to her chin under her dark brown coat and a matching cream-colored scarf. The sky showed patchy clouds. The cool July blew a draft across the table each time the shop door opened mixing the smell of cinnamon pastries with coffee. The sound of people's voices and the cash register ringing filled in the background giving privacy to their conversation.

When they first sat down, Carmen picked up the discussion of faith from yesterday. As soon as she brought it up, Andy wrote something on a napkin and turned it face down on the table.

Carmen said, "So you mean it is the natural consequences of my thoughts. If I think about catching killers then everyone either looks like a killer or doesn't and my chances of identifying a killer increase."

"Yes, but there's more to it."

"You mean there's some magic to it," Carmen said trying to corner him.

"Not magic, consequences. But the consequences are not natural in the way you mean natural."

Several people entered the door and the wind blew in hard. Carmen wrapped her coat tightly at her neck and she threw the scarf around as well. They were lucky to have a seat at all so moving was out of the question.

"Andy, what do you mean by *natural*?"

Andy leaned forward a bit but instantly knew he was too close. Carmen felt it also but decided to let him near. Carmen found Andy to be strange, but she discovered in her dealings with him he had a balance and stability in his own way. He had a peacefulness she found alluring.

"Uh," Andy lost the track of the conversation for a moment. He looked to the empty seat and saw Celeste look down and put a gentle closed hand to her mouth as if she were going to clear her throat. Andy looked back at Carmen quickly. Carmen was still holding her position. She looked at the empty chair and back at Andy "So, Mr. Glover, what do you mean by natural?"

In Andy's peripheral vision, he could see Celeste looking at him and moving her head in Carmen's direction.

Is she coaching me? he wondered.

"Oh yeah, natural. Um, you look at the world," Andy leaned the smallest bit toward Carmen. Her face was serious, but she did not retreat.

"... the natural world," Andy continued, "as everything your five senses report to your brain. There are many things you cannot see, feel, smell your brain recognizes as real, pain for example. You feel it in yourself, and you recognize it in others when they react. When they don't react, you cannot detect the pain, but it's still very real to them. There are things you cannot see all around us: frequencies, patterns, things moving in different time-space dimensions. Even the particles making up this table are undetectable without special and expensive equipment when you get down to the sub-atomic particles: quarks, leptons, and bosons. You are dealing with things passing in and out of existence as we have defined existence."

Andy continued, "Well, having faith in someone or something means you create a partnership with them. My faith in the Lord is an example. He partners with me. I live in His world and by His laws. When I ask for things, in faith, I am subjecting my request for His approval.."

Carmen smiled looking at the napkin, "What if the Lord doesn't like your request?"

Andy shrugged, "I'm like his junior partner. I have to trust him. I believe he knows more than I do."

For a moment, the clouds parted, and the sun shone through the window. The air was clean and crisp while they talked. Andy and Carmen looked out and commented on the beautiful day. People stopped coming in for a moment, and the sun actually warmed their window seats. Carmen felt suddenly warm and took off her scarf and opened her coat.

"So Mr. Faith, are you going to show me what you wrote on the napkin?" Andy smiled and started turning it over very slowly while making a fanfare music and the crowd going wild. While Carmen was waiting, she suddenly felt warm and unbuttoned the top two buttons of her blouse. Andy finally revealed the underside of the napkin.

Carmen's face went blank. She stared at it for a moment and then looked up at Andy. The flush in her face was obvious.

"How did you know I would do that?"

Andy shrugged, "I didn't know. I was just asking, and hoping."

The writing on the napkin said, *I would love to see your beautiful neck.*

30 The Law Firm

Blackford Crighton Law Firm, New York Offices

21st Floor, 206 West 48th Street

Thursday, July 14, 2011, 5:30 PM EDT

Alan Hopkins, Chief Estates Attorney for the New York office, was on the phone.

"Yes sir, I am familiar with the case."

-

"No sir, I am not aware of any document of this nature. It was my understanding ..."

-

"No sir. But if my understanding is correct, there would be no need for ..."

-

"Yes sir. I will have everything ready for you. Will you be here tomorrow?"

-

"Oh, tonight. Very good, sir."

-

"I will have a limousine waiting for you. Very good. Thank you, sir. Good-bye."

The Chief Estates Attorney or Solicitor as he was called in the London office pressed the speakerphone button and dialed zero, "Miss Montgomery, please come in."

Miss Montgomery loved how the British pronounced her name. She entered the walnut paneled office lined with antique law books armed only with her steno pad and pen.

Solicitor (attorney) Alan Hopkins began as soon as Miss Montgomery stopped in front of his desk.

"Miss Montgomery, please reserve the board room for the rest of the evening and all day tomorrow. Put my name on the schedule. Move the proctors' meeting to the Kingston Room. If anyone has reserved the Kingston Room, they can find their own bloody quarters."

"Yes sir."

"Then I want you," Alan said wearily while rubbing his temples, "to place all the paper files we have on the Hollingsworth estate on the board room table. Put the oldest folders at the head of the table, and arrange the rest by the date on the folders around the table consecutively. Then put all the electronic files onto my private shared drive, and make sure all the computers in the room can access my shared drive."

"Yes sir. Is there anything more?"

"Yes, one more thing. Get me an aspirin, make it four aspirin. I'll be working late again. Then call my mother in Bristol, and tell her this is the reason I've never married."

"Sir?"

"No, the last part was a joke. Thank you Miss Montgomery."

Miss Montgomery's face warmed at how Attorney Hopkins pronounced her name.

31 Something Changed

405 West 23rd Street, New York City

Thursday, July 14, 2011, 6:00 PM EDT

Andy held the door open for Carmen and started to let go of it without waiting for Celeste. He quickly realized what he had done and was shocked. He turned to look at Celeste standing inside the coffee shop. Andy looked at her apologetically while passersby ignored the odd situation. This was New York.

Celeste looked carefully at Andy. Then she nodded her head without expression and joined Andy in the street. Andy was relieved. If Celeste had shown hurt, he would have been devastated. He had never been disloyal to her before. What was happening?

The street was packed with people. The clouds were back and it was starting to sprinkle. They walked a block as the light faded quickly and thunder rolled across the sky. There was no use trying to catch a cab with everyone competing with them. The rain started falling faster.

Carmen grabbed Andy's hand and started pulling him. They both started running as the rain turned into a torrent. Two blocks later Carmen pulled Andy under an apartment awning. They could not have gotten wetter jumping into a swimming pool.

"You might as well come up," Carmen called over the roar of the wind and rain.

The doorman was standing inside the door. He touched his cap for Carmen and held the door for her. Andy made sure Celeste walked in ahead of him. The doorman was confused, but Andy smiled and the event was forgotten.

On the thirty-second floor, the elevator door opened, and the three of them exited. Carmen talked over her shoulder as she opened the deadbolt, "Not sure what there is to eat. We could order out, but it will take forever this evening."

Andy walked in after Carmen and held the door for Celeste but he was watching Carmen as she removed her coat and pushed her wet curls behind her ears. He was mesmerized and did not notice Celeste had not entered. When he looked at the open door Celeste and Warren stayed in the hall. Celeste, of course, was not wet at all or even cold. Andy was afraid he had hurt her feelings twice now. Celeste frowned and shook her head *no.* Warren reached for the outer doorknob and ripped it out of Andy's hand.

The door had jerked closed so hard Andy's fingers clicked together as the knob left his hand. The door slammed shut with astonishing force. Carmen's head appeared from around the corner of the kitchen. She was toweling off her dark brown curls. "Is everything okay? I heard a crash?"

Andy was stunned. He thought, *That had never happened before. What is happening?*

He turned to Carmen with a weak smile, "Uh, I'm fine. The wind must have caught the door."

Andy thought, *Was she telling me I shouldn't be here?*

"Well don't just stand there. Take off your wet clothes and, I mean your coat, just your coat. Hang it on the hall tree there," She pointed to the far corner of the room and disappeared down the hall.

Andy stepped into the warm cheery apartment and hung up his thin coat. He thought about removing his wet shoes but his pants were dripping as well. He started looking around for some place safe to stand.

Carmen found him shivering in the kitchen, standing on old newspapers.

"Andy, you better take a hot shower. The bathroom is down the hall."

She led him down the hall.

"The towels are in there," she said pointing to the cabinet next to the shower. "Soap and shampoo are in the shower. Hand out your pants and shirt. I'll see what I can do with them."

Andy finished his shower and heard Carmen knock on the bathroom door, "Andy! Your pants are hanging on the doorknob. I'll have your shirt ready in a minute. Then you can take care of the rest."

"Thanks," Andy sighed, caught between his obvious attraction to Carmen and feeling something significant had changed with Celeste, but he had no idea what.

32 Reversal

Fourth Floor, 252 West 22nd Street, New York City

Thursday, July 14, 2011, 7:10 PM EDT

There was a pounding on Carmen's door. Carmen checked the peephole and saw a NYPD uniform. She opened the door without lifting the chain.

"Yes, Officer?"

"Ma'am, are you Dr. Carmen Andriano?"

"Yes I am. Is there something wrong?"

The officer said, "Maybe. I guess your boss at the FBI wants to talk to you real bad. He needs you to call him ASAP."

"Well the phones are out in the building and our cell phones got drenched. So they aren't working either. I'll call him as soon as I can get to a phone."

The officer handed his cell through the crack in the door, "Here ya go Ma'am. Mine's good."

"Thank you, Officer."

Andy came out of the back hall, "Who was at the door?"

"It was the police telling me to call Agent Edwards. I called him and he wants us in his office as soon as possible. I don't think he's happy."

***

Tommy stood as Carmen and Andy walked over to the White Collar office space. It was late. Only Tommy Edwards and his team were present. Tommy's face was dark.

"Let me get this straight, Dr. Andriano," Tommy said a bit too loud, "you and Mr. Glover were in your apartment this afternoon ... alone."

"Yes Sir, but he's not a suspect, so I don't understand why ..."

Tommy cut her off, "Suspect at the time? No he wasn't. But if I remember correctly, he is a patient of yours. You are in violation of ethical conduct both as a psychologist and an FBI agent."

Carmen's face instantly turned bright red. She said nothing but stood waiting for Tommy to pronounce judgment.

"I could and probably should have you brought up on charges, but not today. You were assigned to us temporarily, and now I no longer need you. You are dismissed."

Tommy's word was the gavel. Carmen knew she was lucky to keep her job and license. She had screwed up in a BIG way. She said nothing. She turned and left. As she was leaving, Andy heard a man's voice behind him, "See ya later, asshole!"

He jerked his head around in time to see a hand in the doorway giving him the finger.

Warren was leaving. Celeste was leaving! Andy's slide into despair was interrupted by Tommy's voice.

"Mr. Glover, as a child, how many people have you seen killed?"

"I don't know, uh, maybe a hundred?"

Tommy stood squarely facing Andy, "You got used to dealing with death and dead bodies, correct?"

"Well, yes, but I had to. I didn't have a choice."

"And now, Mr. Glover, it has come to my attention you were in New York City the day before the Rossetti murder." Everything suddenly turned around. Andy was the prime suspect again.

"No, wait, I was on a plane. I can prove it!"

"You were in Sullivan's Bar-B-Que on Delancy on July fourth, the day before the killing. I have several witnesses including the Catholic priest you met there."

"Yes, I was! But I flew out the same day! I had to go back to Colorado! I was on a plane when the killing took place."

Steve stepped forward leering, "You almost fooled me, Prissy. I don't know how you did it, but we'll figure it out."

Tommy stood next to Steve facing Andy. Carlos and Angela stood behind him.

"Andy, we will request airport security footage of you getting on a plane and an in-depth forensics report on Mr. Rossetti. Until that time, you will be kept in custody as a dangerous felon. I also need to tell you anything you say can and will be used against you in a court of law. You have the right to an attorney. If you cannot afford one, and we all know you can, one will be assigned to you." Steve turned Andy around and put handcuffs on him.

The rest of the Miranda speech faded into the background. He had been part of a team. They were making progress. He was contributing. He belonged. For the first time in his life, he had belonged!

Now everything was gone. The little he had in his life important to him was gone. Carmen was gone. Celeste was gone. Even Warren was some comfort just by his constant presence. Andy sat in a cell in the secured area underneath Federal Plaza alone and once again a prisoner.

***

"Hey Tommy," Angela said, poking her head into Tommy's office an hour later.

"Yeah Ange. What do you got?"

"Tommy, it turns out Andy and I were right. One of Mr. Maxwell's kids confessed. All three of them were in on it. They had tried to copy the Barkley slice and dice from last month."

"Great, but it still doesn't make him innocent, Ange."

"No, I was just saying ..."

33 Eye of the Storm

Fourth Floor, 252 West 22nd Street, New York City

Friday, July 15, 2011, 8:00 AM EDT

Carmen knew it was a lie. She wasn't sick but something was wrong. Her direct supervisor at the FBI CIRG Center also knew something was wrong even before he got her call. He heard a rumor from the day before about unprofessional behavior.

Carmen was a rarity among psychologists he worked with, her professional practice and career always second to her FBI work. She had worked tirelessly on every assignment. She was one of the most driven people he had the honor of working with at the FBI. She had campaigned for months to work with the Serial Crimes Task Force headed by Tommy Edwards. For now, he was willing to give Dr. Andriano some time off, get her act together. She probably just needed some rest and relaxation.

Carmen did need rest, but she sat on the floor next to her bed feeling her life drain away.

After Tommy dismissed her Thursday night, Carmen caught a cab back to her apartment. It was cheaper and safer to leave her car in the FBI Center Garage. After she paid for the cab, she turned and saw a lovely woman in a cream-colored dress without a wrap. Carmen also noticed she was barefoot. She reached for the cab door to open it for her, but when she turned to look at her, there was no one there, only a few people walking by on the sidewalk. An uneasy feeling settled on her already dejected state of mind.

When Carmen reached her apartment door, she dropped her keys. She picked them up and then dropped them again. The next time she picked them up, she gripped them in her fist. As she reached the keys toward the deadbolt, she couldn't get the key to go into the lock. Finally, she cursed and the key went in but wouldn't turn. Now she was angry. She grabbed the key ring to force the lock to turn. It started to but then turned back as if someone was arm wrestling with her.

She twisted the lock and kicked the door viciously and the lock turned but her arm hurt. When she stepped into her apartment, she saw a drop of blood dripping from what looked like a small bite mark. Her bad feeling increased and she wished Andy were there.

Carmen crossed the living room into the kitchen and laid her car keys on the counter. She heard a retching sound behind her and screamed when she saw a humanoid type creature spewing some type of goo and walking toward her.

Without thinking, she sprinted down the hallway toward her bedroom. The bedroom door slammed shut behind her as soon as she crossed the threshold but the door quickly shattered into thousands of shards as a crowd of hideous creatures fought frantically in a bizarre melee six feet from where Carmen had hunkered down on the floor in the small space between her dresser and bed. Carmen squeezed her eyes shut trying to force the nightmare in front of her out of her reality.

To Carmen's relief, the sounds of the battle moved out into the hall. She opened one eye to peek out of her pretended concealment. The beautiful, stately woman Carmen had seen on the street earlier was sitting on the edge of her bed and looking sideways at her, but now the woman was mostly transparent.

Carmen screamed as a sharp point pierced her back and was now protruding from her chest.

Later, as Carmen was in the space next to her bed waiting to die, her mind wandered to the small details of her surroundings. There should have been blood. She had forgotten to take her shoes off. She always removed her shoes when she entered her apartment. Carmen now stared vacantly at the woman standing on the other side of the bedroom. The woman was fading in and out of focus. She still had no shoes on.

When the woman was visible again, Carmen asked, "Where are your shoes?"

A man stepped between Carmen and the woman. The man was brandishing some kind of metal weapon at Carmen as if she were a threat. Carmen was unconcerned as she felt herself sinking down into darkness.

34 Dressing Down

Blackford Crighton Law Firm, New York Offices

21st Floor, 206 West 48th Street

Friday, July 15, 2011, 9:00 AM EDT

Alan Hopkins stood at attention while one of the senior partners from the home office in London gave him a thorough dressing down for incompetence in the handling of the Hollingsworth situation.

"I've never seen the like. Seventeen years with the firm and you've bungled the whole affair!"

Sir Wynton Smythley, Senior Partner for Blackford Crighton's and his personal secretary, Niles Bagley, finished reviewing the Hollingsworth files just as the office staff came in early Wednesday morning.

Sir Smythley twisted the waxed end of his white handlebar mustache before continuing, "You've entrusted the whole of our most important North American client to a single, handwritten slip of paper! They didn't even have the decency to use a typewriter at the very least. Bloody colonials! Think they're still in the dark ages!"

Alan said, "But Sir, I had no reason to suspect he was adopted! And there is certainly no evidence of it in Hollingsworth's personal papers. On the contrary ..."

"Contrary be damned!" Sir Smythley pronounced, slamming his hand on Alan's desk where he sat while Alan stood. "This was why you were placed here. You've handled all the details in the past. You took care of every contingency. Something you now seem to have forgotten!" Sir Smythley said glaring at Alan.

"And now," Sir Smythley concluded, "there is only one course of action to take."

"Very good, Sir," Alan said snapping to attention again. "I will tender my resignation to the home office this afternoon."

"Nonsense!" Sir Smythley said, "You'll do nothing of the sort." He waved away the suggestion and then pointed at Alan, "You will fix this mess you've made. You will hunt down the evidence - and you will take care of it promptly!"

"Yes Sir."

Sir Smythley rose from Alan's chair and stepped around the desk, "Bagley, get my coat."

Sir Smythley spoke while Bagley helped him with his coat, "Hopkins, I expect you to have this straightened out in seven days. I want a report on my desk promptly."

"Yes Sir," Alan said starting to follow him to the door.

"And don't bother seeing me out. Bagley and I can find our own way. You get cracking!"

"Yes Sir."

Alan did not move until the door shut. He quickly returned to his desk.

"Miss Montgomery," Alan spoke into the phone, "please place a call to a Mr. Roscoe Tanner, and route it to my desk. He is in the Rolodex under Tanner and Associates. And hold all my other calls, and cancel all my appointments for the next two days."

***

"Bagley, have you ever seen the like?" Sir Smythley asked as they rode the elevator down to the waiting limousine.

"No Sir. How did this Hopkins get this position anyway?"

"Some relative of Lord St. Claire. No importance in himself, mind you. I believe St. Claire sent him to the states to be rid of him. Not that I blame him. Boy has the breeding of a goat. That was why I 'cut his rope short,' as they say, and not a damn thing he can do about it."

35 The Cattleman's Club

The Harriman Building

301 East Superior Street, Chicago, Illinois

Friday, July 15, 2011, 1:00 PM EDT

The door of the elevator opened on the 49th floor of the Harriman building in downtown Chicago. The staff welcomed the two gentlemen by name, coats taken, and then the discretion The Cattlemen's Club was known for took over.

The original Cattlemen's Club moved lock, stock, whiskey, and beer barrels to this location in 1990. The original club building was over one hundred and fifty years old. The old location was becoming known in some political and media circles. The club was open only to the current thirteen members. Guests had to be cleared prior to arrival.

The decor similar to an upscale old west saloon circa 1900, had a pool table, fully stocked bar, complete restaurant, and a cigar vault. This was one of six private rooms or clubs existing in America. The same thirteen members owned, supported, and frequented them as needed.

The two men walked into the lounge area where eight other men sat sipping hundred and twenty year old whiskey from a small distillery in County Cork. Each of the ten exchanged greetings, not like old friends but like old business partners.

Joseph Harriman began the official conversation, "Gentlemen, thank you for coming on short notice. Gould, Stanford, and the representative of the Walker family could not be here, so let's get started. First on the agenda is the good news. Andy Glover has reconsidered our proposal."

A general sound of approval spread around the group.

Mr. Harriman continued, "I understand he spent a night in the FBI lock up in New York. This had an impact on his decision. I was certain after the meeting Bob Stanford and I had with him in Denver on July 5th he would need to be replaced. He will still need guidance and most likely large segments of his holdings will stay with O'Bannon, the current caretaker. There is the possibility we can provide another caretaker. Andy is bright but I am sure it will take years before he can take a top spot in his own ventures, let alone working with the rest of us."

Will Vanderbilt asked, "What about the Brits? How are they taking this?"

Fred Crocker responded, "Harriman, the real question is, what are they doing about it."

Mr. Harriman replied, "Good question Fred. Our best intel comes from the British law firm, Blackford Crighton. We know they are hiring a private investigation firm to look into whether Andy was adopted. If he was, I'm sure they will find a basis for a legal challenge. The next in line for the estate would be Dudley Hollingsworth. He's a British citizen, and if I were on the other side of the Atlantic, I would have been grooming him for decades by now.

Fred fired back, "The Brits are also getting very chummy with the White House Chief of Staff. We need to do something about it."

Aaron Fridman said"Yes, Mr. Crocker. I can take care of Mr. Robins, but I will need a hand from you Harriman."

Harriman nodded his assent.

"How do they know Andy's adopted?" Will asked.

"No one is talking yet but they are hot on this as if it were a fact," Harriman stated.

"The trust is scheduled to be distributed on Andy's thirty-second birthday, August 1st. The Brits will want to move before then. After Andy is installed, it will be very difficult to remove him in a way allowing Dudley to take over the estate."

Will Vanderbilt quickly added, "What's our move?"

The senior member of the group, Aaron Fridman, spoke up, "Our move is the same as it always has been. Let them do their dirty work, and we'll help the authorities expose them. They get punished publicly and, if we choose, privately. Keeps our hands clean, and the authorities take care of our dirty work."

"Very good, works best for the Crocker Group," Fred replied, and there was general consent from all.

"The only other major news," Harriman continued, "is the planning for a military coup in Venezuela. We are looking at a two-year time frame. It will look good for business at first but then get worse. Stan, you were the lead on this. What's the big picture?"

Stan Cooper looked up from a note he pulled from his pocket, "Initial forecast is a short turn gain and a long down turn affecting Venezuela, of course, along with Columbia, Ecuador, and Panama."

"Who's promoting this?" Ed Kartcher of the Flagler group asked.

Stan continued, "This came from a meeting I had with families from Brazil and Paraguay. They are concerned about the large cache of foreign currency and oil reserves in Venezuela disrupting their balance of power and influence. The coup and economic downturn will cause the reserves to be tapped."

"Thanks Stan," Harriman said. "Is there any other business we need to discuss?"

36 CIA Headquarters

Langley, Virginia

Saturday, July 16, 2011, 10:02 AM EDT

"Gentlemen, please be seated," the Assistant to the Director of National Intelligence said to the four men entering the small meeting room in the CIA's Langley office complex.

"My presence here is to make sure everybody shares the information they have. As overseer of major sections of the budgets from both organizations, I do have considerable leverage to make sure everyone plays nice."

Tommy Edwards reminded himself once again he was involved in something he did not understand going to highest levels of power. The assistant director would never stoop so low as to referee a low level meeting like this unless ordered to by higher powers. There weren't many people higher in national intelligence.

Carlos started the discussion as Tommy had directed him, "The CIA visited a priest named Father Rand in East New York twice in the last two months, questioning him about Andy Glover. Andy has been instrumental in helping solve some serial killings."

"So you threw him in the lockup?" one of the nameless CIA agents sneered.

Carlos cocked his head and gave a leveled response, "No, we arrested him because of his intimate knowledge of a murder, and we proved, contrary to his alibi, he was ten blocks away from the crime scene within a reasonable window of opportunity."

"What happened then? Why did you release him?" the senior agent asked.

"He had more to his alibi that he didn't give us at first and it seems to hold. There wasn't one plane flight but three flights and he gave us no story to explain why," Carlos responded.

Tommy leaned forward, "So why are you investigating him?"

The senior agent said, "We aren't investigating him now. We were directed to drop all efforts to look into Mr. Glover's life."

The assistant director rose to his feet, "Gentlemen ..."

Tommy was sure the meeting was over.

"... I'm going to get some coffee. Would anyone else like some? No? Well, I'll be right back." Then he exited the room. The door clicked shut behind him.

The junior agent started, "This is a safe room. All electronic signals are blocked, wireless and wired. The directive to halt all investigation into Andy Glover came from someone high up in the White House."

Tommy raised his hand, "It was probably Robbins the White House Chief of Staff. Don't ask how I know."

The senior agent leaned forward, "It would make sense. He has a lot of connections in, well, in other places. How did you get involved with Glover?"

"He volunteered," Carlos said. "He visited a crime scene and seemed to know all about it. He provided a lot of evidence forensics missed. After reading the report on his evidence I doubt the FBI could have gotten most of it."

"Kind of like a cross between a psychic and a savant," junior agent added.

The senior agent said, "We started looking into Glover after his name turned up in some interesting places."

"How interesting?" Tommy asked.

"Scrambled communications by private citizens in Europe, Asia, South America. There were others. We checked our databases for past references and found nothing."

Carlos asked, "When did this start?"

Senior responded, "Last question before you answer some for us."

Tommy nodded, "Agreed."

"The first instance was in March of this year, four months ago. The second was in mid-April. Since then his name has been turning up repeatedly. Now your turn. We were prevented from talking to Glover. What's his real name?"

Carlos shook his head, "We don't know, but we figured out early on it's not Glover."

"We had a little come to Jesus meeting with him," Tommy added. "He told us about growing up in a big house with a lot of parties, wild parties, the kind with ritualistic human sacrifice. He doesn't know where he lived. He was a slave working all hours of the day and night as a small child. He not only witnessed the killings but had to take part and clean up."

Senior agent leaned back in his chair, "Whew. And you think he is living out his childhood. I know you had a psychologist talk to him. Does he show any bizarre behaviors: sociopathic tendencies, schizophrenia, voting for independents?"

Tommy and the junior agent chuckled.

Carlos began, "He had symptoms of schizophrenia, invisible friends for the most part. But we saw some serious physical evidence his invisible friends are probably real. Even our former special ops agent was convinced."

Tommy pointed out, "We had a language expert listen in on conversations. He said his speech is a mix of Midwestern, Northeastern, and Queens. We also know he has a lot of money. He has an account at First Republic Bank. We have the name of a trust fund owning several million dollars of real estate. Two of them are where Andy lives. Here is a copy of property tax statements from three properties we know of."

Tommy took papers out of his coat pocket and slid them across the table.

The senior agent sighed, "A couple of other things you should know. I can't tell you any specifics, but Glover was mentioned in a discussion of the disappearance of Celestina Cassanzo. That took place in May of '87, twenty-four years ago. The other thing you should know is some very serious people want him dead."

37 Interstate 95 North

Maryland

Saturday, July 16, 2011, 1:25 PM EDT

Carlos read the green sign over the freeway: "I-95 North, Warwick, Churchville Road Exit 1 mile." On the five-hour trip back to New York City, Carlos and Tommy discussed the meeting with the CIA. They laughed about the feigned surprise the assistant director showed when he came back from getting coffee twenty minutes later and found them leaving.

Carlos watched farms and small towns drift by the window he was leaning against. Tommy was driving.

"Psychopath not Sociopath," Carlos mused.

Tommy was shaken out of his thoughts, "What?"

"The older CIA agent asked if Andy showed any sociopathic tendencies. I'd call Andy more of a psychopath. He's technical, gets the details right."

"No," Tommy said, "Andy's very emotional, almost needy. When I left him in the cell, he was crying. Psychopath's don't cry."

"Maybe he's both," Carlos offered.

Tommy sighed and gritted his teeth. He hated being screwed with. He hated being manipulated. But even more, he hated being wrong. Every time he got a read on this guy, some piece of evidence proved him wrong.

Finally Tommy said it out loud, "Maybe he's neither."

"Boss, he's a perfect suspect. He had the opportunity. He definitely has the knowledge and resources. His background provides the motivation. What more do you want?"

"It's not what I want, Carlos. What Andy wants is the key."

"Ok, what does Andy want?"

"That's easy, he wants family."

38 Andy's New York Townhouse

329 West 89th Street, New York City

Wednesday, July 20, 2011, 2:25 PM EDT

The rooms were dark. The security system was set, and nothing moved in the spacious townhouse. The telephone next to the bed rang three times. On the fourth ring, the answering machine picked up the line "This is Andy. Leave me a message ..." (beep)

The voice on the other end sounded far away. "Andy, this is Tommy Edwards. I'm sorry things worked out the way they have. This is not an official call. I just wanted to tell you I am sorry. You fit the evidence we had at the time. Anyway, the team has another serial event in the city you could help us investigate. Call my cell number if you're interested. Thanks." (click)

The open hand lying next to the phone never moved.

39 Roscoe Tanner

Thursday, July 21, 2011, 2:30 PM EDT

"Alan Hopkins please," the thug-like voice spoke through thick lips. "This is Roscoe Tanner."

No one would ever see the summa cum laude designation on Roscoe's diploma he received from Brown University for economics. He liked to get it out of his bottom desk drawer at times to remind himself he was more than the intimidating hulk other people saw.

Alan Hopkins knew the first time they had met there was intelligence and a quick sense of humor behind the scowl. Alan sent as much work as he could to Tanner and Associates.

"Hey Alan, 'ow you doin'?"

-

Roscoe switched the phone to his other ear and flipped open his notebook.

"Look Alan, ya didn't give me much to go on, you know?"

-

"Yeah, I know it's all ya got, but here's what I found out. The hospital that wrote this birth certificate don't exist no more. Burned down in '85. I did run across several birth certificates that looked identical—same paper, same ink, even one had the same signatures."

-

"Yeah, Alan, lucky for me but don't do you no good. I tracked down the nurse and doctor who signed it. The nurse thinks she remembers the family, but the doc's pretty old. He don't remember too much.

The nurse says it looks authentic. She says it's definitely her signature and handwriting."

-

"Yeah, yeah, I thought of that, and my associates and I was able to track down twenty-seven girls who had unwanted pregnancies in this and surrounding counties. All their kids are accounted for or aborted except for two little girls I can't find. What do you want I should do?"

-

"Okay, because you are asking me, here's what I would do. You say somebody's got evidence this guy was adopted. Fine, let's talk to 'em. Find out what they got. 'Cause if I have to start searching down to the city for kids put up for adoption? Fa get aboud it!"

-

"Yeah, I got all this written up. You'll get the report with my bill. Good talkin' to ya, Alan."

40 A Second Phone Call

Andy's New York Townhouse

329 West 89th Street

Friday, July 22, 2011, 6:15 AM EDT

The telephone next to the bed rang three times. On the fourth ring the answering machine picked up the line, "This is Andy. Leave me a message ..." (beep)

A clipped male voice on the other end said, "Mr. Glover, there is a message for you in the pre-arranged location." (click)

Andy forced himself out of bed and went to the kitchen. He got a screwdriver from the junk drawer and went back into the bedroom. There were no more tears to shed. It was all over. Harriman and Stanford, the group in Denver, was not a team, not a family, but it was the only thing Andy had going. He took the cover plate off the outlet next to his bed. Inside there was a folded piece of paper.

Andy replaced the cover plate and went back to the kitchen. He opened the paper and blinked. It seemed simple enough. If the message hadn't been secreted in the location he gave to the two men in Denver, he would have thrown it away. But there it was. The only thing for him to do was follow the simple instructions. If Andy wasn't numb inside, he might have wondered how long the message had been there, but he didn't.

Andy placed a call to the limousine service on the instructions. Fifteen minutes later, he was escorted to the limousine by a muscular man sporting a military haircut. Andy watched the road signs and wondered again why he was alive. What was the meaning of all the crap in his life? What was the point? His parents called him "Mistake." The other adults called him "Trash." The kids in all his schools hated him. The small town in Colorado didn't want anything to do with him after the dog incident.

"God!" Andy screamed. "I just want to help people! Is that too much to ask? I just want to help."

The driver didn't turn around or even look in the rear view mirror. It was not any of his business.

Andy remembered the guy with dog again after his emotions settled down. Everyone in town knew Old Pete and liked him. Andy knew him too by a different name from a long time ago.

After a forty-five minute drive in the limousine, Andy found himself at Teterboro Airport. The limousine pulled up to a private Gulfstream jet with an open door and a flight attendant waiting at the foot of the stairs.

"Good morning, Mr. Glover," the attendant said. "We'll be leaving as soon as we get clearance from the tower."

Andy's eyes were still red as he wiped them climbing the stairs. He stepped on board and sat in one of the deeply cushioned leather seats. The door to the cockpit was closed, and only the attendant was with Andy in the passenger compartment. The plane started moving immediately.

"Can I offer you something to drink? We have a complete bar and also quite a selection of breakfast or lunch choices."

"A bottle of water would be nice."

"Water it is," she responded with a warm smile.

Andy had never been in a private jet before, and though he didn't know it, this jet was a step above everything else. The design was elegant. The seats flowed in matching arcs on either side of the plane so you could face the people across from you or the seats on the same side with minimal effort. Real wood paneling, gold fixtures, convenient but hidden storage compartments, large flat screens with remote controls built into the walls were accessible from every seat.

The flight landed in an airport Andy did not recognize but a short drive quickly told him he was in Washington, DC. The limousine pulled up to the iron gates at 1600 Pennsylvania Avenue. Andy was impressed.

The driver gave the guard Andy's name, and the gate swung open, no identity check, no vehicle search. A full dress Marine opened the car door at attention at the side entrance. Andy was escorted inside to an office. When the door to the office opened, Andy first noticed the presidential seal on the floor and the oval shape of the room. Now he was truly impressed.

41 The Short Leash

Cambourne Hall Near Oxford, England

Friday, July 22, 2011, 1:20 PM GMT (8:20 EDT)

"I don't give a damn where he is. He will be here tomorrow by afternoon tea if he knows what's good for him!"

Lord St. Claire slammed the phone down and let out a sharp cry of pain while reaching for his lower back.

"This damned back of mine will be the death of me yet."

Sir Wynton Smythley sat across from Lord St. Claire sipping a short scotch, "William, does Hopkins know how to find him? He could be anywhere."

"Hmm, what's that? Oh, yes. Hopkins came up with it. Very simple really. He sends a message to Matthew's cell phone. If Matthew doesn't respond in five minutes, Hopkins closes all his accounts. Miss one message and you learn to respond quickly."

42 The Oval Office

1600 Pennsylvania Avenue

Washington, DC

Friday, July 22, 2011, 10:00 AM EDT

At a side couch sat Mr. Harriman while another gentleman stood with a Marine guard. Mr. Harriman signed a form and handed it to the man Andy did not recognize. The man handed Harriman a very formal looking envelope closed with a large red seal. The Marine escorted the man out and closed the doors behind him.

"Andy, thank you for coming. I hope you don't mind the clandestine arrangements, but it was convenient for me, and we need to have a little privacy," Harriman said as he opened the sealed envelope and pulled out a single sheet of paper.

"Will the President be joining us?" Andy asked overawed at his surroundings.

"No, he is in Los Angeles doing some fund raising. This will just be you and me."

Andy remembered his manners and walked over to shake Mr. Harriman's hand, "Thank you for taking time for me."

After they shook hands, Mr. Harriman looked at the paper he had just received turning it over to look at both sides. Andy could not see any markings on either side of the paper.

Harriman held it up to the light and said, "Looks like someone just spent a lot of money to send a diplomatic courier from England to give me a blank sheet of paper. Hmm ..."

Then he switched his attention to Andy, "No, Andy, this meeting is for me, and others. You need to learn this. Everything I do is for my own benefit. It may benefit you also and others. I tell you this for our long term relationship if there is to be one."

Andy sat in a chair opposite Mr. Harriman "If?"

Mr. Harriman, "Yes. Something has come up you need to know about. The distribution of your parent's trust could be delayed. A challenge to your adoption is being put forward by a second cousin of yours. Actually, it is being put forward in your cousin's name."

"I didn't know I had family of any kind."

"Well, you do, a cousin, Dudley Hollingsworth. I need to give you a little background to help you understand."

"And this is for your benefit, Mr. Harriman?"

"Yes, mine, yours, and other people as I will explain. Mr. Stanford and I asked you to join a group of businessmen. All of us are American citizens. Our business interests lie chiefly in America, though we are all diversified around the globe. The future of America is of great interest to us. As the base of our operations, it is important America remain secure. Our group acts as a unit for our own benefit when it is critical for us to do so."

"This sounds like a conspiracy," Andy pointed out.

Mr. Harriman laughed and shook his head, "You give us credit for too much cooperation and organization. We are still subject to the laws of the land, in as much as they apply to us, and we still compete against each other in every business venture. When we must act together for mutual benefit, our combined wealth and influence determines the scope of much of our success and sometimes size of our failures."

"It is critical for us," Harriman continued, "and America, we, as a group, remain strong. Your father was part of our group at one time. As I told you, your family name was Hollingsworth. Your great grandfather came from England during the Second World War. His purpose was to protect his family and wealth during the war. Your great grandfather loved America but your father liked being English and was considering moving his wealth back to England which would have weakened our group."

"So you had him killed," Andy stated flatly.

Mr. Harriman pursed his lips, "No, killing him would not have kept his estate in America. The British have a group of businessmen similar to our group. We did find out Hollingsworth, your father, was grooming a young British man as his heir prior to his death. We never learned his name. The addition of the Hollingsworth estate to their group would have increased their strength and been troublesome to the balance of power in Europe."

Andy's face took on a troubled look.

Harriman noticed it replying, "Yes, there are several groups of 'businessmen' in Europe and elsewhere. An unfortunate event happened, however, we had nothing to do with. A young lady from one of the key Italian families disappeared. Her grandfather was central to the Italian group of businessmen."

"Do you mean Celestina Cassanzo?" Andy asked incredulously.

"Oh, you remember the event. It was in the news, but you would have been pretty young. Did you remember hearing or seeing anything about Celestina at your house?"

"I was seven or eight at the time. I don't remember much of anything," Andy said trying to cover his astonishment.

"This Italian business group did not go to your father who was rumored to have something to do with her disappearance. They went to the British group and demanded satisfaction."

"You mean revenge."

"Some Italians have a long standing tradition for such things but the Italians were hampered by the disappearance of many of their key business leaders in North America and Europe and Africa. This stalled a majority of their businesses and prevented them from taking action on their own. There were also some interesting interactions with groups from South America and Asia who were looking for a reason to pressure Britain and Europe, to keep them from regaining control of the Hollingsworth estate. Business people around the world get nervous hearing talk of a one-world government centered in Europe. Anyway, the British group let the police handle your parents to satisfy the Italians."

"The British control our police?"

"No, Andy," Harriman was amused with Andy's naivety. "It only takes a phone call to the right authorities with the proper information. Someone may have phoned the mayor of New York or the Governor of New York or even the FBI to get the right wheels turning. Also, the press were kept in the dark about what went on at your house."

"That was not my house. I was worse than a slave there."

"None the less, the police raided the house, and both your parents were shot resisting arrest. It was interesting your father never had an autopsy. They would have seen marks from the handcuffs he was wearing when he was resisting. Apparently, no one wanted them talking."

Andy shook his head, "I don't care about them. I have forgiven them even though they hated me. What happened to them was, well, it's just what happened," Andy forced the words out while getting teary.

"I think you do care about what happened to them. They were your parents."

"I only regret I wasn't more important to them," Andy said clearing the mist from his eyes.

"Regardless, we thought at the time the British group let the matter go a little too easily. They must have had an ace up their sleeve. And now they are playing it - this second cousin of yours and some knowledge about your adoption. Did you know you were adopted?"

"People keep talking about this like it's a fact. I have no idea. It could be true," Andy replied giving up the point.

Mr. Harriman leaned forward, "Here is why you need to know this. The unknown Brit may have been named as the principle beneficiary of the trust your parents set up. If not, the British group will challenge your adoption if you were adopted. The adoption opens up many options to challenging your claim to the estate. There are many options they may use to bring this to a court battle. To the British mind, the blood line is all important."

"Wait a minute. What if I don't want it? What if I just say 'screw it' and go get a job and try to live a normal life? Wealth doesn't define me. I don't need a big payday to find meaning in life."

"Bravo. Well spoken, Mr. Glover," Mr. Harriman said sardonically, "but it doesn't change anything. If you leave the choices to others, then some pretty nasty people get to make those choices for everyone. Is that what you want?"

"I just want to live my life. Not some life I didn't ask for!" Andy looked down, and he felt down, let down, lied to, abandoned, alone.

Mr. Harriman looked at Andy. He saw a young man with great promise but no compass. His heart went out to him.

"Andy, how do you know you were not born for this purpose? Is it possible that whatever you went through was to prepare you for this role?"

"What role, Mr. Harriman?"

"Andy, you have the opportunity to help steer the course of many."

In Mr. Harriman's words, Andy heard the distant echo of his earlier cry for meaning.

43 Matthew Sutton

Cambourne Hall Near Oxford, England

Saturday, July 23, 2011, 9:00 AM GMT

Rare morning sunlight poured through the large windows warming the small breakfast table the servants brought out for such occasions. The breakfast was set out. Lord St. Claire preferred coffee in the morning to start his day.

"Good morning, Grandfather; you're sleeping later, I see," the man eating a poached egg and toast said but did not stand.

Lord St. Claire walked awkwardly with a cane into the morning room and grumped, "It's about bloody time you showed up. Where have you been hiding, and what have you been up to?"

Lord St. Claire's grandson, Matthew Sutton, tall, good looking, rich, and arrogant had the smooth manners of a well-bred Englishman still in top physical form from his daily routine of doing whatever exercise suited him. He ran, skied, fenced, played polo, swam, mountain climbed, lifted weights, martial arts of several flavors, or anything else he could find to do.

Matthew sipped his coffee and said, "Oh, I've been gadding about in the colonies taking care of affairs. And, if it hadn't been for your lap dog, Cousin Alan, I would be enjoying a rather pleasant affair this evening."

Lord St. Claire pounded his cane on the stone floor, "That's not good enough! That damned Italian Cassanzo is still hounding me for a solution. We are running out of time, and you have not produced anything. Senor Cassanzo is going to outlive me just for spite, and everything will be ruined."

"Nonsense, Grandfather," Matthew said, "Everything is going to be fine. Senor Cassanzo will get his revenge, and we will step in and pick up the very large pieces."

St. Claire pointed with his cane at Matthew, "Your cousin Alan has not been able to produce any evidence young Hollingsworth was adopted. How certain are you that he was adopted?"

Matthew eased back in the seat feeling the heat of the rising sun warm him, "Oh, I am very certain."

"Not good enough, young man. I need something Alan can take to court. How do you know?"

"It is very simple, Grandfather. Hollingsworth, senior, was only married once. There were no affairs ... on his part, no requests for child support, no quiet payoffs. He was surprisingly monogamous. Of course, with a wife like her, I can see why. And she certainly had no children."

Lord St. Claire's nose went up in the air, "How can you be so certain of her?"

"Let's just say that I had intimate knowledge of her body. Many things passed between her legs, but none of them were children, this I can assure you."

"Hmph," St. Claire snorted. "I can't exactly take that before a judge, can I!"

Matthew sat forward, "Tell cousin Alan he is missing something. Mrs. Hollingsworth investigated her husband regularly. She assured me there was no unfaithfulness on his part. I always found it odd she was so keen on making sure of it so often."

The old man looked over his glasses, "Not good enough, young man. Who investigated? I need a name."

"Well I don't have a name, Grandfather," Matthew insisted over the top edge of *The Times*. "You'll just have to tell Alan to dig it up. He's got a bloodhound for this sort of thing."

"There's another matter you need to be aware of," St. Claire said moving on. "There were several inquiries into young Hollingsworth's past. We put a stop to it quickly enough but it appears young

Hollingsworth is now assisting the FBI. He was working on some task force nonsense."

Matthew looked up, "Seriously? The FBI? My, the young man does get around." Matthew shifted his attention back to the financial section of The Times. Turning a page he continued, "With his upbringing, I'm surprised he's not locked up somewhere."

"Now Matthew, I'm tired of your presence here. Give me the run down, and then you can be off. I know you want to get cracking on your affairs."

Matthew bowed, "Certainly Grandfather," and Matthew folded the newspaper and proceeded with his presentation.

"The Cassanzo foundations are starting to crack. Their support in Italy is on the verge of collapse, and their resources will be diminished soon enough. Cousin Alan will work the adoption angle. Dudley Hollingsworth has signed the contracts last month to give us management rights to all his financial affairs. So even if Cassanzo targets Dudley for revenge, we will still retain control. If young Hollingsworth gets the estate, Cassanzo will end his short reign and a new 'last will and testament' will miraculously be found and put the estate in our hands."

"Very good, Matthew, now get off this estate before I set the dogs on you."

"I love you too, Grandfather," Matthew said dropping the paper and picking up his suit jacket." Matthew added, "But you don't have dogs anymore, remember?"

St. Claire added, "If you don't leave quickly, Martin will get some. And don't stay away so long."

Matthew turned back at the main hallway and said with a grand bow and sweep of the hands, "As you wish, Lord St. Claire."

44 Caldwell Murder Site

900 Block, East 34th Street, Brooklyn, New York

Saturday, July 23, 2011, 10:00 AM EDT

Tommy's cell chirped. Tommy looked at the number, excused himself from the agents and police gathered around the outline of a body. Tommy answered in his official manner.

"Agent Edwards."

"Tommy, this is Andy Glover."

"Andy, thanks for calling. I've left you a few messages. I could use your help. We are spread pretty thin out here."

"Tommy, I've got something that might help. I believe I know a clue linking the Random murders together."

"Well, don't keep me guessing kid. What do you have?"

"This is about money. It's not about stealing money but moving it or keeping it from moving."

"How do you know this, Andy? Don't hold back on me."

"Tommy, I can't tell you. It's for your protection and mine. I need to see the Rossetti inventory list and everything you've got on the Caldwell site."

"I'm standing at the Caldwell site. It's still fresh. How'd you find out? No, don't tell me; just get your butt over here."

"On my way, Tommy. Apology accepted," Andy said with a laugh.

"Go to hell," Tommy closed with and hung up.

He hated being wrong.

45 Reporting In

Blackford Crighton Law Firm

New York Offices

Saturday, July 23, 2011, 10:20 AM EDT

"Yes, Sir Smythley, I am still working on it."

-

"No, nothing has changed since my last report from yesterday."

-

"No Sir, I was not being impertinent, Sir."

-

"I only ... Yes Sir, we have a very good bloodhound."

-

"Were you able to find out what we need?"

There was a pause in Alan's office while he took notes.

-

"Yes Sir, very important piece of information. I will get the bloodhound on it straight away. Yes, thank you S ..."

"He hung up on me," Alan said to the empty office. He took a deep breath and blew it out.

"Miss Montgomery," Alan sighed into the phone.

Miss Montgomery walked in smiling as usual and carrying a fresh coffee across the large office.

"I appreciate you coming in on Saturday and ..."

Alan noticed the coffee and his mood brightened, "You know, any one of the paralegals can bring me coffee, Miss Montgomery," Alan said.

It suddenly occurred to Alan he seemed to say that quite often. He looked at Miss Montgomery as she approached his desk; conservative business suit, naturally red hair cut short, thin but athletic with enough curve for a woman. Alan smiled as she set the cup down. She was pretty in a straightforward way, no frilly fanciness about her, a quality he admired.

"I don't mind getting you coffee, Mr. Hopkins."

"You didn't spend buckets of money on your education just so you could bring me coffee. Where did you say you graduated?"

"Dartmouth, Sir."

"Top of your class, as I recall."

"Yes Sir."

Alan forgot himself for a moment, "Oh, right! You're probably wondering why I called. I need Mr. Tanner's cell phone number and ..."

"Here you are, Sir," Miss Montgomery handed a slip of paper across the desk.

Alan was surprised at her forethought, "Right. Very good, yes, very good indeed. That will be all. Thank you ... um ... Miss Montgomery."

Their eyes met. Neither spoke. Miss Montgomery broke the silence by smiling again. Then she turned and walked toward the doors. As she turned to close them, she smiled and nodded saying, "You're welcome ... Mr. Hopkins."

Once again Alan took a deep breath and exhaled but for a very different reason, "That must be what the yanks call 'having a moment.'"

His morning suddenly seemed a little brighter.

Alan dialed. (ring ... ring ...)

"Mr. Hopkins, what can I do for you?" the thick Brooklyn accent asked.

"Mr. Tanner, I heard back from the home office. They could not give us much to go on, but I did learn this. Mr. Hollingsworth was being investigated by a private agency for domestic issues, fidelity, what have you. I understand this happened regularly. It would benefit us greatly to talk to the investigation staff and acquire their records and findings, even have a chat. Do you think you could find them?"

"Yes Sir, Mr. Hopkins. Take me three phone calls to find out who. The talkin' and acquirin' will take some negotiatin'. I'll let you know in two hours tops."

"Very good, Mr. Tanner. A pleasure doing business, Sir."

46 Andy is Back

Caldwell Murder Site

900 Block, East 34th Street, Brooklyn, New York

Saturday, July 23, 2011, 10:30 AM EDT

The cab dropped Andy at the corner. It was as close as he could get with all the police and emergency service vehicles. Tommy walked over to meet Andy outside the ring of reporters, neighbors, and emergency personnel.

"Hey Tommy, what can you tell me?"

Tommy stopped Andy's forward progress with a hand up signaling him to stop, "First things first. Okay, you didn't tell me everything you know, but you were straight with me. I'll do the same. I had a conversation with some CIA agents. They told me some people want you dead. They didn't say who, but you need to know. I couldn't tell you until I knew no one was listening."

Andy nodded, "I just found out myself. Nothing's happening yet. My birthday's not until August 1st."

"Your birthday?" Tommy looked confused but then put his hands up, "I know, I know. You can't tell me."

"Whose house was this?" Andy asked changing the subject.

"Wait until we're inside," Tommy replied and escorted Andy past several reporters and the uniforms guarding the steps to the house.

As they crossed the threshold, Tommy started giving Andy the run down, "Walt or Walter Caldwell, sixty seven, union guy, Boiler Makers. His throat was cut, but he's got the beginnings of the same design cut into one of his arms. That's why I called."

Andy put praying hands up to his mouth, but he wasn't praying, his eyes wide open as he surveyed the room with the predator's look. He looked down at the victim. The body had been left as it was found by Agent Edwards' orders. The left arm showed the beginnings of smoothly curving lines cut into the skin starting at his right wrist. The lines showed the same artistic flow. They never touched or overlapped. The space between the flowing lines never varied but became as much a part of the pattern as the lines. Andy gazed around the room past the dwindling number of police uniforms and forensics winding up their collection process. After two minutes, he started walking around the living room in a circle pointing at things and shaking his head. He walked to the kitchen and looked into the room.

"Tommy, did you have them check out the pots and pans? The knives, cutting board and spoons? Or the drain boards?"

Tommy walked toward the kitchen, "Sure, Angela Ricchetti knows the routine. She's already headed back to the lab. Why?"

"Tommy, get Angela back. Something different happened here. We might have a shot at getting a print."

"Angel," Tommy spoke into his cell, "Andy says we need you back at the Caldwell site. Yeah, okay. I'll tell him. Hey Andy, Angela says you're a real pain in the ass. She also says you need to tell the two techs still on site what you want."

Andy rolled his eyes and nodded.

"He knows, Ange. Thank you, and you're welcome."

47 Cassanzo Villa

Rambling One Floor Villa on a Working Farm in the Hills

Near Orsara di Puglia, Province of Foggia, Italy

Saturday, July 23, 2011, 4:30 PM UTC +1 (10:30 AM EDT)

(Conversation in Italian)

"Is that him?" the old winemaker asked shielding his eyes against the sun.

The wheat fields were white for harvest adding to the afternoon glare. The smell of ripe wheat, grape vines, and dust floated on the breeze flowing up the hill to the villa and barns at the top. Three men walked the dirt road toward the bridge over the stream.

One of the young workers shouted, "It is him! Look how he walks. Alberto must be on his left. Look how short he is. Let's harness the horse to the cart and get them."

Agosto squinted his seventy five year old eyes while still seated in the shade of the ancient barn. "By the time you get a horse and put the harness on it, they will be here." Agosto wiped a faded red handkerchief over his sweating forehead. He and the two younger men spent the morning hauling the vine cuttings and orchard pruning to the burn pile behind the barn. If there were to be a celebration in the evening, Agosto would be ready for a bonfire.

A well-dressed man in clean beige pants and white short-sleeved shirt walked up behind Agosto.

Agosto said, "Stefano is here," pointing down the dirt road.

"Good, now we can get started. I will tell the others to get ready."

"Roberto, what can I do to help?" Agosto asked.

Roberto put his hand on Agosto's shoulder, "Agosto, you can pray my father will listen to him before the other families force us out."

Roberto turned and walked back through the barn toward the villa. As he entered the door nearest the kitchen, he felt the cool breeze coming through the open windows. An elderly woman asked about Stefano as she kneaded more flour into the bread dough.

"He is here, almost to the stream," Roberto said as he passed.

The large table sat in an alcove to the large great room supported by dark brown carved columns. He called to the maid, "Tell the sisters and their husbands Stefano has come. Tell them to meet us here."

Elena scurried off to the living quarters on the south wing of the home. Roberto heard laughter of the younger children in the olive grove growing up the hill to the back of the villa. Roberto put his hand on one of the oak pillars supporting the great room. He looked up into the vaulted ceiling his great, great grandfather had built. How much longer would their family last here he wondered. His father's past refusals brought them to this precipice. Now the family had to act together.

Roberto's thoughts were interrupted by the three men entering the main door.

"Stefano!" Roberto called out and walked over and embraced his older brother.

Roberto was tall, thin, good looking in classic Mediterranean manner and coloring. Stefano was just as tall but sturdily built with a more serious demeanor than his younger brother.

"Good to see you, little brother," Stefano replied.

"Cousin Alberto!" Robert continued, "I didn't know you were coming until I saw you walking to the house."

Stefano introduced the third man with dead eyes and many scars, "Roberto, this is Salvatore. He will be helping us work out the solution to our problem."

Roberto held out his hand and said, "My brother brought you so you are welcome in our home."

Salvatore took his hand and said, "Thank you."

Roberto turned to Stefano, "We will meet here and then go talk to father. I want us to be in agreement in case, well, just in case."

Stefano walked into the great room and looked around at family portraits, pausing in front the picture of his own daughter Celestina playing with her cousins.

48 Jimmy

Jersey City, New Jersey

Saturday, July 23, 2011, 11:00 AM EDT

A wiry man with a face much older than his fifty plus years walked out of the bank and crossed Washington Boulevard followed by Roscoe Tanner. They climbed into the dark limousine, and the car pulled away from the curb.

Alan spoke first, "Are you satisfied Mister ...?"

"Jimmy, you can call me Jimmy," the wiry man said.

Alan sat facing Jimmy with Roscoe seated on Jimmy's right.

"Yeah, the money's good. You just bought one hour of my time so start with the questions."

Alan opened a small notebook, "I understand the firm that employed you in 1987 was contracted by Mrs. Randall Hollingsworth to investigate her husband. Is this correct?"

"I suppose you could say dat," Jimmy sniffed. "Truth is, she dint contract wit nobody dat I know of. It was always some other guy."

"Do you recall who?" Alan asked.

"Yeah, it was a couple a guys everyone was bowing down to, ya know, like dey was important."

Jimmy continued, "So we are watching dis guy, you know, the husband. Well, one night we see him banging the wife, you know, like everything's okay, I'm thinking. So later, we're supposed to be watching the husband, but he's sleeping. So the wife leaves the room and we catch her in another window humping some other guy. And she ain't just lying there. I mean this girl's got stamina, if you know what I mean. And dat wasn't the only time."

Alan needed to keep on track, "Yes, thank you Mister, uh, Jimmy. Could we get back to Mr. Hollingsworth? What did you learn about him?"

Jimmy smirked "The guy was a dullard. I mean he gave his lady a good run most nights. Not that it was ever enough for her. She was . . ."

"Jimmy, please. Mr. Hollingsworth?" Alan reminded again.

"Oh yeah. Well, we hear him talking about some group called 'The Order,' see. And I'm thinking he might be into some weird shit, right? Turns out, when he ain't in the room these two guys laughing that they made up the whole 'Order' business to convince Hollingsworth to cap some people for 'em. They said they was stopping money. Whatever dat means. But these two guys, they told Hollingsworth he was way up in da chain of command in 'The Order' 'cause he was willing to take care of business for 'em. We guessed stopping money was their business. It must a been pretty profitable."

Roscoe asked, "Take care of whose business?"

Jimmy shook his head, "Dunno, but seems Hollingsworth went out and got a lot of people involved into the 'Order' thing. I mean, Hollingsworth took it seriously, but these guys was laughing at him the whole time. Hey, I'm no boy scout. I seen some bad stuff. I been in the service, and I worked for one of the New York families for a while, and I'm telling ya, it was hard watching some of the shit they was doing."

Alan winced and forced a smile, "Jimmy, I need to know about a little boy who lived at the house, the manor. Do you remember seeing any children?"

"Yeah, there was one little guy there. Didn't see him much and not for long. I mean like, we would see him for a second, and then he was gone. It was one of the games we played while watching the house, you know, catching the wife screwing somebody or seeing the kid. The wife, she was easy, I mean, wow ..."

"Jimmy!" Roscoe ordered.

"Oh yeah, but it was the kid who was tough to catch. They called him Trash or 'The Mistake.' I never did catch his name. It was tough for me to take. I had small kids at the time and I hurt pretty bad for the little guy, but you know, there was nothing I could do."

Alan leaned forward, "What I am looking for is evidence of whether he was adopted or was he their natural child."

"Let's see," Jimmy rubbed his chin, "I don't remember hearing nothing about him being adopted, and I pray to God they wasn't his real parents! I mean, no parents should treat their kids like dat."

"How did they treat him?" Alan asked.

"Kept him up all hours of the night. Making him work all the time and cleaning up their parties." Jimmy used two fingers to make the quotes when he said parties.

"What do you mean by parties?" Alan asked leaning forward.

"What! You don't know?" Jimmy gasped. "Oh, my fricking Aunt Gertrude! I thought that was why you hunted me down. Man, they was killing people! I mean one or two a week, sometimes more."

Alan was stunned. He looked at Roscoe for some meaning. He felt his eyes tearing up involuntarily.

Roscoe noticed the shock registering on Aslan's face so he took over.

"Okay Jimmy. So you're telling me they were killing people, and you never reported this?"

"Naw man. The pay was more than double. Sometimes a LOT more, and I seen people killed before. At first I was trying to be all tough, but it wasn't until we seen this little boy, I'm talking six or seven maybe, cleaning up blood. That was it, man. I started to break. I had to get out and didn't want the money no more."

"You were paid more than double?"

"Yeah, the company paid us our regular rate, and then the Brit paid us even more."

Alan snapped out of his daze wiping tears from his eyes, "Brit? What Brit?"

Jimmy slapped his forehead, "Oh yeah, the guys laughing at the husband, dey was Brits."

Roscoe looked to Alan who was still shaken.

"Who were these Brits?" Roscoe asked.

"I dunno. I only saw 'em at a distance. Charlie was who dealt with 'em. The kid paid us in cash. The old guy I only saw once or twice."

Alan was now looking down at his hands. He then asked the question he did not want to hear answered, "Can you describe them?"

"Oh yeah, the kid was maybe twenty, blonde wavy hair, six foot even, one seventy-five pounds. Definitely a poodle kinda guy. We caught him banging the wife more than a few times. The old guy was same height, had a big white mustache though."

This was roughly the answer Alan did not want to hear.

"And one more thing you might want to know," Jimmy added. "The wife liked this Brit kid a lot like dey had a thing going, you know, more'n just sex. I personally overheard her talking to her husband about training this Brit kid to be their successor in 'The Order.'"

Roscoe asked, "Since 'The Order' was a hoax, why would it matter?"

"'Cause it started a big fight. Probably the only real fight I heard between 'em. The husband says the kid, the Brit, would have to inherit everything. She says she already got the wills written up. Then the heat really turned up. We didn't need no bugs or cameras to hear 'em yelling then. Finally, she tells da husband he would be welcomed into the highest social circles in England. That's when he starts calming down."

"Do you know if they signed the wills?" Alan asked still looking at his hands as if they also were covered in blood.

"Dunno. They killed some Italian princess one night and made the little boy clean it up. I left. I mean, I took off. That job wasn't worth it."

"So you never went back," Roscoe said.

"Went back? I never went back to my apartment. I hid out in a buddy's garage in Hoboken. These were some serious freaks. Charlie should a done the same. Police found him in a vacant house on Long Island all cut up. Dis job screwed everybody: me, Charlie, everybody. And if the little boy survived, he would be one screwed up individual."

49 Still at the Caldwell Murder Site

900 Block, East 34th Street, Brooklyn, New York

Saturday, July 23, 2011, 11:30 AM EDT

Andy walked into the living room where they were packing up their equipment, and he explained to the forensic technicians he wanted them to look for prints on the kitchen faucet, the rim of the kitchen sink, the dish soap bottle, any other surfaces in and around the drain board or close to the stove.

After describing the task, Andy stood and faced the wall above Walt Caldwell's desk. He stopped, but his mind raced through what he had seen and heard.

"Tommy," Andy began, "you said Mr. Caldwell belonged to the Boiler Makers Union." Andy pointed to several service awards and commendations on the wall.

"Where was he working?"

"He retired last year, but pay stubs show he was working part time at the Cribbs Tower in the Financial District."

It clicked in Andy's head, "That's it Tommy! We've got to find out what money managers, brokers, investment bankers are in that building. I'm pretty sure that the killer was looking for access to the building, blue prints, anything like to ..."

Andy's face showed surprise for a second time, then a worried look. "Tommy, I need to find out if Radic and Feld has an office in the Cribbs Tower."

Tommy flipped his cell open and spoke while he speed dialed Carlos, "Andy, who is Radic and Feld?"

"They're some kind of ..."

Tommy held up a finger, "Carlos, I need to find out if there is a Radic and Feld office in Cribbs Tower. Yeah, right now." Tommy gave Andy a questioning look.

There was a moment's pause, "Okay, great. Give me the office number and phone." Tommy scribbled in his notebook.

As soon as Tommy hung up, Andy started again: "Mr. Rossetti had a bunch of financial papers on his desk. I saw several envelopes from Radic and Feld. The address was Cribbs Tower. I think they handle international money transfers."

"So you also have a photographic memory," Tommy said looking up after dialing the number Carlos had given him.

"I only remember some things. I thought the financial angle might be important."

Tommy listened and then hung up and dialed Carlos again, "Carlos, the office is closed for the weekend. Give me the number for Cribbs Tower Management Office." After a pause, Tommy wrote the number in his notebook and started dialing.

"Andy, you think this Radic and Feld group is the link to the Random killings?"

Andy nodded, "Whoever handled the Cassanzo holdings will be the next victim. If they worked for Radic and Feld, it will link Rossetti and Caldwell to the Cassanzo family."

Tommy held up a finger again to pause the conversation, but his mind raced back to his meeting with the CIA where they mentioned Andy was associated with the famous Celestina Cassanzo disappearance.

"Mr. Maynard, this is Special Agent Tommy Edwards of the FBI. I need to contact the person in charge of the Radic and Feld office ..."

-

"Yes, I know you cannot give out the information. Write this down. This is a matter of life and death. I need you to contact the Manhattan FBI office. Ask them to put you through to Agent Tommy Edwards, that's me. My badge number is 2850 M. Please do this immediately. Lives are at stake ..."

Tommy closed his cell and turned toward Andy, "Tell me about the fingerprints."

"The psycho," Andy said turning toward the living room, "got interrupted."

Andy walked over to the body and picked up the right wrist. The blood had been wiped away revealing the cuts. "Look! See how even the pattern is here, through these lines and here, more here. Then, here, see how the pattern has a jagged cut here. It's like something surprised him. He takes the body out of the chair and ... *coup de grâce*," Andy pretended to hold a knife and sliced it across the victim's neck.

Andy continued explaining while walking into the kitchen, "Then he went into the kitchen and cleaned up. The sink still has a strong scent of dish soap. Whatever he cleaned, he didn't clean the surface of the sink like he did at Mr. Rossetti's. He was hurrying."

Tommy's cell rang and he opened it, "This is Agent Edwards ... Mr. Maynard, thank you for calling back. Give me the name, number, and address." Tommy wrote frantically.

-

"Got it. Thanks."

Tommy dialed the number. There was a pause. "Nathan Kahn? This is Special Agent Tommy Edwards of the FBI. We have credible evidence someone from your office is in serious danger."

-

"What? Do NOT return to your house! Get to a police station as quickly as possible."

-

"Yes, fine, go there. Mr. Kahn, are you responsible for the Cassanzo holdings?"

-

"Oh! Who else? Can you give me his address and cell number?"

-

Tommy wrote in his note pad with his cell held to his ear with his shoulder and started walking toward the front door. He motioned Andy to follow him while talking, "Thank you Mr. Kahn. We will have someone contact you at the police station."

Andy followed Tommy down the steps. Two reporters followed them for half a block asking questions, but Tommy had dialed and was again on the phone. He put his hand up signaling no response. The reporters asked Andy the same questions, but Andy held up his hand also, and they stopped following.

"Steve, I need you to get some agents and local police to this address on Long Island. I think this is the next victim. Here's the address ..."

50 This Old Man

Cassanzo Villa

Orsara di Puglia, Province of Foggia, Italy

Saturday, July 23, 2011, 5:50 PM UTC +1 (11:50 AM EDT)

The old man had an oxygen tank attached to the side of his wheelchair. He watched the children playing in the olive grove from under the ancient grape arbor. He heard people come out the door and tried to turn to see who was there. His thin lips drew tight when he saw his oldest son Stefano. "So you finally have come back. Where is your wife?" he demanded.

"She will not come, Father," Stefano said.

The old man looked around at his two sons and three daughters with their husbands. Roberto's wife stood in the doorway of the house.

"You look like a mob come to kill me," Signore Cassanzo stated. "What do you want? Why is Alberto here? And who is this stranger? He looks like Mafiosi," he said pointing at Salvatore.

"Father," Stefano began, "I have come to keep the oath you made me take."

The elder Cassanzo looked suspiciously, "What oath, and who is this stranger?"

Stefano knelt on one knee, "Father, when I was twelve I was standing with you under this grape vine. You held me by both shoulders and made me swear to you I would do whatever was needed to protect our family."

"So who threatens our family?"

"You do, father."

"What are you talking about?"

"Since my daughter Celestina was taken from us, you have refused to attend to our family's business. You moved here, our summer home, and now you never leave. You want revenge for her death, but you won't take revenge, and you won't let us live."

"Bah! You talk like your worthless brother."

Stefano glanced apologetically at Roberto then back to his father.

"Father, the other families have met. They say they have waited long enough. Our money cannot be moved because of problems in America with the fund managers."

"What problems?" Signore Cassanzo demanded.

"The same ones Roberto and the others have been telling you about. Someone has been killing or threatening the people who manage our assets or their family members. Our businesses are handicapped because we cannot use our own money."

"Then get new ones and then find me Celestina's killer! The same thing I have been telling you all!" He waved a gnarled finger at his children.

"Father, this isn't a fruit cart in the market. These are multi-national businesses. You can't just move to the next stall. Agreements need to be negotiated. Trust needs to be built, but you are holding us back from moving. Our money is the blood of our business and of the other families. If it doesn't move, we will die, and the other families will remove us from our place. All we will have left are fruit carts in the market and the land around us."

Stefano stood up, "Father, because of my oath to you, because I love you and this family, I am asking you to step down from being the head of the family business."

The father squinted his eyes, "Very smart, very loving you traitor, you Judas! I will not quit, and you cannot make me while I still breathe," the old man ended with a sneer.

Stefano looked down at the ground, "Father, we must in order to survive."

"Then I will curse you all and your children and grandchildren. Do you want that?"

"No Father," Stefano said shaking his head, "I do not want that, and the other families will not accept us if you do, but I've come today to make you a promise. In exchange for this promise, you will allow Roberto and me to get our family's assets under our own control."

"So are you finally willing to take revenge for your own daughter?"

Stefano and his father locked eyes. With a strained voice Stefano said, "I will do whatever is needed to protect our family."

The father's eyes narrowed and he hissed, "I will tell you what you must do. First," his teeth clenched, "you must visit Carlo Vendante. He will be our messenger."

51 Carson Murder Site

Glen Cove, New York

Saturday, July 23, 2011, 1:30 PM EDT

The mood was somber as the forensic teams moved around the house. Agents Angela Ricchetti and Carlos Barrera talked outside on the walk as Tommy Edwards and Andy pulled onto the gravel drive of the large home in the small town of Glen Cove. Andy saw a swing set in the yard, and his stomach twisted in a knot.

Tommy walked up to the agents trailed by Andy, "Tell me," he said with resignation.

Angela looked up from the ground. Her eyes were moist but under control. "The wife and little boy were in the back den on the first floor, single shot to the head for both of them. William Carson had run some errands but the perp' was waiting for him. Carson dropped a bunch of items from hardware and paint stores in the side entryway when he was shot. There was no sign of a struggle. Not the same MO."

"It doesn't matter," Tommy said, "Andy made the connection. We know it's our random."

Carlos asked, "So what is the connection for Rossetti, Caldwell, and Carson?"

Tommy turned to Andy, "Correct or add anything I miss."

Tommy faced the team, "It appears Rossetti was a signatory for some large financial holdings for a wealthy family in Italy, named Cassanzo. How Random found out about Rossetti, we haven't figured out yet, but Caldwell was working part time as a maintenance man in the Cribbs Tower where Carson worked. He and a ..." here Tommy looked at his notebook, "Mr. Nathan Kahn were the principal account managers for Cassanzo."

Angela asked, "Why were they killed? What's the motive?"

-

In a bar in Jersey City, New Jersey, Roscoe Tanner sipped his tequila while Alan knocked back his third shot of Johnny Walker.

"It's about the money," Roscoe said as he set his tumbler back on the table.

"But why? That doesn't get them any money?" Alan said with the slightest hint of a slur.

"Money's like oil," Roscoe started. "When it's in the ground, worthless. Put it in a barrel and people will be fighting for it. Money's only valuable when it is available. When countries can't move money, wars start. When companies can't move money, they go under."

Alan was leaning back in the booth in a back corner. Only two other customers sitting at the bar watched a ball game with the bartender.

"When did you get so smart about money? I can't imagine this comes up much in your line of work, no offense."

Roscoe smirked, "None taken. I got a subscription to *The Economist*, and I read a lot. I even started working on my master's thesis in economics on this very subject when I was still on the force in Albany. I called it 'The Pillars of Civilizations.'"

"Why in blazes didn't you complete it, man?"

Roscoe appreciated the fact that Alan was letting his guard down and getting more personal.

"I didn't complete it 'cause no one took me seriously, not my profs, not the guys on the force. Even my family used to crack the only job I could get in economics was doing collections."

Alan raised an empty shot glass, "Well Roscoe, in my book, you are aces. I believe that is how Bogart would say it."

Roscoe smiled and stood up, "C'mon Mr. Hopkins. No more for you. We gotta get you back."

Roscoe put a big arm around Alan's shoulders when he first tried to stand.

"You really must call me (hic) Alan. Really."

52 The Edge of Memory

Carson Murder Site

Glen Cove, New York

Saturday, July 23, 2011, 1:30 PM EDT

Andy followed the last forensics technicians out of the house. Tommy saw Andy walking down the steps, "Anything we miss?" Angela and Steve looked at each other. Steve was particularly annoyed Tommy seemed to seek Andy's opinion exclusively.

"No, just like Angela said."Andy returned with a frown.

"But what?" Carlos said.

"Probably nothing, but I feel like there is something I am supposed to remember. I don't know why, but there is something familiar here."

Carlos said, "Familiar good or familiar bad?"

"Familiar scary," Andy replied as Tommy's cell chirped. Tommy turned away from the team and answered.

The group collectively held its breath. They could see by Tommy's shoulders and frozen stance he was listening intently.

-

"Okay, got it. We'll look into it."

Tommy spun back around, "This may or may not be about the case but Doctor Andriano is missing. No one has seen her or heard from her in a week. The assistant director sent a couple of uniforms to her apartment, and they couldn't get in the door and refused to go back without support. Steve, take Andy over to her apartment. Have a couple of uniforms meet you. Find out what's going on."

53 The Confession

Cassanzo Villa

Orsara di Puglia, Province of Foggia, Italy

Saturday, July 23, 2011, 7:30 PM UTC +1 (1:30 PM EDT)

"Those are my terms!" the elder Cassanzo pounded on the old oak table with his gnarled fist.

A stunned silence followed.

Stefano broke the silence, "Papa, my Teresa hates you for what you said to her and to us all. She will never come back to me if I conspired with you to take revenge for Celestina's death."

Signore Cassanzo said, "She will come when we bring her daughter back for burial here. A mother's heart. She will come. I don't care what she thinks of me."

Roberto spoke up, "Father, it has been more than twenty years. If the British could not find her killer or her body in all those years, how can we find them?"

"Because," Signore Cassanzo said flatly, "things have changed. I never thought the British were working hard to find the killer. I always asked myself why. Why do they not want the killer found? Were they helping the American?"

Wine and cheese had been brought out, but no one was eating or drinking. Signore Cassanzo looked around the group sitting around the oak table under the lights strung through the ancient olive tree. He leaned forward, "Now I will tell you a secret you will not believe, but it is true. I swear it."

"The killing of the Americans, the burning of their house ..." Cassanzo paused as all gathered waiting to hear what they already knew but no one admitted.

Signore Cassanzo continued, "I had nothing to do with those things."

There was uncomfortable shifting as confusion filtered through their minds. This was not what they were expecting.

Roberto spoke up, "Of course you had this done. You even said so once. You bragged about it."

There was talk all around the table until Stefano held up his hand, "Father, if you did not do this, then who did?"

"Maybe your friend here knows," Signore Cassanzo said pointing to Salvatore.

Salvatore held up his hands, "I was seventeen when it happened. I know nothing."

Signore Cassanzo offered, "Then maybe it was the Vendante family. Maybe it was another American family. Maybe it was the British."

54 Carmen's Apartment (Reprise)

Fourth Floor, 252 West 22nd Street, New York City

Saturday, July 23, 2011, 3:10 PM EDT

The stench was apparent in the hallway. There were no sounds from the apartment but an unease flowed out with the stench beyond smelling and hearing.

The second day after Carmen came back, all the tenants in the surrounding apartments left. The sights, sounds, and smells frightened them off. The small group consisting of two uniformed policemen, the super', Carmen's sister Natalia, Andy, and Steve Haskins approached the apartment.

The super's hands were shaking as he tried to insert the key into the dead bolt. Andy reached out and took the keys from him. The super gladly surrendered them and stood back.

Andy bowed his head praying. The police looked at Steve for an explanation. Steve shook his head with a look of disgust and smacked the back of Andy's head.

Andy spun back to Steve. His eyes flashed anger, "Don't ever touch me again."

Steve leaned into Andy's face, "What're you gonna do? Turn the other cheek?"

Andy's face showed fury, "No, something simple even you can understand. I can make sure you don't sleep for the next two decades. And I won't have to lift a finger."

Steve leaned into Andy, "You don't scare me."

Andy smiled, "I don't need to scare you. I only need you to understand."

Andy turned back to the door and stuck the key in the lock and grabbed the door handle. Steve moved his hand to his holstered service weapon and unsnapped the safety catch. Andy said quietly,

"Lord, you've brought me through all this before. Help me to do right. Thanks."

Carmen's sister Natalia said, "Amen."

Andy unlocked the deadbolt and stuck the key in the doorknob. The lock turned slowly, but Steve could tell Andy was having a hard time turning it. They heard the door start to move. Everyone tensed.

The door swung open. The apartment looked like a scene from a war zone, furniture overturned holes in the walls, clothing, dishes, and pictures had been thrown about, but it was the smell of rot that took their breath away.

Carmen's sister said, "I should go in first and make sure she's decent."

A spectral image of a headless man stood in the dim light near the middle of the living room. Natalia froze in the hallway.

Andy stepped past Natalia and said, "Don't worry about it. I'll take care of her. You stay here."

Andy walked three steps toward the image and turned to Steve, "Welcome to my world. Are you coming in?"

Steve could not force himself to move. Andy turned away from the door.

When he got to the middle of the living room, Steve heard Andy say, "Hey Headless. I see you're back. Where's Fatso and Mama?"

Andy stepped around what looked like vomit. "I assume Big Ugly is back here," he said walking down the hall. An inhuman scream was heard coming from the bathroom. When Andy looked in, a jar flew out of the door and smashed against the wall. Andy ducked in time and hurriedly stepped past the bathroom.

The last thing the group in the hall saw or heard was Andy calmly stating, "Real nice Harriet."

The apartment door slammed shut with force enough to move the doorjamb outward.

The keys, still in the lock, were thrown onto the floor when the door slammed. The super' picked up the keys and tried to put them in the lock, but for some weird reason, he kept dropping them. Steve could see the guy's nerves were shot. He didn't blame him. This was too much for anyone, even him! The police and the super slowly backed toward the end of the hall.

Steve heard sobbing in the apartment from time to time. It sounded like Carmen, but Natalia was not going near the door even if they could get it open. There were sounds of things moving around. After fifteen minutes had passed, the door opened. Andy asked Carmen's sister for the clothes she brought. Another thirty minutes passed and then Andy opened the door. His arm was around Carmen, but even her sister would not have recognized her. Her skin was a sickly pale, and her hair looked like whitened straw and was missing in places. There were sores, cuts, and what looked like small bite marks on her arms and legs.

Carmen clung to Andy's arm with her eyes closed. She repeated in a quiet voice, "I knew you'd come. I knew it. I believed. I knew you'd come. I had faith ..." Her voice trailed off.

Steve's skin started tingling as soon as he saw Carmen. Something was wrong with her. His hand moved involuntarily to his side arm. Her sister Natalia stepped forward to take Carmen's arm, but Carmen froze. Carmen's head jerked up, and her eyes were crazed.

Natalia fell backward, passed out. To Steve, Carmen's movements were out of sync with his senses. Steve looked at Natalia quickly and then back to Carmen as his arm slowly started to draw the weapon out.

"No!" Andy said quickly and firmly, "Steve, do not draw your weapon. It will only make it worse."

Steve kept his hand on his holstered weapon, and put his left hand out straight. The walls and floor were moving disjointedly.

Carmen was looking at him. Her mouth was not moving, but Steve heard her voice behind him. Steve looked over his left shoulder and saw someone behind him. He spun around to find Carmen standing solidly while the walls moved behind her. When he looked forward again, Carmen was with Andy, leaning on him, but the edges of her body were in constant motion. An image of Carmen moved out of her and forward with her arms held out.

Steve felt nauseous. He heard Andy speaking, but it was far off, "Breathe Steve, breathe slowly. If you feel like throwing up, go with it. Relax, you will get the hang of this, but it takes time."

Steve went to his hands and knees and started vomiting. As his whole body wretched, he became aware he was moving. Sounds were dulled as if a flash bang had stunned him.

Steve was then aware of the two police officers supporting him. They were outside and walking to their squad car.

His head and gut ached but he asked through the fog in his head, "Where's Dr. Andriano?"

"Easy big guy, you took a nasty fall," one of the officers said.

When they got him in the back seat of the squad car, Steve lay down on the seat and asked, "Where's the doctor and Andy?"

An officer got a white bag out of the trunk and was shaking it and rubbing the sides of it vigorously. The officer held the bag out for Steve.

"Agent Haskins, here, hold this on your head. It's cold. It'll help. Andy and the doctor were picked up by a priest and nun about 30 minutes ago."

"What happened?"

The two policemen looked at each other. Then one said, "We were watching through a crack in the door. The nearest we can figure is the doctor or part of the doctor reached out and touched you, and you fell through the floor. It took us a while to find you 'cause the floor below ain't laid out the same. You ended up in some old lady's living room."

"Did the floor break?"

"That's the freaky thing. There ain't no hole in the floor, or the ceiling downstairs. You just slipped through a solid floor."

55 Melt Down

Blackford Crighton Law Firm, New York Offices

21st Floor, 206 West 48th Street

Saturday, July 23, 2011, 6:00 PM EDT

Alan rubbed his forehead with his right hand. His left hand fingered the short tumbler with one finger of scotch remaining from the three he started with. Alan rarely drank, but today it seemed to be appropriate. During his interview with Jimmy, Alan realized the person who arranged for his position, Lord St. Claire, seemed to be an accomplice to crimes more heinous than Alan could have imagined. St. Claire's grandson, Matthew, was also deeply involved.

Ceiling lights off, Alan's desk lamp and the low table lamp next to the sitting area in the middle of the room provided a low, somber light to match Alan's state of mind. Alan slouched on the leather sofa furthest from the lamp with his back to the door. The door opened slowly.

"Mr. Hopkins?"

"Yes Miss Montgomery?" Alan said drearily without looking up or even moving.

Miss Montgomery walked to the sitting area, "Is everything all right, Mr. Hopkins?"

Alan looked straight ahead with tired eyes, "If this were a court of law, Miss Montgomery, I would be required to say 'No, your honor, everything's not all right.'"

"Did you have a bad day?"

Alan rubbed his forehead again, "No, a bad day is when you wake up late and lock your keys in the car. This was more of a finding out my father was a transvestite kind of day, and no he wasn't. It's just an example of ... of ... well, something much worse than b-bad."

"Mr. Hopkins, you probably shouldn't sit in the dark and drink alone. Don't you have some friends you can go out with?"

"Hmmm, friends! Did you know I was, I was the chief solicit ... solicitor, is British for attorney you know, solicitor."

"Yes, I know."

"I was the chief solicitor for estates and, and trusts in the home office. Then they sent me here."

Miss Montgomery walked around and sat on the front edge of one of the chairs demurely crossing her legs at her ankles. Alan could not help but notice.

She replied, "New York's not such a bad place. I thought you liked it here. You've done very well for yourself."

"Sure," Alan flung his head and one hand up. "I've done well. Worked my fingers to the bone for, for what?"

Miss Montgomery sat upright on the front half of the chair, "If you don't like it, why don't you quit?"

"Oh well, bloody easy for you Americans. You just go where you want, do what you want, set up shop in the middle of the wilderness, have a wolf for a pet."

He pointed at Miss Montgomery, "You know your whole economy is built around that."

"Sir?"

"It's why your houses are so far, so far, far apart and (burp), and outside of New York, there's no decent public transportation. Everyone has their own car and drives wherever they damn well feel like! Every store caters to anybody's idea of a good product even if it makes no sense at all. Pet rocks, your country invented pet rocks."

"Is that bad?"

"Bad? It's bloody brilliant! Something doesn't suit you, and you say 'take this job and shove it.' You don't have to be a tailor just because your father was a tailor. By the way, what was your father, Miss Montgomery?"

"My father is a potato farmer in Ohio."

"See? Exactly what I mean! Potato farming didn't suit you, so you run off to find your dream in New York City. You eat where you want and nobody tells you you can't." Alan shook an unsteady finger at Miss Montgomery, "It's not easy being British, you know. It's all 'stiff upper lip' and being a steady chap, 'Queen and country', being prop ... proper."

"Mr. Hopkins, if you could do anything you want, even if it's not proper, what would you do?"

Alan's head rocked back, "I know exactly what I would do. I would eat a whole pizza with all those different kinds of meat on it. Then I'd eat a gallon of vanilla ice cream ... and I'd stay up late and watch Casablanca three times."

Miss Montgomery grinned, "Why, Mr. Hopkins, you are a romantic."

Alan sighed, "Yes, a helpless ro- romantic. A lot of bloody good it does me. Doesn't fit in with being proper, unfortunately."

Miss Montgomery stood up and held her hand out to Alan, "Mr. Hopkins, if you come with me, I will take you to the best pizza shop I know and it's open until 2:00 AM, but you can't tell anyone we went out, and you must call me Alicia once we are out of the office."

Alan looked up at Alicia's hand and paused. Then he said, "What the hell. I'm in America."

He took her hand as he stood unsteadily, but he felt a jolt of electricity shoot through him when their hands touched. He quickly looked up at Miss Montgomery, Alicia, and apparently, she felt it too. Her stunned look quickly faded into a shy smile. Their hands let go as soon as they left Alan's office, and they walked out toward the elevators.

56 Cambourne Past and Present

Cambourne Hall Near Oxford, England

Saturday, July 23, 2011, 11:45 PM GMT (6:45 PM EDT)

Martin the butler walked through the dark and nearly vacant estate fondly remembering the large family that had once lived here. There were many parties and guests constantly coming and going at proper hours. He had been Head Butler in this house most of his adult life. His son and wife had both been employed on the estate. His life had been idyllic even if the hours were long. The previous Lord, William Sutton's great uncle, had been a large jovial man people loved to be around.

Martin's footsteps echoed off the stone walls and pillars as he made his way to Lord St. Claire's private study. For him it was a relief his wife had not lived to see the great house so empty. *She would have hated it.*

Martin knocked on the heavy oak door.

"Come in, Martin. You don't need to wait in the hall. The staff has left, and it is only the two of us here."

"Yes Sir. A cable arrived for you Sir."

Lord St. Claire waved an impatient hand, "Well, get on and read it."

The truth was it was an email Martin had printed out. Explaining this to Lord St. Claire only invited more ranting about the false promise of technological advances.

"This is from Foggia, Italy. It says Stefano Cassanzo has arrived at the villa along with his cousin Alberto and an enforcer."

"Well," demanded Lord St. Claire, "does it say who the enforcer is?"

"Yes, Sir. It says, em, yes, here it is. He is a former Mossad agent. He goes by the name Salvatore."

"Of course he does. He is the savior," Lord St. Claire said wearily in a mocking tone.

"Martin, in the morning have Alan Hopkins send a message to Matthew. Tell him Cassanzo brought in an enforcer. Matthew will understand."

"Very good, Sir. Will that be all?"

"Yes, good night Martin."

"Good night, Sir," Martin said closing the door. He made his way back through the drafty halls to his private quarters in the back of the east wing.

"All this cloak and dagger nonsense. Bessie would certainly not approve nor my son Adam for that matter. Good thing he is safely away in London."

57 The President's Daily Briefing

The White House, Washington, DC

Sunday, July 24, 2011, 9:50 AM EDT

Ed Garibaldi, the Director of National Intelligence, sat waiting patiently across the desk from the President. The President was reading the Presidential Daily Brief assembled by the CIA for the President's eyes only. Ed Garibaldi's presence was to provide any additional background information, answer questions, and initiate any follow up requested by the President.

"What are we doing about the Italian assassins?" the President asked without looking up from the report.

"We will be updating the FBI within the hour, Sir."

"Ed, I see Italy's economic problem is on the report again. This doesn't seem to warrant my attention. What is the problem I am supposed to be aware of?"

"Mr. President, it would take me an hour to scratch the surface."

"I don't have an hour, Ed. Readers Digest version."

"Okay, their economy is in the crapper. Many problems. Some of their resources have been sitting in US treasuries and institutions for a long time. Simply put, they have resources but aren't using them all. If the leaders of industry in Italy get their act together, they could start moving in a positive direction. The down side is some US institutions have been relying on Italian resources sitting still for too long. If their money gets put into circulation, our economy would take a small hit. If they start dumping treasury notes, it hurts our ability to borrow. Republicans and Democrats will cause trouble for the budget you just gave to Congress."

"Ed, does this have anything to do with the diplomatic pouches my Chief of Staff is getting almost daily from Europe?"

"I'm sorry, Mr. President. I can't tell you much about the them. We are aware they are coming more frequently. Most of them are from England. Our best guess is they are mostly dealing with requests for financial information on institutions and individuals. Short of interfering with their delivery, we haven't seen any of the requests yet. We only see the results. We also are aware Mr. Harriman received a diplomatic pouch sent here with his name on it."

The President's eyes narrowed, "That is a clear violation of international law! How dare he have it sent here! What else can you tell me about it, Ed?"

"Same as the others, it came from Whitehall, the British Foreign Offices."

"I'm going to put an end to this. I'll not have anyone using this office to commit crimes against this nation. Is the Chief of Staff breaking any laws?"

"None we know of. The EU has strict laws about them sharing a citizen's personal information, but the US does not."

The President pursed his lips and spoke, "Ed, Jim is an old friend, but if any of this is heading south, I want to know pronto!"

"Yes Sir, Mr. President."

"One last thing Ed. Did the technicians sweep for bugs after Harriman left? I'm sure they did, but I have to ask."

"Yes Sir. We started sweeping before he got to his car."

"Well, I want this office fumigated and disinfected too. I swear I smell cigar smoke every time he comes here."

"Yes, Mr. President."

58 Alan's Apartment

Sutton Place, New York City

24th Floor, Suite 3

Sunday, July 24, 2011, 10:49 AM EDT

Alan was now aware he was, in fact, alive. The pounding in his head was proof. He also knew he was not in a movie. If this was a movie, the beautiful, leggy red head would be lying next to him in bed, but she was not.

The one truth now outweighing all others, and the focal point of his whole existence, drinking beer after an afternoon of scotch and whiskey was a bad idea. The pizza and ice cream didn't help either.

Alan was pretty sure he waited until Alicia got him home before he vomited on the floor. This must be, Alan thought, how Americans feel about themselves: enjoying their over indulgences to the hilt and then feeling foolish about it later.

Obviously, not all Americans felt foolish later, but Alan did.

59 A Clear Message

Lord St. Claire's Estate

Cambourne Hall Near Oxford, England

Monday, July 25, 2011, 6:00 AM GMT (1:00 AM EDT)

The ambulance quietly pulled to an easy stop in front of the steps of the main doors of Cambourne Hall. Martin, the Hall's butler and manager, was in the kitchen reviewing the staff's responsibilities for the day. The morning light made the room cheery, and the coffee was handy. He drank tea during the day but had learned to drink morning coffee during his time in the army. Martin made notes for each of the staff to allow them to carry out their duties with minimal bother to him and impacting his own responsibilities. He heard the heavy door knocker being pounded and rose quickly to silence the intrusion to the morning solitude before Lord St. Claire was disturbed.

Walking quickly through the formal dining room that led into the grand entry, Martin, thankful a second round of knocking had not started, swung the heavy door inward revealing the presence of no one. There was only an ambulance with flashing lights. No driver or medical personnel were visible.

Andrew assumed the driver and EMT were in the back of the vehicle. He walked briskly to the back of the ambulance. No one was to be seen, so he opened the back door.

"Good God!" he shouted and stared.

A man was stretched out by his arms between the top shelving units up against the far wall. His dark hair was caked with blood, and both eyes were blackened and swollen shut. His mouth had duct tape over it. One arm was broken so badly the bone had pierced through the skin. The remnants of a once expensive suit had been sliced and torn to pieces along with the underlying skin. The exposed skin visible through the blood showed deep bruising. The head was held upright with a strap under the chin fastened to the ceiling. The bones of the face were shattered making the face look twisted. There was a large envelope attached to his feet. Martin saw the blood was fresh, the wounds were very recent. Then the body moved.

Martin put two fingers in his mouth and blew and astoundingly powerful whistle. A young man in his early twenties poked his head out of the large garage and stables at the far end of the house. Lights from the ambulance and Martin waving frantically brought him running with unbuttoned shirt and untied shoes across the white graveled drive.

Before the young man got to the ambulance, Martin re-directed him, "Timothy! Run and wake Lord St. Claire at once. Tell him this is an extreme emergency, and he must come quickly. Then call for an ambulance and the police. Quickly now!"

Timothy heard the urgency in Martin's command and complied without question, flying through the entry and up the staircase, he did not bother to close the door to the house.

Martin returned to the back of the truck and removed the envelope. Its contents were thick. He hurried to a bin of salt in the next to the steps. He lifted the lid and deposited the envelop. He closed the lid and smoothed the dirt to remove his footprints.

Other than the envelope, he did not touch anything for fear of causing the poor man more injury.

60 Intolerable

Cambourne Hall, Lord St. Claire's Estate

Monday, July 25, 2011, 10:25 AM GMT (5:25 AM EDT)

The intercom screamed, "Martin!" through the long stone and oak paneled hallways of Cambourne Hall followed by an uncustomary silence.

"Where is the blasted man!" St. Claire stormed to himself.

He sat at the large table in the Hall's business office Martin had managed for the last three decades. In front of him, he had spread out the contents of the large envelope Martin had wisely hidden. The envelope contained a note along with a pile of photographs. When the constables arrived with the ambulance followed by detectives from The Met (formerly Scotland Yard) an hour later, there was enough activity to obscure Martin secreting the envelop inside his coat.

Sitting at Martin's desk, St. Claire saw an additional small white envelope off to one side with Lord St. Claire's own name written in Martin's firm script. St. Claire opened the envelope. Inside was Martin's letter of resignation. *He deeply regretted ... and firmly resolved ... and circumstances being unsuitable . . .*

St. Claire let out a snort of disgust, "The man survived a war in the Middle East and one bloody body sends him running. Damn! This is the worst. Damn, Damn!

There was a knock on the office door.

"Come in, come in!" St. Claire stormed.

The young man from the garage poked his head around the corner.

"Begging your pardon, Lord. It's me, Timothy, your driver and mechanic. Martin asked me take him into Oxford, to the train station. He said you might be needing m' help. Is there anything I can do for you?"

"Yes, damn it. Here is a phone number in the states. Place this call immediately."

Timothy took the number and dialed from the phone on the desk.

Matthew answered his cell, "Hello, Martin?" Timothy handed the handset to Lord St. Claire.

-

"Matthew, where are you right now? Never mind, it doesn't matter. You must leave there immediately. Someone is watching you. Yes, I have pictures of you in the lobby of the Peninsula Hotel."

Timothy overheard Lord St. Claire say, "Cassanzo sent Carlo Vendante to my home. He was nearly dead. Wasn't he the one who was with Celestina the night she disappeared? There was a list of demands and photographs attached to him. There were pictures of our entire family including you.

-

This photograph shows you at a marine supply house. Someone wrote Jamaica, New York, on it. When were you there?"

Timothy, feeling very uncomfortable listening to this conversation, started to slowly back out of the room. He had only begun retreating when he heard St. Claire say, "Yes, they want her body back. They also want to end the blood ... Yes, they want her body. They are demanding an end to the name ..."

-

"I don't care what it takes ..." was the last thing Timothy heard as he quickly retreated to the privacy of the barn serving as a garage.

***

In the presidential suite at the Peninsula Hotel in New York City, Matthew Sutton tried to explain to his grandfather why this was impossible "... because Grandfather, her body was burned to ashes and the bones were ground up and spread around the estate! This was done with all the bodies. I saw her in the fire myself. We will have to give them a different body. How will they know? What choice do we have?"

-

Matthew heard static on the line and asked, "Grandfather did you call me on the secure line? Where is Martin? Let me talk to him. When did he leave? Grandfather, you must call Sir Smythley at once. Do you have his number? Tell him Martin left us. Call him as soon as we hang up. Good bye Grandfather."

Matthew pulled a duffel bag from the bedroom closet and headed toward the elevator. Matthew stepped off on the fourth floor. He walked to the service closet at the far end of the hallway. He opened the duffle bag and donned maintenance overalls, work boots, a hard hat, a lineman's tool belt, and sunglasses.

Matthew rode the service elevator to the garage level dressed as a telephone lineman. He stopped outside the elevator in the underground garage and lit a cigarette. Without a morning shave, he very much looked the part. He stood smoking while looking around. Satisfied no eyes were on him, he walked to a dusty white utility van. He drove slowly to the guard booth watching for any movement. The guard waved to him and lifted the gate. Matthew turned left onto West 54th Street and right into the one-way traffic on Fifth Avenue and was gone.

61 Forced to Wait

Cassanzo Villa

Orsara di Puglia, Province of Foggia, Italy

Monday, July 25, 2011, 12:10 PM UTC +1 (6:10 AM EDT)

The old man's wheel chair was under the grape arbor on the patio. The early green grapes hung down through the wires supporting the vine. The afternoon was quiet. Only the breeze and an occasional humming bird's flutter could be heard. Stefano stood in the doorway with the villa's great room behind him. The old man sipped red wine from a juice glass. A platter of different cheeses and hard salami were on the table next to him.

Stefano walked onto the patio and sat on one of the benches next to the ancient table. He picked up the knife and cut some cheese and salami. His father watched him.

"Father," Stefano said between bites, "the shooters are in place. One of them is missing. We assume he was picked up by the police, but he won't talk. Carlo Vendante will be eating through a straw for the rest of his life."

Signore Cassanzo sipped his wine and nodded.

"When can we start transferring control? The other families are ready to move against us."

Signore Cassanzo looked at his son sideways with a sharp expression. Then he turned to look at the olive grove growing up the hill in the back of the villa. He put one hand down flat on the table. This was his gavel. A decision was coming.

"We will start the process. The families will be satisfied for now. I will not hand over final control until the day of Celestina's funeral."

There was a pause for several minutes, then Stefano spoke, "Father, Papa, I know you are certain Celestina's body will be found. What if she is not found in time?"

Signore Cassanzo answered slowly, "That is my decision."

Stefano knew not to argue the point any further. He stood and said, "I will call the attorneys to start the paperwork."

He exited praying silently for his wife and also for Salvatore.

62 The Daily Run

Riverside Park, New York City

Monday, July 25, 2011, 6:45 AM EDT

"Tommy!"

Tommy Edwards thought he heard someone call but kept running.

"Tommy Edwards!"

Tommy looked over his left shoulder. He saw a white male, six foot, two inches, weight approximately one ninety, late twenties.

"Mind if I run with you?"

Tommy turned and continued running while the white male caught up to him.

"Do I know you?" Tommy asked without looking at him.

The runner was struggling to keep up and talk at the same time, "No, but (breath) (breath) some friends of mine (breath) met you once."

"CIA, right?"

"Yeah (breath). Got some intel (breath) on your boy (breath) (breath) and a rumor (breath)."

"I'm listening," Tommy said easily.

"It's gonna cost (breath). We want (breath) an interview with (breath) Glover."

"Give me the intel and rumor. I'll get Andy to sit with you. Can't guarantee he'll talk."

"Stop for a minute (breath)."

Tommy stopped running, "You guys are out of shape."

"Yeah, well, (breath) I'm not as tall as you, and I never played college ball. Let's (breath) keep walking (breath) up to the bench."

"Is this your kill zone?" Tommy asked.

"Kind of," the runner said. "I can guarantee this spot is safe (breath). Anywhere else (breath) is unknown."

They reached the bench and stood behind it. Tommy pointed out, "You're making me cool down before I'm done, so make it quick."

"We picked up an unencrypted phone call from England to New York about an hour ago. Mr. Glover is to be assassinated, priority one plus. They also said they want her body. And a couple of other things we don't understand: 'end the blood' and 'end the name.'"

Tommy looked out across the river, and the CIA agent flinched, "Agent Edwards, keep your eyes on me. Don't look at the river."

"Why? Who is watching?"

"I don't know if anyone is watching, but we can't risk it."

Tommy flinched again, and he was angry, "Risk what?"

"The rumor I mentioned. I was told a 'cease all activity' order is coming down for any activity concerning Mr. Glover. The rumor is solid because the section chief for DC received it early this morning and promised he would inform me immediately. I was standing in his office when he got the call. I powered down my cell phone and set this meeting up. I would bet even money you are about to get a similar order on Glover."

Tommy asked, "Whose body are we referring to?"

"Not sure, but it's likely referring to Celestina Cassanzo. She disappeared twenty-four years ago, and her body was never found. The guy she was last seen with, a Carlo Vendante, showed up in Oxford, England, this morning barely alive."

"And what's 'priority one plus'? I never heard of it."

"It means don't wait for a perfect shot. In this case, it pretty much means shoot on sight, multiple times if possible. Any more questions?"

"Too many," Tommy answered.

The agent pulled a cell phone from his jacket and flipped it open. He hit the power button, and the phone started its power up cycle.

"One last thing, Tommy. We nabbed an Italian businessman on a flight from Paris. We handed him over to Federal Marshals at Kennedy this morning. He's a world ranked sniper, former Italian military. "

The agent's cell phone rang and he answered, "Yes? I understand. I will comply."

The agent flipped the phone closed, "Sorry Agent Edwards. I can no longer talk to you. Have a great morning."

He tucked the phone away and started running back in the direction he had come.

Tommy pulled his cell phone out and sent a text to his team to power their cell phones down and meet him at Andy's townhouse at 10:00 AM.

63 Andy's New York Townhouse

329 West 89th Street

Monday, July 25, 2011, 10:10 AM EDT

Agent Tommy Edwards, flanked by his dwindling Serial Crimes Task Force team members, Angela Ricchetti and Carlos Barrera, rang the doorbell to Andy's townhouse on West 89th Street. Steve Haskins had been ordered by his doctors to rest after his encounter with Carmen on Saturday night. Tommy agreed.

As they waited on the steps in front of the door, Carlos stood behind Tommy and Angela. He felt his skin start to crawl. There was something causing one of his senses to tingle. He opened his mouth to ask if the others felt it too, but no words would come. From the corner of his left eye, he saw a woman. He turned and found Carmen standing next to him dressed in a nightgown. Andy opened the door, and the others started to walk inside. Carlos could not move. The others didn't notice.

Carmen looked mostly solid, but Carlos could see the planter and stone work through her. The door closed. His face could not register the shock he felt. The facial muscles refused to obey, but tears started trickling down his cheek.

Carlos felt his skull beginning to rip apart like two hands had worked their fingers into the middle and pulled, suddenly and violently. The pain was excruciating but it did not end. His brain was being pushed and pulled and squeezed, and ... as quickly as it started ..., it suddenly stopped. The apparition in front of him walked up two steps and turned to look at him. She had no eyes. Carlos could see the door on the other side behind her eyes.

Words came to his mind his ears did not hear, "She likes you."

Carlos was confused. He did not understand what the words meant. The apparition with empty eye sockets descended a step and leaned her face close to his.

"The woman, Vivian, you were thinking about her on the drive here. Do you like children?" came to his mind.

With a great effort, he forced his mouth to say "Y-Y-Yessss."

The face withdrew, and Carlos heard the word, "Good."

Carmen turned again and walked up the steps and stood by the door while Carlos heard, "Watch out for the handcuffs."

Carlos stood frozen in place staring at the door where the apparition vanished. Angela suddenly opened the door and sneered, "What are you doing? Get in here. There is some weird shit going on. Hey, are you okay? Man, for a Texican, you look white!"

Carlos finally got to the door and reached out for the frame to steady himself.

"I'm okay. I'm okay. Yeah, I'll be all right. Where is everyone?"

64 Diplomatic Communication

The White House

Washington, DC

Monday, July 25, 2011, 10:50 AM EDT

The Marine guard escort watched as James Robins, White House Chief of Staff and longtime friend of the President, signed for another diplomatic pouch. Mr. Robins handed the signed form back to the courier, and the courier handed a sealed envelope to Mr. Robins. The Marine guard escort followed the courier out of the room and then off the White House grounds.

James Robins watched the courier exit and noticed two other Marine guards in the hallway. The Marines entered his office and stood at attention.

One spoke clearly and definitively, "Mr. Robins, the President is requesting a meeting with you immediately in the Oval Office."

Jim Robins started writing in a notepad and said, "Tell the president I am coming immediately."

The Marine who spoke took one official step forward and replied, "We are here to escort you to his office, and please bring the envelope you just signed for."

Jim Robins swallowed hard. His whole political career could be on the line. He had only done what others before him had done. The President himself had given him general guidelines about these relationships and he had followed them closely. He had not broken any laws, but if his actions became publicly known, it would cause damage to the President. All these thoughts raced through Jim Robins' mind as he walked the thirty feet to the Oval Office with one Marine in front and one trailing. The leading Marine knocked on the office door and opened it without waiting for a response. The

Marine saluted and announced, "Mr. President, Mr. James Robins to see you."

The President said to his administrative assistant, "Tammy, that's all for now."

She hurriedly reminded the President, "You have a briefing with the Joint Chiefs in ten minutes, a meeting with the French Ambassador at 11:00, and lunch with the First Lady at 11:35 in the family dining room."

The President addressed the Marines, "Please wait in the hallway."

The Marines snapped salutes and exited closing the door and taking up posts on either side in the hallway.

"Jim, I've got nine minutes to take care of this. Tell me what you are holding in your hand."

Jim Robins stepped up to the desk and placed the envelope within the President's reach, "Sir, this was a job I inherited from my predecessor. I get these envelopes with requests for obtaining information or for squelching information. I was told we send the same kinds of requests to governments friendly to us. You, yourself told me to help facilitate open communications with the European Commonwealth. I also intentionally did not inform you in case there were negative repercussions."

The President picked up the envelope and saw the address of the sender was Whitehall Road, England, the location of Parliament and other British government offices.

"So what's in this one?" the President asked.

"I never know what they will send. Let's open it up."

65 Carmen's Condition

Andy's New York Townhouse

329 West 89th Street

Monday, July 25, 2011, 10:55 AM EDT

The nurse and psychiatrist were hurrying to leave and rushed past Carlos and Angela. Carlos heard Tommy ask Andy, "Where is she?"

"She's in the bedroom, but they just gave her some heavy sedatives. She needs to recover physically before she'll have the strength to deal with her other problem."

Carlos interrupted nervously, "Are, are you sure she's in there?"

Andy shot a glance at Carlos and snapped, "What happened, Carlos? Where was she? What did she say?"

"She was out there, on the steps. She read my mind and told me things," Carlos said pointing back toward the front door.

"What did she say?" Andy persisted.

"I was thinking about ... about a woman on the drive over here. She told me the woman liked me."

"She said nothing else?"

"Yeah, that was it."

Andy knew from experience there was more, but he also knew how invasive a demon can be to anyone unsuspecting or unprotected. He knew the messages were intimate and seductive. Carlos would not easily divulge them.

Tommy looked puzzled, "Do you mean to tell me she can read minds now?"

Andy shook his head, "No, it's not Carmen. She has multiple spirits inside her. They were projecting her image short distances before, but the distances seem to be getting farther. "

"Can we use her to read someone's mind?" Tommy asked quickly.

"No!" Andy replied, "She needs to rest. Then we need to deal with these spirits hanging onto her."

Tommy said, "Andy, there are snipers sent here from Italy to kill you. We have one of them in custody. If Carmen can read his mind we could protect you and get to the bottom of this."

"It won't help you protect me, and it won't give you any usable information. This is not Carmen you are dealing with. These spirits are like wild animals. They won't follow your rules, you can't control them, and they lie. They almost killed Steve, and they were just getting started, and you are putting Carmen in harm's way."

A voice came from behind the group, "She has an ability we can use."

They all turned and saw Steve Haskins with his head wrapped leaning against the bookcase by the door.

"You were ordered to rest," Tommy demanded.

"I slept in. It's the best I can do," Steve returned. "Also Tommy, the assistant director wants you to call him ASAP. He said it was urgent, but then you already knew it. That was why you had us turn off our cell phones."

Then joining the conversation Steve added while limping forward, "As for Dr. Andriano, she's a committed FBI agent. She would want to use every resource to crack this case."

Andy said throwing his hands up, "What kind of logic is that? I'm glad you didn't find any uranium lying around. You'd be trying to make an atomic bomb because it might help. Well, it won't help, and, 'Mr. Special Forces,'" Andy continued, "You aren't checked out on this weapon. You have no idea how it works or even how to point it, and there is no safety!"

66 Contents

The White House

Washington, DC

Monday, July 25, 2011, 10:55 AM EDT

The President broke the seal on the envelope and pealed back the tamper proof security flap. He looked inside while Jim Robins looked on. He looked up at his old friend and then reached into the envelope and pulled out a half sheet of paper and laid it on the desk.

The Royal Bank of Scotland was emblazoned across the top of the form. The second line in bold letters said, "Wire Transfer Notice." Jim could see sending and receiving account numbers, verification, and audit instructions, but it was the bottom line that Jim was staring at "£150,500." Total focus on the document absorbed both men.

The President broke the silence, "If my math is correct that is about a quarter of a million dollars, US."

He looked up at Jim with no expression showing, but his stare was piercing.

"That is not mine! I have never received money for doing my job! I never asked for it! This is a frame, Sir! You have to believe me. I have no idea what this is about!"

"Keep your voice down, Jim," the President said firmly, "Money leaves a trail. I will have this investigated by the experts. If this is a frame, we will get to the bottom of it."

"I swear to you this is not mine!" Jim Robins said as he flopped into the chair in front of the desk Tammy had left there.

The President took a letter opener and slid it under the paper. Using a pen, he lifted the flap on the large envelope and tucked the paper inside without touching it again.

"Honest, Sir, I had nothing to do with this!"

"Jim," the President began, "this is bad. This is bad for you, but it's bad for me on a dozen levels. My fingerprints are on the paper. I know about this piece of paper. Laws have been broken, and I am trying to keep the biggest economy in the world from sinking any lower."

The President stood and started pacing while talking, "Jim, what was the last issue you were dealing with in these correspondences?"

"Uh," Jim's brain was searching, "there was a US citizen, Hollingsworth, who had applied for British citizenship, but he died while under investigation. There was a missing person report. Nothing was proven, but some elements in the British Conservative Party had asked me to take some steps to keep Hollingsworth's son out of the news and government dealings. They thought it cast a bad light on them because of business dealings with the family. This is a very short version of the story, but this is the reason for the majority of the diplomatic pouches I have received in the last six months."

The President stopped pacing and folded his arms while looking out the window, "What actions have you taken?"

Jim Robins spread his hands, "Well, the latest was having a private conversation with the Director of the FBI and the head of the CIA asking them to drop any non-essential dealings or investigations into the son."

The President nodded to himself. His course was set. "Jim, go back to your office and call them both personally. Tell them you need to retract anything you said or requested previously. Tell them any directives you gave them, any hints or impressions you might have communicated are to be ignored. Tell them the President says, 'business as usual.'"

The President sat down at his desk and leaned forward, "This is designed to hurt me. I need to be above board on this. Somewhere there is a torpedo honing in on this money, and we need to be clear of it when the shit hits the fan. When you talk to Scott at CIA, tell him I want this covered in tomorrow's daily briefing. Send him all the documents you have received to date."

There was a knocking from the side door. Tammy was reminding the President of his next meeting.

"That's all, Jim. We'll get to the bottom of this, don't worry."

"Thank you, Mr. President," Jim Robins said as he stood and exited through the door he had entered.

67 Facing the Music

Blackford Crighton Law Firm, New York Offices

21st Floor, 206 West 48th Street

Monday, July 25, 2011, 11:00 AM EDT

"Miss Montgomery, can ... can you come in please?"

A moment later, the door opened and Miss Montgomery walked in showing no expression as Alan anxiously watched her. Alan shifted in his seat dreading having to face his one-woman judge and jury in regard to his behavior Saturday night. As she neared his desk, Alan stood.

"Yes, Mr. Hopkins?" Miss Montgomery said flatly.

Alan looked at his shoes and then stood up straight, shoulders back facing Miss Montgomery squarely, "Um, Miss Montgomery, I owe you an apology for my behavior Saturday evening. I showed you the worst treatment humanly possible."

Alan attempted to stand even straighter, "Can you forgive me?"

Miss Montgomery looked at Alan standing before her with his heart in his hand. She smiled, and Alan felt a rush of relief. He felt that at a minimum there would be no lawsuit.

"Mr. Hopkins," Miss Montgomery began, "you are my boss. I am required to be under your authority at work. While I am at work, I will comply with all your requests and demands falling within the confines of my employment here at Blackford Crighton."

Alan steadied himself for the 'but' clause of her statement.

"But," she continued, "when I am not working, my time is my own. I am no longer under your authority and can do as I wish within the confines of the law and my own conscience. Your actions Saturday night were unfortunate ..."

"Yes, yes, I am incredibly stupid, stupid, stu ... I am so sorry."

Miss Montgomery held up her hand for Alan to allow her to finish.

"I'm very sorry," Alan snuck out.

"Mr. Hopkins, I saw a side of you I thought I would never see in a man."

"So sorry you had to ..."

"You were kind," Alicia stated.

Alan stopped talking and snapped his head to the side uncertain of what he just heard.

Alicia continued, "Under the worst possible circumstances, you were a complete gentleman. You were funny. You made up a poem for me that was so sweet."

"Good Lord, I was not doing that again. Oh, that is SO embarrassing."

Alicia opened her notebook and pulled out a half sheet of paper and showed it to Alan. "See, I wrote down the poem and had you sign it. I didn't think you would remember any of it in the morning. Saturday night also showed me you don't drink as a habit, very important to me."

Now Alan was hopeful, "Alicia, uh, Miss Montgomery, If I might boldly go where no Alan has gone before, would it be within the realm of all possibilities I, I mean we, could try again?"

Alicia smiled and said, "Alan, I still owe you part of an improper evening. You were in no shape for it Saturday. Are you free tomorrow night?"

Alan returned the smile replying, "As of right now I am."

"Good. Tomorrow, my place, seven o'clock. We'll have pizza."

Alan held up one finger, "Could we not have pizza? Recent bad memories, you know."

"Chinese?" Alicia suggested.

"Yes, I love Chinese."

Alicia held up her pen and steno pad, "Did you need me for anything else?"

"Yes, I mean no, uh, not right now. That will be all Miss Montgomery."

68 Hiker

A Low Mountain Ridge in Upstate New York

Monday, July 25, 2011, 11:30 AM EDT

A lone hiker with a straw of wheat in his mouth easily gained the top of the ridge. The view was beautiful with the other mountain ridges fading to the west and the quiet water of the massive lake to the east. He stopped to admire the setting a moment before continuing his hike south along the ridge. He crossed over the ridge and looked about for a small hollow. He spotted it just ahead and climbed down into the hollow. He then turned toward the steep side of the hill facing him. He pushed the bushes and weeds aside from what looked like an edge of a shallow opening. Instead of finding a rock face, he found a metal door. He produced a key and fit it into the lock with some difficulty. The key finally did go in but would not turn.

The hiker stepped back and considered the situation. After some thought, he stepped forward and pounded his foot into the door close to the doorknob. The door budged slightly. He stepped back and kicked again making sure his foot was flat against the door when he made contact. The door moved another half inch.

A third kick sent the door flying back on its hinges revealing a passageway running ten feet before being blocked by a jumble of rocks and timbers. The hiker took off his backpack and pulled out an object about the size of a cigar box. He put on latex gloves and then took the plastic bag off of it revealing old, dirty burlap coverings around the object.

He walked to the opening and using a small stick carefully lifted the blanket of roots and spider webs just inside the opening. Behind this were old wooden shelves still well preserved. An old metal box was among the debris on the bottom shelf. The hiker opened the metal box with his gloved hands He put the object into the box and closed it. Then he replaced the roots and webs that had obscured it, stepped outside, and pulled the door closed.

Once more standing in the hollow, he removed the latex gloves and secured them inside the backpack before putting his arms through the shoulder straps. He looked at the door. Not liking what he saw, he stepped forward and pulled the bushes and grass back into place concealing the opening.

The afternoon was beautiful as he descended the west side of the ridge. He took a deep breath enjoying the fragrance of the mountain rhododendrons.

69 News from DC

Andy's New York Townhouse

329 West 89th Street

Monday, July 25, 2011, 11:30 AM EDT

"Thank you, Sir," Tommy spoke into his cell phone. "I will convey your compliments to the team."

Tommy ended the call and pocketed his cell phone while turning to the group.

"Good news, team. Our budget has been guaranteed for the next two years by the director himself."

Carlos and Angela whooped and gave each other a high five. Steve just smiled and nodded to Tommy as he sat wearily in one of Andy's kitchen chairs.

Tommy continued, "That was Assistant Director Snyder. We have been given a green light to pursue the Random killer with every means at our disposal. Dr. Andriano has been placed on our team again as long as we need her."

"It doesn't change anything!" Andy challenged. "She still needs Father Rand and me to deal with her 'problem.'"

Father Rand who had been keeping to the background and out of the argument spoke up, "Agent Edwards, I've had enough experience with Andy and others to know you are putting her eternal soul at risk."

Steve responded to the both of them, "This changes everything. We will prove their trust in us is well placed, and we will bring Dr. Andriano back here this afternoon unless you want to go with us."

Andy turned to Tommy, "Let me get this straight. You want me to help you, to advise you, but you are going against my advice to keep Dr. Andriano here. You want to take her out into the city and use the evil spirits inside her to help you solve murders. Did I get that right?"

Steve said, "Yeah, that's pretty accurate."

Tommy added, "I think your personal feelings for Dr. Andriano are clouding over the good she can do."

Andy followed with, "Oh, so you are using the evil spirits to do good now?"

"It sounds bad when you say it like that," Father Rand said quietly.

"Tommy," Andy argued, "these evil spirits are not machines. They have their own agenda, their own personalities."

Steve stood and pointed a finger into Andy's chest, "You're just mad because you are losing control over the doctor."

"Andy, the decision has been made. Are you coming?" Tommy concluded.

Father Rand put a hand on Andy's tense shoulder, "Andy, you go with them and watch over her. I have to get back to the shelter."

Father Rand stepped his large frame in front of Andy eclipsing the rest of the group, "Just make sure you don't fall back into darkness. There won't be any rescue for you."

Andy looked up at Father Rand and sighed, "I know I have to go but this is so stupid."

Steve spoke up from behind the Father, "You couldn't keep her anyway. We are taking her whether you like it or not."

Father Rand continued to Andy, "No more complaining. Just do your work. Take it one step at a time."

70 FBI Holding Cell

Federal Holding Cells Underneath Federal Plaza

Lafayette Street, New York City

Monday, July 25, 2011, 1:20 PM EDT

Dr. Andriano was still heavily sedated when Angela finished dressing her and brought her out to the standard issue black Chevy Suburban. Angela reported no problems, or in her words, "she didn't show any type of weirdness."

The ride down to Federal Plaza seemed uneventful to everyone except Andy. He kept seeing the image of Carmen walking down the sidewalk or sitting on a bench, always looking at him. Andy tried once to point her out but no one else saw her, so Andy just kept it to himself. The only problem was Andy saw the image of a woman he deeply cared for, but the eyes were the eyes of a well-known enemy.

The Suburban pulled into the underground parking lot beneath Federal Plaza. A wheelchair was brought for Carmen. Carlos and Steve lifted her limp body out of the car. Carlos kept a close watch on Carmen for any movement still remembering his earlier encounter with her or it. Steve was simply taking care of business. Carlos looked down to verify the location of the wheelchair. When he looked back at Carmen, her eyes were wide open staring at him. He jumped back dropping Carmen roughly into the wheelchair.

"Barrera!" Steve barked, "What the hell's wrong with you? You almost dropped her on the ground!"

Carlos was embarrassed and fumbled for an answer while looking quickly from Steve to Carmen and back, "I don't, I didn't mean, sorry."

Andy looked at Tommy and said, "This will get worse. Count on it."

Steve started pushing Carmen's chair and replied, "That's what you're here for, Priss."

The ride up the elevator went smoothly with Carlos standing as far away from Carmen as possible.

The group passed through several security checkpoints with metal detectors inside the offices. They arrived at a heavily protected area surrounding a single elevator that went down into the holding cells. Andy recognized the entrance to the Federal Containment Area where he had spent a night. That was two weeks ago, but it seemed like a lifetime.

The contents of the elevator were visually inspected from several camera angles and thermal imaging before the doors were opened. A plastic wheelchair was brought out, and Carmen was transferred to it before descending into the cell area.

Once in the cell area on the lower floor, a guard escorted them to an observation alcove overlooking a bare interrogation room. In the room was a square metal table and two chairs. In one of the chairs sat a dark haired man in an orange prisoner jump suit.

Tommy turned to Andy, "Ok, how does this work?"

A tearing scream from the interrogation room stopped all conversation. The guard jumped forward to open the door, but Carlos grabbed his arm, "Wait. He'll stop in a second."

Tommy asked, "Carlos! What's going on?"

Carlos looked in the window of the door, "She's already reading his mind. This hurts like hell. I probably didn't mention it."

Just as Carlos predicted, the screams tapered off. The prisoner was still writhing in the seat as much as his chained hands and feet would allow. His mouth was wide open as terror played across his face. His eyes were wide open but not seeing.

Carlos continued, "This should be over in a ..."

Carlos watched as Tommy's eyes went wide. Tommy grabbed the top of his head and dropped to his knees.

"Get her out! Get her out!" Tommy shouted.

Steve had been standing on the other side of Carmen's wheelchair. He turned his attention from the prisoner to Tommy. Then he looked at Carmen. Carmen's chin was still on her chest due to the sedation. Steve backhanded Carmen's head. Tommy fell to the ground in agony. Steve looked at Tommy and reared back to strike Carmen again. As his hand came forward again, it was grabbed from behind with a vice-like grip on his wrist spinning him around. He was facing Carmen or something that looked like her. Carmen opened her mouth. Steve Haskins, former Special Forces task group leader, saw double rows of needle-like teeth. The stretched skin on Carmen's neck showed the image of large scales just under the surface.

All sound stopped, and motion slowed. Steve was alone in a different time and space with this creature. A pen was lifted from Steve's pocket without being touched. A communication was established. Haskins was drowning in thoughts he could not escape. He felt his mind being poisoned, and he had no defense. Wave after wave, over and over, he was inundated with a vision of hell consuming him, his mother, former commando task force members, and the Serial Crimes unit members. His face burned while he could not escape the vision.

As suddenly as it started, it stopped.

Steve, Angela, Carlos, and the guard looked around. The wheelchair was empty. There was no sign of Carmen.

"Where did she go?" Steve demanded looking at Andy who was the only one seemingly unaffected.

"Where did she go?" Steve asked a second time grabbing Andy's arms.

"Don't touch me!" Andy screamed as he grabbed Steve by the throat and viciously slammed his back down to the cement floor.

"I am not your enemy," Andy said letting go and trying to calm himself. "I am not your enemy." Andy sat down on the floor a let out a deep breath. He screwed up. He couldn't let his anger control him again.

Carlos and Angela were stunned. Angela said to Andy, "Holy hell, how did you do that?"

Steve was rubbing his face and throat and starting to sit up, "He got lucky. The priss' will never do that again."

Andy laughed, "Look who's calling me a priss'. You meet one demon face to face and you're balling like a baby, and, oh, look, you pissed your pants! Also, by the way, your face now has a tattoo."

Steve looked at his crotch and let out, "Oh shit!"

Angela knelt by Tommy, "Are you okay, Sir?"

Tommy was laying on his back with his eyes closed still holding his head, "No," he said through gritted teeth.

Andy stepped up and knelt on one knee next to Angela. He spoke softly, "Your head will throb for an hour or two. Aspirin will help. Do you feel nauseous?"

"Where's Carmen?" Tommy asked sneaking a peek at the wheelchair.

"Don't know, Sir, but we need to start looking for her," Angela responded.

Carlos said to the guard with them, "Check on the prisoner. I'll call Security."

The guard had stepped back out of the area when Tommy went down. He now opened the door and went in to check on the prisoner. He came out of the room and flatly stated, "The prisoner is dead."

Carlos picked up the wall phone and dialed one, "Security, this is Agent Carlos Barrera. There is a prisoner down. The location is interrogation room number 4. We are missing FBI Agent Dr.

Carmen Andriano. She is not a suspect but is under the influence. Consider her dangerous but not a criminal, repeat not a criminal.

-

Yes. Please locate and advise."

Angela was pointing at Steve, "Oh hell, look at his face!"

71 Permission Granted

New Hope Homeless Shelter

Sutter Avenue, East New York City

Monday, July 25, 2011, 3:20 PM EDT

"Yes, I know, I understand His Eminence is a busy man, but this is an emergency. All I'm asking for is permission to administer the sacrament of Confirmation to a person in trouble."

-

"Yes, yes, highly unorthodox. No, Father Fitzgerald. I don't think the bishop needs to attend."

***

(Diocesan Offices, 1011 First Avenue, New York City)

The Archbishop walked into the anteroom to greet some guests and stopped to listen to the conversation.

"Father Fitzgerald, what do they want?"

"Pardon me, your Excellency, it's the priest who runs the New Hope Homeless Shelter. He wants permission to administer the sacrament of Confirmation. It's for a person in trouble."

"Can he schedule it through this office?" the Archbishop asked.

Father Fitzgerald spoke into the phone, "Can we schedule this for the Archbishop to ..."

-

Father Fitzgerald turned to the Archbishop with the phone still at his ear, "No, Sir. She is in the Federal Lockup, but they can't find her at the moment. One person is dead, and she has multiple demons and ... (turning to the phone), yes, Your Excellency, the priest says they will need to move quickly when they find her."

The Archbishop quickly returned, "Oh my, yes, permission is given. Here, hand me the phone. (To the guests waiting) I'll be with you shortly. (To the phone) Uh, Father Rand isn't it? You're the big fella with the tattoos. Yes, you have my permission under canon 884. Father Fitzgerald will take care of the paperwork. When you are done, make an appointment with me. I would like to hear how this turns out. Thank you. God bless."

Archbishop said to Father Fitzgerald as he was leaving, "We all have our place in God's kingdom. He is certainly the right man for that shelter."

72 Blue Ink

Federal Holding Cells Underneath Federal Plaza

Lafayette Street, New York City

Monday, July 25, 2011, 4:00 PM EDT

Steve winced, looking in a mirror at the dark blue lines in his face. The lines hurt before, but were now on fire.

Carlos pointed out, "At least it was a blue pen in your pocket. It would really look weird if it was red."

Angela added, "So much for undercover work unless you're working in New Zealand."

One side of Steve's face had delicate blue lines not tattooed but literally carved into his face forming ridges in the skin from the right side of his forehead, down his temple area, on his cheek to his jaw line.

"Hey, I know a Maori guy in the Village," Angela added, "he's into this kind of tattoo stuff. I'll get him down here to look at it. Maybe it can tell us something about it."

"Meanwhile," Tommy said, "we need to go over the cell area one more time. And this time, I want Andrew Glover to be allowed to participate."

The last sentence was directed at the Federal Marshal acting as the Incident Officer.

"Not on my watch," the Marshal countered. "No civilians. End of story. Now let's get moving. We're wasting time. I want groups of three this time. Each group gets their own thermal imager."

"Elevator up," the Marshal shouted to the officer in the security booth.

The Incident Officer shouted, "Groups one and two front and center!"

The officer in the security booth checked the monitors for the hundredth time and saw the static on the screens, but the thermal screen showed no heat signature.

The elevator doors opened, and freezing cold air flowed out followed by the image of Carmen. Her skin was sickly white. Her eyes were white with wide black pupils. Spectral images flowed out from her central body touching the security personnel sending them through the floor to the basement below. Carmen stepped forward toward the door leading out of the secured area. The Incident Officer pulled his weapon and fired point blank into the shade of Carmen reaching for him. The bullet passed through the shade and struck another security guard's lower abdomen sending him to the floor. The Incident Officer disappeared from sight.

Steve did not draw his weapon but jumped out of Carmen's way and kept looking over his shoulder to see if she was behind him too. Carlos and Angela ducked behind the registration desk.

Tommy and Andy had been on the far side of the security booth to look at the monitors. Carmen walked quickly through the door with a cloud of images surrounding her. Resistance melted away as she neared the front of the building, agents and officers scrambling out of her way.

Andy ran to keep up. He was twenty feet behind her when she blew open the front doors. Andy saw all the images suck into her as soon as she cleared the doors. She ran to the sidewalk and was quickly lost in the foot traffic along Broadway.

Andy gave up trying to find her after fifteen minutes. He walked back to the entrance of the building. The guards were back at the metal detectors as if nothing had happened. Andy was still wearing his visitor ID badge and was admitted up to the second floor where the elevator security booth was located. Tommy was there with the team.

The Incident Officer had been replaced because the escape was considered a separate incident. In the first incident, a prisoner was killed and another FBI agent went missing. In the second incident, two security guards were killed when they landed on the floor below them in space occupied by metal bars. A third security guard was in critical condition from the shot fired by the first Incident Officer.

Tommy Edwards was holding his head. The headache was less but still present. All of the team was stuck there answering questions and filling out Incident Reports. Steve was wearing borrowed security pants.

Forty-five minutes into the red tape and paperwork, Angela stood and started walking to the Broadway Street entrance, "I'll be right back she yelled over her shoulder."

Angela brought back a large man, tall and wide with dark skin and long braided hair past his shoulders. The most distinctive feature about him was the tattoos on his face. They looked similar to the blue lines on Steve's face. Angela introduced him, "Team, this is Joseph Maaka. He tattoos people with Maori designs from New Zealand."

"Naw, I'm not allowed to do that," Joseph said. "My grandfather would fly over here and kick my ass. I just do the tourist version."

Joseph walked right up to Steve, "Scuse me, Bra. Can I touch your moko?"

Steve put his hand up, "Hell no! What's a moko?"

Joseph pointed to Steve's face, "The lines on your face are your moko. They tell about you but you already know that. Who did this work? It's the best I've seen. How long ago did you get this done?"

"I'll be asking the questions," Steve snapped.

Andy stepped forward and said, "He got it about four hours ago."

Steve gave Andy a withering scowl.

Andy said, "Look, we want the guy to help us. Level with him."

Andy turned to Joseph, "Four hours ago."

Joseph was shaking his head, "Naw man, you're shitting me. I couldn't do it in four weeks. I've never seen anyone do the hammer lines this close and fine. Even my grandfather on North Island couldn't do lines so tight and even. It's weird you chose blue, not very traditional."

"I'm not Maori," Steve said, "and I didn't have a choice."

Tommy spoke up, "Joseph, what can you tell us about the design?"

"Well, it's a ... hmm. It shows here on your cheek you are a warrior, a badass warrior too. Look how deep the lines are here. That must have hurt like hell."

Carlos intervened to keep the information flowing, "Joseph, we swear to you this guy walked into this building at 1:30 PM today without a mark on his face."

Joseph looked at the faces around him. He could see the whole group was telling the truth.

He frowned and thought for a moment then said, "Okay, tell me what happened. How did you get this?"

Tommy was shaking his head, but Angela spoke up this time, "We are running out of time. We need all the information we can get. Tommy, clear him!"

Tommy looked wearily at Steve, "Give him the short version, Steve."

Steve started telling what happened. He sounded like he was reporting an engagement to a commanding officer using very choppy but accurate narrative.

At the end, Joseph thought for a minute and then asked, "This lady, Carmen, tell me what you saw that told you she was not herself."

Steve described the parts of her that would flow out, some of the tricks she did, the double rows of needle-like teeth, and what looked like scales under the skin.

"Whoa Bra, it sounds like you're describing some kinda moko-nui. It's like a demon lizard. Moko-titi, moko-moko, those are other names but that's just old stories, Bra. And, by the way, the story on your face says your mother was a good lady, but there's nothing about your father. Is that true? 'Cause if you all are not jus' pulling my chain, you know? This thing read your whole life."

The group looked at Steve. Steve pursed his lips, looked down and nodded but said nothing more.

"Great," Andy said pacing around the group. "Now the demon has a name. We took this demon out of a trashed apartment and turned it loose on the whole city, and we gained nothing! Oh, but we did manage to loose Carmen."

Tommy looked up, "Andy, remember what Father Rand said, 'no complaining and take this one step at a time'. Also, you're wrong. We did gain something out of this. That thing read the prisoner's mind. I saw images of who we are looking for, how many there are, and where they probably are. I also have a mental picture of one of them. We can move in the morning."

"What else did that thing tell you?" Andy queried. "They don't give information out without a lie built in somewhere."

"That was all I got from Carmen," Tommy responded.

"Hey Carlos," Andy called out, "do you believe Tommy told us everything?"

Carlos looked at Tommy and shook his head no.

73 Between the Lines

The President's Daily Briefing

The White House, Washington, DC

Tuesday, July 26, 2011, 6:30 AM EDT

"Moving on, Mr. President, the diplomatic pouches Mr. Robins was getting all came from the same office in Whitehall. It is likely they all came from the same person. Also, we are now sure there is a connection between the diplomatic pouches and the problems in Italy we have been reporting to you."

"I see. So what you are really telling me is the messages from Whitehall to my Chief of Staff stopped you from reporting to me directly about this guy, what was his name?"

"Hollingsworth, Sir."

"So instead, you were trying to salt my reports with enough information to let me connect the dots. Is that correct?"

Ed Garibaldi looked at the President and said, "Sir, we had to assume his directives came from you. There were implications, however, you needed to be aware of."

The President leaned forward, "Next time, Ed, be straight with me, or I'll find someone else that will."

"Yes, Mr. President."

The President nodded to himself thoughtfully then said, "Ed, I would like us to discreetly reach out to our British cousins and find out why someone in their government is paying my Chief of Staff. Also, let the CIA know Italy is also our friend. Just tell them that. It should be enough."

"We will start the ball rolling today, Mr. President," Ed Garibaldi, the Director of National Intelligence replied.

74 Soldiers and Sailors Monument

Riverside Drive and West 89th Street, New York City

Tuesday, July 26, 2011, 8:10 AM EDT

It was a beautiful morning for a stroll. Salvatore, though, had been trained long ago to ignore beautiful scenes, scents, and tastes. They created diversions from your surroundings. Every detail was analyzed. The boots on the concrete workers were checked for long-term wear and concrete stains. Did they wear rings? Concrete workers never wear rings or watches. Did the cop's uniform look new? Shoes and jewelry were two of the best ways to spot undercover police or intelligence agents.

A third way was the face. Undercover agents or officers needed to have a nondescript face to fit in with the crowd. Even though nothing about them could make them stand out, it was the way their eyes were always moving; that was the giveaway.

The lady leveling the concrete had boots for the job and knew how to use the bull float. She also directed the other workers to keep them moving. The guy with the blue face tattoo jogging in camouflage shirt and shorts was too obvious and had stopped to check his heart rate. The businessmen two blocks ahead spread out on both sides of the street were to be avoided. They looked too fit and aware.

"Hey Buddy! Watch where you're walking, huh? That cement is fresh!"

Salvatore smiled and waved to the workers. He got too close to the 'Wet Concrete' sign for their comfort. He detoured around the truck and headed deeper into the park.

"Hey Ese!" The bloodshot Hispanic yelled, "Next time, watch where you walking! *Este es mi lugar!*"

Salvatore knew as soon as he turned his head to look back, he had made a mistake. The large black man came out from behind the truck and hammered the back of his head with something metallic. Salvatore leaned to his left half an inch at the last minute by instinct.

He went down but came flying up only to have the lady concrete worker snap a handcuff onto his right wrist. The next thing he knew his arm was hoisted into the air lifting him off the ground. He swung his feet to push off the side of the truck to gain height on his attackers but the guy with the blue face had a wire loop waiting for the foot and pulled Salvatore's leg sideways so he was now suspended in midair with several weapons pointed at him.

Salvatore was captured alive and unharmed except for getting tasered. It allowed Tommy's team to bind him securely without worrying if he had hidden weapons.

Carlos climbed down off the truck bed where he had hoisted up the arm of the shooter. Walking around the truck, he said, "Detective Vivian, that was some handcuffing job. How did you do that so fast?"

Vivian squinted one eye and smiled saying, "Why don't you come over some night and I'll show you."

Carlos smiled broadly. Viv walked past him and whispered, "I'll let you practice on me."

Carlos eyes went wide suddenly remembering his conversation with Carmen or Moko-whatever it was. He stood there stunned.

Steve noticed Carlos standing by himself, not moving.

"Hey, Carlos, you okay?"

"I'm not sure," Carlos breathed.

75 The Interrogation

Federal Holding Cells Underneath Federal Plaza

Lafayette Street, New York City

Tuesday, July 26, 2011, 12:30 PM EDT

"Okay, Enrique, or should I call you Salvatore? Or should I call you Yoel Frankel, your birth name."

Salvatore relaxed and smiled, "So you know my name. So do all the children from my kibbutz. This is not an accomplishment." The chains he wore joined his handcuffs to the chains between his feet were also locked into a ring in the floor.

Tommy and his team were once again in the Federal Containment Area in the lowest level of New York's Federal Plaza. As he was starting to question Salvatore the door to the interrogation room opened, and the two CIA operatives Tommy and Carlos met with ten days earlier walked into the room.

Tommy said, "Gentlemen, thank you for coming. Let's get started."

Tommy started, "Yoel."

"Please, call me Salvatore."

"Okay Salvatore, you are being detained on espionage and weapons charges. If you cooperate, you could be deported to Italy, the country issuing your passport."

Salvatore spread his hands as far as the chains would allow, "Gentlemen, why should I help you. What incentive can you offer me to tell you anything?"

The senior CIA agent held up a hand and said, "Agent Edwards, hold on a minute. Let's put some information on the table. I think we can have a dialog here."

"Go ahead."

The senior agent turned to Salvatore, "We know you are here representing the Cassanzo family. They want their daughter's body, and they want to kill Andrew Glover, the son of Randall Hollingsworth. I am assuming this much is correct."

Salvatore shrugged and said, "I have no idea of what you are talking about, but go on."

The senior agent continued, "Would it make a difference to the Cassanzo family if Randall Hollingsworth was not the killer?"

Salvatore shrugged again, "I don't know this family, but I can imagine if a tragedy took the life of such a beautiful young daughter or granddaughter, it would not make any difference. The family would just want revenge."

The younger agent stepped forward, "So then, if this family, or any family, were to get their revenge, and if the body of the daughter or granddaughter were to be returned, then a family would be able to carry on with their lives?"

Tommy watched the faces wondering where this was going.

The senior agent added, "We, the American government, are friends of Italy and their families. It would be very upsetting for us to have families destroyed over such matters. Such a change hurts everyone."

There was a pause while all watched Salvatore considering his options.

Salvatore finally nodded, "Yes. A change like this can hurt, but sometimes these things cannot be avoided. I happen to know it is not possible to recover the cherished remains of a loved one after so many years."

***

Behind the glass Steve asked, "C'mon Priss, you were there. How'd they dispose of her body?"

Andy stared ahead blankly.

Steve continued, "The guy in there is an expert assassin. He's got a team of assassins here to kill you. You might want to help us and yourself."

"I don't ..." Andy grimaced and shook his head.

Angela asked, "What was she wearing? Let's start there."

"White, not white white. More like a cream color."

Steve asked, "You talked about a party room with a big table. Did they put her on the table? Did they cut her throat? There would have been lots of blood."

"No, her dress is clean, I mean was clean."

Carlos asked, "How did they kill her, Andy?"

Steve said, "You told Carmen she died peacefully."

"Yes, she was calm and smiled at me."

"Is that when she asked you to take her with you?" Angela said.

"Yes ..."

"Just before they killed her," Steve added.

"No ... yes, she was ..."

"Where was she when she said that?" Carlos said, "Was she in the cage? Was it dark?"

Angela said, "Was is bright? You saw her smile? Was she laying down or standing?"

Steve asked, "Did they cut her heart out or slit her throat? Cracking her rib cage would be noisy, slicing through bone. Cutting her throat would be quiet, but a lot more blood." Angela gave Steve a scowl.

Andy looked up confused, eyes darting across the blank walls and ceiling.

"Did they dismember her and make you carry parts to the burn pile?" Steve demanded.

Angela held up a hand to slow Steve down. Then she asked, "Something simpler, what color were her shoes?" Did they match her dress?"

Steve threw his hands up and said, "What kind of stupid question is that?"

Andy quietly said, "She doesn't have shoes."

"She had shoes," Angela said, "A classy lady would have nice shoes to go with the dress. What happened to her shoes?"

"I took them," Andy said looking guilty. "They got dirty. I had to clean them."

"Why clean the shoes," Carlos asked.

Andy whispered, "So they wouldn't know."

Steve and Angela asked, "Know what?"

"Where she was."

***

Steve opened the door and said, "We know where her body is."

"That is not possible," Salvatore said. "There were witnesses who saw the body burned. Later, we know the bones were ground up and spread around the gardens."

The junior agent squinted at Salvatore, "How do you know this happened?"

Salvatore stated, "I had a brief conversation with Carlo Vendante before his unfortunate accident. He told me everything."

Steve shook his head and said, "He was fooled by an eight year old kid. They cut her throat on the big table then took her down to the burn pile. There was another body on the pile. The kid rolled Celestina off the pile and down the hill, put her shoes on the other body, covered it with firewood, and poured gas on it. Carlo only saw the shoes.

Steve continued, "Carmen is still out there. She has Celestina with her and the Warren thing."

Salvatore said, "She has a guard?"

"A guard," Steve said eyes wide, "yes Warren is her guard."

"What are you talking about?" Tommy said impatiently.

"Warren," Steve said eyes wide said, "the one who attacked me, Warren is not his name. It's Celestina's guardian. He only protected Andy to protect Celestina."

"To find Celestina we have to find Carmen."

"You are talking riddles. If you want to make an agreement with me," Salvatore stated flatly, "you will find the girl's body first."

***

During the negotiation with Salvatore in the observation room Andy continued with Angela and Carlos.

"I was standing next to her at the end. She told me she could not die there. She asked me to take her with me. They dumped her on the pile. I didn't want her burned and forgotten like all the others, but I couldn't move her and started crying. Someone heard me and helped me roll her over the edge and roll her down the hill. There was a uprooted tree down the hill. I rolled her into the hole the tree's roots left. I covered her with dirt and leaves. I took off her shoes and put them another lady and covered her with fire wood and branches."

"Celestina has been with me twenty four years until the night you arrested me. And now she's gone with Carmen. We need to find Carmen."

Carlos asked, "Won't Warren protect her?"

"Warren will protect Celeste, not Carmen."

76 Recovered Evidence

Blackford Crighton Law Firm, New York Offices

21st Floor, 206 West 48th Street

Tuesday, July 26, 2011, 2:10 PM EDT

"Come right this way," Miss Montgomery told the two men and woman in black suits, white shirts, and black ties.

"Mr. Hopkins, the FBI agents are here."

Alan stood, "Come right in, please. Have a seat."

Alan grabbed another chair and brought it up to his desk so they all could sit."

"No thank you, Mr. Hopkins," Tommy said, "we won't take up much of your time. We understand your firm represents the Hollingsworth estate. Is this true?"

"Yes it is. How may I be of service?"

We need to know the location of the Hollingsworth home. We were not able to find it listed. Can you provide the location for us? Also, for our records, do you have a copy of the birth certificate of their son?"

"On the first point, I'm afraid I can't help much. I can tell you it was near Canaan, New York. The Hollingsworths had significant land holdings in the area but the house burned down in 1989. Most of the land was donated for state park land as part of a tax settlement which included reclamation of the house's remains. I can have my secretary provide you with a map detailing the holdings."

"Thank you. That would be helpful," Tommy said.

"On the second point, I have a photocopy of young Hollingsworth's birth certificate right here. You may keep this one."

"It's strange that you have it on your desk," Angela said, "Why is that?"

"Because there is a trust distribution coming up on Master Hollingsworth's birthday."

Tommy looked at the copy in his hand and straightened up suddenly, "Mr. Hopkins, this copy says the date of birth is August 1st. We were never able to verify that. Are you certain this is his valid birth certificate?"

Alan nodded, "Oh yes, quite sure. We had it authenticated by the attending nurse."

Tommy remembered something Andy said once about his birthday, "Mr. Hopkins, if something were to happen to Mr. Glover or Hollingsworth, if he were killed, does the reaching of his birthday change who benefits after he passes away?"

Alan paused in thought and then smiled, "Sorry, client confidentiality and all. I'm sure you understand."

"A simple 'yes' or 'no'?"

"Sorry," Alan said with an apologetic smile.

Tommy pulled a card out of a small leather case and said, "Here is my card in case you need to contact me for any reason. Thank you for your time."

Tommy reached out and shook Alan's hand.

***

The door of the elevator closed on them.

Angela said, "Did you see the looks between Hopkins and that leggy secretary? Whoo hoo!"

Carlos shrugged and said, "I didn't see any looks."

"It wasn't the expression. It was the long look," Angela said nodding.

"Did you see Mr. Hopkins answer my last question?" Tommy asked.

"No," Carlos said thinking he had missed everything.

Tommy smiled, "The troubled look on his face means that it does make a difference when he dies, before or after his birthday."

77 Hollingsworth

Blackford Crighton Law Firm, New York Offices

21st Floor, 206 West 48th Street

Tuesday, July 26, 2011, 5:20 PM EDT

Alan's phone rang. "Hopkins," Alan answered.

-

"Yes, good evening Sir Smythley. I was just ..."

-

"No Sir, no news on the adoption, but we have ..."

-

"Another will? No Sir. I have not seen or heard anything about another will. There certainly is not another will later than the one executed on the Hollingsworths' demise."

-

"Sir Smythley, as the legal representative of the estate, I need to ask how we came by this information."

-

"No Sir. I am not being impertinent. It is my job to ask such questions."

-

"Is this the same eye witness that swears Mr. Hollingsworth is adopted?"

-

"Yes, I can send the bloodhound round to look for it."

-

"Yes, Mr. Tanner is quite capable. I'm sure he can find where the house was."

-

"Sir Smythley, if the house is no longer there, how can we find papers there?"

-

"Yes, a basement might be left. I will tell him to look for a basement."

-

"One thing more, Sir Smythley. The courts will be suspicious of any later wills coming forward at this time. We do need to be ready for opposition if we believe any new found will is the final desire of the senior Mr. and Mrs. Hollingsworth."

-

"While we are on the topic, Sir Smythley, the FBI was here today also asking for the location of the home."

-

"Please don't shout, Sir. My hearing is quite acceptable."

-

"I had no legal basis for withholding the information. I told them the nearby town, but I don't exactly know where the house stood."

-

"As a matter of fact, I swore an oath to uphold the laws ..."

"He hung up on me again. Of all the impertinence!"

Miss Montgomery responded, "He's always like that, isn't he?"

"Yes, tonight more than usual, I'd say."

Alicia had both hands behind her back, "Are you still free for our improper evening?"

Alan smiled, "Oh yes. I have been looking forward!"

Alicia coyly said, "Alan, I bought you something for our evening."

She held out a thin, white box tied with a white bow.

"Alan, you must bring this with you, but you cannot open it until you get to my apartment. Promise?"

"I promise. What's in here? It's so light."

78 Alicia's Apartment

39 West 19th Street, Manhattan, New York City

Tuesday, July 26, 2011, 6:30 PM EDT

Alan got out of the cab and was surprised Alicia was able to afford such an expensive neighborhood. She must have twenty roommates he reasoned.

He nervously knocked on her door. There was no turning back now.

Alicia opened the door wearing blue jeans and a blue jean shirt. With her red hair, she looked the perfect picture of American femininity: cute, shapely, smart, and tough.

"Come in, Mr. Hopkins," she cooed.

"I brought you a gift," Alan held out the lightweight box Alicia gave him.

"Yes," Alicia said as she closed the door and locked it, "but this gift is for you. The Chinese food is here. The whole night is ahead of us. Come in and open your present.

Alan carefully untied the bow, lifted the lid. He lifted the white tissue paper and exclaimed, "Oh you dear girl!"

Alan lifted up a DVD of the movie Casablanca. On the front was a note that simply said 'for Alan.'

Alicia grabbed his arm as he stood staring at the box, "Come on Alan. The food is in front of the television, and we've got a long night ahead of us if we are going to watch it three times."

79 British FCO

British Foreign and Commonwealth Office, or FCO

Sir Jeffereys Stype, Department Business Innovation and Skills

FCO Main Building, Whitehall, King Charles Street, London, England

Tuesday, July 26, 2011, 6:30 PM GMT (1:30 PM EDT)

"Sir Jeffereys, thank you for making time for me at this late hour," said the elderly gentleman in the tweed sport coat and proper British-winged mustache.

"Not at all, Mr. Wynton, though I do have a pressing engagement, so if we could keep this short."

"Yes Sir, to the point. The American government wants to know why the British government is sending scads of money to the American President's Chief of Staff. The Chief has received quite a lot of diplomatic pouches from this office with instructions, and the latest one had a wire transfer receipt for over 150 thousand pounds sterling."

"This is preposterous, Sir! I assure you this office sent no receipts for any kind of wire transfer to anyone. You are MI-6, are you not? I believe that is your department, sending illegal funds out."

"Sir Jeffereys, the Chief of Staff for the Americans has received no less than twelve diplomatic pouches in the last year, all from this office. Surely you are aware of what your office is sending out?"

Mr. Wynton reached into his coat pocket and brought out a folded piece of paper and placed it on the table. "This is a list of the pouches the Chief of Staff has received from your office along with our tracking numbers and the dates received. I have no doubt your office will be able to explain in great detail the nature and purpose of each pouch."

Sir Jeffereys' face got red, "My office will do nothing of the kind. You have no right to order me about. Your superiors will hear about this tonight!"

Mr. Wynton looked down apologetically then said, "This is a bit awkward, but it was your superiors that requested you and I discuss this privately. My superiors were in agreement. This way we avoid the need for a full investigation."

The mention of Sir Jeffereys' superiors meant this had already been discussed on Downing Street.

Sir Jeffereys picked up the piece of paper without opening it and tucked it in his own coat pocket.

Finally, Sir Jeffereys said, "I will consider it. That is all I can promise."

Mr. Wynton stood up and said, "Thank you ever so much, Sir Jeffereys. That is all I could ask for. I shan't keep you from your engagement any longer. Good evening Sir."

The two men shook hands politely.

80 Fire Drill

Outside White Plains, New York

Wednesday, July 27, 2011, 9:10 AM EDT

"Damn!" Tommy shouted as he slammed his fist on the steering wheel of the Suburban and pulled to the shoulder of the Interstate.

"Who was on the phone, Tommy?" Angela asked.

"Fire drill everyone! Angela, get in the back. Carlos, you drive. We're going back! Use the siren," Tommy ordered.

The Suburban had been headed to Canaan, New York, to look for the Hollingsworth Manor. Now it skidded to a halt in the gravel on the freeway shoulder. The three flew out and ran to their doors. Rocks flew when Carlos hit the gas of the modified engine and transmission. Siren blaring, Carlos raced toward the next service vehicle crossover.

Andy sat quietly in the back to allow Tommy and Carlos maximum focus on the emergency at hand.

"Steve," Tommy barked into the cell phone, "something's happened to Nathan Kahn. I just heard from CIRG that he's in a coma in North Shore University Hospital. Get two uniforms over there now! I want 24/7 protection. No exceptions! Get him to a room with no windows. I want a list of all staff caring for him with everyone's photos! Get the list to everyone on guard."

-

"No, I want you to get over to Great Neck Estates. Call for local back up, fully armed. This is the next person in charge of the Cassanzo holdings: Marta Liebowitz. Here's the address: 55 Shore Road, Great Neck Estates."

-

"We will meet you there. Ok, out."

Carlos looked over to Tommy, "What happened, Tommy?"

"Our field trip to Andy's old house is postponed," Tommy proclaimed as he dialed the next number on his list. He needed to update the CIA agents.

As soon as Tommy stopped dialing and put the phone to his ear, Angela said, "You know I can drive too."

Tommy rolled his eyes and said, "Okay, next time you can drive."

Tommy was still listening on the phone so Andy added, "Are we there yet?"

Carlos snickered, and Tommy glared at him.

81 London Office

Blackford Crighton Law Firm, Home Office

15 Upper Bank Street, London, England

Wednesday, July 27, 2011, 2:20 PM GMT (9:20 AM EDT)

"Sir Smythley, Lord St. Claire on line two. He says it's urgent."

"Please excuse me, won't you?" Sir Smythley said to the meeting of the law partners in the boardroom.

He stepped out and into an empty office and pressed the button for line two.

"Smythley here. William, what can I do for you?"

-

"Now William, slow down. What in blazes is wrong now? Did the young man I sent you arrive?"

***

At the other end of the line in Cambourne Hall ...

"Yes Smythley, he has arrived, but he has everything fouled up! I told him I wasn't to be disturbed, and he didn't tell me you called until just now! Everything is coming apart, and he left me napping! Martin would have known the urgency ... "

-

What's that?"

-

"No! I'm referring to the FBI. The latest will is our best option, but Hopkins is interfering. I want you to get over there as quickly as possible. I'm told Hopkins is seeing one of the office staff."

-

"Yes, and she is living beyond her means. Who is paying her? Look into that. It's possible she is compromising him. Be quick about it, and get that new will in place!"

82 Communicating with Salvatore

Federal Holding Cells Underneath Federal Plaza

Lafayette Street, New York City

Wednesday, July 27, 2011, 2:30 PM

Salvatore put his hands through the slot in the bars and one of the guards produced a key and unlocked the handcuffs. Salvatore moved to different cells at irregular intervals to prevent him from escaping or communicating with the outside world.

As he always did when put into a new cell, he started shouting, "I AM HERE. I HAVEN'T ESCAPED YET!"

He reached under the bed and found an earpiece taped inside the angle iron bed leg. He put it into his ear and yelled, "THIS IS SALVATORE! I KNOW YOU CAN HEAR ME!"

In his ear he heard, "Good afternoon, Salvatore. What is the status?"

"I LIKE IT HERE IN PRISON. I GET TO REST. MAYBE WE CAN FIND THE BODY. MAYBE WE WON'T. ANDY KNOWS. ANDY KNOWS."

"We cannot afford any more delays. If Cassanzo cannot get his granddaughter back, then we will risk moving against him."

"I KNOW YOU AMERICANS ARE TRYING TO HELP. IT WAS THE BRITS THAT DID THE DIRTY WORK."

"It doesn't matter. The old man won't care."

"I WILL GET OUT. YOU KNOW I WILL. I ONLY NEED TWO DAYS."

"You've got two days to deliver."

Salvatore took the tiny earpiece out and placed it under the leg of the bed and pulled the leg back and forth across it grinding the pieces to unrecognizable debris, easily concealed in cracks and corners.

"TWO DAYS. THE AMERICANS WANT TO HELP," he kept shouting as he scooted the few tiny bits of wire into a pile. He paused his shouting to lick his finger and pick up the remaining wire pieces.

"MAYBE WE CAN FIND THE BODY. ANDY KNOWS," were his last shouts as he inserted the wire bits into the locking mechanism for his cell, too tiny to clog the gears and surrounded by metal to avoid detection.

***

"Two days? What does that mean?"

The senior CIA agent smiled and said, "We will find out, probably later today."

83 Marta Liebowitz Home

Great Neck Estates, New York

Wednesday, July 27, 2011, 2:50 PM EDT

The voices hushed.

(click) "That's the second time the phone truck circled the adjoining block. Over."

(click) "Did you see a parabolic mike or any kind of listening device? Over."

(click) There's some kind of signal capture antenna lying flat on top of the van. Wait. The van is slowing. It's right in front of me. Can you see it? Over," Carlos whispered from an empty house just behind Marta's.

A whispered command was given by Steve Haskins, "Angela, get Marta to the top of the stairs. I need her to make a business call."

A few moments later Andy heard some shuffling and saw a figure just below him on the carpeted basement stairs. Marta was there and Angela was right behind her giving her instructions.

"*Guten abend, Gunter Uhlbrick, bitte*?" Marta spoke into her cell phone.

A brief pause and then, "Gunter," Marta's voice quavered, "this is Marta Liebowitz calling for Radic and Feld. I will be ... handling all transfers for Cassanzo holdings for this week."

After a short pause, Marta nervously said, "Yes, we've had many changes again. I am sending over the codes, the EFT authorization codes. The transmission numbers will, uh ..."

Marta squeezed her eyes shut, and her hands shook as she continued, "... the numbers will start from the next number after the last transaction. We, ah ..." Marta's voice faltered. The pressure was getting to her.

Marta's hands shook so hard it was getting difficult for her to hold the phone. "Gunter, I will call you back after ... I need to ... send the codes ..."

Steve gave the cut sign and Angela grabbed the phone from Marta and hustled her back to a lighted room in the basement without windows.

(click) Carlos voice whispered from the house behind, "A man in work clothes exited the van. He's leaning against the van smoking a cigarette and looking around. Over."

Tommy keyed his radio and spoke low, (click) "Everyone hold. We need him to enter the house."

Andy wore a side arm before. He reached down and unfastened the safety catch on the holster. He lifted the gun up to make sure it would slide smoothly in the holster.

Carlos had one uniform policeman with him, and the other one was with Tommy and Steve. All official vehicles were shuttled out of the neighborhood. More Great Neck police were waiting inside two fire stations to the north and south of the Liebowitz home.

Carlos radioed from across the backyard, (click) "The driver is moving to the back of the van. He's opened the ... HOLY SHI ..." The radio went dead.

(click) "Carlos. Carlos, come in," Tommy called into the radio quietly.

"Steve," Tommy whispered, can you see Carlos? What's happening?"

Steve used the scope on his sniper rifle to scan the fence and thick bushes separating the yards.

"No activity. Limited visibility on north side," Steve whispered back.

Tommy turned toward the basement stairs, "Andy, get upstairs. Eyes on the neighbor's house. Give me a status. Stay low."

Andy quickly climbed the carpeted stairs and into one of the back bedrooms. The Venetian blinds were slightly tilted to let in light but keep out the sun light. This allowed Andy to see only the back yard but not as far as the bushes or the fence beyond. Andy raised the bottom of the blind to the bottom of the window to get a sliver of a view of the house behind. He pulled the cord slowly so the blinds above stayed motionless. Andy kept his eyes trained on the bottom of the blinds. As soon as light was visible under the blind, the window exploded. Bullets shredded the blinds and pieces of brick from the outer wall, like shrapnel, ripped through the room.

Steve and Tommy looked toward the stairs to the second floor, but Steve turned quickly back to his scope only to see Carmen walking through the bushes with creatures flowing out of her in all directions. Steve flipped the safety and fingered the trigger, but before he could squeeze, several of Carmen's creatures burst through the wall in front of him throwing Steve and Tommy against the brick kitchen wall with solid thuds, debris filling the air.

Carmen stepped slowly through the opening she had just created followed by Matthew Sutton carrying an M95 assault rifle and slamming home a new clip.

Tommy was out cold. Steve was only dazed, his rifle was lost in the fall. He wasn't sure which way was up but reached for his side arm.

Matthew stepped around the Carmen creature to her left and leveled the rifle at Steve and Tommy. From Carmen's right, on the stairs, a bloody face appeared.

"Hey, Big Ugly!" Andy yelled.

Matthew looked up. The largest of Carmen's projections raced toward Andy. The face was wide and covered with dark lines and eyes that moved and flowed into smaller faces with leering eyes and needle-like teeth. When it reached Andy, it froze. The eyes on the projection and Carmen's eyes went wide. The smaller faces flowed away from Andy.

Andy leered at the hideous face, "Remember me? I'm not a kid anymore!"

A shiver ran through the creature as it drew back. The shiver was mirrored in Matthew as he faltered in his mind. The assault rifle clattered to the floor, and Matthew was dismayed. His confidence shattered. He looked around wildly. His hands started flailing at the air around him as he started backing away toward the new opening in the wall. Andy stepped forward toward Carmen. The projections flowed at him again and reached for him with their tentacles and hands, but touching Andy only brought howls and shrieks of pain from the projections.

Matthew panicked and took his first side step toward escaping. Steve popped to a kneeling position and leveled his side arm at the fleeing Matthew. All of Carmen's projections fled from Andy and attacked Steve. Steve closed his eyes and fired into the mass of hideous faces and claws. He was slammed again into the brick wall now only two feet behind him.

Andy drew his pistol with grim determination and a straight arm. Firing, he hit Carmen high in the chest, just under the collarbone, and again in her thigh.

The projections vanished like smoke. Carmen teetered a moment and faced Andy with a look of confusion. Then she quietly fell in a heap.

84 Cut Off

Cambourne Hall

A Private Estate Near Oxford, England

Wednesday, July 27, 2011, 8:00 PM GMT (3:00 PM EDT)

"What's that Wallace?" Lord St. Claire asked the new man Sir Smythley had sent over to replace Martin.

"A visitor Sir, from Whitehall. It is Sir Jeffereys' aide. Should I show him back?"

St. Claire waved Wallace off, "Of course, show him back. I cannot get out of this damned chair until the pills take effect."

A minute later, the door to Lord St. Claire's private study opened, and a smartly dressed young man stepped into the room. The door shut behind him.

"Lord St. Claire, good evening."

"Yes, what is it?" St. Claire said impatiently.

"Sir, there's been a bit of a row over the diplomatic pouches Sir Jeffereys' office sent out for you, which he did in good faith."

St. Claire looked suspiciously at the young man, "Row? What kind of row? The pouches were harmless enough."

"Yes Sir," the young man said with determination, "except for the last one containing a wire transfer receipt for a large sum of money given to the American President's Chief of Staff."

"I did no such thing!" St. Claire stormed. "That was not anything from my office!"

"Yes Sir, we know. The wire transfer form was a fraud."

"Well then, why all this bother?"

The young man shifted his feet, "It seems Sir, in the investigation of the fraud it was discovered the account numbers were real. They led the authorities to uncover amounts you had actually paid to the Chief of Staff."

St. Claire was stunned. All the careful planning, all the quiet arrangements now open to the sky.

"Yes Sir," the young man continued, "I am here as a last favor from Sir Jeffereys to let you know he will be handing you over to the authorities."

St. Claire was stunned.

He did not hear the young man end the conversation with, "Good day, Sir."

The door opened and closed. St. Claire sat alone in the silence.

85 Priest on Deck

Great Neck Estates, New York

Wednesday, July 27, 2011, 5:30 PM

"Whatever it takes to get him here quickly," Tommy told FBI CIRG Charge Officer.

That was the reason for the helicopter setting down in the Upper Roosevelt Park's practice football field on the edge of Great Neck. A big, thick, tattooed man in a priest's cassock and a bandana around his head stooped as he ran to the waiting black Suburban.

"Father Rand, come this way," Carlos shouted over the helicopter's rotor noise and dust.

The door closed, and the Suburban headed off quietly six blocks to the crime scene.

"How is the patient?" Father Rand asked with concern.

Carlos looked over and back to the road, "She's groggy but alive. Andy tranq'd her with some special brew they used in Colorado. Andy mixed it up himself."

"How's everybody else?"

Carlos sighed, "It was rough, Father. Tommy got slammed against a brick wall and had twelve punctures needing stitches. I think Steve got a separated shoulder, but he did something to put it back in place. Andy lost a lot of blood with multiple head wounds. The medics had him on an IV for a while. They stitched him up on site because he wouldn't leave until you got here. He will have a strange haircut for a while."

"And what happened to you? You look like you went ten rounds with Mike Tyson."

"Carmen dropped a house on me or at least part of one."

The Suburban pulled up to the back of the Liebowitz house.

"They are all in the garage, Father," Carlos said pointing to the detached garage.

Father Rand found a small operatory set up in the garage. There were three gurneys used for beds. Tommy lay on the left one. Andy was sitting on the middle bed, and Carmen was laying on the right bed with her hands and feet strapped to the sides. Steve Haskins was sitting calmly eating a sub sandwich and running a finger across the blue lines on his face. He looked up as Carlos and Father Rand appeared in the doorway.

"Hey Andy, your priest is here."

Andy stood and continued the introductions, "Father Rand, this is Carmen. Carmen, this is the priest I told you about."

Carmen's eyes shot open, though her body did not move. Red swirls started filling the whites of her eyes. Father Rand jerked back.

"Don't worry Father. She's calm enough. It took a lot of energy for Big Ugly to get to the surface. He won't stay there for long."

Carmen's eyes softened and the red swept away like a wind had blown across the inside of her eyes. Father Rand came close again, towering over everyone. He pulled a small candle from one pocket and two vials from another. From a bag, he took out bread and a small bottle of wine.

"Can someone get me a bowl? A clean bowl preferably."

One of the police officers found a stack of small terra cotta dishes for potted plants. He wiped it out with his hand. "Will this do, Father?"

"Yes, that will work. Thank you."

Father Rand poured water into the clay dish.

The same policeman asked, "Andy here says you're going to perform a confirmation on her. Don't you have to be a Bishop to do that, Father?"

Father Rand smiled and said as he laid out the bread on a white cloth, "Yes, except in cases of extreme emergency, like someone dying or this poor girl who might recover at any second and tear your throat out. The Archbishop gave me a special dispensation to perform the sacrament."

These were not idle words since the police were standing between two brick houses torn apart and seasoned FBI agents thrown about like rag dolls by this same poor girl. The officer stepped back from Carmen's gurney. Andy and Father Rand shared a secret smile, but it was still true.

The priest poured water from the vial and sprinkled some on Carmen while praying audibly. He then turned to sprinkle Angela and Carlos who had drawn close. For an added effect, he flicked some water at Haskins who looked up with an annoyed expression.

The prayers and motions of the mass started and were taking a little too long for Andy's comfort. Carmen was getting restless, and Andy kept his pistol close by. He kept giving Father Rand the *speed up* signal. There was a careful balance needed between keeping Carmen's body somewhat sedated but having her aware enough to understand and communicate.

Finally, Father Rand said, "Carmen Lucia Theresa Andriano, do you reject sin so to live in the freedom of God's children?"

Carmen struggled but finally said in a raspy voice, "I do."

Father Rand smiled and told her, "Good girl. Carmen, do you know what the sacrament of Confirmation is for?"

Carmen looked scared as she replied, "It will make me a better Catholic?"

"Yes, little one. It will, but the main purpose is for you to receive the indwelling of the Holy Spirit. This won't make your life easier, but it will give you a partner in God so you won't have to go through your trials alone. The Spirit will remind you of what God's word says. The Spirit will also show you areas in your life that need attention and His help."

"Carmen," Father Rand put a hand on Carmen's shoulder and continued, "Will you receive the Holy Spirit?"

Andy's hand went silently to his pistol.

No sound came from her open mouth. Her breathing stopped, and a wisp of vapor came out. Carmen exhaled forcefully followed by her words, "I have received the Holy Spirit. He's here!"

Tears started flowing out of her, "I have received the Holy Spirit!" she repeated as she sobbed for joy.

"Welcome back, dear," Father Rand said as a tear flowed over the jagged scar under his right eye.

"I am back," Carmen sobbed again, trying to catch her breath.

Andy turned to Steve, "We can let her up now. The thing is gone."

Steve turned away from Andy and gave a disgusted wave of his hand.

Andy and Carlos started removing the leather restraints on her hands. Angela and Father Rand removed them from her feet. Father Rand helped her sit up and she hugged him.

The priest separated himself from Carmen, "Before we get too far, let's make this official."

He took the other vial. Opened the lid and put a drop of oil on his finger. With the oil he made the sign of the cross on Carmen's forehead and said, "Live well in your new relationship with God. Let the Holy Spirit guide you on your journey through life. Amen."

Father Rand made the sign of the cross in the air and said, "That's the shortened version, but it's official. How do you feel?"

"I feel like crying," Carmen said as she laughed and sobbed at the same time. She reached over and hugged Angela and then Carlos. The hug she gave Andy was noticeably short and a little awkward on both their parts.

Carmen noticed Steve sitting on the side and said, "Steve Haskins, you are one of the bravest men I have ever known. That was an amazing shot you made."

"You mean the one where he was trying to shoot the demon?" Andy laughed.

Carmen smiled, "No, the one where he shot through the demon and hit Random as he was running away. The demon was trying to cover his escape."

Carlos and Andy looked at each other with raised eyebrows.

"I got some blood samples off the ground," Angela bragged, "We're gonna bag this ..."

Steve interrupted by asking Carmen, "Did you have to give me this tattoo?"

Carmen smiling said, "The pen was supposed to go through your eye and out the back of your head. I was able to distract the demon with the idea of drawing on you. It was all I could think of to save your life."

Steve lightly touched the raised lines on his face with a grimace, "That's the second time! Your life saving techniques are going to kill me."

86 The Beginning of Understanding

Cassanzo Villa

Orsara di Puglia, Province of Foggia, Italy

Wednesday, July 27, 2011, 11:45 PM UTC -1 (5:45 PM EDT)

"Can't sleep, Brother?"

Roberto saw the outline of Stefano in the shadows just inside the open barn. The cool night air was a relief from heat of the July sun just as the quiet of the barn was a relief from the tension of their childhood home. Roberto walked over to sit on a hay bale across the opening from his brother. Wan light from the sliver of moon rising lit the sloping vineyard and the woods beyond them. Frogs and crickets singing set the mood.

Roberto shook his head, "No, I do not have peace."

Stefano nodded, "I also am troubled more than usual. There is too much that does not make sense."

"Have we heard from Salvatore?"

Stefano looked out across the mist-shrouded vineyard as he spoke, "When I was in town today I spoke with Domenici. He said Salvatore needed two more days before he would know if my daughter's body can be recovered. They say he found an eye witness."

"Do you think they will try violence?" Roberto asked.

"Against the family here?" Stefano replied. "No, they will go through the courts. There are enough broken contracts and promises to take away everything."

After a pause in the conversation, Roberto finally asked the question that kept him awake, "Stefano, if father did not kill the American Hollingsworth, who do you think did it?"

After some silence Stefano said, "When Carlo came back without Celestina, I knew she was dead, even though he would not say what happened. He was more afraid of the people responsible than he was of me, her father. I was completely empty. I had nothing left to live for. My Teresa was the same. When Hollingsworth was killed, it meant nothing. Celestina was gone. Revenge could not bring her back."

"Years later I saw Teresa at the street market in Bari. She looked tired but still beautiful. I asked her to have coffee with me and we started talking again. I saw this beautiful woman so hurt, so desperate to be whole again. She made me wake up from my grief. So we have dated for the last five years. I have been dating my own wife!"

Stefano continued, "A few years ago I started thinking about Celestina again. The pain was less and it occurred to me someone killed my daughter, my only child. They killed her intentionally. This was no accident; otherwise, Carlo would not have been afraid. I started looking into the history of our business dealings around the world. I found information but no answers. We had very few dealings with or direct competition with the American's companies. Now father says he did not kill the American. It can only mean that there is another person or business or family connected with the American and with us. One family name kept coming up in our businesses, a British family named Sutton."

87 Getting Directions

State Route 295

Canaan, New York, 4 Miles from the Massachusetts Border

Thursday, July 28, 2011, 9:15 AM EDT

"Can't say I remember the place," one of the three old men said.

They were sitting in wooden chairs on the front porch of the general store at the crossroads of State Route 295 and County Road 5.

Carlos was getting nowhere with them. The Chevy Suburban sat idling with the team checking and re-checking all the possible locations the Hollingsworth Mansion may have stood and comparing the list with the places they had visited since 6:30 AM.

Another of the old men replied, "You might need some fancy electronic gadget to find that place. I'm sure they got one in the big city but not here, stranger."

Steve had been watching Carlos. He shook his head and got out of the back seat. He walked up to the group and said, "We're from the FBI. We're investigating voter fraud. There's a bunch of Democrats from New York City voting in this county. They claim the Hollingsworth Mansion as their local address."

Three fingers all pointed in the same direction with a flurry of descriptions of things to look for including fallen trees, a split rail fence, large boulders, and a broken signpost.

88 Didn't See that Coming

Blackford Crighton Law Firm, New York Offices

21st Floor, 206 West 48th Street

Thursday, July 28, 2011, 9:30 AM EDT

Sir Smythley arrived by private jet the night before. He walked out of the elevator and walked straight up to Miss Montgomery's desk. The door to Alan's office was open, and Alan could hear Sir Smythley talking angrily.

"So you are the whore trying to seduce Alan!" Sir Smythley stated with disgust.

Alicia looked up from her desk with eyes open wide, "Excuse me! What did you call me?"

"A hooker or prostitute, if you prefer," Sir Smythley restated, "It doesn't matter. But let me tell you it won't work. You are to leave these offices immediately, or I will be forced to call the police!"

Alicia turned bright red and stood to her feet, "How dare you, you impotent, spineless, little ..."

"Miss Montgomery, please!" Alan stated with alarm as he hurried out of his office.

Sir Smythley added while walking away, "Yes, please! Please run to the loo for a cry, and then clear out."

"Sir Smythley!" Alan commanded, "That will be all from you, Sir!"

Alicia stormed out from behind her desk. Alan took a quick look to make sure she wasn't carrying a paperweight or anything.

"You, Sir, are a coward," Alicia proclaimed. "You hit girls and run away. Well, you're not running away from me!" Alicia followed Sir Smythley into Alan's office. "I would think someone of your caliber would know all about prostitutes. We know Bagley sets you up with hookers every time you come to New York."

"Alan, order this bitch out of the office! We have discovered people in Washington are paying her rent. She is a kept woman."

Alan stood up straight and said, "Sir, you do not have the authority to fire staff in this office. I will not have you ..."

Alicia shouted over Alan's shoulder, "You have offended me for the last time, you bastard! You know what I'm going to do?"

Alan stepped between the two combatants checking the content of Alicia's hands once more.

"You're going to leave!" Smythley said firmly.

"No, I'm not going to leave. I'm going to write my congresswoman," Alicia said determinedly, "and you know what I am going to say?"

Smythley rolled his eyes and said with a mocking air "Oh, please tell us."

Alicia stopped her advance and said loud enough for all to hear, "I'm going to say 'Dear Mother ..."

There was a brief silence in the room while the men struggled to understand. Then Alan's eyes flew open, "Your mother is Macy Montgomery, the bulldog of Capital Hill? The co-chair of the House Ways and Means Committee?"

"Yes," Alicia stated, "and the Republican Lead on the House Foreign Relations Committee."

Alicia now owned the floor while Alan and Smythley stood dumfounded.

Alicia paused and then said, "You don't have any business interests in the US you are concerned about do you Sir Smythley? Oh wait, you have this office, and the office in DC, and Los Angeles, and San Francisco."

Alan tossed in, "There are offices in Atlanta and Chicago also, and a little one in Denver."

Alan and Alicia were now both looking at Sir Smythley. There was a short silence broken by Smythley's defense, "Alan, I'm telling you I saw the payments ... from multiple places in Washington DC. Her housing, her rent, her clothes, they were all paid for!"

Alicia turned to Alan, "I came to New York to make it on my own, but my mother wanted to help. I finally let her help me with rent. I was having a miserable time finding a decent place to live. She also annoys me by paying for other things. She's my mom. What can I say?"

Alan smiled, "I think you've answered for yourself quite well, Miss Montgomery. Don't you think so Sir Smythley?"

Smythley knew retreat was his only option. He grabbed the coat he had put down and stomped back out of the room speaking as he passed them, "You have not heard the last of this - either of you!"

Just before he got to the door Alicia called out, "Next time, do better research asshole!"

Alicia took a breath to calm herself. Her face was still flushed red enough to match her hair.

"One would think," Alan said looking at the closing door, "I would have known by your name and red hair. You look just like her, only thinner, and prettier."

"Well, one would think," Alicia said in her best British accent, "if someone were paying for my clothes, I would dress nicer. By the way, Alan, uh, Mr. Hopkins, may I go back to my desk now?"

"Yes, Miss Montgomery, please go back to your work."

Alicia started walking back to the door and heard Alan say, "I also need the O'Bannon files as quickly as you can find them."

She turned at the door and replied, "They are on your desk Mr. Hopkins."

89 Following Directions

Stony Kill Road

Outside Canaan, New York

Thursday, July 28, 2011, 9:40 AM EDT

"There's the broken sign post," Tommy called out. "Pull over here."

Angela pulled the black vehicle as far off the road as she was able. Tommy and Steve got out and were searching the shoulder of the road ahead of the vehicle. Andy sat with Carmen in the third bench seat. Andy sat against the driver's side. Carmen sat in the middle and the passenger side was seemingly empty.

"I thought you were crazy, I mean seriously damaged," Carmen said as she reached over and took Andy's hand. "Thank you for coming for me."

"I had to," Andy replied. "I needed to fire you as my shrink so we could have coffee again."

Carmen said, "If you had told me the woman's name was Celestina instead of Celeste, I would have a basis for believing you. I have known about her since I was four. My father worked for the Cassanzo family. Celestina's disappearance was the reason I became a psychologist and wanted to work for the FBI."

Andy said, "I had been threatened many times that if I ever told anyone, they would be killed," Andy replied. "These people were killing all the time. It was not an idle threat."

"Hey, why don't you guys get a room," Angela complained. "Could you possibly sit any closer?"

"For your information, Miss Nosey," Andy sneered, "someone is sitting on that side. You just can't see her. You do believe in spooks now, right?"

Angela held her hands up, "I was in the basement, remember? Only you and Steve saw anything, and both of you are psychos as far as I'm concerned."

Carlos protested from the middle seats, "I saw the 'Big Ugly' too."

"I rest my case," Angela laughed.

Carmen whispered to Andy, "Celestina left when Steve got out," and she squeezed his hand.

Andy felt warm all over and then a thought troubled him, so he asked in a low voice, "Am I still your patient?"

"I don't care," Carmen said smiling warmly, "but no, you aren't. I terminated our doctor-patient relationship the night it rained. You are still entitled to a thirty days' notice if you desire, but if you fire me it's effective immediately."

"You're fired. I like the immediate termination. I do have another question. Celeste and Warren never liked any of the girls I asked out. He would freak them out non-stop. Is she okay with you and me?"

Carmen smiled smugly, "Does it matter?"

"No, not to me, but it might matter to you."

"Good," Carmen said, "and it was her idea to have me sit next to you. I don't think I would have risked it on my own."

Andy smiled and squeezed Carmen's hand.

Tommy came hustling back to the Suburban. "We found it, Angela," Tommy stated.

"Drive up to Steve and turn into the gap in the bushes. There are tire tracks in the grass."

Andy asked Carmen, "Where are Celestina and Warren? Did they make it back?"

"I don't see them, but I'm sure they are around," Carmen said gazing around.

Angela pulled the Suburban into the bushes, but some small trees were close to the track preventing the large suburban from getting through. Steve and Carlos got tools out of the back and went to work on removing them.

"I saw you, you know," Carmen said to Andy, "in the Federal Plaza and at the house yesterday."

Andy's curiosity was piqued, "What did you see?"

"It felt like I was in a well of water, and I had to fight to get to the surface to breathe or see or talk."

Andy nodded, "I know the feeling."

"But I saw through the side of the well if people came close. When the big one picked up Steve, I could see him through the side. But you, I could see you across a room. You shone like gold. I could see your light. When you came for me in my apartment, I could see you through the walls as soon as you came through the front door. They are afraid of you."

90 Blue Garden Inn

250 Northern Boulevard

Queens, New York

Thursday, July 28, 2011, 10:10 AM EDT

Matthew lay in bed with a phone to his ear. The *doctor* had just checked the stitches he put in the night before and left Matthew with some pain pills. The entry and exit wounds were clean, no organs or bones involved. All was paid in cash - no prescriptions, no records.

"Wallace, I need to speak to Grandfather at once."

-

"I don't care what he is doing! Tell him this is urgent!" Matthew urged with labored breath.

***

At 3:10 PM Greenwich Mean Time in Cambourne Hall, Wallace knocked on the study door and opened it.

"Phone for you, Sir. Your grandson says it is urgent," Wallace said handing the phone to Lord St. Claire.

Wallace looked briefly at the solicitors from Blackford and Crichton's London office briefing St. Claire on the up coming hearing.

St. Claire took the phone and asked the solicitors if they might wait in the library for a moment. The door closed, and St. Claire held the phone tightly.

"Matthew, what is so urgent? Did you get to her, the last one?"

-

"She is alive?"

-

"No, no, if she takes some time off it might be all we need."

-

"How did she sound when she called the office?"

-

"Unnerved? Good, good. I think we may break them yet."

-

"You sound hurt. What happened?"

-

"Well, get some rest. You only have five days until the trust is distributed. We need that new will and testament in place. Has it been retrieved yet?"

-

"I will contact Smythley. He is in New York. Call him if you need anything. He can be reached at Cousin Alan's office."

-

"Yes, yes, excellent work, Matthew. Good bye."

91 Mio Amico Luigi

Bar Pyper

Corso Pietro Giannone, 27

Foggia, Italy

Thursday, July 28, 2011, 4:10 PM UTC -1, (10:10 AM EDT)

"Eh ciao, Stefano!" the short, large man with a wide grin said as Stefano approached the street corner in front of Bar Pyper.

"Luigi Ciulli, ciao!" Stefano returned as he met the big man's hug.

Luigi Ciulli stood five feet eight inches tall. He was almost as wide as he was tall, but every inch of his massive girth, arms, legs, hands, neck, and head was rock hard muscle. He could afford to have his clothes tailor made these days. In his youth, he dressed shabbily in anything he could find to wear. Too slow for football (soccer) or rugby, Greco Roman Wrestling was his savior. In school and at university he never lost a match. His girth was surpassed only by his omnipresent smile and laughter.

"Let's go inside, my friend," Luigi said as he put a hand on Stefano's back and helped him toward the door.

The bar was classic in its simplicity. It was a place for friends to meet and talk without loud music or televisions blaring except during World Cup.

"Luigi, why is the old man behind the bar staring at us?" Stefano asked.

"Oh, that's old Pietro," Luigi said loud enough for all to hear. "He's been here so long he even remembers when I robbed this place."

"You did what?"

"It's ok, it's all right. I paid them back. I was young and stupid, but old Pietro thinks I'm still up to no good."

"But you're a rich man! You could buy this place if you wanted to. You could buy the whole block," Stefano argued.

"True, true, but that old man, he is something I need. He doesn't have his hand out. He tells me what he thinks. All my money means nothing to him. Additionally, he still thinks I am a kid. Where can you buy that much honesty and still feel young, eh? And slim!"

Stefano laughed, "You were never slim!" as they sat down at a table.

Stefano ordered a local red wine, Don Marcello. Luigi ordered a Budweiser beer.

Old Pietro angrily yelled, "Why can't you be a good Italian and order an Italian beer! Be a good Italian like your friend."

Luigi laughed and said in his booming voice, "Do you sell Budweiser?"

"It doesn't matter. It's not Italian!"

Luigi continued laughing and said, "Yes, you do! I see it on the wall!"

"It's not Italian!"

"You have it on tap! Take my money and give me my beer!" Luigi laughed.

The whole room was laughing at them as they spoke over each other. The argument ended with the woman behind the bar pouring the beer and bringing the beer and wine to the table. Old Pietro continued mumbling as Luigi and Stefano talked in private tones.

"Luigi, I understand you are selling New Zealand beef to Algeria and Syria on a regular basis."

"Sure," Luigi shrugged, "regular business, no secret."

"So you buy it from the British and re-sell it to these countries."

"Yes, though most buyers only know it comes from New Zealand. These countries are funny about buying from America or England."

Stefano nodded, "Of course. I also know you sell a lot of beef for the Sutton's of England. Do you get a good price from them?"

Luigi leaned his massive head to the side, "This is a touchy discussion. If we were not friends, I would be angry about your question. I may give you the answer, but you need to tell me why you want to know this."

Stefano leaned closer, "Luigi, you know the majority of the Italian families give very little shipping business to my family anymore. Now we are getting squeezed out in agriculture, farming equipment, shoes, and many other items. It seems the Suttons are always the ones in the right place at the right time beating us out. I need to know how they are doing this and why!"

Some men walked in and greeted many others. Stefano and Luigi were expected to greet them also.

"Salute," they said raising their glasses before going back to their conversation.

Luigi reached a big hand across the table and put it on Stefano's shoulder, "This is a cry from your heart. A friend cannot turn away from such a thing. I will tell you what you want to know, but it probably won't help. Several Italian families are planning to take your ships and some of your land holdings in payment for broken contracts. They have held off for over twenty years but the older generation is turning over control to sons who don't remember. They don't remember when your father came to their family's rescue after the Second World War. Some don't care."

"Just tell me, Luigi. Maybe I can do something."

Luigi nodded, "First of all, the question you asked before, 'Do I get a good price?' the answer is no. I am selling almost at my cost, sometimes under. I barely break even on the beef but the shipping is free and I ship many other goods at the same time. So I make no money on beef but make a killing on selling produce, farming and construction equipment, clothing and many other things I could not sell before. All the goods we used to buy from Cassanzos and ship with Cassanzos we now buy or make ourselves and ship with Sutton with enough profit to resell in other places."

"But," Stefano said, "how do they do it?"

"That's easy," Luigi said, "Your father was in business with William Sutton, Lord St. Claire. Sutton's son and wife died and Sutton got custody of the grandson's. Sutton and your father had some big plans. I don't know what they were. I'm only telling you what I heard. Sutton's second grandson is next to take over the business."

Stefano said, "Second grandson? I thought he only had the one grandson?"

"No, there were two boys, The older one, Brian, died about the same time as, and forgive me friend, but it was about the same time your Celestina disappeared. Matthew, the younger, will be taking over."

A memory was triggered in Stefano. A brief conversation he overheard that ended when he walked into his Father's office in Bari. Stefano heard his father say, "This will kill that old bastard ..."

Stefano returned to the present.

"How did Brian die, the grandson?" Stefano asked as he looked out the window at the late afternoon sun shining on the Via Salvatore Tugini.

Luigi finished his beer, set down the mug, then said, "He died in an automobile crash. He hit a rock or tree or something."

"How do you know these things about my father and Sutton? My father has never spoken to me about them."

"Hey! Andrea Marie, can I have another beer please? I don't want to upset Pietro again. You better get me a Moretti. Oh wait, that's German. How about a Baladin?"

Andrea Marie put a fresh mug on the table and turned away, Luigi said, "I went to New Zealand many times on business trips. I visited a couple of the ranches. The two Sutton boys had been raised in New Zealand after their parents died. I think the Grandfather was trying to keep them out of trouble (burp) in the big cities. You know how kids are with a lot of money and no parents. The ranch was proud of the boys. Treated them like family. I guess the boys went pretty native too."

"What do you mean?"

"I was told they lived up in the mountains and took part in native rituals. They even got some native tattoos. The older brother went to work in America. After he died, the younger replaced him."

"My friend, Luigi, this may be what I need. I may not be able to save anything, but at last I think I know some of the things that have been kept secret from me."

"Stefano," Luigi said apologetically, "when the families come to take your operations apart, I will be there too. I have to do this."

Stefano stood and put his hand on Luigi's large shoulder, "Luigi, you do what you need to do. We will still be friends. I hope someday we can work together again. Ciao, my friend."

"Ciao Stefano."

Stefano walked to the door and heard Luigi's booming voice behind him, "You see that, Pietro. I bring you good business. Why are you still mad at me?"

92 Hollingsworth Estate

Stony Kill Road

Outside Canaan, New York

Thursday, July 28, 2011, 10:30 AM EDT

The Suburban climbed the slope where the drive had once been. There was no sign of the drive or anything man-made. With some small detours for brush and trees, the vehicle reached the top of the ridge. A wheel chair was brought out for Carmen who could walk but still unsteady on her feet. A trail could be seen along the top of the ridge. By the visible tracks it was mostly used by deer.

"So, if there was a large mansion here, where was it? Angela asked. "I don't see anything."

Tommy said looking into the distance on the west side of the ridge, "The attorney said the State had reclaimed the site. We can check their records and find it that way. We may have to come back."

Andy pushed Carmen's chair along the ridge trail while he looked east, "We don't need to check with the State. Some things never change."

"Like what?" Carlos asked.

"Like that," Andy said pointing down the steep eastern slope.

All eyes followed his direction. Through the trees, you could see sunlight shining off a large body of water.

"I used to come out at night and sit and watch the moonlight on the water," Andy said.

"Are you telling me we're gonna be searching for dead people by moonlight?" Angela gasped.

"Don't be stupid, Angela," Steve smirked. "There's no moon tonight."

"Oh, fantastic," Angela threw up her hands. "In the dark! Now I got nothing to worry about."

"Hey, there's a brick!" Carlos said, "And here's another one."

"Those are paving bricks. They must have been part of the drive," Steve said.

Andy walked slowly along the path pushing Carmen ahead of the rest.

"She will be over here," Andy said pointing ahead of them to the south.

Andy walked past a small hollow then tilted Carmen's chair back and slowly lowered Carmen's chair and himself down the slight incline. He turned to the left and entered into the hollow.

"I know where I am now," Andy said pointing northward along the ridge. "The house stood along the ridge there. The end of the house was over there not too far. This spot marks the end of the basement, which was longer than the house. A door opened into this hollow. The door should be right there."

Steve pushed some overhanging bushes and grass away revealing a battered door in the steep side of the hollow. Angela and Carlos gasped. Tommy and Steve felt the same way. This house and all the evil that had happened had all been hearsay and rumor until now.

Tommy stepped up and pushed the door open. Steve's hand went to his holster. The door swung easily on the old hinges. Tommy produced a flashlight. Andy stepped up also.

The hallway or tunnel went about ten feet and then was blocked by stone blocks and rotted timbers. Clearly visible on the floor were fresh shoe prints made by very large shoes.

"Someone was here recently," Steve pointed out.

Andy pointed to the debris in the hallway, "The thin metal you can see under those stones was one of the smaller cages."

"Andy! Tommy!"

All eyes turned to Carmen, "Celestina's body is down there, just before the small mound."

"How do you know?" Tommy asked.

Andy asked, "How do you know? Do you see Celestina?"

"No, I see Warren. He's pointing."

Within twenty minutes, Carlos yelled back up the hill, "We've found a skull! And there's a bracelet."

"Steve, radio for assistance and the coroner," Tommy called out.

93 Files

Blackford Crighton Law Firm, New York Offices

21st Floor, 206 West 48th Street

Thursday, July 28, 2011, 11:15 AM EDT

Alan Hopkins pushed himself back from his desk and the files in front of him. He let out a huge sigh. The pressure from the home office to complete the Hollingsworth trust dispersion was more than he had ever experienced. Strange history and events surfaced concerning the trust didn't make sense.

Alan's tremembered the verbal attack from Sir Smythley just this morning. Alan's thoughts started churning now as he allowed himself a few moments of freethinking.

Just bizarre! Why would Smythley even notice my secretary ... other than the usual kind of ...? I should talk to her, make sure she's not too put off by any unpleasantness.

Alan walked out of his office to Miss Montgomery's desk just outside his office doors. As soon as he opened the door, he saw Alicia turn toward him with a shy smile that shone right through him, lifting the weariness and pressure from his mind. He didn't even notice her arm closing the file on her desk and covering the name on the file.

"Miss Montgomery, I do hope you were not too put off by Smythley's unseemly rancor. I have no idea why he even bothered coming here other than to cause a row."

"Don't worry Mr. Hopkins, I will get over it. Oh, by the way, I am having lunch with my mother. She's just in town for today and shoved me into her schedule. Would you like to meet her?"

Alan was taken aback on two levels and fumbled through his thoughts quickly enough to get out, "Your mother? I ... I ... No, I have work, and you, you need to spend time with your mother. I would love to meet her, of course, but could we wait for another time?"

"You are so sweet. Yes, there might be another time."

Alan's elevated mood went considerably higher.

Alicia continued, "I might be gone for more than an hour, maybe more like two. Would that be okay?"

"It would be acceptable considering you are having lunch with your congresswoman."

Alan's spirits were flying when he closed the door and returned to his desk. The nuance of words was his life. She had said "yes" regardless of any other qualifications or disclaimers that followed; he knew Alicia wanted him to meet her mother. This was definitely going in the right direction. The pressure he had felt earlier slid off his shoulders and into the waste bin.

94 News from the Crime Scene

Federal Holding Cells Underneath Federal Plaza

Lafayette Street, New York City

Thursday, July 28, 2011, 11:45 PM EDT

"Salvatore," the senior CIA agent said to the prisoner, "apparently the girl's body was found. What is the plan now?"

The agent was standing outside of Salvatore's cell. The prisoner was stretched out on his metal bed with his hands under his head and eyes closed.

"My plan," Salvatore returned, "is to finish catching up on my rest. I haven't taken any time off for many years."

"We already started the paperwork. You will be released to the FBI for deportation. There will be no hearing. What else do you need?"

Salvatore sat up and stretched saying, "There is nothing else, but I recommend we move quickly."

"What about Mr. Glover?"

"I don't know. Some things have changed. This is not for me to decide. When I return with the body, I will speak to the people who sent me."

The agent asked, "To the Cassanzo family?"

Salvatore smiled and said, "Cassanzo did not send me."

"I was wondering," the agent said. "You are wrapping up this situation for many families."

Salvatore stood and walked to the door of his cell and stuck his chained hands through the slot. The agent stepped out into the corridor and called to one of the guards.

As the guard was unlocking the manacles, Salvatore said, "I was brought in to address a problem for several families in Italy. They had been helped by the Cassanzos and later were willing to be patient.

But business is business, and a new generation is in charge. So to honor their obligations to the Cassanzo family and continue on with business they brought me in to move things forward and give the Cassanzos, I think the correct word is 'closure'. I will tell them what I have learned and the girl's body has been found. They will confer with Cassanzos, and a decision will be reached."

Salvatore rubbed his wrists to get the feeling of the manacles off them.

"And if they still want Mr. Glover killed?"

Salvatore looked grimly at the agent, "You cannot protect him. He may even be dead already and not know it."

"What does that mean?" the agent demanded.

"It means I won't have to lift a finger, or even be in the country," Salvatore said, sitting and then lying down on his bed. "Please have my pants and shirt pressed before you bring them to me."

The conversation was over.

95 Lunch with Macy

Wolfgang's Steakhouse

250 West 41st Street, New York City

Thursday, July 28, 2011, 11:50 AM EDT

Alicia easily spotted her mother's table from the crowd of business people packed in closely listening and waiting for an opportunity to get the congresswoman's attention. The restaurant was noisy and vibrant. It suited her mother well.

The congresswoman spotted her daughter through the throng and raised a hand. Talking around the table stopped, and Alicia heard her mother say, "Sorry ladies and gentlemen, my daughter is here, and the rest of the lunch hour is my time with her."

Macy Montgomery rose from the table as Alicia made her way through the retreating people. Macy's bright red hair made her easy to spot in any gathering.

"Oh Honey, give me a hug Alice, but don't mess my hair."

Alicia complied. Macy then held her daughter at arm's length.

"Look at you, just lovely, Alice."

Alicia was well acquainted with the routine: big greetings followed by pleasantries, then light conversation and posing for the paparazzi without looking like you are posing. After the cameras were out of sight, the real conversation, complete with hardball positioning and strong arming, would start.

Macy was a substantial woman, sturdily built with a healthy constitution and strong voice, Alicia's hero, larger than life and full of energy. In some ways, she was the opposite of Alicia who found herself too shy and quiet. Alicia did share her mother's voracious intellect and intensity, though, with subtlety instead of pretention.

"It's not fair, Alice. You have your father's build, tall and slender."

Mother, you can call me Alicia. That is the name you gave me."

"I know dear, but in Ohio it didn't fit well, and now this is how I know you. You still dress like you're from Ohio. What did you do with the money I gave you for clothes?"

Alicia could feel her mother's feelers reaching out and searching for data points for the real discussion that would follow in private.

Alicia countered innocently, "I like simple styles and colors and clothes easy to care for. It's so good to be able to see you, Mother. How were you able to get away from DC?"

"Oh Honey, sometimes I think I have more work in New York than Washington. Why didn't you come to Washington last weekend? I had some delicious parties you would have loved."

Alicia patiently replied, "Like I told you, I had to work last weekend. I need to pay my bills. You get paid to attend parties. I have to work."

Macy sat straight up, "You don't think what I do is work? I would like to see you ..."

"Calm down Mother. I know you work very hard, and, yes, I am glad I don't have to keep your schedule. I'm not sure how you had time to have kids."

A waiter walked up to the table.

"If you had seen your father when ..." Macy said fanning herself with her menu.

"Excuse me, Ladies, are you ready to order?"

"Oh, nothing for me, but this skinny girl needs some real nourishment," Macy gushed.

"Please, I would like a steakhouse sandwich to go without the pickles," Alicia said to the waiter.

When she first entered the restaurant, Alicia had seen the waiter clear off a plate containing whatever could not be eaten from a filet or rib eye steak. A lunch hour with her mother was always less than an hour. Alicia accepted it. It came with the job.

"Very good," the waiter said moving quickly away.

"As I was saying, I would see your father back home taking off his shirt with all that muscle and would just go weak at the knees."

"Mother! I really didn't need to hear that."

"It's true. You might as well know it. Sometimes I think of him and just need to catch the next flight home. Whew! I might need to go home this weekend, and meet with his constituency."

"Mother! That is so gross! Just stop."

Macy was fanning herself now with energy. "You need to find yourself someone like that."

Very little was said until Alicia's sandwich arrived, but Macy continued fanning herself until they stood to leave.

In the limo, Macy told the driver to take them to the airport, but Alicia insisted she go back to work.

"The trip to the airport will give us more time to talk, Alice."

"Mother you will have to get your point across quickly. I have to go back to work, you can drop me off. Besides, your phone has been buzzing nonstop since I sat down in the restaurant."

"It always does, dear. So, Tammy tells me you are sleeping with your boss."

"That is not true," Alicia vented. We've had two dates, well, two and a half. He has been a perfect gentleman. Even Daddy would approve."

"Then how do you afford the posh apartment? You aren't making that much money as a secretary."

"Mother, you know who I work for. You introduced me to Mr. Harriman."

"I introduced you so you could learn about foreign trade not to be a spy for Harriman! And now you are in bed with your mark."

"Alan and I aren't sleeping together, Mother!"

"You know what I mean. You are emotionally involved. This is the big leagues, Alice. You're swimming with the sharks, and you are covered with bacon!"

Alicia smiled, "Mother, Alan Hopkins is a British attorney. He likes me. I like him. I keep my boundaries straight and everything is simple, straight forward."

"Alice Honey, when Harriman pushes you for more, and he will, your boundaries are gonna crash together with you in the middle. You will get crushed."

"Yes Mother, unless I have a sponsor bigger than Harriman who will give me carte blanche. And yes, I am lining one up. The situation is fluid."

The limo pulled in front of the Blackford Crighton offices on 48th Street.

Macy Montgomery sat open mouthed for a split second while Alicia opened the door and stepped out.

The congresswoman said to Alicia through the open door, "Maybe I should be concerned for the sharks!"

"I am your daughter."

96 More Work at Hollingsworth Estate

A Ridge Above Stony Kill Road

Outside Canaan, New York

Thursday, July 28, 2011, 2:20 PM EDT

The body of Celestina Maria Cassanzo was uncovered easily due to the shallowness of the grave and the loose soil. Angela supervised the Coroner's team. A careful inventory was made of the jewelry found with the body; after twenty-four years, little remained but the bones and jewelry.

Steve had driven back into town and brought back lunch for all, even the sheriff and the two people from the coroner's office. When Steve returned, Tommy had gone back to the Suburban to update CIRG on the progress of the Random case.

Andy saw Carmen staring at the basement door. "Carmen, what are you looking at?"

"Celestina is pointing at the ground in front of the door."

Andy called out, "Angela, ask the coroner's staff if they have a metal detector."

Directions were given and a Sheriff's Deputy brought a metal detector over. Andy asked the Deputy to scan the area in front of the door.

"Yeah, there's something metal down there. Probably a good size, not like a button, or fork, or anything. Probably a foot across."

Carlos and Andy got shovels the coroner staff no longer needed and started digging.

"What are you digging for?" the Sheriff's Deputy asked.

Andy replied, "I'll tell you when I find it."

After Carlos had dug a three-foot hole with no results, the deputy brought back the metal detector and confirmed the object was close. Andy started digging.

At about the four foot level, a metal surface was uncovered. Angela and the coroner's staff had come up the hill with Celestina's remains. All were looking into the large hole Andy was digging. Andy uncovered the edges of the metal object twelve inches square. Andy dug down and around the edges to find the bottom of the metallic box. The box was freed and lifted out of the hole. Under the box were bones. Angela ordered Andy out of the hole, and she took over.

Angela ordered the hole to be expanded to uncover all the bones.

97 The Arbiter

Blackford Crighton Law Firm, New York Offices

21st Floor, 206 West 48th Street

Thursday, July 28, 2011, 3:30 PM EDT

Miss Montgomery opened the door to Alan's office and announced, "Mr. Hopkins, Mr. Vargas is here from O'Bannon Management Group."

A tall, dark haired man in an expensive suit followed Alicia into Alan's office. Alan walked to the middle of the room with his hand outstretched.

Mr. Vargas shook Alan's hand but looked over his shoulder toward Alicia as she left the office closing the door behind her. His quick glance immediately put Alan on edge.

As the two men walked back to Alan's desk, Vargas said, "A very attractive woman."

Alan gave a forced smile and a curt, "Yes," as a response.

After the men sat Alan said, "Mr. Vargas, I understand you will be attending the trust distribution and the execution of the transfer documents."

"Yes, the O'Bannon Group has been managing the Hollingsworth assets in trust for almost twenty-five years. I am here to make certain the trust is dispersed in accordance with the final wishes of Mr. and Mrs. Hollingsworth."

Alan looked askance and said, "And Blackford Crighton is the guardian of the remainder of the estate. Are you in doubt as to the named beneficiary of the trust?"

"The trust document," Mr. Vargas responded, "specifies the beneficiary will be named in the will. We have been notified the will currently in place may not be the ultimate will executed by Mr. and Mrs. Hollingsworth."

"I have heard a rumor another will may exist," Alan said cautiously, "but any court would be highly skeptical. I myself only heard this rumor for the first time on Tuesday. May I ask the source of your information?"

Mr. Vargas nodded and responded, "A colleague in our London office told me about it. Our executive management directed me to move cautiously and not start the transfer process until the issue of the will is settled."

"At this point, Mr. Vargas, I am not in favor of delaying the dissolution of the trust for mere rumors. Also, as custodians of the trust, you do not have the right to delay dissolving the trust beyond the date specified without a court injunction."

"The injunction has been filed, Mr. Hopkins, but will not be ruled on until Tuesday of next week. We would ask for a day's leniency just to be certain."

Alan stood and pronounced, "I am sorry Mr. Vargas, but rumors do not constitute evidence, and I must oppose your injunction. Let me walk you out."

Mr. Vargas paused ... then he stood and shook Alan's hand saying, "I can see myself out."

Alan smiled and said, "Oh no, I insist."

98 Built on the Past

Cassanzo Villa

Orsara di Puglia, Province of Foggia, Italy

Thursday, July 28, 2011, 9:10 UTC -1 (3:10 PM EDT)

The night breeze was cool. There were orange, pink, and purple clouds fading to the east. The remnants of the evening meal were put away and so were the smaller children. Life was simple here at the villa ebbing and flowing with the growing seasons. The family was more peaceful here than when they had all lived in the city of Bari decades ago, hardly a memory. The villa had been a weekend getaway for the family then. Stefano walked up the hill, through the barn, and into the dark kitchen lit only by the fading light in the sky.

As he entered the great room, he heard the rough voice of his father, "There you are! Where have you been? You missed the family meal!"

There were several table lamps lit around the great room where older children played cards and another group a board game. Agosto and Roberto sat outside under the olive tree with a lantern flickering between them. Stefano's sisters, Theresa and Lucia, talked in a quiet huddle. They looked up when they saw him enter. They smiled and waved then went back to their private conversation. Stefano dropped himself into an easy chair next to his father.

"So where were you?" Signore Cassanzo repeated.

"I went into Foggia. I met Luigi Ciulli and had a glass of wine with him."

"Why did you talk to him? He is a thug."

"No Papa, he made mistakes when he was young, but he has paid for them. He is doing quite well."

Signore Cassanzo shook his head, "People don't change. He is still a thug, but now he is a rich thug."

Stefano sat quietly turning over what he had heard today and on his trip to Foggia two days ago. He thought about his daughter and how much he missed her still. The ache he felt put him on edge.

His father picked up the conversation again, "Luigi is just like Alfonso Tucci. Both of them are bullies. They don't change."

Stefano's anger boiled over, "What about you, Father? Did you change? You were a great man during and after the war. You sacrificed everything to help others. Everyone knows what you did."

"Bah, no one cares."

Stefano was on fire, "When did you stop being a great man?"

Signore Cassanzo jerked his head toward Stefano, "What are you talking about?"

"You ran an empire!" Stefano continued without stopping. "You controlled shipping. You sold goods to people who needed them. Yes, you made money doing it, but those people had nowhere to turn, and you did business with them."

Stefano sat up and on the edge of his chair, "Why did you run away from the world? Why do you hide here where no one can get to you? Why don't you let vehicles drive up to this house? What are you so afraid of?"

Signore Cassanzo reached his hand back to smack Stefano across the face.

"Go ahead! Go ahead, you old coward!" Stefano said through gritted teeth. "You are a bitter old man who is so afraid of something you cannot even talk about it!"

"You know nothing, nothing at all, and you want to lecture me! You lose one child, and you run away. I have lost many children and at least I can face my own family!"

"That was in the war. You were great then, but you have changed. You were a leader of men. Now you won't lead, and you won't let us lead! What are you so afraid of?" Stefano guessed, "Is Sutton the one who you are afraid of?"

Signore Cassanzo's eyes flared in hatred. He picked up his heavy glass tumbler and threw it, but he had been drinking, and Stefano easily dodged it. The glass smashed on the tiled floor.

"That's it;" Stefano understood, "it's William Sutton. You were in business together, but he cheated you. Isn't that right? I said isn't that right?"

"You know nothing," Signore Cassanzo replied quietly.

"No, I don't know, but you are going to tell me. You are going to tell us all."

Roberto and Agosto had come in when the shouting started. The sisters were watching but not getting any closer. The teens were chased out of the room into the dining room by one of the matron cooks who was reading in the great room when the argument began. Lying underneath the dining room table, the teens could see and listen but not be seen.

"He cheated you," Stefano repeated, "he started taking your business away. What did you do to him?"

Signore Cassanzo stared across the room at nothing and refused to talk.

"You had his son killed, didn't you?"

No response but a collective gasp from the family.

"You killed his son, and then his grandson. It was Sutton who arranged to get Celestina to America with Carlo Vendante. Carlo's family did a lot of business with Sutton. She followed Carlo to America, and Sutton had her killed."

Still no response.

"And that is not all, is it Father? There is more, I know it."

The father said nothing.

"You were a great man once, but you have changed, and I am ashamed of you, of what you have become."

Stefano started to walk away and then he turned back, "Go ahead and curse. Your curse means nothing now. I don't ever want you to speak to me again until you are willing to tell me the truth, all of it."

Stefano walked out through the dining room and into the kitchen. The outer kitchen door closed. The family started walking away. When the room was empty, the teens hiding under the dining table heard the old man crying quietly.

99 The Bear

Stony Kill Road

Outside Canaan, New York

Thursday, July 28, 2011, 4:15 PM EDT

The dirt had been cleared away and the body exposed. There was nothing extraordinary about the body, no clothing remnants, no jewelry. The coroner staff was preparing to remove the bones when Carmen asked Andy, Do you have any idea who this is?" Carmen asked.

"Not anyone I know of. I walked in and out of this door all the time, and I don't remember it ever being dug up. What was in the box?"

Carmen had the box open on her lap and listed the contents as she sifted through them: "Photos, a baby spoon, a plastic cup, a small stuffed bear, more photos. You know who this looks like?" She continued and then gasped. She held up an old photo of a woman holding a baby.

"Andy, is this your mom?"

Carmen looked up, and Andy's eyes were tearing up. He reached for the bear and picked it up. He held it to his face and smelled it. A flood of incoherent memories, more like feelings poured through him. He started crying and then sobbing. Carmen stood from the chair and leaned into him, holding him.

100 The Will

Blackford Crighton Law Firm, New York Offices

21st Floor, 206 West 48th Street

Thursday, July 28, 2011, 7:45 PM EDT

"Yes, please let him come up," Alan told the security desk on the main floor.

Alan had stayed late at the office. He and Alicia had a quiet conversation and then she had other plans that night. Alan heard a knock on his office door. The door opened and in walked Roscoe Tanner.

Alan watched him approach the desk and then set a plastic trash bag on the desk.

"Did you have any problem finding it?" Alan asked.

The large man's furrowed brows told their own story. "Not too much, but I gotta tell ya, Alan, this stinks. There's something goin on here I don't want no part of."

"What is it you see going on that bothers you, Roscoe?"

"I seen the FBI nosing around dis place right after I left. I watched 'em for a while. They were diggin' up bodies. I don't have a problem doing the work, ya know? But I won't cross the line for nobody. This box I took is probably crossing the line with the FBI, you know, withholding evidence."

"I could not agree more," Alan said rummaging in a desk drawer and pulling out a business card. The card read:

Federal Bureau of Investigation

Tommy Edwards CIRG Division

Agent in Charge 26 Federal Plaza

Serial Crimes Task Force New York, NY 10278

ofc (212) 384-4073 cell (563) 285-0224

Alan turned the phone on his desk around and pushed the speaker button.

"Roscoe, dial 9 for an outside line and then dial the cell number. I'll do the talking, but let's tell him know what we found."

Roscoe dialed the cell number.

Tommy answered, "Agent Edwards."

"Agent Edwards, this is Alan Hopkins. I am the attorney for the Hollingsworth estate."

Tommy answered, "Yes, Mr. Hopkins. What can I do for you?"

"Someone who does investigative work for me uncovered a box from a hillside in upstate New York outside the town of Canaan."

Tommy asked, "Does your investigator happen to have size 15 shoes?"

Roscoe replied, "Yes, I do. Did you happen to play for Penn State?"

"Yes, I did. Did you happen to remove evidence from a crime scene?"

"Yes, I did but I felt really bad about it. Actually, it wasn't a crime scene when I took the box. I saw you drive up as I was leavin', and I wasn't too sure who you were at first or why you were there."

"Minor details," Tommy said. "I will need to see what you took and ask some questions."

Alan spoke up, "Agent Edwards, that is actually why we called you. Mr. Tanner is above the law at all times and was threatening to quit if we didn't come clean."

"We'll stop by in the morning. Mr. Tanner, can you arrange to meet us there at Blackford and Crighton's office at 9:00 AM?"

"Yeah, no problem."

"Thank you. We will see you in the morning."

"Good night, Agent Edwards," Alan closed with.

***

Tommy ended the call on his cell phone and turned to Carmen, "So what you are telling me is Andy's father killed his mother and replaced her with another woman."

The team was meeting in Tommy's hotel room.

"It seems like the most reasonable explanation for the box and the bones. The box contained photos of a woman and a child. The child in the photos was a male from birth to approximately two years old. The woman does not match the pictures we have on file of Mrs. Hollingsworth, but our images are all after 1980. If the woman in the grave is Andy's mother, she would have been killed around that time. This does fit with what we know of Andy's earliest memories."

"Why bury her there," Carlos asked, "by the basement door?"

Carmen shrugged, "Possibly to keep her close to Andy. The items in the box show a form of affection, personal items, memories of intimate moments between mother and child, the child's favorite play thing, eating utensils. The eating utensils wouldn't need to be destroyed. Why bury them?"

Angela said, "Is there any significance to laying her the way they did with her head toward the door?

"I don't think so. In American and European culture, we have a general aversion to stepping on graves. Putting her body there was more likely a way to show disgust. The people who used the door were servants and her son."

"Isn't that contradictory? He respected her, but was disgusted with her," Tommy pointed out.

Carmen responded, "It sounds like a lot of marriages. It probably reflects the conflicting feelings Mr. Hollingsworth had for his wife."

Carmen looked over at Steve Haskins who was deep in thought on the far side of Tommy's hotel room. Given what little Carmen now knew of Steve's past, the image of a mother buried under a son's feet had to be very disturbing. Andy, though, was her main concern. Andy hadn't spoken a word on the whole drive to the hotel in New

Windsor where Tommy authorized another night's stay at one of the major chain hotels right off the freeway. Just before the meeting in Tommy's room, she watched Andy walk away from the hotel.

101 A Field of Lights

A Hill Overlooking Stewart International Airport

New Windsor, New York

Thursday, July 28, 2011, 9:05 PM EDT

The field of blue, yellow, and red runway lights against the black night sky provided a surreal landscape punctuated occasionally by the roar of jet engines taking off.

In the silence between planes, Andy heard someone climbing the hill behind him. He turned to see the most disappointing sight he could imagine; Steve Haskins was walking up the hill.

"I know you wish it was the Doc and not me. The Doc was starting to head out to look for you, but I told her it wasn't safe."

"Wasn't safe? You can see the door of the hotel from here!" Andy said trying to understand.

"Sorry kid," Steve apologized as he sat down on the grassy hill. "The Doc isn't ready to start hiking around in the dark just yet." Steve continued, "And a few other minor details you missed because you decided to skip our team meeting..."

Andy caught the implication. Steve included him as part of the team.

"The Doc told Tommy her family could be connected to the family of the murdered lady we dug out of the hillside today. They came from the same province. Tommy's not sure what to do about it yet."

Andy sighed looking straight ahead. That was not what he wanted to hear. Just when things might be turning his way, another emotional disappointment seemed in the cards.

"Wait," Andy said in a confused tone, "Carmen and Celeste are connected?"

"Yeah, Carmen's father is from the same town in Italy as Celestina's grandfather. Carmen said her father had worked for the Cassanzos at one point."

Andy shook his head, "That is so weird. What are the chances?"

"About a hundred percent according to Tommy. He said something about a law of attraction."

Andy sighed, "Anything else?"

"Yeah. Apparently you have a birthday next week, and there's some distribution of a trust meeting you need to attend."

This comment reminded Andy of another looming emotional obstacle - someone wanting to kill him.

Andy sighed and mumbled, "If I live that long."

Steve exhaled, "Oh, so you knew."

"Yeah."

They sat in silence until a jet took off a little to their left. The sound was deafening.

When the quiet returned, Steve said, "I'm sorry about your mom. I was pretty sure that's who it was once we knew there was a body in the hole."

"How did you know?" Andy asked.

"I didn't know. It was a feeling. Let me see the bear."

Andy reached into his jacket pocket and pulled out the small stuffed bear and reluctantly handed it to Haskins.

Steve looked at the animal for a minute and said, "Mine was a train. I slept with it every night for years. I guess that makes me more mechanical, and you, well, you're just stupid."

Andy laughed out loud, and it felt good. It relieved a lot of built up tension.

Steve chuckled too and followed with, "I don't know if you heard the Maori tattoo guy talking about my mom and dad."

Andy said nothing, waiting for Steve to continue.

"My dad was abusive. One night he came home drunk. Which was almost every night. I was crying in my room, and he wanted to hit me. My mom wouldn't let him go into my room, so he shot her in the head. Once he sobered up enough to realize what he had done and why the police had surrounded the house, he ate a bullet. I was seven at the time. I lived with a drunk grandfather for a couple years then got sent to a string of foster homes. When I turned seventeen, I enlisted in the Army. I just wanted to kill people but there weren't any wars, so I decided to become a Ranger. I took the most dangerous assignments I could find. I think I was trying to commit suicide by heroism. I thought I could be a better man than my father."

"I've never seen you drink."

Steve's eyes momentarily flashed anger, "And you won't, not ever. Anyway, I wanted to tell you I know what it's like to lose your mom."

They sat in silence for fifteen seconds, then Steve added, "Don't you ever tell anyone what I told you. This is between you and me."

A jet took off again. At the tail end of the roar, Andy replied, "Between you and me."

Steve nodded and then stood up.

He handed the bear back to Andy saying, "C'mon, Priss'. We need our beauty rest if we're gonna catch bad guys."

Walking back to the hotel Andy asked, "Did the tattoo hurt? I've never seen a tattoo that raised lines on your skin."

Steve nodded, "Like the big guy said, it hurt like hell. Still does."

102 History

Cassanzo Villa

Orsara di Puglia, Province of Foggia, Italy

Friday, July 29, 2011, 5:10 AM UTC -1 (11:10 PM EDT)

The sunrise was dimmed by the early morning clouds. Stefano saw a dark figure stooped over something in the morning mist. This was his family's land. He approached boldly.

"Hey! Who are you, and what are you doing?" Stefano called out.

The dark figure on one knee straightened up and a gnarled hand waved "Ciao, Stefano. A beautiful morning."

Stefano recognized the gravel voice of Agosto.

"Agosto, what are you doing out so early?"

"Oh, this vine got hit by an ax yesterday. I had to make sure it was cared for, to make sure the wound was sealed correctly. Help me up, please."

Stefano pulled Agosto's arm as the old man struggled to stand. Once he was upright, he stood like an oak.

"Will the vine survive?"

"I don't know yet. It has been badly damaged. I have done all I can do to help it, but now it is up to the vine. If it wants to do the work of restoring the flow of nutrients and water, it will live. If not, there are many other vines here. But look around us. It is a beautiful morning and only you and me to share it. Why should we talk about vines dying?"

Stefano looked at the southeastern facing hillside, the rows of vines already heavy with young grapes. It was almost an hour before the sunrise. The air was cool, and the day was new.

Agosto put his ancient hand on Stefano's shoulder, "I never tire of seeing this land. It saved my life. It saved all the lives of my family and other families too."

"I know your family lived here during the war. How did you come to live here?"

Agosto looked Stefano directly in the eyes and smiled. Then he waved his hand out toward the hillside and down to the tree line hiding the stream. "This was a haven for us, for many people in those days. During the war, after Italy surrendered to the allies, the German army took over everything. They were brutal, killing and capturing anyone who could be a threat. My father took our family from Foggia and fled into the hills. He brought his wife and seven children to this place. We built a one-room shack in the trees behind the olive grove. We heard rumors of whole villages being shot or burned alive. The Germans came here and put a mean old man in the main house here. He was responsible for making wine and olive oil for the Germans. No one liked him or his wife."

"In the fall of 1944, after the Germans had been pushed out of this area, an old truck drove up the hill and stopped in front of the house. Some very tough looking men with guns rounded up the families living in the woods. They brought the man and woman out of the villa and shot them. Your father came with these men in the truck. He was twelve years old and carried a machine gun and smoked and cursed. They were partisans, and we were very afraid of them. The men told us your father's family owned this land, and we all had to work for him. We heard rumors that all the people in your grandmother's village to the north were killed. We didn't know what to expect."

Agosto asked and looked into Stefano's face, "Did your father ever tell you about the war?"

"No, he never spoke about the war," Stefano said, looking out over the fields. "If we brought it up, he became angry."

Agosto turned away and looked across the fields again, "Last night when you and your father were arguing, it reminded me your father never talked about the war, even then."

Stefano remarked, "One thing he said puzzled me. He said he had lost many children. He must have been referring to the war."

"That was probably what happened to your grandparents. We never met them. They never came here. All the pictures of them are from before the war."

103 Legal Update

Cambourne Hall Near Oxford, England

Friday, July 29, 2011, 8:45 AM GMT (3:45 AM EDT)

"Yes Sir, quite serious," Christopher Turner, the chief solicitor for Blackford Crighton's London office criminal law division, told Lord St. Claire and the small group convened in the immense library at Cambourne Hall. The room was rarely used except for serious discussions requiring formality.

"Whitehall has turned the incident over to the Metropolitan Police SCD7 unit. This is now a criminal investigation."

"SCD7 is the Specialist Crime Directorate unit charged with investigating organized crime," solicitor Niles Bagley clarified.

Bagley was a partner in the firm and Sir Smythley's second in command.

"Organized Crime! This is preposterous! On what grounds?" St. Claire remonstrated.

Solicitor Bagley said, "On the grounds persons in your employ knowingly violated British law and sovereignty by using the controlled communications services of the British Foreign Office for your personal gain. Businesses you control have been bribing foreign diplomats, and these are only the first issues the 'Met' is investigating."

"The Met! Bah! Why can't you call it Scotland Yard so we all know what you are talking about," St. Claire scoffed. "What else could they possibly find worth prosecuting?"

"The Met also wants to know why an Italian citizen was kidnapped off the streets of Florenc, and left on your doorstep half dead."

St. Claire pounded on the table, "I had nothing to do with him!"

"There are also reports," Bagley continued, "of illegalities involving your shipping and related businesses."

"These are groundless, Sir. I assure you. Nothing more than a slap on the wrist should suffice."

104 Errands

A Hotel Near Stewart International Airport

New Windsor, New York

Friday, July 29, 2011, 6:20 AM EDT

Tommy met his team in the lobby at a small table in an alcove for a short meeting.

"Angela," Tommy started handing her the business card for Alan Hopkins, "Get over to the attorney's office and get whatever was taken from the Hollingsworth crime scene. Be sure to find out all you can about what, why, and when it was taken. I assume they didn't know about it until recently, or they would have removed it sooner. Ask how they found out about it."

Angela pointed out in a respectful but annoyed tone, "Tommy, I know how to do my job."

Tommy smiled and said, "Yes, you do. Pick up a rental car at the airport."

Tommy turned to Carlos, "Go to the North Shore University Hospital and visit Nathan Kahn. Make sure our security instructions were followed to the letter. If Mr. Kahn can speak, find out all you can about what happened to him. Get a rental car."

"Yes Sir," Carlos replied, "but you will have to drop us off at the terminal."

"Steve, Carmen, and Andy are with me. We are going to guard the remains of Celeste and assist the CIA in expediting the release of her remains to the family."

Steve raised his hand, "Why do you need me to help with the coroner's office?"

"You'll be riding shotgun," Tommy answered.

Steve raised his eyebrows with a questioning look, "You want me to come with you so I can sit up front?"

Tommy gave an exasperated sigh and explained, “No, well yes, you get to sit up front, but ‘shotgun’ as in the original meaning of the phrase.”

Carlos and Angela looked blankly at each other.

“On a stagecoach!” Tommy said with a raised voice, “The guy sitting next to the driver with the big gun! Am I the only one who watched or read westerns as a kid?”

“I don’t read anything that’s not military,” Steve said with a hint of disgust.

“Get out to the Suburban!” Tommy ordered.

Everyone started moving toward the door. The vehicle was parked right outside. Steve punched Carlos in the arm remarking, “How come you never watched westerns? That’s up your Texas alley.”

Carlos batted Steve’s hand away, “Man, this Texican grew up in Miami. My parents were from Texas.”

105 Strengths and Weaknesses

A Hotel Near Stewart International Airport

New Windsor, New York

Friday, July 29, 2011, 6:30 AM EDT

Tommy concluded the call on his cell phone, "Thank you, Mr. Hopkins. Angela should be at your office in about two hours."

Tommy hung up and asked Andy, "Okay, explain how this demon possession thing works."

Tommy asked as they waited outside the car rental agency. Later, they would drive back north toward Hudson, New York, county seat of Columbia County. Angela and Carlos leaned in the two passenger side windows while they waited for their cars to be brought up. Tommy was behind the wheel with Steve next to him. Carmen and Andy sat on the middle bench seat but not too close.

Steve followed Tommy's question with, "Yeah, how could Carmen blow a hole in the Liebowitz brick house and then get taken out by your little dart gun?"

Andy exhaled, "I'd be lying if I told you I know all the answers. I have experience with this stuff, a lot of experience, but it still baffles me."

"A few things I know," Andy continued, "demons and people both have strengths and weaknesses. When there is a possession, a demon is using a person. The possessed person sort of has the strengths and weaknesses of both."

Andy took a deep breath and continued, "But either of them can override the other. It's a battle for control if the person is willing to fight back. The stronger one will win the battle, but the control can flip at any time to the other one."

Carlos asked, "How do you get possessed at all? Why did they pick Carmen?"

"Possession happens usually by invitation; you intentionally invite the spirit or demon into you. I know a few times where someone was so involved in drugs and other things it lowered their defenses. In those cases, the spirits can sometimes walk right in."

Tommy asked, "What do you mean 'lower your defenses?' So we have defenses against these spirits? Then why Carmen?"

"I don't know. Carmen must have a family connection with Cassanzos. That's why Celeste attached to her. Then the spirits attacked Carmen because of Celeste. I'm guessing here."

Angela asked, "What about silver crosses and stuff like that? Does it help?"

"They only work on vampires, and only in the movies," Andy smirked, "since there aren't any real vampires. We should probably stick with reality."

Steve didn't even turn around when he said, "Chasing demons isn't exactly like reality."

Andy quipped, "It's been a big part of my reality, and, by the way, you have a blue tattoo on your face, in case you forgot."

106 Too Obvious

Blackford Crighton Law Firm, New York Offices

21st Floor, 206 West 48th Street

Friday, July 29, 2011, 9:10 AM EDT

Roscoe Tanner and Attorney Alan Hopkins sat in Alan's office watching Angela dial her cell phone. The contents of the metal box that Roscoe had retrieved lay open on a well-lit side table.

"Tommy," Angela said with some excitement, "you asked me to call as soon as I knew. The object removed from the Hollingsworth basement was a metal box with papers in it."

Alan next heard Angela say, "Well, one thing was important. There is a will from Andy's parents in there. It's dated a week before their deaths."

Alan tensed waiting for any information about the will.

-

Angela answered Tommy's next question, "The answer is 'no' with a probability factor of ninety nine percent."

-

"Sure, I'm leaving for the lab now. Yes Sir, I'll let him know."

-

Turning to Alan and Roscoe, Angela asked, "How did you learn the location of this metal box?"

"A call from a partner in our home office in London," Alan said, "suggested there might be another will. The partner was Sir Wynton Smythley. He also told us about the presence of a basement where we could look for it."

Angela spoke into the cell phone, "Yeah, a Wynton Smythley from Blackford's London office."

Alan interrupted with a raised a finger, "*Sir* Wynton Smythley. I am afraid he will insist."

"Sir Wynton Smythley, got it. Tommy, also these guys had a very interesting conversation with a guy named Jimmy."

107 The High Cost of Favors

Cambourne Hall Near Oxford, England

Friday, July 29, 2011, 2:50 PM GMT (9:50 AM EDT)

Constant pain in Lord St. Claire's back strained his physical reserves. The mounting legal charges being read to him were further draining his ability to keep a grasp on what was happening. St. Claire braced himself for a final effort for the day to start his defense and attack strategy.

"Wallace!" St. Claire demanded with half closed eyes.

"Here, Sir."

St. Claire pointed toward the open door while pausing. Finally he continued, "Go to my, my office. Bring the leather satchel from my bottom left drawer."

"Very good, Sir"

"Wait, you will need this key," the Lord said pulling a chain from around his neck with a single cylindrical key.

"Thank you, Sir," Wallace answered. "I will be back shortly."

Wallace walked hurriedly out of the room, and returned ten minutes later, but instead of bringing a satchel, he held the door open for a well-dressed elderly gentleman. All discussions instantly stopped and everyone present except Lord St. Claire rose to their feet. If St. Claire was angry or disturbed, he did not dare to show it.

"Please Gentlemen," the visitor said softly, "Lord St. Claire and I will require some privacy. Please allow us a few moments, and then you may return. Wallace, please remain to wait on the Lord's pleasure."

The four solicitors from London filed out of the room. Wallace stood at attention near the door.

As soon as the heavy oak doors closed, St. Claire turned to the visitor and stated, "I was told there would be no interference with my affairs as long as I brought the Hollingsworth estate back to England."

The elderly gentleman patiently answered, "And you have been left to your own affairs. You turned your affairs into such an ugly disaster with this revenge business no one was willing to get involved with you. It even looked for many years you might actually succeed."

St. Claire's chin lifted as his eyes allowed his anger to surface. "I have increased my holdings more than tenfold in the last thirty years, and the Hollingsworth estate is within my grasp. The court has no reason to interfere now."

"Yes, you benefited from keeping the Italians off balance with your reign of terror. Unfortunately, William, we have reason to believe Hollingsworth monies will be staying in America and ..."

"No!" St. Claire erupted. "A new will has been found, and the trust assignments will bring the entire fortune back to where it belongs!"

The visitor looked down his nose at Lord St. Claire allowing a silence to settle between them.

At some length the visitor replied, "Interrupt me again at your peril."

Silence followed the visitor's remark.

Lord St. Claire reluctantly apologized, "Yes, thoughtless, please forgive my rudeness, but we are days away from concluding the Hollingsworth transfer to a British national."

"You would like, of course, to have Dudley Hollingsworth inherit the entire estate with you managing for him. It would be a considerable increase in your power base in The Court."

"For queen and country, of course," St. Claire agreed.

The visitor stood and straightened his waistcoat proclaiming, "Unfortunately, your little fairy tale will not come true. The Americans have already proven the new will to be false, the Italian assassins have failed, and your mess has grown so large we were unable to see any way clear of it until now. We have a small window of opportunity to salvage your holdings from complete annihilation and gain some inroads with the Americans."

"But I witnessed the signing of the will myself. It is valid!"

Wallace opened the door for the visitor who turned back to face St. Claire, "This last statement I would not repeat in case the Americans hear you. They are looking for someone to prosecute, and you have enough legal troubles already."

St. Claire assured his visitor, "We can handle these charges easily enough."

"Possibly, but there are more coming. Also, your selection for a successor is unacceptable. Pick someone else."

St. Claire lost any semblance of propriety and stormed, "You cannot tell me what to do! I will manage my own affairs!"

The visitor said ominously before walking out, "You will replace him or we will, for queen and country."

One of the junior solicitors came back into the room, "Lord St. Claire, forgive me but a chap I know at the International Maritime Organization called. He let me know Interpol has boarded one of the Sutton container ships in the Port of Oran in Algeria. They found refugees from the country of Columbia in some of the containers, all of them were young girls and women. Interpol agents have evidence they were being sold as slaves."

108 A Short Call to Light the Fuse

Blackford Crighton Law Firm, New York Offices

21st Floor, 206 West 48th Street

Friday, July 29, 2011, 10:10 AM EDT

Alan Hopkins dialed the phone number Alicia Montgomery had just handed him.

"Good morning, Mr. Vargas. This is Alan Hopkins at Blackford Crighton."

-

"Yes, quite well, thank you. I am calling to let you know we will need you here at our offices Monday morning at ten o'clock to begin the dissolution of the Hollingsworth trust."

-

"We had a visit from the FBI this morning. It seems, not only is the new will not valid, but it is evidence in an ongoing investigation."

-

"Very good, we will see you then. Thank you."

-

Alan hung up the phone and looked up at Angela seated next to Alicia, "Does that suffice?"

"Perfect, thanks," Angela replied standing to her feet. "It's all we need. We will be back on Monday with Andy. Also, my boss asked me to stay here for the rest of the day, if you approve. More evidence may turn up, you know, conversations, phone calls, visits."

"I will not have any of our clients' privacy compromised," Alan stated emphatically, "but you may stay in my office and listen to anything pertaining to your Hollingsworth case."

"Thanks," Angela said through her sneaky smile, "but I have a better idea."

109 Reaching for Closure

Cambourne Hall Near Oxford, England

Friday, July 29, 2011, 3:15 PM GMT (10:15 AM EDT)

"Matthew," Lord St. Claire said into the phone with a forced calmness.

Wallace had just dialed the phone and handed it to him before exiting.

"I say Matthew, I know you are still healing, but we have a crisis. Matthew, can you hear me?"

-

St. Claire continued, "We are running out of time. Our ships and planes are being grounded. Warehouses in Africa, Europe, and South America have been seized. I am certain the oriental locations are next. We need the Hollingsworth funds now."

-

"No, there is a problem with the new will. I just got off the phone with O'Bannon's London office. I fear old Hollingsworth may have been on to us."

-

"The FBI has taken the will as evidence. The fact that I signed it as a witness, and you are the sole heir, could implicate us. Our only hope now is for young Hollingsworth's demise so Dudley can inherit. Matthew, do I hear a woman's voice?"

***

In a large estate overlooking Long Island Sound, Matthew Sutton spoke quietly to the middle-aged beauty trying to pull him further down into the already crumpled bed.

"Sorry Love, I must take this call, foreign trade and all. It never sleeps."

-

"Why yes, Grandfather, you hear the voice of a very charming friend. She volunteered to assist with my mending process."

-

"I am feeling very fit. Marissa was a dear to give me some clever pills ..."

-

"Of course Grandfather, I will do whatever it takes."

-

"I won't have to even put on shoes. Salvatore and another were captured, but the rest of the Italians are still here. We just need to give them young Hollingsworth's location."

-

"No Grandfather, I don't know his location. Ask Smythley to get it. All we need is his cell phone number or the number of someone traveling with him. I believe he is moving about with some FBI people."

-

"Call Brian's pet? It's not that simple. We lost my brother's pet when I got shot. My pet is a bit more unwieldy. She will take some coaxing."

-

"Grandfather, we only need to survive until Monday. After ..."

-

"Then have Smythley call cousin Alan. Can one of your people pass the number to the Italians?"

-

"Yes, let the Italians take care of Hollingsworth or whatever he calls himself."

110 Cassanzo

Cassanzo Villa

Orsara di Puglia, Province of Foggia, Italy

Friday, July 29, 2011, 11:50 AM UTC -1 (3:10 PM EDT)

"Who was that who just left?" the old man demanded.

Stefano had just walked out to the veranda. His eyes were red and still wet. The day was very warm, and the still air offered no relief from the heat. Stefano took a seat across from his father.

"It was a messenger from Luigi Ciulli, Father."

"He is not welcome here!"

"He knows, Father. That is why he does not come but sent a messenger."

"Well, are you going to tell me what he said?"

Stefano wiped more tears away and said, "The Americans are certain the body they found is my daughter Celestina."

Stefano choked up and could not speak for a moment. He sat silently while his father watched the sparrows taking dust baths in the dirt at the edge of the olive grove that grew down the hill behind the veranda.

"The Americans will not release the body because they are investigating her murder. Luigi was able to delay the seizures of our businesses but it won't delay the others for long."

The old man did not move or say anything.

"I was also told to tell you Luigi sent William Sutton a present. The messenger could not explain what it means but said you would know."

The old man's face eased into a crooked smile.

111 Stirring the Pot

Cambourne Hall Near Oxford, England

Friday, July 29, 2011, 3:15 PM GMT (10:15 AM EDT)

"Sir Smythley, this is Wallace, Lord St. Claire's butler," Wallace spoke into the house phone in Lord St. Claire's bedroom.

Wallace continued, "His Grace is indisposed and asked me to pass some information to you. He says we need Mr. Hollingsworth's cell phone number or the cell phone number of one of the FBI agents traveling with him."

-

Wallace kept his professional demeanor and responded, "Sir Smythley, His Grace is leaving the acquisition of the information in your capable hands."

-

The conversation ended with Wallace adding, "Very good, Sir. I will let His Grace know. Thank you."

Wallace knocked on the bathroom door and waited.

From behind the door St. Claire answered, "Wallace, I cannot get up. I will need your assistance. What did he say?"

"Sir Smythley said your nephew Alan may have information. He will contact him promptly."

112 Small Town Fun

City Hall

Coroner's Office

Hudson, New York

Friday, July 29, 2011, 3:15 PM GMT (10:15 AM EDT)

"I am so sorry, Sir, but we just received the body last evening," the receptionist repeated to Tommy what she had already told Steve. "Dr. Carver is on vacation and will not be back until Monday."

"Are you telling me there is no one else who can sign off on the remains?"

"You can get a habeas corpus writ but we still need an inquest, after all, this poor girl was murdered, even if it was a long time ago."

"Not a problem, Miss Hatcher, I'll have a writ faxed here within the hour. Where is the body now?"

"I'm not sure. It may be at County General pathology lab, that's where Alvin likes to take bodies late in the day. They are open twenty-four hours. If Marcus was driving, it may be in the city morgue, unless the drawbridge was up, and it might have been. There was a lot of boat traffic on the river last night. Oh, but from Canaan, he could have gone through Mayfield. It's a little out of the way, but you don't have to worry about trains or the boat traffic."

"All right, look, if the draw bridge was up, where would it have gone?" Tommy asked exasperated.

Miss Hatcher looked through her inbox again for the fourth time, "Like I told the other agent, I don't have any paperwork. It was only yesterday. We usually don't file the paperwork until the next day or the day after. If Alvin drives, Marcus does the paperwork, and vice versa. The paperwork is probably still with the body."

"Exactly, so how do we find out where the body is?" Steve interrupted.

"Well, with Dr. Carver out of town, the boys won't need to turn it in until Monday. Dr. Stimson could be called in a pinch. He's Dr. Carver's backup when he's out of town, but, of course, he's ..."

Tommy cut her off, "Can you show me to the city morgue?"

"Actually, no, I can't. I mean I don't have the keys," the elderly Miss Hatcher replied. "I loaned my set to Marcus since he uses them all the time, and I don't have any need to ..."

"Are they the only ambulance drivers in the county? Can you call Marcus?" Steve asked brusquely.

"No, they aren't the only ones. They work for the county and don't charge us. All the other companies charge a small fortune that frankly ..."

"Can you call Marcus or Alvin?" Tommy asked reinforcing Steve's request.

"I can call Marcus, but he may not pick up. He takes Friday off because he works Saturdays. Alvin may answer if he is in the truck. I know he is on call right now."

Steve threw his hands up, "I can't believe we found a body that's been missing twenty-five years, and now we lost it again!"

113 An Easy Call

Blackford Crighton Law Firm, New York Offices

21st Floor, 206 West 48th Street

Friday, July 29, 2011, 11:30 AM EDT

"Good morning, Blackford Crighton, Alan Hopkins office," Miss Montgomery answered the call the front desk had transferred to her.

-

Alicia pursed her lips and frowned as she listened. Finally she responded, "Sir Smythley, Alan is not here."

-

Alicia moved the earpiece from behind her ear to avoid dismissive abuse she could still hear an arm's length away.

-

"May I take a message, Sir," Alicia asked replacing her earpiece.

-

"Yes, I will have him contact you. Sir, I believe you have his cell number, but I can give it to you if you need ..."

-

Angela also had an earpiece and silently shook her head when she heard Sir Smythley's request.

-

"Uh, no Sir, I do not have a cell number for Andrew Glover, and I believe the FBI agents can be contacted through their office. Can I give you their numb ...?"

"He hung up," Alicia said to Angela. "Why would he need to talk to the FBI or Mr. Glover?"

Angela shook her head and said, "Not sure, but I have a guess. Where is the business card Agent Edwards left with Alan?"

"It's in his desk drawer," Alicia said standing and walking toward Alan's office.

Angela stood and followed.

As they approached Alan's desk, Angela sniped, "Seems like you know where Alan keeps everything."

Alicia stopped looking through Alan's desk drawer and stood upright looking slightly down into Angela's eyes, "I know where enough things are for my position here as his assistant."

"Hey you can assist him with anything you want. It's your business, sister, but I saw how he looked at you, and you weren't exactly turning a cold shoulder."

Alicia reached down into the drawer and took out the business card Tommy had left with Alan.

"I have been professional and business like in all my dealings here. The fact that I happen to admire Alan does not affect my work."

Angela accepted the card from Alicia and then held her hands up, "Put the guns down, lady. When I smell smoke, I don't need to see flames to know there's a fire. Personally, I'm happy for you. I hope it works out."

Alicia read sincerity in Angela's smile and said simply, "Thank you, I hope so too."

114 Don't Forget to Write

Federal Holding Cells Underneath Federal Plaza

Lafayette Street, New York

Friday, July 29, 2011, 1:00 PM EDT

Processing day for Yoel Frankel, a.k.a. Salvatore, had come. His deportation to Italy was not contested by himself or any of the other parties. It had been hurried through channels as part of his deal with the FBI and CIA.

"Has your team found their target yet?" one of the CIA agents asked casually as if they were looking for a gas station.

Salvatore smiled and replied, "Because you asked the question, I know the answer is 'no,' but trust me, they will. They are very patient and thorough."

"Patient, maybe, but the clock is ticking, a very loud clock," the agent said returning the smile as the federal marshals put handcuffs on Salvatore's wrists and manacles around his ankles.

Salvatore asked one of the marshals, "Is this really necessary?"

The CIA agent laughed, "Think of it as a going away present. We wouldn't want you to forget us." The agent added, "This team was trained by you, wasn't it?"

Salvatore smiled again, ignoring the question and simply said, "It has been my pleasure, Sir."

Then Salvatore was led away toward the elevator up to basement level one where the marshal's Suburban would take Salvatore to the airport.

115 Hand in the Cookie Jar

Blackford Crighton Law Firm, New York Offices

21st Floor, 206 West 48th Street

Friday, July 29, 2011, 11:30 AM EDT

Alan opened his office door after a short standup lunch with court officials to update them on the coming trust distribution for Hollingsworth.

"Sir Smythley, stand away from my desk!" Alan demanded.

Several of Alan's desk drawers had been emptied out on his desk and a side table. Smythley was bent over the most recent pile of papers and business cards going through them one at a time.

"There is no time for this Alan. I must have that cell number for the FBI. I know you have it here somewhere."

For the shortest moment, Alan froze. He knew the card to be on his desk under the pile of papers Sir Smythley had created. Then he realized Smythley couldn't find it, so it might as well not exist for this conversation.

"This is most unprofessional! I'm not sure who told you I have such a card, but apparently, they were mistaken. This will be presented to the Board of Partners for redress, I assure you."

Smythley continued going through notes and cards in the pile saying, "I must have that card, Hopkins."

Alan strode up to the frantic man and grabbed his arm pulling him to the side of the desk.

"You can see for yourself, Sir Smythley, there is no business card from the FBI here. Leave these offices at once."

Alan's commanding tone and steady glare brought Smythley to the realization that further efforts here were fruitless. He pursed his lips to say something, but no words came to him. He stormed out of Alan's office past Alicia and a frumpy twenty-ish year old bobbing her head to music in her earphones.

The elevator door opened, and Smythley stepped forward.

"Sir Smythley," Alicia called in a sweet singsong tone, "are you looking for this?"

Sir Smythley turned around to see Alicia holding a business card and waving it in the air. He took a half step toward her and stopped.

Her arms visible from her sleeveless top were not the skinny arms of a model. They were thin but muscled like the arms of a farm girl who worked out. More daunting then the definition of her strong arms was the heavy glass paperweight she was holding at her side with the other hand.

Smythley gritted his teeth and stepped backward into the waiting elevator.

The doors slid shut. There was a moment of silence while the elevator car dropped a couple of floors. Then Angela took out her earphones and roared with laughter.

Alan came out of his office looking puzzled and expecting Sir Smythley to be causing more trouble.

Angela was still laughing.

Alan asked, "What did I miss? What is so funny?"

Alicia had quietly put the paperweight and arbitrary business card she had used back on her desk.

"It was nothing, Mr. Hopkins," she said with a mischievous smile.

Alan looked at Angela askance and replied, "Well, um, Miss Montgomery, can you assist me in reassembling my desk?"

After Alan walked back into his office, Angela laughed, "Sister, you are my kinda girl!"

Alicia gave a timid high five to Angela's waiting hand but said, "That was probably not my finest moment."

"Like hell, it wasn't!" Alan heard through the open door of his office.

116 Confirmation

Blackford Crighton Law Firm, New York Offices

21st Floor, 206 West 48th Street

Friday, July 29, 2011, 11:50 AM EDT

"Tommy, I was right. Some old guy from Blackford's London office was rifling through the attorney's desk trying to find your cell number. It was that Wynton Smythley guy, I mean Sir Wynton Smythley. He didn't get the number, but he's going to keep trying," Angela said quietly into her cell phone so no one else could hear.

-

"Okay, Tommy, I'm staying here for now."

-

"Oh yeah, Jamal owes me a few favors. The signature was bogus, and there was talcum powder on the box from latex gloves. The powder was made in the last five years."

-

"How did I know about the husband's signature? No, the wife's signature didn't match from the older signatures on file, but we knew it wouldn't. It was the husband's signature that aced it."

-

"Yeah, because he signed with his full middle name, Douglas Rogers Hollingsworth."

-

"Because he made some of the letters darker than others."

-

"Yep, those darker letters were D-U-R-E-S-S. Hollingsworth was forced to sign the document, and he was trying to let everyone know."

-

"Right, I'll start calling Steve's phone. Tell him to start answering it."

-

"Okay, I'll tell the attorney. Okay, bye."

-

"Mr. Hopkins, Agent Edwards told me to tell you this new will you retrieved from the Hollingsworth estate has major legal complications I need to tell you about."

117 One More Favor

Cambourne Hall Near Oxford, England

Friday, July 29, 2011, 7:15 PM GMT (2:15 PM EDT)

"One more favor pays for all, Smythley." Lord St. Claire called Smythley on a special cell phone that scrambled the signal, preventing electronic eavesdropping.

-

"Offer him more money. It's all he ever wanted, and he will need more if he is about to be sacked. Go as low as possible, but you may offer him up to ten million, in dollars of course."

-

"Fly there tonight. Get this taken care of and no excuses!"

-

"Give the number to the Italian Embassy in Washington, the main switch board. That is all he needs to know."

118 One for the Money

A Private Residence

Georgetown, Washington, DC

Friday, July 29, 2011, 6:05 PM EDT

"Yes Sir, this is Jim Robins, White House Chief of Staff. I need to talk to one of your agents."

-

"No, he is in the field right now, and I need to get a message to him."

-

"It's actually very important that I speak to him right away."

-

"Okay, I have an idea. This is for Tommy Edwards. You tell Tommy he needs to call the Italian Embassy as soon as possible. This is very critical."

-

"Yes, this is about the Cassanzo girl's body. Have him call the embassy."

-

"Yes, thank you."

Jim Robins hung up the phone and turned to Sir Smythley, "I hope that helped. The President did have me pass the message that Italy is our friend. Our friends at the embassy will be relieved to know the FBI will be calling with the news."

Sir Smythley slid a set of instructions across the small kitchen table and said, "Thank you ever so much, you have no idea how much this small gesture of friendship means."

The note contained a phone number to a Swiss bank, a number for an account containing five million dollars, and instructions for changing the pass code.

Sir Smythley offered Jim Robins his scramble phone.

119 Two for the Show

Da Ba Restaurant

Hudson, New York

Friday, July 29, 2011, 7:10 PM EDT

Tommy shook his head while he hung up his cell phone.

He looked across the table at Andy and Carmen explaining, "The CIRG office wanted me to call the Italian Embassy in Washington for an update on Celestina's remains. The embassy didn't know anything about it, at least not before I called. They sure know about it now." Tommy added in a worried tone, "They are very excited."

The three of them looked at the menu in silence until Steve walked in followed by two other men about Steve's age, obviously active or former military.

"Tommy, Priss, Doc, this is Larry Evans and Chris Boydelatour. We served together in Desert Shield. You won't believe what they have in this backwater town. Hey, but first, tell 'em I didn't volunteer for this tattoo. They don't believe me."

Carmen confirmed, "The tattoo was definitely forced on him."

Steve followed with, "Hey you guys, grab some seats. I'll get the beers."

Carmen quickly followed with, "The empty seat is taken."

"Don't ask," Steve answered Chris's questioning look.

Larry and Chris pulled chairs from another table as Steve walked to the bar.

"So you guys are Steve's new family," Chris said to start the conversations.

Larry added, "We were worried about him after they broke up his unit. He's not what you call a 'people person,' but you all have warmed him up a bunch."

Andy shook his head frowning and asked, "You think Steve is warmed up?"

Larry looked over his shoulder to make sure Steve didn't hear then said quietly, "Don't get me wrong. We like Steve. Solid guy. When you're in a fight, you want him covering your six, but after a battle, we couldn't get two words out of him. Trust me; he has come a long way."

"A long, long way," Chris agreed.

Steve came walking back to the table, "Can you believe it? The bartender wanted the waitress to bring the beers. I told him, 'Just give me the bottles.'"

Chris then started the conversation heaviest on his mind, "So why are the Feds in our quiet little town? Don't tell me you're here to soak up the ambiance."

Steve said, "Larry and Chris work for the Sheriff's office. They run the SWAT team for the county."

"Steve tells us you're into some weird shit. Anything we should know?" Chris asked.

Tommy gave a heavy sigh and said, "We aren't sure yet. We found two bodies on top of a ridge outside the town of Canaan. One of the bodies was the daughter of an Italian industrialist. She has been missing for over twenty-five years. The coroner's office lost the remains. Also, there is a team of Italian commandos, all former military, with a contract on Andy here."

Andy smiled and waved.

Tommy continued, "Some British attorneys are working hard to find my cell number, probably to locate me. My office asked me to update the Italian Embassy in Washington about the girl's body, but the embassy claimed they didn't know about it, but are very excited we discovered her body."

Steve sat bug eyed then said, "Crap! I left you guys alone for one hour and everything went to hell."

"The commandos are using your cell phone to track you. That's easy," Chris said. Tommy nodded..

Larry leaned forward focusing on Steve and Tommy, "It's a fair assumption they are in route now. I would prefer no action takes place in Columbia County, but we may not have a choice. How do you want to play this?"

Tommy said, "If we leave here with Andy, the team will probably come and leave, and you'll never see them."

Steve sat up saying, "Unless they start looking for him here and get mean. Then you have an angry hornet's nest right in your kitchen, and they would be hard to get out without causing damage."

Tommy's cell rang.

"Angela ..."

-

"Yes, we know about my cell number. What's up?"

-

"Now? Which channel?"

-

"Oh, the breaking story is on all the major networks," Tommy said to others at the table with mock enthusiasm.

-

"Where are you now?"

-

"Why are you with Alan Hopkins' secretary?"

-

"How did she do that?"

-

"Oh, well tell her I said thank you for the attempt."

-

"No, I need to remain here for now."

120 On the Sidelines

Mile Marker 14, Snowmass Creek Road

A Large Estate Near Aspen, Colorado

Friday, July 29, 2011, 5:30 PM Mountain Daylight Time (7:30 PM EDT)

"Harriman, are you watching this?" Fred Crocker asked, alarm in his voice.

Fred Crocker stood in front of the massive picture window, which perfectly framed Burnt Mountain. The ski trails of the Snowmass Resort on the mountain were bright green in their summer foliage.

Fred added, "This means the Italian commandos have found Glover."

-

"What are we doing to help?"

-

"I don't think a limited response is sufficient! I told you all along we needed to take a bigger role in his ..."

-

"Yes, we left him alone and now the major play for him is in progress and we are on the sidelines picking our nose!"

-

"Well give the Governor my regards and then find out what ..."

-

"Who's helping him?"

-

"At what level?"

-

"That is not enough!"

-

"Yes, I promise, no intervention on my part, but Harriman, this screw up is on you!"

121 Hemmed In

Da Ba Restaurant

Hudson, New York

Friday, July 29, 2011, 7:50 PM EDT

Larry Evans broke into the conversation, "Not that it matters right now, but the remains you are looking for are in the county's cold storage locker on the north side of town. It's next to our training facility. We saw Alvin drop them off."

"That phone call," Tommy continued, "was from one of my team in the city. Apparently the Italian authorities were so excited about resolving the Celestina Cassanzo disappearance they called a press conference to announce it and the press is eating it up."

Steve said, "A beautiful Italian princess abducted and murdered twenty-five years ago? What's so interesting about that?"

Carmen said, "Stories don't get any hotter than beautiful kidnapped princesses."

Tommy spoke from experience, "Here's how this will play out with the press. The big city talent is driving here now. These are the second stringers pushing to make the starting lineup. They will be aggressive and manipulating. First though, the networks will call their local affiliates to get first feet on the ground here."

Chris asked, "How do we control this thing with the commandos on their way just ahead of the press?"

"You underestimate the ability of the media," Tommy said pointedly. "The trucks and talent from the city may be ahead or surrounding the commandos. Also, we can't control this, but we can manage it."

"Manage it how?" Steve asked.

"We let people know," Tommy answered, "what to expect, when to expect it, with known options when things don't go as planned.

We put up signs to manage the vehicle and foot traffic. We define the options for the onlookers, the press, and the commandos."

"Should we move Andy?" Carmen asked.

"It's too late," Tommy answered. "We assume the commandos were in the city, but if they have spread out, well, we can't take that chance. Andy is safer here with us."

Tommy took a breath and started outlining, "First, we get a hold of Miss Hatcher at the coroner's office and get her out of town. Next, nobody, and I mean nobody, can find out where the remains are."

Tommy pointed at Larry, "Is the cold storage facility secure?"

"Yes and no," Chris stated, "but it will be completely secure within thirty minutes."

Chris stood, drew his cell phone and walked away from the table to call his team."

Tommy continued, "Okay, that's taken care of for the moment. We need to set up a media communications center, a small office with as many phones as we can get and people we can train to answer calls. We need to direct activities and narrow people's options. We need to have a press conference to give the media controlled information. I will contact CIRG and get them up to speed. I may be the one to speak to the media, but it is their call. They may want to send more agents, but," Tommy spoke to Chris and Larry, as they returned, "I want to avoid a firefight in the center of a crowd of civilians."

"You are going to need spotters," Chris said. "Larry is a top pro, and we have trained four others."

"Good," Tommy agreed. "Now, we need a location for the press conference. What is the weather for tomorrow?"

122 Dining In

A Large Estate Overlooking Long Island Sound

Rye, New York

Friday, July 29, 2011, 8:45 PM EDT

"You're back!" Marissa said in a shocked tone.

"Of course, Love. We can't have a romantic dinner without proper food," Matthew Sutton answered in a matter of fact tone.

"But," Marissa intoned, "the last time I told you I wasn't ready for you to meet my friends you left suddenly and I didn't see you for a year! And then you left again after we had our discussion this afternoon."

Matthew was unloading groceries from bags and placing them on the counter. He stopped and looked at her, "Are you ready yet for me to meet your friends?"

Marissa felt caught between her social circle and this British millionaire charmer who might slip away again. Experience won out, and she spoke from her heart, "I'm not ready to be seen with another man yet, but I am getting closer."

Matthew smiled and continued unloading the groceries, "Good," he said. "We are making progress. Now run along and slip into something more suitable to food preparation."

Marissa gave Matthew a pained look, "You are making me cook?"

"Don't worry, Love. I will do all the cooking. You can be my assistant. It will be fun, and I have a special dessert."

123 On the Steps

Steps in Front of City Hall

Hudson, New York

Saturday, July 30, 2011, 8:00 AM EDT

With spotters in place at 10:00 PM the evening before, the SWAT team operated on hand signals, radio silent. Only normal police, sheriff, and EMT communication were allowed for traffic and crowd control. Steve and his buddies rigged up markers using something no one could possibly notice if they were uninformed - beer cans.

The press conference was set to take place on the front steps of the city hall. The historic stone building had wide sweeping steps leading up to the front door. Tommy was approved by CIRG executives to handle the press conference.

One team of four additional FBI agents was dispatched to cover the far side of the Hudson River in case commandos used the river for an escape. This avoided coordinating with other municipalities.

Andy and Carmen kept out of sight in the upper floor of city hall directly behind Tommy's podium at the base of the steps.

Tommy looked out the door of city hall where he was preparing himself. He was amazed at the number of network news vans with their high-powered antennae and remarked to Carlos, "This has turned into a circus. There's even food trucks."

Carlos and Tommy were both exhausted. Carlos from driving to Hudson last night and then taking his turn standing guard inside city hall where Andy spent the night. Tommy played liaison between the press, the mayor's office, police and sheriff's offices, while also trying to get the coroner, Dr. Carver or Dr. Stimson on the phone to schedule a quick examination of Celestina's remains.

"Holy ..." Steve gasped. "Is that Celestina, that picture on TV? That's her?"

"Yeah, that's her," Andy confirmed.

Steve was stunned but not into silence, "And you have been looking at her face and body all your life?"

Carmen rolled her eyes.

Andy responded, "Ever since I was eight."

"Man, if I ever had the least inclination about feeling sorry for you, I take it all back!" Steve concluded, "Wow, tell her I think she is the most ..."

"Tell her yourself," Carmen offered pointing at an empty chair. "She is sitting right there."

Steve quickly looked at the empty chair expecting to see something.

Andy said, "I have a suggestion, Steve. If you want to impress her, don't tell her how beautiful she is. I'm sure she would like it, but she has heard that from anyone whoever saw her."

"What should I say?" Steve asked like a flustered grade-schooler.

"Look for her character, things under the surface."

Steve continued looking at the empty chair but said to Andy, "Like what?"

"Like you admire her character for reaching out to befriend a little boy when her life was at risk. Like how she faced her own death with courage."

Carmen added, "She was only twenty-two years old. They cut her throat, and she didn't cry or whimper or blame anyone. She reached out to the only friend there."

Steve, a hardened soldier, faced death before. He trained for it, lived for it, but not this beautiful girl. She faced her own death as Steve knew he would someday.

Steve's eyes misted over and he mumbled, "I'm sorry Celestina. I didn't realize ... That's, that's pretty damn impressive. I wish I could have known you. I mean, well, that's what I mean."

Steve turned away and ran a sleeve across his eyes.

Carmen eyebrows at the tenderness Steve showed to a woman he could not even see. "Steve," Carmen said in a whisper, "Celestina just put a hand on your shoulder."

Steve, with his back to the room, stood up straighter saying, "Tell her I said 'Thank you.'"

"You just did," Andy replied.

124 Meet the Press

City Hall

Hudson, New York

Saturday, July 30, 2011, 8:50 AM EDT

Tommy reviewed his notes one more time inside the main doors of city hall. The cameras were already recording the empty podium at the bottom of the steps. News anchors got last minute make up while perfecting their look in front of the selected backdrop shots. Each network kept maneuvering for the perfect background that would be interesting but not cluttered, expansive but slightly out of focus, and certainly with no other news crews or their satellite vans in view.

Upstairs in city hall, Steve reminded Andy, "Look Priss', one last time, stay out of sight. If you want to look, stay behind the screen. That will let you see but, under no circumstances are you to step in front of a window."

The mayor's administrative assistant stood ten feet away from Tommy and said, "Three minutes, Agent Edwards."

Tommy nodded.

Public safety was the number one concern. Nothing was controlled but everything was being managed. The players were all in their places. It was out of Tommy's hands now.

He didn't pray. That was his mother's thing, not his, but an unrequested suggestion came out of his childhood that he should pray. He decided, *No, I don't pray.*

Another memory came to him, his moment of mental and emotional nakedness when the possessed demon inside Carmen pried into his mind and heart. Tommy pushed it away. He didn't have time to deal with it now.

"Thirty seconds, Agent Edwards."

Tommy took a deep breath and stepped out of the doors and walked down to the podium.

125 Twenty-Four Hour News

Multiple Locations Around the Globe

Hudson, New York

Saturday, July 30, 2011, 9:00 AM EDT, 2:00 PM in England, 3:00 PM in Italy

Luigi Ciulli balanced himself on a bar stool at the Bar Pyper in Foggia. He wanted to be close to his childhood home and he couldn't say why. He offered to buy old Pietro a beer. Pietro accepted the offer, and no one took notice.

All eyes were on the TV mounted high up on the wall across from the bar.

Stefano Cassanzo and Roberto his brother walked into the bar and were allowed to stand behind the bar so they could see above the crowd. This was one of many restaurants and bars in town that were crowded. People could have watched at home, but many felt the need to be around family and neighbors.

Matthew Sutton lounged in bed with Marissa snuggled up to him, both of them watching with interest.

Roscoe Tanner sat in a diner discussing a case with a new client. When he heard the announcement on the TV behind the counter, he flipped back to an older page in his notebook and found Celestina's name.

Alan Hopkins sat with Alicia and the rest of the office watching in the Kingston Conference Room. Angela watched from the doorway.

Lord St. Claire sat alone in his personal study in front of the small TV he kept, wishing he could see old Cassanzo's face.

The news coverage was playing in Carlo Vendante's private room, but he was sleeping as he did most of every day.

Mr. Harriman and his team of analysts paused their weekly Saturday review meeting to watch the press conference.

Several key members of The Court, a collection of key families in England, watched intently.

FBI Agent Tommy Edwards stepped up to the podium and silence fell across the town square in Hudson, New York, and tens of thousands of large and small gatherings across the world.

126 Fiasco

Steps in Front of City Hall

Hudson, New York

Saturday, July 30, 2011, 9:00 AM EDT

"Ladies and gentlemen of the press, I am FBI Agent Thomas Edwards, Director of the Serial Crimes Task Force, a branch of the Critical Incident Response Group.

I have a short statement to read, and then I will take some questions."

All eyes of the press and the world were on Tommy. Tommy opened a black leather notebook and placed it on the podium. He looked down at the words and then looked up at the reporters. He gave the announcement from memory.

"On Thursday, July 29th, the FBI, following leads gained during the investigation of a related case, uncovered the remains of Celestina Cassanzo of Foggia, Italy."

Tommy looked down and then back up. "Celestina's remains were found in a shallow grave on a ridge outside the city of Canaan, New York. Her identity has been verified by forensics."

Tommy paused, "The cause of death was a deep laceration of the throat by a curved knife."

The crowd audibly gasped.

"This has been verified by an eyewitness to the murder who has recently come forward."

Reporters started yelling questions. Tommy might have lost the crowd, but he raised his hands for silence. His intimidating stature and calm demeanor stopped the reporters.

Carmen was pushing forward to see and hear better. Andy was slightly behind her and could not make out much of anything. Steve bounced back and forth between the windows and the television.

Tommy said, "Based on eyewitness testimony and physical evidence we have gathered, we were able to make one arrest and more are planned. We also want to question a Matthew Sutton, a British citizen now residing in the United States ..."

A car parked on the street behind the mass of reporters and onlookers exploded into flames with a deafening concussion wave.

Steve jumped to one of the windows to check on Tommy. Tommy looked up over his shoulder in time to see Andy in another window.

No one heard the two silenced shots. Tommy watched in horror as Andy fell away, small splatters of thick red could be seen spattered on the glass near the bullet holes. Above the din, Tommy heard Carmen scream.

127 Repercussions

Steps in Front of City Hall

Hudson, New York

Saturday, July 30, 2011, 9:00 AM EDT

In England, a single member of The Court set down his tea and dialed a number.

In Foggia, Italy, Bar Pyper was a scene of weeping and consolation that was stunned again to silence as the explosion shook everyone's sense of order. They did not know what to make of it.

Alan and Alicia had met Tommy once. They had no idea what was happening.

In Colorado, Fred Crocker lifted the phone to call Harriman, but he dropped the phone back onto it's cradle. What was the point?

In Cambourne Hall, Lord St. Claire smiled. Then he rang the bell for Wallace.

In Rye, New York, Marissa lay unconscious on her bed with a bruise to her temple. Matthew Sutton walked calmly to his suitcase while talking on his cell phone.

"Grandfather, I don't care what you saw. Sniper's bullets do not throw blood forward. I will finish this. I don't know how they did it but I know Master Hollingsworth is just fine.

128 Shattered

The Upper Floor of City Hall

Hudson, New York

Saturday, July 30, 2011, 9:20 AM EDT

"No, I'm not all right!" Andy grimaced.

Carlos smiled at Andy's annoyance and pulled out his cell phone.

Andy pulled another half-inch long shard of glass from his cheek complaining, "Look at me! I could have been blinded!"

"He got a few cuts, that's all," Carlos told Tommy.

129 Reading the Signs

Town Square in Front of City Hall

Hudson, New York

Saturday, July 30, 2011, 8:00 AM EDT

Before the press conference got started, a large number of pickup trucks could be seen mixed in with all the news vans and vehicles. Each of the trucks had a group of locals sitting in the bed of the truck drinking beer and being neighborly. They talked to the reporters and the camera crews as they set up their equipment. Some of the men set up folding chairs or lawn chairs in and around the people spread out on the grass.

One of the sheriffs used the term "Bubba Power" looking at all the blue collar types who generally don't show up to press conferences. But then press conferences don't generally come right into where they live.

The first issue was to identify the people who didn't fit.

Under a black shroud in the library next to the city hall, Larry Boydelatour looked out his spotting scope watching beer cans in and around the crowd. He was one of four spotters deployed, each with a limited view of the scene. The limited view would lessen the likelihood of them being spotted by commandos who always preferred the widest view possible.

Larry's cell phone had a wired ear bud with a microphone.

"Domestic in C2, domestic C3, water in C4. I need a walk by in C4."

Two men hopped off a truck and carried two six packs of beer to the C4 location. Larry watched them as four men from the lumber mill accepted the beer and set them on the ground."

Larry continued, "Domestic in C5, domestic C6, dropping a row. "Domestic in D1. I've got a Carlsberg in D2 and a Corona, repeat, 2 foreign beers in D2. There's a cameraman right behind him, blond hair, six foot even. No reporters seem connected. He's got an earpiece and a mike. There's an antenna on the battery pack. No weapon visible."

In Larry's ear bud he heard, "We're watching him Larry. Move on."

The process was repeated constantly until two commandos were clearly identified in the crowd. That meant two shooters or one shooter and one cover man to cover the getaway.

On the edge of town, a three-quarter ton van was on the side of the road with its hood up. It had been noticed by the Bubba guys as they drove in to town. A couple of local mechanics offered to help the man sitting on the side of the road. The man told them he did not need any help. When they insisted on helping, he became angry and threatening. After they drove off, Chris Evans peered over the bank of the creek bed and shot the man dead but only after Chris had removed the tripping mechanism from the explosives attached to the bottom of the bridge.

Just before Tommy started giving his statement, the two cameramen surrounded by foreign beer started trying to fix problems with their earpieces.

After the vehicle exploded on the far side of the green, one of the two cameramen stood up and pressed a button on his camera mount that automatically elevated the angle of the mounted camera. Another cameraman saw him and pointed his shoulder camera up to the center window of the upper floor. He filmed a man approaching the window and bullets ripping into him in a cloud of mist and blood. Later this footage would be played over several times on Albany's News Channel Ten and then on the ABC national feed to all their affiliates. It was posted to YouTube within an hour of the event.

The major questions were always, "Who is the unidentified man in the Hudson Shooting? What is his connection to Celestina? And who shot him?"

Fox and NBC crews were able to film the FBI arresting three men sitting in a truck that wouldn't start. The only statement the FBI agents made to the press was that members of the Columbia County SWAT Team were to be commended for their quick thinking and coordinated efforts resulting in the arrests.

130 Clean Up

The Upper Floor of City Hall

Hudson, New York

Saturday, July 30, 2011, 9:55 AM EDT

Tommy walked up the stairs and through the tall doors to the large meeting room where Andy had been shot. The floor of the room had a V shape of blood spattered away from the window where Tommy had seen Andy standing.

"How's the patient?" Tommy asked Carmen.

"He's still breathing, but whiny about everything," she answered winking at Andy.

Andy protested, "Hey, glass cuts hurt, and I got about thirty of them. And how long do I have to be dead anyway?"

"Washington wants us to sit on this for twenty-four hours," Tommy said looking around the room. "I think this will help you, Andy. Random is still out there. He may have watched the show we put on this morning. If he did and he buys it, you will be in the clear until you show up at the attorney's office on Monday."

Carmen asked as she dabbed at blood leaking from Andy's cheek, "How will Random be able to match the shooting with Andy or match Andy with Celestina for that matter?"

Tommy said, "And we can start using his real name, Matthew Sutton."

"I like 'Random' better," Steve snarled, "It's more anonymous. I don't want people remembering his name."

Tommy shrugged, "Fine with me; I don't care as long as we catch him."

Tommy walked over to the panel Steve had made. It was eight feet high and four feet wide, made of one-inch thick plywood over laid with a heavy mirror on the front. The mirror had two large craters where the sniper's bullets had struck and the glass shards had peppered Andy's face and clothes.

Andy walked over and looked at it closely for the first time and said over his shoulder,

"Hey Steve, you could have warned me this would happen."

Steve answered without looking up, "It didn't happen last time we used it."

There was a sudden silence while everyone looked at Steve. Steve looked up and around at the unexpected quiet.

Then he went back to cleaning his gun and said, "Can't tell you. It's classified."

131 Feeding Frenzy

The Park in Front of City Hall

Hudson, New York

Saturday, July 30, 2011, 9:55 AM EDT

While Tommy's team was safely hidden from public, the media frenzy caused by the unearthing of Celestina's remains increased exponentially as live reports and live footage of the shooting swept across TV networks, coffee shops, hair salons, and back yards. Still photos of the three men arrested swamped the internet as people searched for their identities.

An after shock floated through the story when a bomb disposal unit was followed out of town by camera crews. The explosives under the bridge was only the first of three bombs set to slow down any pursuit. The removal of all three kept news crews busy for the reminder of the day.

The cameras were also on site to film the FBI taking jurisdiction over the entire operation. The FBI threw the first cold water on the story by moving camera crews back to a half mile from the bombsites.

Still the questions reporters continued to ask the FBI and local law enforcement were,

"Who was the man upstairs?"

"Is he expected to live?"

"What is his connection to Celestina Cassanzo?"

"Was he the witness?"

"Who were the men arrested?"

The media initially presumed and broadcast that the man was dead because no ambulance left the scene.

The sheriff's department squashed the story by calling Alvin and Marcus. Marcus drove to the back of Town Hall where a body under wraps was removed from the building and driven to Columbia Memorial Hospital. A squad of police and sheriffs formed a human shield to keep reporters away as they wheeled the very live body of the town hall's janitor into an interior room. After being released, the janitor walked out the front door and got a ride back downtown. The room was kept under guard.

Police arrested several paparazzi and confiscated their equipment as they tried to sneak into the hospital wing where the body had been placed.

The extra duties were not an unreasonable burden for the City of Hudson. The fines the police charged were stiff and many. All in all, trespassers and violators of the peace more than paid for the officers overtime.

When the FBI took over the scene, the black SUVs with tinted windows came and went frequently enough that when a reporter finally got near the room, she found it empty. Another missing body only added to the mystery keeping the media firestorm white hot.

132 Setting the Stage

US Route 9 South

Two Miles Outside Hudson, New York

Saturday, July 30, 2011, 11:30 AM EDT

Tommy met with and transferred FBI control to one of the CIRG assistant directors. The assistant was only too glad to get his hands on such a hot case, and Tommy was only too glad to get rid of it. Both had separate jobs to do.

"This way, Tommy," the FBI agent motioned to him and the four members of his team present.

Andy held a baseball cap over his face to cover up the butterfly bandages. His ten-yard walk to the waiting Chevy Suburban went unnoticed and the black SUV moved smoothly through the town and on toward US Route 9.

Tommy dialed his cell phone and listened. After several rings, Tommy said, "Angela, find Wynton Smythley and have him arrested. Attempted murder, no wait, make it murder one, conspiracy. We don't want anyone to know Andy is still alive, not yet."

-

"He's across the street? Okay, very convenient."

-

"Are you still with Attorney Hopkins and his girlfriend?"

-

"I don't care what they are. Are you with them?"

-

"Good. Tell them we would like to enlist their help in catching the person or people who are behind the Random killings."

-

"Yes, we need Attorney Hopkins to go ahead with the trust settlement but we need him to move the location. Tell him we will reserve one of the FBI offices in the Javits Federal Building, Monday at 10:00 AM."

"Yes, tell him to set up everything and notify all the people who need to be there with all the correct paper work."

-

"Thanks, Angela. We are about two to three hours away."

-

"Okay, we will see you there."

After Tommy hung up Andy sheepishly said, "Tommy, I know you guys all have travel bags with you at all times but I don't. Could you ask Father Rand to pick up some clothes for me and my shaving kit?"

"Do you have his number?" Tommy asked.

"Sure, wait! No, my cell is dead."

Steve said, "No problem, I have his number."

Steve dialed and then spoke very officially, "Father Rand, this is FBI Agent Steven Haskins."

-

"Father, I'm afraid I can't answer your question, but if you would not mind, can you get some clothes Andy could be buried in?"

-

"Yes, a suit would be fine," Steve answered, smiling at Andy who was furious, but couldn't talk and give himself away. Andy kicked Steve who only replied, "Yes, something very colorful would be great. Thanks Father. Can you bring them to the Federal Building downtown? The address is 26 Federal Plaza. If you use the main entrance on Lafayette, the guard will take them from you. Thank you so much for your help. Good bye."

"Forget it!" Andy stormed, "I'll just keep doing laundry every night."

Steve just laughed over all of Andy's complaints.

Andy jerked his head toward Carmen sitting next to him with a confused look, "Wait, I don't have any suits!" Andy put his hands to his face, "Oh no, what if he gets a suit from out of the clothing donations?"

Even Tommy laughed at that comment.

133 Orsara di Puglia

The Street in Front of the Post Office

Orsara di Puglia, Province of Foggia, Italy

Saturday, July 30, 2011, 5:30 PM UTC -1 (11:30 AM EDT)

The first foreign reporters arrived in Bari at the offices owned by the Cassanzo family. They found the offices empty. Cleaning and maintenance staff pointed them to the small town of Orsara in the hills outside Foggia.

The Yonhap News Agency from South Korea was the first van to climb the long hill from the plains up to the highland town. They would be the first to discover there was very little parking anywhere in the town. They stopped in front of a white and red monument with a brass angel on the top. There were several pipes coming out of the hillside with water running out of them making the monument look like a large drinking fountain.

When they got out of the van, they noticed the large eight-pointed star in the middle of an intersection, plus the fact that a large red and white sign across the street from their van said "Bar" told them this was the town square.

The reporter and a single camerawoman would find the beginning of the story they were looking for in the bar. The other two set up cameras next to the van when a small car with "Daunia News" on the doors drove up. The woman reporter saw the other van and the camera rigs being set up. She immediately pulled her cell phone out and checked the signal. There was one bar, but she doubted the signal was real. She also walked across the street to the bar to use a landline to call her office.

134 In Hand

Crowne Plaza, Times Square

1605 Broadway, New York City

Saturday. July 30, 2011, 12:20 PM EDT

Smythley and his assistant exited the elevator. They had lunch reservations and were anxious to arrive on time. Smythley thought he recognized the frumpy twenty-ish year old walking toward him from Hopkins' office, but this time, she was wearing a dark windbreaker with FBI stitched into the fabric and accompanied by two other agents wearing the same jackets.

"Sir Wynton Smythley," Angela pronounced loudly and clearly, "you are under arrest for conspiracy to commit murder."

Angela spun Smythley around and tossed him easily on the carpet while she snapped handcuffs on the arms she twisted behind him. His face was shoved hard into the plush carpet within sight of his waiting limousine.

Angela started quoting his rights, "You have the right to remain silent ... Hey FBI!" Angela shouted to the agents accompanying her while she pointed to Smythley's assistant, "Grab that guy!"

Smythley's personal assistant, Niles Bagley walked away while all the attention was on Smythley. The agents quickly caught Bagley and brought him back to Angela who was completing the review of the Miranda rights for Smythley.

135 Restraint

A Shallow Alcove in the Peers Lobby

Westminster Palace, London, England

Saturday, July 30, 2011, 6:35 PM (11:35 AM EDT)

The Lord Chancellor spoke quietly into his cell phone as he walked through the lobby, and most public rooms were empty this late on Saturday. All sounds echoed well off the vaulted ceilings. The guards swept the last of the audio tour guests out of the buildings hours before.

"Restraint be damned, I want a resolution today!"

-

"What's that?"

-

"How big an opportunity?"

-

"Very acceptable. Set the wheels in motion right away. We need to salvage some good out of this disaster."

-

"Hmm, what's that? Arrested? Arrested by whom?"

-

"Well, he bloody well should have thought of that before he started playing Sutton's games!"

-

"Yes, I agree, we simply can't leave Smythley with the Americans. Make a deal for him. All record of wrongs expunged. I insist."

-

"I don't know! Smythley has been mucking about for Sutton. I'm sure he has picked up some information to trade, but we need to make that offer, not Smythley."

-

"Go through diplomatic channels not the police. It will be quicker."

-

"Very good. Tell your son I still owe him a thrashing at tennis."

-

"Yes, yes, convey my best also."

136 Form and Process

Blackford Crighton Law Firm, New York Offices

21st Floor, 206 West 48th Street

Saturday, July 30, 2011, 3:20 PM EDT

"So now that the pressure is off, and you and Alan are snuggled away in your own private office with three mountains of legal forms, a nosey FBI agent, and a finance creep," Angela Ricchetti verbally jabbed at Alicia who kept herself busy printing and collating papers.

Alicia looked up at Angela and then back to the work assigned her by Alan Hopkins and Mr. Vargas, the financial representative of the trust fund.

"I do my work," Alicia responded controlling her emotion.

Alicia liked this FBI agent, but Angela was annoying with her suggestive remarks concerning her and Alan.

Angela looked down at Alicia's desk and the stacks of papers. A particular folder at the bottom of the stacks caught her attention, and she pulled it out.

"Oh ho! What is this on the secretary's desk?"

Alicia snatched it out of Angela's hand, "That is not about this case. It needs re-filed."

"And here's another one," Angela pulled out another thick folder.

Angela kept this one out of Alicia's long reach and said, "A folder for Smythley and one for Sutton? What gives, Sister? And don't bother with any re-filing noise. You tell me straight, or you and Alan are going into my private confessional right here."

Alicia looked through Alan's open office door. She saw Alan and Mr. Vargas continuing through a long checklist of forms and procedures at Alan's desk.

She looked back at Angela, sighed, and explained, "When you pick a fight with someone bigger than you, you better have all your ducks in a row before the fight. Alan challenged Sir Wynton Smythley, who is his superior. We know Smythley won't fight fair, so I was trying to even the odds."

"But Alan can look at those files any time he wants," Angela countered.

Alicia shook her head, "No, these are from the confidential files Alan would never see. Even if he found them, he would not use them for his own defense. That's the kind of man he is."

Angela finished the statement with, "Stupid."

"Honorable," Alicia corrected.

Angela pointed at Alicia, "If he is so honorable, this information won't do him any good. He won't accept it."

"Not directly," said Alicia, "but I can use what I learn to nudge him in the right direction. It's not a great plan but I wanted to do something to help. Alan has been accused of insubordination. About an hour ago, he got a phone call that he is being recalled to London."

"When is he supposed to leave?"

"They wanted him on a flight this afternoon but Alan refused. He told them he was needed here to finish the Hollingsworth trust transfer. He just wants to do what's right for this transfer. Afterwards, Alan told me they can do anything they want."

Angela reminded her, "But Smythley is in jail now and will be for a long time."

"It doesn't matter to the British. Alan broke proper etiquette, not once but many times, including his refusal to leave today. He will have to face a board of inquiry for his actions. Now, I just need to get the files back before Alan finds out I have them."

"Oh Sister," Angela sighed, "You've got it bad."

137 Safe Haven

FBI Offices

26 Federal Plaza, New York City

Saturday, July 30, 2011, 6:40 PM EDT

"You took long enough," Andy complained as Steve tossed him the bag of clothes Father Rand left at the security desk for Andy's funeral.

"Hmph," Steve responded, "I guess I shouldn't have suggested something colorful. The priest also brought your shaving kit."

"Awesome!" Andy got up from the cot that had been borrowed for him.

Andy walked down the hallway to the men's bathroom to take another turn washing up at a bathroom sink. At least this time he would not have to also wash his clothes.

Tommy was waiting for him when he returned.

"Tonight and tomorrow, Andy, then it will be over. Once the trust proceeds are in your name and your will designates your heirs Random won't have any reason to try coming after you. Killing you won't get him the money."

"How about revenge for pissing him off," Steve suggested.

Carmen threw in, "It won't be long before he is found and locked up."

Andy pointed out, "I don't know, he got in and out of all those crime scenes without being detected."

Steve objected, "He used a damn utility van, no mystery there."

Andy thought about it a few seconds and then said, "He needed the van to transport Carmen. I'm pretty sure he moved about on his own before that."

138 The Monument

The Street in Front of the Post Office

Orsara di Puglia, Provencia di Foggia, Italy

Sunday, July 31, 2011, 12:50 AM UTC -1 (6:50 PM EDT, Saturday)

The village garda had completely stopped traffic from flowing into the tiny town. Cars and vans filled with the world's press representatives were diverted to the town's maintenance lot and the cemetery's parking lot north of the town. This forced the crews to carry equipment the third of a mile to the fountain square on Corso della Vittoria.

The company, Monte Maggiore, set up temporary toilets near the post office in a profit sharing agreement with the Comune, or municipal government.

Candlelights burned brightly surrounding the three-foot tall portrait of Celestina set on an easel next to the fountain. Flowers and cards poured in by private carriers. When the Italiane Poste opened on Monday, it would certainly be flooded with packages and letters.

Some residents rented out their balconies overlooking the square. Some rented out rooms or provided meals.

The world demanded more coverage and answers. Coverage they got, answers - not yet.

139 Proper Form

Blackford Crighton Law Firm, New York Offices

21st Floor, 206 West 48th Street

Saturday, July 30, 2011, 10:10 PM EDT

Mr. Vargas had left an hour before satisfied Alan had all the proper forms. The only task left was to make sufficient copies for each form according to the list attached to each form. For the seventy-two forms, it would be a large task for tomorrow.

Angela napped in the outer office.

"The State of Connecticut is over there," Alicia said. Alan placed the forms for Connecticut next to the other state forms bringing the work to a close. He had stalled long enough. He stood straight and opened his mouth.

"Yes, I will go with you," Alicia said, glancing quickly up at Alan and then back down at her notes for the next day.

Alan closed his mouth and his eyes went wide.

"You have been trying to ask me for the last hour," Alicia spoke with her matter of fact tone, "When you stood up straight, I knew you had made up your mind to ask me. You're too easy to read. We'll need to work on that."

Alan stammered, "It won't be all tea and pinkies. There should be a proper row with me getting the pasting. I didn't want to drag you into the ugliness."

Alicia walked around the desk saying, "Nonsense, Alan Hopkins. You'll need a friend."

She stepped up to Alan and put her hands on his shoulders, looking him squarely in the eyes, "You didn't flinch for Smythley. You won't flinch for your inquisitors either."

Alan heard Alicia's words, and he felt stronger, determined to face the board without apology. He set his jaw saying, "You're right, of course. I did the right thing. It is the best I can give anyone."

Alan's hands bravely wrapped around Alicia's waist and pulled her body close. Alicia slid her hands up Alan's shoulders and wrapped arms around his neck as she leaned into Alan's kiss.

The kiss filled their senses, their thoughts, all of their awareness.

Alan was intoxicated by her breath, the warmth of her lips, the feel of her back through the cool smoothness of her blouse. Alicia fell into Alan. The longer the kiss lasted, the more she wanted to never recover her balance. Down and down she floated, surrounded by a man she desired.

All time stopped for the two new lovers but not for the rest of the world. The phone rang on Alan's desk.

Alicia pulled back slightly with Alan's arms still around her. She started to stumble but Alan caught her. Over Alicia's shoulder, Alan saw Angela holding her cell phone next to her ear.

"Sorry kids but I may want to retire some day. I didn't know how much longer you were going to last. After twenty minutes I was getting worried."

Alicia was embarrassed but not enough to let go of Alan.

Angela kept going, "I figured you would notice the cleaning crew, but they finished up and left without you noticing."

Alan looked into Alicia's eyes while he still held her but spoke to Angela, "I do apologize for keeping you so late and this inappropriate display of affection."

Alicia looked into Alan's eyes without flinching.

"No, no," Angela countered, "For a kiss, that was proper form and delivered with real heat!"

140 The Process

A Large Estate Overlooking Long Island Sound

Rye, New York

Sunday, July 31, 2011, 9:30 AM EDT

Marissa slowly became aware of her surroundings. She could hear Matthew's voice but could not make out any of the words he was saying. Her eyes didn't focus on him standing in front of her. She seemed to be seated in her own antique desk chair unable to move.

A vague impression of fear and something terribly wrong troubled her, but she could not retrieve the memory yet.

Two black cases spread out in front of her. She recognized a rifle with a scope in the larger one. The other had small bottles and hypodermic needles along with knives and other sharp objects.

Matthew's face came close, and Marissa could finally focus on it and hear what he was saying.

"Ah, there you are, Love. I apologize, but I sedated you more than usual. I needed to leave and get supplies."

Marissa could move her eyes but not her head.

"Yes, you are quite strapped in, Love. Your head is taped to the back of your chair. Don't worry; I was careful not to muss your hair. Must be looking our best now, shouldn't we?"

Marissa started to gag. There was something in her mouth.

Matthew stated, "I put clean socks in your mouth so you won't be able to scream out and alert the neighbors."

Marissa tried to spit out the socks but could not.

"Oh, and I have tape over your mouth to keep them in place."

Marissa's eyes went wide when Matthew picked up a scalpel and held it close for her to see.

"Ah, that is what I needed to see, your fear. This won't work unless you are afraid," Matthew said unfolding drawings of a pair of hands on heavy parchment. The two hands covered with intricately curved lines tattooed into them.

On the drawing the fingers were extremely long making the arms look odd. Other drawings of tattoos on a woman's neck and face. The woman's facial features were not in the drawing, but lines surrounding the features were included giving an impression of a very gaunt face. The hair was represented by lines sticking out in jagged angles from the head.

Matthew was finally ready and said, "Sorry, Love, but this is the part where I hurt you."

Matthew ran the point of the scalpel blade along Marissa's index finger reproducing the intricate curving lines in the drawings. Marissa's eye registered unlimited panic. She pulled at the zip ties that held her arms to the chair, shaking the chair with all the force she could muster.

Matthew cut the next line and looked up at Marissa's face.

Seeing her eyes filled with terror, Matthew cooed, "Good girl, Marissa. Keep that up, and she will be here shortly."

141 Chatty

A Large Estate Overlooking Long Island Sound

Rye, New York

Sunday, July 31, 2011, 2:15 PM EDT

Marissa awoke with a jolt. She was still strapped to the antique French dining chair.

"Welcome back, Love," Matthew said softly. "I think you fainted again."

Marissa's right arm felt like it was on fire. She looked down to see the hundreds of delicate lines Matthew had skillfully cut into her hand and arm. The cuts were superficial; very little blood was lost, but each small amount of pain , each violated nerve compounded into a crescendo of agony.

"I am afraid the chair will need some professional cleaning," Matthew pointed out casually as he dabbed at a drop of blood that was in the way of the next line he was starting.

The scalpel went into the top layer of skin covering Marissa's bicep. Matthew chatted nonchalantly as he cut and soothed and wiped. "It is crucial that we get the patterns right; otherwise, she may not show up at all."

"I once worked on a woman for two days, and she never came. That was quite a nuisance getting out of that neighborhood. Apparently she had family she never told me about living close by."

Matthew set one scalpel down and picked up another. "In my experience, a number twelve is better for this area. By the by, I happen to know why you didn't want your friends to meet me. You have that other chap you've been seeing when I am not around. Very naughty, this one!"

"I hear you two are very serious and he has proposed at least once. Actually, that was why I chose you. I didn't really want to meet your friends. At least I didn't want them knowing about me."

Matthew finished a spiral cut and braced himself for the next line. As usual, Marissa screamed into the socks stuffed into her mouth. She was now fighting for her existence with all the strength she could bring to bear on the many ties holding her arms and legs.

Matthew kept cutting her deftly moving with her efforts or sometimes forcing her to sit still.

"You are going to miss a wonderful dinner tonight. I was planning on lamb shank with mint sauce and a light spring salad with pears. I was debating on the rice dish, but no matter. You won't be sharing it with me, I'm afraid."

Matthew looked back to the drawings and nodded, "Almost done with this arm. No crying now. You are past pain. You feel rage. Feel that rage. Hate me. Wish me dead. Let your anger pour out like water."

Marissa bit down on her gag. Her eyes flared as she struggled against bonds but could barely move.

"I used to simply draw the lines while my victim was in pain and invite her to come and she would come. Over time, she has become more reluctant to appear. I tried other methods, but carving the lines has been the most effective as of recent. I should mention, she is a little unnerving at first, but she is very effective. Bit of a bloodhound, literally. I give her a scent of blood, and she can track it down anywhere."

Matthew switched to the finer scalpel blade and started on the fingers of the left hand.

"Your blood, for example, could be used if I wanted to find your offspring or your parents, cousins, uncles, aunts, as long as there is a blood connection. Also, she can follow the lines of power in a family. She has the ability to sense the people in authority for a given blood line even if the person married into the family. She is quite gifted that way."

"This is one of my favorite ... Oh you have fainted again."

Matthew picked smelling salts and waved them under Marissa's nose. She responded quickly with her eyes looking wildly about.

"I was saying this part of the hand is exceptionally painful."

142 Crossing the T's

Blackford Crighton Law Firm, New York Offices

21st Floor, 206 West 48th Street

Sunday, July 31, 2011, 4:20 PM EDT

"And I want to tour the Parliament building."

Alan said while completing the copies of signature forms for the American Stock Exchange, "The name of the building is West Minster Palace. The American Stock Exchange forms are complete. What is next?"

Alicia sat next to Alan and gave him a slow, light kiss on the cheek then said, "We only have the European exchanges, and then we are done.

Alan floated through the day. The euphoria Alicia brought to his life made the coming partner review seem meaningless.

Alicia, for her part, felt anything was possible with a life with Alan. It brought an overwhelming sense of security, a feeling of safety and warmth for this very good man. She could see Alan standing taller as he started standing up for himself.

143 A Nation Grieves

The Street in Front of the Post Office

Orsara di Puglia, Province of Foggia, Italy

Sunday, July 31, 2011, 11:00 PM UTC -1 (5:00 PM EDT)

"Good evening all of Italy; this is Antonia Anabellis reporting live from the town square in Orsara di Puglia, ancestral home of familia Cassanzo and the famous industrialist, Vincente Cassanzo."

The news anchor for TM News out of Rome opened the eleven o'clock news with the latest chapter in the Celestina Cassanzo kidnapping / murder case.

"This evening I have Roberto Cassanzo, uncle of Celestina, here to talk to us and make a statement from the family. Roberto?"

Antonia and a dozen other reporters pointed microphones at Roberto. The family had been keeping all outsiders off the grounds of the villa. Several intruders had been threatened. A notorious paparazzi had been beaten severely and then arrested for trespassing. The family members present agreed Roberto should say something to the news reporters camped out in the tiny town of Orsara. Roberto was escorted to the square by the local garda.

Roberto now looked out at the candles and flowers spread out around the square. The photo of Celestina, now eight feet off the ground to accommodate all of the gifts of sympathy, and illuminated by candle stands. Roberto took a deep breath and read the family's statement from a paper in front of him.

"The Cassanzo family wishes to express our gratitude for the wonderful show of sympathy and support from all over Italy and even the world. My brother, Stefano, and his wife finally have knowledge of the fate of their beloved and only child Celestina who disappeared from their lives over twenty-five years ago.

"The family also asks a small favor. You have been so kind to us in our grief. May we ask one more thing from you all? Please pray for the evil ones who perpetrated this crime to be brought to justice and bring closure to the family. Thank you."

Roberto was asked many questions, but instead of answering them, he shook hands with the people close by he recognized. A dear old grandmother from Orsara who had known the family and Celestina beckoned to Roberto. Roberto bent down to give her a hug. The cameras focused on the old woman's grief stricken face.

Roberto hugged many more people, but the old woman's face and grief were played over and over. This was the picture that pierced the souls of all who knew the story or had seen Celestina's photo.

The heart of Italy knit together in sorrow with the Cassanzo family.

144 Distance

FBI Offices

26 Federal Plaza, New York City

Sunday, July 31, 2011, 6:00 PM EDT

"Okay Priss', you are on your own for tonight. I'll see you here tomorrow at 9:00 AM. Clean up all your shit before everyone gets here. Don't embarrass me."

Andy's bag of clothes and shaving kit were laying on top of the conference table occuping the middle of the large meeting room where the trust transfer would take place the next morning. The majority of the leather seats around the table were placed uniformly except for the few occupied.

"Thanks Steve," Andy replied somberly without looking up from the floor where he was staring.

"Come on prissy boy, tomorrow you'll sign some papers, get a bunch of money, and you can be done with all this crap. You can go anywhere you want, do anything you want to do."

Andy's head lifted, "Really? I can do anything I want?"

"Forget it," Steve said flatly. "You can't stay here. You need to go out and have a real life."

"But I feel like I make a difference here. I'm doing something valuable."

Steve shook his head, "Your expertise was needed because all this crap was from your life. We've solved this case. It's over. The next case will be completely different. Besides Priss, that doctor needs you to sweep her off her feet and ride away with her into the sunset." Steve pointed to Carmen sitting across the room listening and waiting for Steve to leave.

"Okay, okay!" Steve said responding to Carmen's silence. "I'm leaving. See you two in the morning." Steve walked out, and Carmen walked over to sit by Andy.

"Andy, we need to talk."

"That sounds ominous," Andy replied.

"What is going to happen after tomorrow? You will have money, I'm guessing a lot of money, hundreds of millions?"

"Something like that," Andy guessed. "Even now I still have no idea. They kept me in the dark about everything. I only got a monthly allowance for living expenses. I persuaded the trust to buy some real estate so I wouldn't have to pay rent. I guess it was considered a good investment."

Carmen pressed her question again, "So what happens after tomorrow? What are you going to do with your life? You can't tag along with Tommy's team. Like Steve said, your subject expertise is limited. Also, the money will bring you other responsibilities, a lot of responsibilities."

Andy admitted, "Carmen, I don't know what will happen. I like being a part of this team. After tomorrow, you and I will need to accompany Celestina's remains back to her home, but afterwards I don't know."

Carmen looked puzzled, "Why? Why do I need to go back to Italy?"

"To take Celestina home," Andy said. "She's attached to you for some reason, and you need to take her home."

Carmen looked at the empty seat across the conference room table from her and next to Andy.

Andy asked, "What does Celestina think?"

"She doesn't talk, remember?" Carmen said with anger.

"Whoa, Carmen, it's me, Andy. I'm on your side. What is going on with you?"

Carmen's hands started gesturing then she began, "Look, I like you, a lot. You're strong in your own way. You're kind, maybe too kind. I don't know, but tomorrow you are leaving, and I am staying. Tommy offered me a permanent position on his team. This is my dream. I don't want to run off to Italy, not now. The day after tomorrow will be Tuesday. I need to be at work on Tuesday here in this building or wherever Tommy tells me. You don't have any idea what you will be doing."

Andy was taken aback. "Carmen, we can figure it out as we go. We have options. Let's see what happens before we make any decisions."

"Flying by the seat of your pants, is that how you operate? Well I don't work that way. I have order in my life. I need order, a plan."

Andy shook his head and defended, "My whole life has been out of control; people have been doing things to me, hunting me, hurting me, rejecting me. I learned to deal with the chaos and make a life. It's been a miserable life, but it's mine. Now, I finally have a chance to change it and possibly help other people. I would like to do that with you, not without you."

"I'm not going to Italy. Celestina can fly there without me."

Andy sighed, "What is the expression on Celestina's face?"

Carmen glanced over to the empty seat, then she looked at Andy with narrowed eyes, "If you are so concerned about her, why don't you take her? You two could be very happy together living in a crypt in Italy."

"Are you jealous of her?" Andy asked in disbelief.

"Look," Carmen said her anger rising even higher, "you and these invisibles get along great. Me, I'm more than a little freaked out every time I see her or Warren. And Warren talks all the time! Even when I can't see him, I can hear him! I never know if what I'm hearing is heard by anyone else, and I have zero privacy!"

"You get used to it after a while."

"Well I don't want to get used to it!" Carmen stormed. "I want them out of my life! I want my life back!"

Andy leaned back in his chair and said evenly, "Then go to Italy. See this thing through."

"Fine!" Carmen answered.

Andy said, "Now you sound like Steve."

Carmen was not amused.

145 Apparition

A Large Estate Overlooking Long Island Sound

Rye, New York

Monday, July 31, 2011, 6:15 AM EDT

A head splitting screech rent the morning quiet rousing Matthew from sleep on the couch. He sat up and held his hands over his ears trying to block out the piercing sound. His eyes were squeezed shut and mouth open letting out a scream no one could hear above the cyclone of sound pouring out of the dimensional rift opening in Marissa's living room.

A jagged vertical line appeared in the middle of the room and started to spread sideways revealing its true nature. It was a tearing, a rending of space, a pulling apart of the world complete with cracking, popping sounds. Then the hands appeared.

Long thin fingers with lines carved into them reached from within the dark grabbing the edges and spreading the gap wider. Then a long thin foot appeared through the gap, followed by the face, almost a woman's face, but long, gaunt, and pale white. Her eyes didn't close or squint. Matthew never knew if she had eyelids. Her eyes were always wide open. Her head swung quickly back and forth while her eyes darted about. She stepped through the opening and moved quickly to Marissa.

Matthew stood apart from Marissa as the creature drew near to her. Marissa had been listless but now tried vainly to back away with her last effort.

The creature's hair and skin did not have solid boundaries. They faded unevenly into thin air giving her the appearance of having a jagged edge. The hair flowed straight out from her head with changing lengths of hair. If her hair had not been a muddy brown, it would have looked like electricity was flowing out of her or into her. The hair grew longer as she approached the bound and gagged Marissa as if the creature was drawing energy from her.

Matthew cautiously watched the creature while picking up a glass tube filled with a dark red almost black substance. He carefully pulled the cork from the top and used the dropper he had prepared earlier to add a clear liquid to the tube all the while he kept looking back to the creature bent over Marissa. Matthew shook the tube as soon as he had the cork back on the opening. The creature shot a frightening glance at Matthew while he kept shaking the tube. This was the part where he would feel pain.

The creature shot out her hand and grabbed Matthew's wrist of the hand holding the tube. Her crushing grip burned him.

With his free hand, he pulled the cork off.

The creature sniffed the air and moved her face closer to the vial.

"We need to find this blood," Matthew proclaimed. "Find this blood."

Matthew took the tube and poured it out onto a white plate from the kitchen.

The creature moved to the plate and sniffed the air all around the reconstituted blood.

Matthew kept an eye on the creature. While she sniffed he picked up his sniper rifle and put the strap over his shoulder. He also reached down to retrieve the pistol next to it. Both were freshly cleaned and loaded.

The creature raised herself, reached out with a powerful arm, grabbed Matthew around the waist, and carried him like a sack of groceries to the dark opening in the middle of the room.

The opening slowly closed as Marissa's life ember faded and went out.

146 Appeals

Corte di Appello di Bari (Appellate Court in Bari)

Piazza E. De Nicola, Bari, Italy

Monday, August 1, 2011, 12:30 PM UTC -1 (6:30 AM EDT)

"You are a Consigliere!" the man in the suit shouted as he slammed his hand flat on the desk.

He held a brief case filled with legal filings that had passed through the lower court's hands then the appellate court. All approvals, signatures, and official seals decorated them. All that was required now was a Counselor or Consigliere to authorize the local police to start confiscating equipment, properties, factories, trains, airplanes, and ships. Once the process started, it would be impossible to reverse. He was so close. And so was the group of twenty other suits behind him. Only the Consigliere stood between them and the dismantling of the Cassanzo empire.

The counselor stood up from his chair behind his officious desk, "I cannot sign these papers, as I told you. These rulings are not in my jurisdiction. The men and women assigned these cases have gone home for the day, and I am leaving now. Find them at their homes if you can."

Another man in the second row of suits standing around the Consigliere's desk shouted, "We have been to their homes, and they are not there!"

"This is a day of mourning for the Cassanzo family. I cannot sign anything for you," the consigliere pronounced and stepped up to the crowd and walked through them as they shouted accusations of cowardice and betrayal.

The Counselor got into his car and drove away. He headed, like the other Consiglieres, to somewhere he would not be found. Doing anything against Celestina Cassanzo's family right now would be unwise as all of Italy was mourning her loss even more than when she originally disappeared.

147 Global Reprisal

SIS Building (MI-6 British Foreign Intelligence)

85 Albert Embankment, Vauxalll Cross, London, England

Monday, August 1, 2011, 11:45 AM GMT (6:45 AM EDT)

"Sir, the mere fact I am talking to you about this means the nation's security concerns are at risk."

The two men sat by themselves in a large conference room with a large window overlooking the Thames River. The day was sunny and pleasant in contrast to the gloom settling over the Lord Chancellor who had been called to an emergency meeting at MI-6. His stomach twisted from stress caused by the sudden turn of events.

The Lord Chancellor replied, "The answer to your question is no. No, I am not going to inform the P.M., and I am certainly not going to the opposition. I am afraid that we will need to find our own solution, and Lord St. Claire cannot be counted on."

The section chief leaned forward, "We know St. Claire is being scandalized along with his grandson Matthew. All our stations are reporting this. To be honest, we were completely caught off guard at the global response to the Cassanzo murder."

"You could not have known a twenty-five year old murder would pop up and threaten our defense initiatives so thoroughly," the Chancellor replied.

The section chief coolly responded, "I need to bring up an indelicate but simple solution to our problem."

"I know what you are going to say, but you cannot involve me in this discussion."

The section chief smiled, "You would like to leave the dirty tasks to others, but this one belongs to you. We are in need of critical materials and equipment for our national security. St. Claire's bungling is shutting down many of them, but Transoceanic Logistics and several other companies all controlled by the Hollingsworth trust could put everything back on schedule and even trim some budgets."

Lord Chancellor sighed, "Yes, Hollingsworth, the web of events keeps pulling us back to Hollingsworth. What is the status on the trust?"

"The trust is scheduled to be distributed to Andrew Glover in two hours. Matthew Sutton seems to have been interested in killing him. Matthew is now missing. He was last reported close to New York City two days ago."

The chief continued, "If Glover receives the trust, it will go to his inheritors upon his demise whenever that might be. It will then pass out of our control. If he does not receive the trust then the trust will be passed to a second cousin who is a British citizen."

"Yes, old Dudley."

"Old Dudley Hollingsworth," the chief went on, "could solve the empire's current lack with St. Claire managing his affairs. The only problem with that is St. Claire is making demands. The first of them is he wants Matthew cleared of all charges in the US and Britain and guaranteed as his successor. His second demand is that he be nominated for position number one in the Chamber."

"For Queen and country, of course," the Chancellor wryly commented.

"You will need to agree to his demands."

The Lord Chancellor gave a strained smile and stated, "For Queen and Country, of course, should anything unfortunate happen to Mr. Glover."

148 In Transit

Blackford Crighton Law Firm, New York Offices

21st Floor, 206 West 48th Street

Monday, August 1, 2011, 8:05 AM EDT

Alan shooed the driver away, and opened the door of the limousine for Alicia. The two boxes of forms already in the trunk, Alan settled himself across from Alicia with his back to the driver as his cell phone rang.

-

"Yes, Alan Hopkins here."

-

"Yes, I understand. That is no problem. Thank you."

Alan hung up the call and turned to the driver, "Small change in plans. We need to go to the Federal Courthouse across Foley Square from the FBI building. You can drop us off at the front steps."

Alicia asked, "Change in plans?"

"Nothing too serious, a power outage. Agent Edwards has secured an office in the courthouse right across the square. This shouldn't put us off our game much."

149 Off Their Game

FBI Offices

26 Federal Plaza, New York City

Monday, August 1, 2011, 8:45 AM EDT

"What do you mean 'We lost power'? This is a federal communications hub, command and control building, thing. You have diesel generators and back up everything!" Andy whined aloud as he pulled on his first shoe.

Battery powered emergency lighting in the hall gave slight visibility in the small office where he and his cot had spent the last two nights.

"The generators are running," Tommy said impatiently, "but no power is getting through to the building. Operations is checking into the problem. Until then, everyone has been ordered to evacuate."

"Where are we going?" Andy asked grumpily.

Tommy was gathering up Andy's bag and shaving kit.

Steve answered, "There's a federal courthouse across the square. It's a short hike. No problem."

Andy sat up straight, "Wait, you mean we have to walk across a New York City square in daylight with Random on the loose and wanting to kill me? Does that seem like a bad idea to anyone other than me?"

Carmen walked in the door breathing heavily, "No good, Tommy. My SUV was appropriated to evacuate directors. Assistant directors and above commandeered all vehicles not used for prisoner transport."

Carmen said to Andy, "I'm glad you were only on the fourth floor. I need to work out more."

Tommy ordered, "Andy, I am going to run over to the courthouse and secure your access. I'll cover your approach from across the street. Steve, Carmen, please escort Andy across the square. Angela and Carlos are downstairs waiting for us. They will cover your flanks. Check your earpieces now. Stay in radio contact at all times. Let's go."

Tommy added, "We will go through the International Court building and exit onto the square. It will shorten our walk by about a hundred yards."

150 Rendezvous

Foley Square

New York City

Monday, August 1, 2011, 8:55 AM EDT

Tommy ran across the square. When he reached the courthouse steps, he turned and waved to Steve and Carmen waiting inside the glass windows of the US Court of International Trade. Carlos and Angela had already exited. Steve and Carmen waited until they were on either side of the fountain in the middle of the square.

Steve exited the building followed by Carmen and Andy.

The limousine with Alan and Alicia drove down Lafayette Street in front of Steve causing him to reach for his service revolver but not draw it. He waited as the long black car passed by him and turned left going around the square and pulling up in front of the Federal Courthouse steps. Steve continued forward ready to draw and fire until Angela spoke on the radio, "Steve, the limo is a friendly. It's Alan Hopkins, the attorney. Get your hand off your gun."

Alicia exited the limousine next and recognized Angela walking toward her. She started to wave but turned her head back toward the courthouse as a vicious scream tore through the air.

A large shadow appeared on the courthouse steps in mid air like a door opening on a darkness behind our world. A bizarre tall woman with crazy hair stepped out of the darkness carrying a man with a high-powered rifle. The traffic kept flowing, but pedestrians on the square froze.

A man in a business suit ten feet from the creature when the man leveled his rifle and shot him through the chest. The bullet passed through him and ricocheted off the concrete and into the side of a passing car. The driver panicked and floored the gas pedal zooming north on Centre Street. The few people present not aware of the apparition were now scrambling for cover or to get out of the square.

Carlos drew his service revolver where he stood and fired at the man with the rifle.

Steve shouted, "Random," into his microphone as he ran forward to the fountain. Steve steadied his arms on the black granite stone of the fountain and squeezed off four shots in rapid succession. Random dove back into the darkness followed by the creature and the gaping wound in our world closed.

People all over the square were shocked and not certain what they had seen. It had happened so fast, they couldn't make sense of it. Some stood to their feet and started walking away. Traffic started moving ever so slowly when the screech hit their ears again.

This time the shadow ripped open on street level next to the stone blocks, left of the steps. As soon as an opening was large enough, Random stepped out and started firing at anyone moving, switching from semi-automatic to fully automatic firing in short bursts at every target. He walked to a security booth on the corner of Pearl Street and gunned down the guard trying to draw his pistol.

Angela pulled a wounded mother and her baby carriage to cover behind the thick stone balustrades leading up to the fountain. Carmen corralled a group of children and rushed them to cover behind some bushes and made them lie flat.

Alicia gasped when Random moved the rifle from hip firing position to his shoulder and zeroed in on Angela. Angela went down in a heap. Random moved on toward the fountain where Andy had taken refuge next to Steve.

Random turned to shoot at Carlos and Steve behind the fountain. Alicia left the security of the limousine and dashed bent over across the line of fire.

Alicia pulled the baby carriage behind the stone barrier, the mother clearly dead. Alicia left her and next pulled Angela to cover.

Alicia sat on a step pulling Angela up to rest on her lap. Angela was making indecipherable sounds. Alicia could see a trail of dark red blood where Angela had been dragged.

Alicia smoothed Angela's hair out of her eyes cooing, "I've got you, honey. I've got you."

Angela looked up into Alicia's eyes. Alicia saw a dullness creep into her expression. Alicia pulled Angela up high onto her lap and held her as Angela's spirit dimmed and slipped away. Alicia sobbed uncontrollably. If Random had stepped around the stone barrier, she would not have cared.

Tommy came bursting out of the doors of the courthouse and down the stairs only to be smashed in the back of his head and thrown down onto the bottom of the stairs. The creature was reaching out and crushing anyone she could reach.

Tommy's bell was rung. His defensive coach stood over him screaming his name, "Edwards, Edwards, Edwards, get the quarterback! Crush him! Kill that bastard! Go, go, go!"

The product of continuous training rose automatically to the surface. Tommy jumped to his feet a split second ahead of the killing blow from the creature. He couldn't get through the linemen in his way so he ran around the end of the line of cars in a blur of motion. He dove at the quarterback, the quarterback holding the rifle. The crushing blow broke bones when the two bodies collided. More bones were broken when Tommy drilled him into the asphalt.

The creature stopped her advance, hesitated, and then retreated to the dark as the fissure closed behind her.

151 Conclusion

US Federal Courthouse

New York City

Monday, August 1, 2011, 10:30 AM EDT

Tommy stood behind Andy with his hand on his weapon as Andy signed paper after paper. Many of the agreements he signed were contingent on other agreements he would need to enter into later.

Carmen sat against the wall in emotional shock from the death of Angela. She wore some of Angela's blood on her shirt when she helped Alicia after the paramedics removed Angela from Alicia's hold. Alicia sat against the opposite wall holding her head and weeping occasionally. Carmen found a gray maintenance uniform for Alicia and helped her out of her blood soaked dress.

After an hour, Mr. Vargas called a halt to the process saying, "There is more to be done, but it can wait. The Hollingsworth trust has officially been turned over to Mr. Hollingsworth's surviving heir, Andrew Glover."

Andy's only wound was a deep gash on his right calf muscle from stone chips thrown by bullet debris.

Mr. Vargas neatly gathered up the agreements he needed and left.

Tommy sat next to Andy. Carlos and Steve had been outside standing guard. They came in and sat at the table. After a long pause, Carlos started the conversation, "We have so much paperwork to do. Can it wait until tomorrow?"

Steve added, "And there is the review board for discharging weapons."

Tommy sighed and said, "CIRG directors will want this buttoned up by end of day today. At least they let us see this through to the end."

Alicia said, "It feels like the end."

"But it's not the end," Andy responded. "There are things we must do today and tomorrow and the next day."

Alicia shook her head at the nonsensical tasks ahead. In light of Angela's death, nothing else seemed important. Not yet.

Alan stated, "Well, I for one, need to go to London to get sacked. Anyone want to go along?"

Alan looked behind him at Alicia.

Alicia shook her head, "No Alan. I'm going to stay here for the funeral. I can meet you later."

Tommy stood and concluded, "Alan Hopkins, it was good to meet you. I hope we meet again under better circumstances."

Tommy and Alan shook hands.

"I agree, Sir," Alan said gravely, "under better circumstances."

Tommy turned to Alicia, "Alicia Montgomery, it is an honor to know you. You cared for Angela with no concern for your own safety. I am in your debt, but I must ask one thing. Can you stand please?"

Alicia stood and Tommy hugged her. They both started crying. All followed the same pattern before leaving the courthouse.

152 Board of Inquiry

Blackford Crighton Law Firm, Home Office

15 Upper Bank Street, London, England

Wednesday, August 3, 2011, 9:00 AM GMT (4:00 AM EDT)

"Sir Smythley!" Alan gasped, "How can you be here?"

Alan had been composed and ready to confidently face his accusers. The fact of Smythley's arrest was evidence in his favor proving he had acted in the firm's best interests. Now even that defense was gone.

Smythley stood up from the row of leather high backed chairs behind the long table Alan stood facing. Smythley wore his formal military uniform complete with all the medals he had garnered.

Smythley lifted his chin higher as he spoke, "Because of my loyalty and long service to this firm and this nation, I have been entrusted with maintaining these same qualities at Blackford Crighton for staff and partners."

Smythley prattled on and on about correct process and lines of authority. Alan was at first appalled and then incredulous at this pompous charade of self-righteousness.

Alan could not hold back, "You broke the law!"

"I did what was necessary," Smythley returned.

Alan fired back, "You helped and encouraged our client to break the law. You condoned and abetted murder as well as concealing evidence. I believe that is against the law of every country in the world."

"I was protecting our client. You have no idea what gangsters the Cassanzos are," Smythley shot back.

Alan returned, "What could they have done that made it acceptable for you to break the laws in America and England over and over?"

Smythley answered, "They killed Lord St. Claire's son; they killed Brian Sutton, my godson."

"They didn't kill him!" Alan retorted, "He died in a car accident!"

"They arranged it. He was drugged and put behind the wheel of his sports car."

Alan shook his head in disbelief, "Did you even know Brian, Brian Sutton, my cousin? He had been driving intoxicated for years. If they wanted him killed, they only had to wait for him to do it himself! It's a miracle he lasted as long as he did!"

Alan pointed his finger at the entire board, "I went on record and was reprimanded for suggesting Brian be forced into a recovery program. The letter of reprimand from this very board is still in my file."

After lengthy acrimonious debate, the head of the Inquiry Board stood and looked at Sir Smythley who took his seat.

The head of the board spoke gravely, "It is for outbursts such as this you are called before this board of inquiry. You have proven in our presence your persistent insubordinate nature."

The old man looked down the length of the table and said, "If there are no objections, we will consider this inquiry closed and your relationship with the firm of Blackford Crighton terminated. You will surrender your keys, credit cards, and identification badge to the security officer as he walks you out of the building."

153 The Mourning After

Green Wood Cemetery

500 25th Street, Brooklyn, New York

Thursday, August 4, 2011, 9:00 AM EDT

The large number of people gathered around the grave sight easily divided into three groups: Angela's Italian family, FBI comrades, and her biker friends. Alicia fit into none of the groups and stood in the back, furthest from the ceremony. Carmen noticed Alicia and pointed her out to Tommy. Tommy stepped back through the crowd and walked around the ring of attendees to where Alicia stood.

As the graveside service was about to start, Tommy walked through the throng of FBI agents escorting Alicia up to the front of the crowd to stand with his team between himself and Carmen.

After the ceremony, Alicia rode in Carmen's black SUV to Ray's Upstairs on Kent Avenue.

"So where is Alan?" Carlos asked Alicia as Tommy's team sat around two tables pulled together. The bar downstairs was full of kids and club music. Upstairs was more intimate, quieter with low lighting. Carmen sat next to Andy but not close to him.

"He's in England," Alicia explained. "He got fired from the law firm. Apparently Sir Smythley got released from custody without any charges being filed. He made trouble for Alan."

"I'm sorry, Alicia," Tommy said. "Apparently Smythley had plenty of money and politics behind him."

Steve said, "I would love to sic Warren on his ass."

Carmen butted in, "Alicia, are you going to see him again?"

Alicia smiled shyly, "Yes, I'm leaving for England tomorrow to see him and meet his parents. Angela would want me to."

Carlos asked Andy sitting across from him, "So what was that thing with Ransom?"

Steve added, "And don't give me any of that 'I don't know' crap. You have some idea."

"I don't know," Andy said adamantly pointing at Steve, "but it might have been an *'ays sheeth-uh.'"*

Carlos protested, "Come on man, what was it?"

"Alright, but no making fun of me," Andy added, pointing at Steve again.

Steve held up his hands, "No promises, Priss."

Andy continued, "There are ancient stories recorded in the Book of Invasions. It's an anthology of the beginnings of the Irish people. It describes creatures across the sea living kind of underground and kind of another dimension."

Tommy turned to Carmen, "I know we haven't had any time to discuss some things, but where were Celestina and Warren when Random and that thing attacked?"

Carmen answered, "They were with me in the park."

Tommy looked at Carmen while saying, "Andy, why did you leave Carmen alone and run across open ground to the fountain?"

"I got confused and ran for cover," Andy mumbled.

Steve leaned forward looking incredulously at Andy, "Not one person here believes that shit. Why don't you put on your big girl panties and just say it out loud."

Andy sighed, "Okay, I ran to the fountain because I knew Random was after me, and I thought if someone was going to get shot, I would rather it be Steve."

Laughter erupted all around except for Steve who only replied, "At least you were honest about it."

Tommy stood and raised his beer, "To the members of the Serial Crimes Task Force! Alicia, get your glass up."

All stood and clinked their glasses together.

154 The Price of Information

Outside Ray's Upstairs, Kent Avenue

Brooklyn, New York

Thursday, August 4, 2011, 8:45 PM EDT

Tommy switched his cell phone to his other side to allow the blood flow back into his left arm. The tension on the call was causing Tommy to grip the phone harder.

-

"Rodney, how I found out was in a life and death situation. A suspect was trying to throw me off balance, distract me from the real issue."

-

"I don't know how they knew, but they did."

-

"No Rodney," Tommy said with strong emotion rising in his throat, "but you are my brother. You're the only family I have left."

-

"I could tell you were avoiding me, but I didn't know why. I think you felt guilty for sleeping with Sharon."

-

"No, no, that is not why I called. I want you to know that I know about it, and I don't want it to come between us. It's ancient history."

-

"Yeah, Mom would have wanted us to be closer than we are. I would like that too."

-

"Thanksgiving? Sure, I think I can make it."

-

"No, it will just be me. I'm not seeing anyone."

-

"Hey, I found a picture of Dad with Martin Luther King and Stevie Wonder at the Chicago Freedom Movement. He wanted to get involved and he did. I'll send you a copy."

-

"He always told me he wanted to do something important with his life and he did. I just wish I could have known him even a little like you did."

-

Tommy's eyes teared up, "Really? You think he would be proud of me? I hope so."

-

"Thanks Rodney," Tommy said wiping his eyes. "It means a lot coming from you."

-

"I've looked for him, for dad. He was last seen in Selma. His body was never found."

-

"Okay, I'll let you get back to your family. Let's talk more often."

-

"No, I won't say anything to anyone else."

-

"Love you, big brother."

-

"Tell your wife and kids I'll see them soon."

-

"Bye."

Tommy felt lighter now the anger he had been carrying around was gone. He had been hampered by it since Big Ugly captured Carmen and showed Tommy images of his ex-wife with his brother.

Tommy took in a big breath of the night air and let it out. He looked up at the few stars visible. He paused and then walked to his SUV and drove to his apartment.

155 Chance Encounter in Middle Earth

Cromwell Green Visitor Entrance

Palace of Westminster, London, England

Tuesday, August 9, 2011, 6:25 PM GMT (1:25 PM EDT)

"Cancelled?" Alan said in a shocked tone. "We paid fifty pounds for the tour, and we've seen scads of groups going through!"

The lady behind the desk at the visitor entrance stoically replied, "Tickets are purchased for specific tours. The guide for the two o'clock tour is not available. Therefore, the tour is cancelled. I can refund your money, or you may apply your refund to another tour time."

"When is the next available tour?" Alan questioned.

The woman looked at the computer screen on the side of her desk, "I have two openings on Monday, nineteen September."

"But my girlfriend is only here for a week!" Alan said with rising frustration.

"Don't you get snippy, your lordship, or I'll have armed security sort you out promptly!" the lady shot back.

"Alan," Alicia spoke quietly but with a hint of warning in her tone.

Alan turned to see two armed palace guards standing behind Alicia.

"You'll have to come with us, Sir, and the young lady also," one of them stated.

"But I was ..." Alan started but abruptly stopped talking when he realized nothing he could say would give the guards grounds for releasing them.

Alan sighed and reached out for Alicia's hand. One of the guards strode in front of them and the other followed behind leading them inside to a cushioned bench along the wall of a long corridor deep inside the Westminster offices.

Alan was still holding Alicia's hand when they sat down. The two soldiers stood on either side of them.

Alan quietly said, "You wanted to see inside Westminster Palace. Well, here we are."

Alicia chuckled and then stopped as she spied an elderly gentleman dressed in a well-worn suit approaching them. His demeanor amiable, but the focus of his gaze was intensely on them. Alan turned to see where Alicia was looking. He quickly stood to his feet as the gentleman approached. Alicia remained demurely seated.

"Lord Chancellor," Alan stammered as the Right Honorable Lord Chancellor held his hand out for Alan.

"Solicitor Hopkins, it is my pleasure to meet you," the Lord Chancellor said warmly to Alan.

Alan pointed to Alicia and began, "Lord Chancellor, this is ..."

"Alicia Montgomery," the Lord Chancellor said smiling mischievously and reached his hand out to Alicia. Alicia stood to shake his hand. She still loved how they pronounced her name. The Lord Chancellor shook Alicia's hand warmly with both of his hands.

"It is my very great pleasure to meet you also. One of my aides showed me the video of you in the New York shooting. You were very brave my dear."

"Thank you, Sir," was all Alicia felt was necessary to say.

Lord Chancellor was still holding her hand when he asked her, "I need to have a private word with Alan. Would you mind if I stole him away for a few short minutes. I promise it will be short. I have a roomful of people waiting for me."

Alicia looked at the man and considered him. Then Alicia turned to Alan, "Alan dear, whatever he offers you, say yes, and we will work out the details later."

Alicia watched as the two men walked into a small lobby out of her sight. She sat back down on the bench.

"Alan, that is a woman of character waiting for you. You are a lucky man."

"Yes Sir."

"Then straight to the point. Lord St. Claire has passed away and claims to his title are now being considered. I would like you to claim his title."

Alan pointed out, "Sir, I am at least the ninth or tenth in order of succession for his title."

"You are the twelfth in line, and you are not the most qualified to take on the burdens of the St. Claire title or the Sutton estate, but," The Lord Chancellor paused, and Alan held his breath.

"A small window of opportunity has presented itself to us."

"Sir?" Alan questioned.

"That young lady outside in the Chairman's Corridor waiting for you, she has lived in the political storm of America all her life. Through her mother, she has connections and experience along with connections of her own that, if she were your wife, would make you by far the most qualified candidate for the title and estate. That is not to say you are not an honorable man in your own right. If you were not, the young lady would not be waiting for you, and you and I would not be talking. You have proven your metal to my satisfaction. Will you claim the title?"

Alan shook his head, "But what about the others before me? What about Matthew Sutton? He could still claim the title and estate."

"Matthew Sutton will not claim the title or the estate, I can assure you. Some of the others on the list ahead of you will need to be compensated. Only two of them will need paid anything significant. The others are asking minor things like help with their mortgages, lifetime flying privileges on British Airways, and one needs significant legal help. I believe another is looking at some well-deserved jail time. Another will want you to pay all his outstanding parking tickets, more than thirty at last count."

A moment of quiet hung in the space between the two men. At length, Alan said the obvious, "As Alicia suggested, I will say yes to the request, but I am curious why you ..."

Alan hesitated and then repeated himself, "Why you, Mister Clark? How does this pertain to you officially or even, if I may ask, personally?"

The Right Honorable Kenneth Clark put a fatherly hand on Alan's shoulder, "That conversation, my boy, will have to wait until you are ensconced in your new role. Nothing sinister I assure you. Now let me walk you and that lovely young Amazon you are courting to the gate, or if you like, I could arrange a private tour with one of my staff. How would that suit you?"

"Alicia would love it."

156 Andy and Carmen

Corso della Vittoria

Orsara di Puglia, Province of Foggia, Italy

Wednesday, August 10, 2011, 9:50 AM UTC -1 (3:50 AM EDT)

The caravan of vehicles stopped in the small town square near the monument the people had built for Celestina. The driver of the van carrying Celestina's remains got out as he had been instructed to do. The three reporters on the scene photographed him walking forward and talking to the Mayor and a few other townsfolk assembled at the small piazza. Carmen and Andy sat in the back seat of a cab Andy hired in Foggia. Andy was still not comfortable with the trappings and necessities of the ultra-rich. Celestina sat between them.

"At least you can guess," Andy said.

"I think Celestina left you because it was time for you to grow up and be on your own," Carmen answered.

Andy's face darkened, and he replied sarcastically, "Nice, thanks."

"Look, you asked me to guess why she left you and attached herself to me. That's what I think."

"Are you going to analyze everything I say and do?"

Carmen gave Andy a hard look, "Only when you are around me. That's who I am. That's what I do. Deal with it!"

After a few minutes of tense silence passed, Carmen offered a conciliatory observation. "Look Andy, you're on edge right now. It's understandable. They did try to kill you two weeks ago."

"And my father was responsible for killing their daughter," Andy added.

"That was Random's arrangement and I think he used the woman who replaced your mother to set up the whole plan that got Celestina killed."

Andy looked at Carmen hopeful her scenario would give some explanation to the horror of his childhood.

"Look," Carmen said, "those people are the Cassanzo family coming into the square."

Andy let out a long breath and sighed, "Okay, let's go meet them and find out if I get to live out the day."

As they exited the backseat of the vehicle Carmen warned, "Stop being so dramatic. Didn't the CIA already contact that Salvatore guy?"

Roberto Cassanzo looked down the line of cars stopped in the piazza and saw a couple matching Salvatore's description. He broke off from the group around the lead van and walked toward Carmen.

"*Benvenuti signora Andriano e il signor Glover*!" Roberto called to them in Italian and then added in English, "Thank you for making this long trip to honor our Celestina."

Carmen looked over her shoulder at Andy. It had not occurred to her Celestina's own family would have any idea why they had come. Andy just shrugged. Carmen did not see any change in Celestina's placid expression. Roberto was confused by Carmen's expression and hesitation.

Carmen finally said, "Thank you for coming to greet us."

"You must come and meet my family," Roberto said enthusiastically.

Roberto walked ahead and led them to his wife and two teenage children. Pleasantries were exchanged with Roberto acting as interpreter. The mayor and others held the focus of the news media reading statements prepared for a larger crowd of reporters. The press was more interested in the murder of Celestina than the resolution of the crime.

Andy noticed a tall, beautiful woman in her fifties walking down the narrow cobblestone street toward the piazza. Roberto stopped talking when he saw her. He immediately excused himself and walked toward her. Roberto and the woman had a brief conversation before continuing on to the group gathered in front of the large picture, flowers, and candles set up by the fountain. As she neared the memorial to Celestina, she opened her purse and drew out a small toy pony with flowing pink mane and tail. She set it on a ledge at the bottom of the photo.

Andy said quietly to Carmen, "She looks so much like her daughter."

A hush fell over the small crowd and several women and men stepped forward to place reassuring arms around her. When signora Cassanzo finally turned around, she looked at the crowd smiling through her tears until her eyes fell on Carmen. Celestina's mother dabbed at her tears with a well-used handkerchief and smiled at Carmen.

The older woman stepped forward saying, "*Mi scusi, non ti conosco?*"

Roberto stepped up and said something to his sister-in-law. Then he turned to Carmen and Andy and explained, "This is Celestina's mother, Teresa Cassanzo. She thought you looked like someone she knows. I explained to her you found Celestina's body and brought it back."

Teresa asked Roberto, "*Chiedete loro se potevano venire al funerale. Essi saranno miei ospiti?*"

Roberto spoke to Andy and Carmen, "Teresa would like you to come to the family's home for the funeral as her guests."

Carmen answered for both of them, "We would be honored to be your guests."

Roberto relayed the message to his sister-in-law. Teresa smiled and touched Carmen's cheek saying, "*Mille grazie, hai portato a casa mia figlia a noi.*"

Carmen said to Roberto while looking at Teresa, "You don't need to translate. I understand."

157 Morning News

Tommy's Apartment

125 La Salle Street, Morningside Heights, New York City

Wednesday, August 10, 2011, 6:40 AM EDT

Tommy sat down with his coffee and morning paper. His morning run had been glorious, cool, and challenging.

Underneath the sex education article, two inches of text quietly announced the resignation of James Robins, the White House Chief of Staff.

The second paragraph of the story read:

Mr. Robins emerged from a lengthy meeting at the White House where the President urged him to 'stay the course,' but the President's long time friend and political ally was determined to pursue some long delayed personal dreams. Jim Robins also announced he would follow through on his pledge to donate one million dollars to the Red Cross for disaster relief.

Tommy shook his head and laughed.

158 Home Going

Cassanzo Villa

Near Orsara di Puglia, Province of Foggia, Italy

Wednesday, August 10, 2011, 2:00 PM UTC -1 (8:00 AM EDT)

The day was thankfully overcast with a light breeze. Carmen and Andy followed Teresa and Roberto down the hill followed by Roberto's wife and two children following well behind.

Andy asked, "What was Celestina's expression when she saw her mother?"

"I don't know," Carmen replied. "I lost Celestina in the crowd. I didn't see her again until we headed back to the car."

"Where is she now?"

Carmen looked over her shoulder and said, "She's right behind us."

"Does she look happy? I'm surprised she is not walking with her mother."

Carmen looked back over her shoulder to see Celestina. Roberto's family saw her turn around and waved to her. Carmen waved back.

"I'd say she looks placid, not happy or sad," Carmen said.

The small entourage followed the parish priest and two alter boys in black cassocks with the simple white linen surplice covering. The group crossed the bridge at the creek and started up the hill to the barn and the villa beyond. At the barn, Agosto welcomed everyone and told them refreshments were being served in the villa while they waited for the last family members to arrive. Roberto translated for Carmen and Andy.

Later, holding their drinks and small plates with cheese and grapes, Carmen followed Andy out the back door to the grape arbor. Andy saw a familiar face.

"Hello Salvatore. I am here if you need me," Andy pronounced with finality.

Salvatore rose as Carmen walked through the door after Andy, "*Buon giorno signorina.* Welcome to Villa Cassanzo."

An old man sitting in a wheel chair with an oxygen tank interrupted the greetings with a grumpy, *"Finalmente siete arrivati. I bambini sono stati in attesa."*

Salvatore looked confused but translated, "Signore Cassanzo says, 'Finally you have arrived. The children are waiting,' but I don't understand ..."

Andy broke in, "He is not talking to us. He sees the spirit of Celestina."

Carmen looked at Andy, "How could you know that?"

The old man snarled, "Lei ha fatto una promessa."

"It's a guess, but it makes sense. Carmen, what is Celestina doing?" Andy said watching the old man.

"She is walking toward the children. Holy ...! They see her! They're coming to her!"

Salvatore looked around and shook his head then asked Carmen, "What children?"

159 Random Traction

Clinton Correctional Facility

Dannemora, New York

Tuesday, August 9, 2011, 2:30 PM EDT

"Tie him down tighter!" the orderly yelled to the nurse who was trying to catch the flying straps the patient attempted to keep out of her reach.

The nurse caught the strap for the prisoner's left hand and pulled with all her strength to secure it to the side of the bed. "There! Now try to get out of that."

The orderly looked accusingly at the security guard, "You could have helped."

"Not my job, brother. Besides Sutton's just gonna get loose again."

The orderly asked the nurse, "Jane, can we sedate him? Is it time yet?"

The patient started howling in a pitiful tone using incoherent sounds through the wiring holding his jaw together.

The security guard asked, "What's wrong with him? Every time he falls asleep he wakes up screaming."

The nurse shook her head, "I have no idea, but twice he woke up choking, and we had to extract a cockroach from his mouth. If this keeps up, he ain't going to last much longer."

160 Engagement Party

Bristol Marriott Royal Hotel

Bristol, England

Wednesday, August 10, 2011, 2:00 PM UTC -1 (8:00 AM EDT)

"But Alan, this is so sudden, and how can we afford this since you've been sacked?"

Alan kissed his mother on the cheek and soothed, "Mum, we will be fine. She said yes, so I wanted to be married as soon as possible before she has a chance to change her mind."

The semi-private conversation between Alan and his parents with Alicia a short distance away was overheard by more than half of the seventy guests. The lofty arched ceilings did little to dampen the fears of Alan's parents or the sound of them questioning their son's motives.

As the guests pretended not to hear Alan's mother fretting about her son getting involved with an American, Alicia greeted each guest personally learning their connection to Alan and her new life. Many discussed the wedding arrangements and the fact that a wedding in England was scheduled for that September.

One very striking couple, Alicia was surprised to find out, was American. After a short conversation, the well-dressed woman mentioned, "Mr. Harriman sends his congratulations also."

Alicia's face became stone, "Please convey to Mr. Harriman that my arrangement with him has been concluded, as I told him."

The woman moved closer, "Your fairy tale story could end here tonight if I let your fiancé know what you were really doing while he thought you were working for him."

"I won't betray Alan, not any more," Alicia trembled as she spoke.

The man leaned in, "You will agree to your previous arrangement to give us whatever information we ask, when we ask. You will agree tonight, right now, or your little love charade with Attorney Hopkins will end in the time it takes me to cross the room."

Alicia swallowed hard as the emotion rose in her throat. She looked nervously over her shoulder at Alan and his parents. She knew this was the perfect time for Harriman to ruin her.

"Say it!" the woman demanded, "Say you will agree! You have thirty seconds."

Alicia's hands started shaking. She opened her mouth but no sounds came out.

The man walked away toward Alan.

Alicia's tears started flowing, and she said through gritted teeth, "I'll do it. I'll do it. Stop him!"

The woman called out, "Edward, Edward darling, Alicia has made plans to come and see us. Isn't that wonderful?"

Alicia started toward the hallway and the ladies' room. She broke into a run as she neared the door sobbing as she ran down the hallway.

Alan asked the couple that had been talking to Alicia, "Is she upset? What was that about?"

The woman put a hand on Alan's forearm, "She was just telling us that she is excited but nervous. The reality of marriage can be overwhelming."

Alan called over his shoulder, "I need to see if she is all right. Please excuse me everyone," as he followed the fading sound of Alicia crying.

"I hope there are no other ladies in here," Alan announced as he entered the no man's land of the woman's toilet.

Alicia was sobbing over a sink as Alan put his hand on her waist, "Dear, what is the matter?"

Alicia spun around and buried her head in Alan's shoulder while she cried.

After a few minutes Alan said, "Okay, not knowing what this is about or what I should do, I am going to let you cry as long as you need to."

Shortly Alicia stopped crying and looked directly into Alan's eyes and said, "We have them. They believed me. We now own Harriman."

"He sent someone here tonight? Of all the cheek!"

Then Alan looked confused and asked, "So how does this work?"

Alicia wiped her nose on a tissue, "When Harriman asks for information, we will know what he doesn't know, and it will tell us the direction he and the others are going. We can stay one jump ahead of them."

"But won't they catch on?"

Alicia sniffled, "Eventually, but by then it won't matter any more. What they have on me will become less and less important as time goes by."

Alan started singing and rocking back and forth, "You must remember this, a kiss is but a kiss ..."

Alicia answered, "A sigh is but a sigh."

They both finished with, "The fundamental things apply, as time goes by," while visions of Casablanca and Humphrey Bogart came to mind. The kiss was epic. Angela would have approved.

161 Celestina is Gone

Cassanzo Villa

Near Orsara di Puglia, Province of Foggia, Italy

Wednesday, August 10, 2011, 8:00 PM UTC -1 (2:00 PM EDT)

Stefano, Roberto, and Salvatore joined Carmen and Andy in a corner of the great room away from the rest of the family.

"So you are saying Signore Cassanzo had all these ghosts around him," Salvatore asked.

Stefano surmised, "The children you saw must have been with my father since the war, over sixty years he lived with them. He must have connected with them in the villages the Germans were destroying."

Andy added, "Carmen, the adults you saw later, they came out of the trees. Who were thcy?"

Carmen looked tired as she tried to make sense of the day, "At least one was in an old German army uniform. I did recognize Mr. Rossetti from the pictures in his case file. Andy, that was your first murder scene, the brownstone on ."

"So all the people killed were coming to Signore Cassanzo?" Andy guessed. "That would make him feel very crowded."

Stefano pointed out, "That was why my father moved here to the villa, to make room for all of them."

Salvatore said, "I heard your father say that Celestina had made a promise. He must have confided to her about the children. I think Celestina may have promised to take care of them."

"And now they are all gone?" Roberto asked.

Carmen sighed, "Yes. Wherever Celestina took them or led them, they are all gone, children and adults."

After a long silence, Stefano stood saying, "It has been a long day, and I promised to drive my Teresa back to her hotel. Good night everyone, buonanotte."

162 Quest for a Good Burger

The Gastropub

Port Angeles, Washington

Tuesday, August 9, 2011, 6:25 PM PDT (9:25 PM EDT)

Steve felt light, light in body, mind, and soul.

He stood at, what looked like the top of the world, the very brink of Hurricane Ridge in Olympic National Park, in the state of Washington. The twenty some snowcapped mountains and deep valleys separating them all led to the ridge where Steve stood. He loved this place, one of the few memories from his family life that brought him real joy.

As an Army Ranger, after his second tour, he challenged his squad to hike down and back in one day. Only he and Sargent Flores made the thirty-four mile descent and climb back up the ridge before the sun had set. This grucling trek was now his de-facto proof that he was in sufficient condition to meet his personal standards.

Steve lingered in the fading light before driving down to the campground. No showers available, but a large utility sink made an adequate washing station. Clean clothes and he was off to Port Angeles to get some real food. The attendant at the gas station rattled off a list of a few of the nicer restaurants or better bars. Steve didn't want any thing fancy.

Then the attendant added, "The best burgers in town are at the Gastropub ... good beer too. It'll be crowded, but it's the best."

Steve found it on the street next to the marina, but any available parking was several blocks away. The night was warm, and some of the non-drinking patrons ate at tables outside on the sidewalk. As Steve walked in the door, he got a lot of stares at his facial tattoo and a stiff greeting from the hostess. "No tables for the rest of the night. I think there is a seat at the bar, but it's crowded."

"Good enough for me," Steve replied as he walked past trying to spot an empty seat.

After many apologies and rude stares Steve was able to traverse the crowded floor and squeeze into the last bar seat sitting shoulder to shoulder with a drunk guy on his right and an annoyed young lady on his left.

The drunk was trying to talk to him, but before he had a chance to get annoyed, the bartender walked over. She looked to be in her early thirties, blond curls past her shoulders, blue eyes with a beautiful figure and face, but a face that had seen tough times and still had a gentle smile.

"Frank, do you have enough for a sandwich?" She asked.

Steve tried hard not to stare.Their eyes met, and she smiled. Steve looked at Frank on his right. Frank spilled a pile of change on the counter saying, "Sandy, I think I have enough for half of a Deli sandwich or some soup."

"Well, let's count," Sandy said leaning over the bar close to Frank.

"Let's put the quarters in one pile," Sandy continued.

Steve realized that the man next to him was homeless. He had been drinking, but he also had some kind of learning or mental disability. Sandy treated him like a person. Sandy made Steve and others see Frank as a real person not just another homeless bum or a drunk on a barstool. Steve felt pangs of guilt for not seeing Frank at first.

Sandy stood, "Frank, you have six dollars and ninety three cents. What would you like to get?"

Steve reached for his wallet, but Sandy, smiling, shook her head "no." Steve slid his wallet back into his pocket.

Steve listened to the conversation between Sandy and Frank all through his burger and coke, joining in when appropriate. All the while, he tried hard not to look at Sandy, but he desperately wanted to talk to her.

While he was trying not to stare at Sandy, a memory came back to him of the town hall in Hudson, New York. In Steve's mind, he could clearly see Andy Glover saying, "If you want to impress her, don't tell her how beautiful she is. She has heard that from anyone whoever saw her. Look for her character, things under the surface."

The next thoughts were pictures of Celestina, the beautiful ingénue, followed by images of her remains and the story Andy told of her courage just before her murder. Steve thought of Andy and Carmen in Italy taking her body back to her grieving parents. Steve was so lost in his thoughts and memories he lost awareness of his surroundings. Sandy was standing in front of him looking concerned, "Hey soldier, are you okay?"

Steve became aware of tears running down his face. He quickly wiped them away, and looked up at Sandy, "Huh? Oh yeah. You just reminded me of someone, someone special. You think of others first, you're very kind, and you work hard. It's very ..." Steve choked and then finished, "You are a rare person."

Sandy's eyebrows went up and her mouth opened..

Steve laid a couple of twenties on the bar as he stood, "Thanks Sandy."

He walked out embarrassed at his sudden rush of emotion.

Steve walked down to the marina to clear his head. The evening was cooled by a breeze blowing in from the water. People milled around looking in the few shops still open or sitting with coffee and friends. The reflection of rigging lights in the marina gave every reflection a carnival shimmer. Two of the large yachts had lively parties casting music into the air. Steve had felt exhilarated after his climb, but now felt loneliness. The parties around him just added to his melancholy.

He didn't want to face the condition of his life, not here so close to where he grew up, not now. Steve headed back to his car.

As he passed the Gastropub, he saw Sandy outside, leaning against a car smoking a cigarette. Two big studs stood on either side of her. Steve didn't want to say anything to her. He just wanted this whole night to become a distant memory, the sooner the better.

"Hey blue face," Sandy called out.

Steve looked over at her as he prepared to pass by.

"Can I talk to you? Do you have a few minutes?"

Steve slowed his pace and turned toward her. Sandy asked the guys to give her a few minutes. They both walked away.

"My name is Steve," he said as he approached her, "not blue face."

"You learned my name, but I never got yours, and you paid in cash."

Steve grinned, "No harm, no foul then."

"So I am dying to know, this special person, did she leave you?"

Steve fought to control the rush of emotion surging back.

"No, she died."

"I'm so sorry. I didn't mean to ..."

Steve put up a hand, "It's okay. It was a long time ago."

"So," Sandy continued, "you are special forces, right? Navy SEAL?"

Steve smiled, "No, Ranger."

"Then why did you get the tattoo? That can't be regulation."

"Actually I'm a former Ranger, no longer active. As far as the tattoo goes, it wasn't voluntary."

Sandy took a drag on her cigarette looking intently at Steve's face, "Not voluntary? Now you'll have to tell me the story. The ridges look awesome. Would you mind if I touched them?"

"Um, sure."

Steve felt her hand on his cheek and jaw line. He didn't mind at all, not at all.

"So some group held you down and stitched this on you? That must have taken hours."

"It was a case I was working on."

Sandy guessed, "CIA? FBI?"

Steve pulled his wallet and showed his ID.

"Okay, so you are the real deal," Sandy said, "but I have to get back inside. What are you doing tomorrow?"

"Flying back to New York."

Sandy dropped her cigarette into the gutter and stepped on it, "That's too bad, now you'll have to call me."

Sandy pulled a blue pen out of the black apron she wore, "Give me your hand."

She turned Steve's hand over and wrote very hard across the bone and tendons.

"Hey, that hurts!"

"Hold still you big baby," she said as she finished writing her name underneath the phone number, "You don't want it to get rubbed off, do you?"

Steve said nothing.

Sandy looked up into to Steve's eyes, "Now call me, and tell me the story."

Sandy started walking back into the pub, and Steve called after her, "I'll also explain why you should quit smoking."

She turned, smiling, "I've been trying. Give me some motivation."

"I'll do my best, Ma'am."

Steve went looking for his rental car saying to the night air, "Best night ever!"

The End

Page of 158

About the Author

The author, Kevin Boyle, comes from an Irish American family of storytellers. Using his exposure to business, ranching, surfing, accounting, farming, engineering, religions, computers and IT, Kevin weaves the facets of life into relatable stories of everyday people in extraordinary times.

www.ingramcontent.com/pod-product-compliance
Lightning Source LLC
LaVergne TN
LVHW090547110826
845146LV00001B/51

9798990783409